A New Life and Love in Montana

BOOK 1 OF THE ELK RIDGE BRIDES

NICOLE COLES

Scene break graphics provided by: https://www.vecteezy.com/

Contents

To my husband,

the one who brings instant peace to my soul

Prologue

"Surely you must be jesting," Emma Barnes said as she rubbed at her throbbing temple, the silk of her glove sliding softly against her skin.

She didn't want to be here right now, listening to complicated legal jargon she barely understood, so soon after her father's sudden, senseless death, but the law waited for no one. Nor did it care that she was being left financially constrained and dependent. Apparently, all the funds her father had accumulated since coming to Colorado—first by opening a general store to sell supplies to miners, then expanding to a second store and investing in the railroad, silver mines, and other ventures—were unavailable to her until she reached the age of majority at twenty-one or married.

"As I said, the will is explicit. You'll have a small stipend for necessities, but you'll have no direct access to your inheritance without authorization from the trustee," Mr. Chapman replied. The portly, balding attorney adjusted his spectacles and cleared his throat, turning the page with deliberate slowness. "Furthermore, the house on Larimer Street must be sold, with the proceeds going to bolster the trust."

Emma grasped the arm of her chair, desperate for something to ground her as the shock of his words sent an icy dread spreading through her chest. "And where am I to live now that my home is being taken from me?" she asked, voice steady only through sheer will.

Mr. Chapman hesitated, her words seeming to form the first crack in his self-possessed composure. "With your father's cousin, Mr. Edward Barnes, his wife, Sarah, and their children in Montana Territory. Apparently, they own a dairy farm. I've taken the liberty of notifying him already."

She stared at the attorney in disbelief. "But I'm nineteen—an adult. Surely I won't be held to that now. In any case, I've never met the man. My father scarcely spoke of him."

"Nevertheless, the will stipulates that you must live under his care until the conditions are met, or your father's estate will be divided between his chosen charities. It was his express wish, and it's my job as executor and trustee to see it carried out."

"I see," she whispered, tapping a gloved finger on the worn leather of her chair in thought.

She was being left without a choice, and while it galled her, she knew her father hadn't done this as a punishment. After influenza had claimed her mother when she was only eight, and her younger sister Abigail had passed a few years later, Emma's father had grown very protective of her.

He'd taken her with him wherever he went when she wasn't attending school or meetings of the Ladies Relief Society. He would have wanted to entrust his only living daughter to someone he trusted implicitly, and if he thought his cousin was the best person to care for her in his stead, she would have to trust his judgment.

After all, there was no other family left in Denver. And after Michael had betrayed her, she didn't even have the prospect of marriage to stay for. Taking a deep breath, Emma stood and collected her white silk parasol and her beaded black velvet purse with trembling fingers.

"Miss Barnes, where do you think you're going?" Mr. Chapman asked, looking a bit annoyed. "We still have more to discuss."

“I’m sure we do,” she replied shakily, her tone polite yet firm, “but I’m going home while I still have one. It seems I have some packing to do. Good day, Mr. Chapman.”

She held her head high as she exited the room, forcing one foot in front of the other and leaving the attorney stammering in his seat at her abrupt departure. As she climbed into the waiting carriage, her heart pounding so hard she could feel it in her throat, she heard her father’s voice close to her ear, whispering, “Onwards, my girl. Ever onwards.” It felt like he was there, giving her courage for what would come next, even as terror clawed at her insides.

Chapter 1

Denver

Late May 1885

As the conductor paced the weathered tracks, bellowing out a boarding call for the northbound Union Pacific train, Emma stood frozen amid the swirl of departing passengers. The cool spring breeze wafted wisps of her auburn hair onto her cheeks, but she made no move to brush them away. Her fingers remained clenched on the handles of her carpetbag, its contents and those of her few trunks all that remained of her old life.

She had fought tooth and nail with Mr. Chapman to let her linger in the hotel while the house sale dragged on, telling the attorney it was only practical. In truth, it had been a reprieve, a way to put off the inevitable. Each day in the familiar town had let her pretend nothing had changed. Here, time had stood still. And in that stasis, she had felt safe.

But the delay could only stretch so far. The papers had been signed, the money transferred, and the tiny town of Elk Ridge now waited on the other side of the journey—along with the extended family she barely knew. She would have to start over and rebuild her life from the ground up. The thought made her stomach churn.

A gentle hand on her shoulder drew her from her musings, and she looked down to see Mrs. Vance, a trim, petite woman in her mid-sixties with curly gray hair. Mr. Chapman had hired her to escort Emma to Montana. The widow was already bound for Missoula to see her son and his new baby, making her the ideal companion in the attorney's estimation.

Emma had bristled at the idea when he first proposed it. After all, she was nineteen years old and perfectly capable of traveling alone. But Mr. Chapman had insisted, noting that it was common practice for a single young woman to travel with an escort. She knew from experience that arguing with an attorney was futile, so instead of wasting her energy, she conceded.

Thankfully, she'd taken to Mrs. Vance upon their first meeting, and the prospect of her company on the train ride had proved welcome.

"It's time to go now," the older woman said, gesturing to the train.

Taking a deep breath, Emma nodded. "You're quite right, Mrs. Vance. I'm sorry for dithering."

"It's fine, child," she replied kindly. "I know how hard it is to leave, but we really must go."

She grabbed her carpetbag from its spot on the ground, and together they set off toward the train, a hiss of steam escaping into the breeze. Though Mrs. Vance stood a good deal shorter than Emma's own five-foot-nine frame, she kept pace without complaint. The platform crowd parted around them as they reached the conductor, who was checking tickets with brisk efficiency.

Emma handed over the sturdy, colored cardstock. After glancing at it to make sure the information was correct, the man tore off one of the perforated sections and tucked it into a pouch. Then he offered a steady hand to help them up the metal stairs leading onto the train.

A friendly porter was waiting just inside to show them to the seats in the Pullman car, explaining that he would be available to help with any of their needs. As they followed him, she admired the lacquered walnut paneling with its carved and inlaid decorations and thick Brussels carpets covering the floor. Chandeliers and polished brass fixtures made it feel less like a train and more like a home on wheels.

When the porter left them to settle in, Mrs. Vance set her carpetbag down on the floor, looked around, and exclaimed, “My, my, child. This is glorious! I thought we would sit on the bench in the other car. You didn’t tell me we were traveling like royalty. I admit, I was worried about how my old bones would fare on the wooden seats.”

“Yes, this is very pleasant.” Emma glanced around the compartment and smiled. Though it had gone against her frugal nature to spend so much on tickets for the sleeping car, it was worth it. “It will be nice to lie down instead of trying to find a comfortable way to sleep sitting up.”

“Why, I didn’t even think of that! I’m so blessed to be traveling with you.” Mrs. Vance leaned in and said, “I was so nervous when Mr. Chapman hired me to be your companion on this trip—you never know how folks will mix. But I’m glad to say he did a bang-up job. We get along splendidly!”

“I agree. This will be a most agreeable trip with you at my side.”

“You’re too kind. Why don’t we sit down and make ourselves comfortable?”

They each took a seat in a wide, upholstered armchair, facing opposite each other, and chatted about the pleasant surroundings. When the train rocked forward and began moving out of the station, Emma leaned to the side and looked out the large window. As the train picked up speed and they left the crowded confines of Denver with its shining electric streetlights glittering in the distance, she felt butterflies fluttering in her stomach.

Emma and Mrs. Vance spent the next few hours talking—mostly about the older woman’s new grandchild waiting in Missoula—and walking the aisles to stretch their legs. It wasn’t until the train slowed for a brief stop to take on water before the last stretch to Cheyenne that Emma realized she was hungry.

During earlier stopovers, they had been content to skip the hurried purchases from platform vendors, but this time, hunger won out. After tucking away their belongings, they made their way to the dining car. They could have asked the porter to bring something to their seats, but neither woman wanted to trouble him.

The dining car's design resembled the sleeping car, featuring the same lacquered paneling and carpets, but here, staff had set several small dining tables with crystal stemware and fine china. The wonderful aroma from the kitchen filled the air as they entered. Emma pressed a hand to her empty stomach and searched for a place to sit. Mrs. Vance found a spot open near a window, and they hurried to claim it for themselves, settling into an upholstered armchair. She lifted the small menu and was debating between roasted chicken and beef stew when Mrs. Vance spoke.

"Do you think they make a decent cup of coffee on this train? I'm dying for one, but who wants weak coffee?"

"I know I don't. My father used to take his black and strong, no cream or sugar." She paused as a familiar wave of grief at the mention of her father rose. When it passed, she said softly, "When I was younger, I tried to drink it like that too, but my sweet tooth outweighed my need to emulate him."

"My dearest John was the same way," Mrs. Vance said softly, probably feeling a similar sense of grief herself. "It was one thing we always disagreed on."

A waiter appeared a few moments later to take their orders, and while they waited for their meal, Emma surveyed the other passengers. Most of the folks she saw in the dining car were well-dressed and obviously well-off, while others were more care-worn in their appearance, their eyes wide as they stared at the opulence all around them. She wondered if they were setting out on a new life for themselves, as she was.

"What's the matter, child?" came the soft question from across the table. "You've hardly spoken more than a few words since we sat down. Still thinking of your father?"

"For once, no," she replied, a wry, weary smile tugging at her lips. "Not this time. I was thinking about starting over. Wondering what my life will look like once I reach Montana."

"It's sensible to ponder such matters. " Mrs. Vance nodded sagely. "It will be quite different. I've never lived on a farm myself. Like you, Denver's always been home, but my son writes to me and tells me of the progress on his homestead regularly."

"What does he say?" Emma asked, leaning forward in her seat.

"That it's hard work," the older woman said with a small chuckle. "There aren't any of the luxuries we're used to—no indoor plumbing, no gas lamps in the home. I don't imagine they have them in Elk Ridge either. Rupert rises before dawn, feeds the animals, and then starts on all his other chores. The first winter nearly broke him, but—"

Suddenly, the waiter appeared at her elbow, briskly setting down their plates of roast chicken, potatoes, and a slice of apple pie before retreating. The interruption broke the thread of her sentence. Mrs. Vance smiled apologetically and picked up her fork again. "Well. You'll see soon enough."

Emma stared at her plate; the food suddenly seemed less appealing. Mrs. Vance's words echoed in her head, but her mind had already drifted somewhere else.

She'd worked hard before. She'd planned charity bazaars for fifty people—coordinated musicians, arranged flowers, and kept the donors smiling through endless committee meetings. Not to mention hosting dinner parties where twenty silver investors shouted over each other, and she steered the conversation without a single plate breaking. If she could manage the late nights tallying donations, arguments over table placements, and the constant pressure to appear effortless while everything teetered on collapse, surely she could manage a quiet farm.

"Quickly, Mrs. Vance! I think I heard the whistle blow!" Emma shouted as she tried to rush her companion along, all the while looking down to make sure she wouldn't trip on her skirts.

They had disembarked in Cheyenne with an hour to spare until the train continued its route, intending only to take a short stroll to pass the time. The town was much smaller than Denver, but despite its size, it was bustling, and signs of growth were all around. Dozens of new wood and brick buildings filled the landscape, and even more were under construction. What began as a simple walk up the road had turned into distracted sightseeing, and they had lost all track of time.

"We're almost there!" she said encouragingly as the train came into view. "Just a little further."

They ran the last few yards, and as they approached the train, a portly man, whom Emma assumed was the conductor, motioned her over and smiled. "I was about to give my last boarding call," he said. "You just made it."

"Oh, thank heavens!" Mrs. Vance huffed as they finally came to a stop.

The conductor chuckled, checked their tickets, and helped them board the train. Both women were still unsteady on their feet after their exertions, but they managed to find an unoccupied berth.

"We made it!" Emma exclaimed, dropping onto a cushioned seat. "Excellent job, Mrs. Vance! What a story this will be to tell your son!"

"He won't believe it! Ha! Me, running to get on a train," the widow panted, still looking rather red in the face. Setting her carpetbag next to her on the seat, she began rummaging around inside, pulling a delicate fan out and waving it in front of her face. "I say, child," she huffed, "let's not wander so far from the train next time. If we do, you can just leave me there lest I expire from lack of air!"

Emma burst into laughter at the melodramatic comment, and as she did, she realized that this was the first time she'd laughed in months. Her father's passing had left her feeling empty, and she'd forgotten how good it felt to find humor in something. It felt almost like the first struggling crocus of spring—its stubborn purple petals bursting through snow and ice after a long, hard winter.

When she finally got herself under control, she said breathlessly, "We'll stick close to the train from now on, I promise."

"Good, good," Mrs. Vance replied as she continued to fan herself. "I think I may need a nap now. Do you mind?"

"Of course not." She said with an understanding smile. "You enjoy your nap. I think I'll read or do some embroidery."

The older woman nodded, leaned her head against the window, and quickly fell asleep.

Emma bent and quietly retrieved *Pride and Prejudice* from her carpetbag. It had been a gift from her mother, and she'd read it so many times that the pages had become worn and brittle. Carefully holding the book in her lap, she read silently while her companion napped. When her neck became too sore to continue, it was set aside. She considered doing some embroidery, but the mood wasn't right, so she rose instead to stretch her legs.

Glancing down at her traveling dress, she cringed at the dust and wrinkles that clung to the fabric. She was not in full black mourning but a dark indigo cotton that complemented her blue eyes, as her father had always detested the rigid tradition of mourning.

"It makes grief more oppressive," he told her after Abbey's funeral, when she had tried to wear full black mourning out of duty. "Wear color when you can, sweeting. Life is short enough without draping yourself in shadows." So she had taken his words to heart, choosing color over convention.

Unfortunately, walking along the dusty roads of rural towns had taken its toll. The delicate lace trim on her cuffs and collar had turned a disappointing brownish-gray rather than the pristine white it ought to have been. She could only imagine what the frantic rush to catch the train had done to her hair. Deciding her first stop must be the ladies' retiring room just down the hall, she slipped inside.

The small room contained little more than a toilet and a mirror. Emma quickly twisted her auburn locks into a simple bun high on her head and secured it with pins. The style wasn't perfect, but since she wouldn't be attending a gala anytime soon, it would have to do.

After attempting to shake all the dust out of her skirts, she made her way to the dining car, settling at a small table near the window. She ordered a coffee and slowly sipped the brew, letting her thoughts wander. From what Mr. Chapman had told her, Elk Ridge was a few hours away from Butte by wagon, with a population of a little over seven hundred. In a town so small, would there still be social activities—church socials, quilting bees, anything to which she could contribute?

And what if she didn't get along with her family? The possibility of living day after day with strangers who might make her life miserable, especially when she had nowhere else to go, was deeply unsettling.

Frustrated with her mind's ability to jump to a worst-case scenario, she pushed the empty coffee cup aside, gathered a few cookies to share, and started back toward the sleeping car. She needed to focus on something else, and thankfully, Mrs. Vance was awake when she returned, knitting a blanket for her grandson.

"Oh, there you are, child," she said with a relieved sigh. "I was just about to come looking for you!"

"Forgive me, Mrs. Vance. I went to get coffee and lost all track of time, but I brought some cookies to share."

"You're forgiven then," the widow said happily as she took the proffered treat.

Emma smiled and took a bite of her own cookie as she sat down. *If only all of life's troubles could be fixed so easily,* she thought wryly. Brushing crumbs from her lap, she retrieved her embroidery frame from the carpetbag and resumed work on the handkerchief she meant for Sarah, the matriarch of the Barnes family in Elk Ridge.

The design was modest but pleasing: tiny forget-me-nots in pale blue silk thread along the edges, a faint trailing vine in green. She wasn't sure the busy farmwife would have much use for such frippery, but it felt like the least she could offer—a token of gratitude for opening her home to a stranger.

Her needle moved steadily despite the train's occasional lurch, and she let the repetitive motion soothe her as the endless grassland rolled past the window.

Mrs. Vance glanced over now and then, offering a nod of approval or a soft, "That's coming along nicely, dear," before she returned to her own knitting. They worked in companionable silence until the afternoon light waned, lengthening the shadows across the seats, and then made their way to the dining car for supper.

By the time they returned to their seats, the gas lamps had been lit, casting a warm, flickering glow across the velvet seats. Porters moved efficiently through the aisle, unfolding berths, tucking crisp white sheets, and drawing heavy curtains. Emma watched the transformation in quiet fascination—the ordinary day car turning into a row of private sleeping compartments, like a stage set changing between acts.

Once their berths were ready, the ladies took turns in the lavatory. When Emma's turn came, she slipped into her nightgown and studied her reflection. She looked tired, but her eyes were no longer quite so haunted as they had been in the weeks right after her father passed. The raw edge of loss had dulled, if only a little. She braided her long auburn hair for the night, fingers moving by habit, then gave herself one last steadying look.

Mrs. Vance had claimed the lower berth—easier for her age and the occasional stiffness in her knees—so Emma accepted the small ladder the porter offered. She climbed up carefully, mindful of the swaying car, and crawled beneath the thin blanket.

"Goodnight, Mrs. Vance," she said quietly.

"Goodnight, child. Sleep well," the older woman murmured, her voice already drowsy.

With the heavy curtains drawn for privacy, she lay on her back, staring up at the close ceiling of the berth as she thought about the days ahead. Tomorrow the train will carry her past Laramie's wide plains, then through the lonely stretches of Rawlins and Green River; past Evanston's silent yards; and into Ogden, where she will change cars for the final push north—Pocatello, Idaho Falls, Butte. Each name felt like a step farther from Denver, from the brick house on Larimer Street, from the life she had known. The thought tightened her throat, but she let the gentle rocking settle her back toward sleep.

Chapter 2

Gabriel Moreau sat on his front porch, lazily rocking his chair back and forth with his foot as he sipped from his steaming mug of coffee and watched the sky turn from murky gray to bright pink and orange as the sun rose. It was a glorious sight to behold, and as the new day dawned, he looked out onto his land and felt gratitude for the new life he'd been given.

It had been more than a year since that fateful morning in Dallas. He still remembered how bone-tired he had been, trudging back to the undertaker's after digging a fresh grave, his arms and legs caked in thick red-brown clay. All he had wanted was to wash up and change into clean, dry clothes. But when he arrived and found a thick manila envelope waiting for him, he forgot all about his disheveled state, just staring at the letter.

No one had ever written to him before.

Full of curiosity, he had wiped his dirty hands as best he could, opened the envelope, and read the letter that lay on top of the stack of papers. It was from an attorney in Butte, informing him that his uncle, Telly, had died and left him the Lucky Strike—a modest ranch in Elk Ridge, Montana. Gabe had stood there for several minutes in shock. He hadn't even known he had an uncle, much less one who would leave him anything in his will.

At first, he had thought that there had been some mix-up, and they'd gotten him confused with someone with the same name. But after sending several telegrams, along with documents verifying his identity, it became official. He owned a ranch. He said goodbye to his boss, Mr. Flemming, packed up his few belongings and took the train north to Montana.

To say it had been overwhelming to learn how to run such a large spread was an understatement, and he knew he wouldn't have made it without the guidance of his foreman, Henry Rollings. The grizzled older man had been a surprisingly patient mentor, and Gabe had worked hard to learn everything he needed to know about ranching. He'd spent his days in the saddle from sunup to sundown: checking water holes, driving cattle to new grazing land, mending broken fences, branding, castrating, and doctoring livestock, only to fall into a deep sleep as soon as his head hit the pillow.

If he was honest with himself, he was only now beginning to feel competent enough to carry on Telly's legacy. He still held the guilt of knowing that the only reason he sat here at all was that a man he had never met had died, but it was also what made him so determined to succeed. He wanted to make his uncle proud.

Gabe continued rocking gently, lost in his thoughts, until the rich aroma of frying bacon, fresh biscuits, and eggs drifted out through the open kitchen window. The savory smell finally pulled him back to the present. Taking a final swig from his coffee cup, he stood and headed inside.

As he stepped into the kitchen, he was greeted by the familiar sight of his housekeeper, Martha May Rollings. Short and matronly, with streaks of gray threading through her once-flaxen hair, she moved briskly about the room, carrying large platters of food to the table. She was so absorbed in her work that she barely seemed to notice him.

He set his cup aside and reached out for a biscuit, still cooling on a tray by the windowsill, but the moment his fingers hovered over it, a wooden spoon rapped his knuckles sharply.

"Ow!" Gabe yelped and yanked his hand back.

Martha May waved the spoon at him like a weapon. "Don't you try to go sneaking any food before grace, Gabriel Moreau," she scolded. "I know your mother taught you better manners."

"Sorry, Martha May. You know these biscuits of yours are the best around. I can't help myself." He grimaced as he rubbed the knuckles on his right hand. "Besides, how will you know if you made them just right unless I test one for you?"

"Oh! You know I always make them the same way every time... perfectly! And don't you go thinking that my husband will back you up on this! That man knows to wait for the blessing before he eats my food. Now, go tell him that breakfast is ready," she instructed as she turned back to the stove and began plating up fried potatoes.

"Don't you go bossing the boss around now, Martha May," Henry cautioned as he strolled in through the back door, scuffed boots and dirt-streaked pants showing that he'd already been hard at work. "He might take offense and decide he needs a housekeeper who doesn't nag him first thing in the morning. Or a foreman who doesn't complain about his aching joints."

Cackling at his own joke, he tossed his wide-brimmed hat on the counter and ran his hands through his salt-and-pepper hair. Then, making sure his wife wasn't looking, he snatched a biscuit and stuffed it into his mouth before heading for the sink to wash his hands.

Gabe stifled his laughter and turned his face so Martha May couldn't see his smile as she set the fried potatoes down on the table.

"Breakfast is ready," she said, wiping her hands on the apron she wore over her pale-yellow dress. "Gabriel, you hurry and wash up, and then we can say grace."

Dutifully, he stepped over to the wet sink and washed his hands, using the cold water piped in from the gravity-fed cistern. When he was done, he took his seat at the head of the table and asked Henry to bless the food.

"Dear Lord," the foreman began. "We thank you for this glorious day. Bless the hands that prepared this meal, and bless this food for our bodies. Amen."

It was a quick, simple prayer, but it served its purpose.

While they passed plates around the table, Gabe looked to Martha May and asked, "Do you need me to get anything for you at the general store? I've got to go to town this week and pick up some things. I figured while I'm there, I should load up."

"I'll make you a list. If I'm going to make your favorite cobbler this week, I'll need some peaches."

"You sure know how to spoil me," he grinned.

"Well, you only get it if you're good." After a few bites, she added, "Did you hear the Barneses are taking in a relative? Edward's cousin died, and the will named them as guardians. By golly, that house is already bursting with nine children in it! How in the world will they make room for one more?"

"Martha May, they aren't all children anymore. The oldest is about Gabe's age," Henry noted.

"Well, yes, that's true. But still!" She put down her fork and tapped a fingernail on the table. "I wonder if Sarah needs any help to get the place ready."

"Maybe you should ask her," her husband suggested. "You could ride over and have coffee with her this afternoon."

"Well, I have to get a few loaves of bread in today and strip the linens off the beds, but I think you're right, Henry. I'll do just that."

Henry gave her a teasing smile and asked, "Can you repeat that?"

"Repeat what?" she asked, frowning in confusion.

"The part where you admitted he's right," Gabe put in helpfully.

"Oh! Why, I never said such a thing!" Martha May squawked indignantly. She crossed her arms, eyes flashing daggers at the pair as they exchanged grins. "I think it's time the two of you headed out. You have work to do."

"I suppose we'd best get to it, then," Henry said, pushing back from the table. He stooped to give his wife a quick peck on the cheek and went to collect his hat, calling out, "Come on, boss."

Gabe nodded and stuffed his last bite of biscuit into his mouth as he left the table. As he grabbed his own hat from a peg near the back door, he said, "I'm going to take Miguel with me to check the fence line along the east side of the property this morning."

"Good," the foreman grunted. "Never hurts to have another pair of hands."

They parted ways at the bottom of the porch steps, and Gabe set off in search of the senior ranch hand. Miguel had been the very first cattle puncher Telly ever hired, and his calm, steady nature, combined with years of hard-won experience, had made him nearly as instrumental in Gabe's ranching education as Henry himself.

After a few minutes of searching, he found the older man in the stable's tack room, mending a bridle at the workbench.

"Morning," Miguel greeted, not looking up from his work, as he punched a new hole through the torn cheek piece.

"Morning. I need you to load a packhorse with supplies. We're going to head down to the eastern fence line of the property together."

Miguel nodded and began packing away his tools. "I'll meet you out front."

With that task delegated, Gabe left him to his cleanup and went about some other chores before going to collect his gelding from its stall.

Xerxes was a beast of a quarter horse, at sixteen and a half hands, with a handsome bay coat that shone like copper in the sun and a long black mane and tail. He had been the first purchase Gabe made for himself when he arrived in Montana, and the two had quickly bonded. So much so that Xerxes would follow him around like a giant puppy, which made Miguel and the younger cowhands laugh.

After grabbing his saddle from the tack room, Gabe led Xerxes out of his stall and loosely tied his reins to a post outside the stable. Knowing the routine, the gelding stood still while receiving a brush down; however, once he felt the blanket and saddle being placed on his back, he began stamping his foot, eager to be off. Gabe gave him a pat on the neck to calm him, and he was leaning down to grab the cinch strap when Miguel arrived.

"I'm ready," the ranch hand announced in his heavily accented English as he led a packhorse and his mount up to the stable doors.

"Good," Gabe said. He double-checked the straps on the saddle and mounted up. "Let's head out then."

Both men were quiet as they made their way through the tall grass and scrub brush to the east. Miguel wasn't the chatty sort, so Gabe let his mind wander as he thought about the ranch. Telly had done the hard work of raising his herd from thirty head of Angus cattle to just over two hundred and fifty head, and while Gabe was proud to carry on his legacy, he wanted to do more with it. He had some ideas in mind, too, but he wanted to discuss them with Henry first. Not that he needed permission, but it would be a lot easier to do if he weren't fighting his foreman every step of the way.

They had just reached the top of a washed-out gully when Xerxes stumbled on a gopher hole, and though the horse righted itself within a few steps, Gabe had been taken by surprise. Unable to catch himself in time, he fell out of the saddle and right over the edge of the steep trench that rainfall and snowmelt had worn into the ground.

Though it took only seconds, it seemed like minutes passed before he felt himself impact the ground, and he hit so hard it knocked the breath from his lungs. He struggled to regain his breath as he rolled several feet down the eroded soil, and when he came to a stop at the bottom of the gully's slope, dust swirling all around him, he groaned in pain.

He lay still for a minute, taking stock of his injuries. Nothing seemed broken. He was fortunate that the gully was shallow, about eight feet deep, with only dirt and small withered roots sticking up from the ground. If he had hit a rock or a fallen log with sharp limbs sticking out, his fall could have been fatal. He was just about to get up when Miguel's worried face came into view above him.

"¡Jefe!" he shouted. "Don't move; I'll come down to get you."

The ranch hand scrambled away, and a few moments later, he came riding down a gentle incline with Xerxes trailing behind him. Seeing only two horses confused Gabe for a moment, but he realized the packhorse must still be at the top.

Miguel swung down from his horse and squatted in front of him. "Are you hurt?" he asked, concern filling the older man's voice.

"I'm fine," Gabe said. "It doesn't feel like anything's broken."

Miguel stood and helped him sit up slowly. A wince escaped despite his effort to hide it, and the ranch hand noticed.

"Jefe, don't be loco," he chided. "Let me help you back to Xerxes."

Gabe held up his hand. "I said I'm fine."

Not wanting to look weak in front of his employee, he struggled to his feet and began swatting the dirt from the seat of his pants. He took a few stiff steps and picked up his revolver where it had fallen from the holster, sliding it back into the molded leather.

"Thank you for bringing Xerxes to me," he said, his voice steady despite the ache in his ribs. "Let's just finish riding the line and head back. I've still got work that needs to be done."

Miguel threw his hands in the air and stomped away, muttering and cursing in Spanish.

Gabe didn't need to be fluent in the language to know what was being said, and he waited until the ranch hand was a few feet away before he lifted his shirt to make sure he wasn't bleeding. The skin on his torso was scraped raw, and even though his entire body would be black and blue by morning, he knew he could work through the pain. It wasn't the first time in his life he'd done so, thanks to his Pa.

Bracing himself, he mounted his gelding and followed Miguel back up the hill to collect the packhorse and continue with their day.

By the time they'd finished the repairs and Gabe returned to the stable to put Xerxes up, he was ready to call it a day. Every part of his body ached, and he was unsure if he could unsaddle his own horse. As he carefully dismounted, he heard the clink of spurs behind him and turned to see Henry, leading his own horse inside the large double doors.

"Are you all right, son?" asked the foreman. "You're moving kind of funny."

"Yeah, I bruised my pride mostly. I took a fall. I'll be fine by tomorrow."

Henry grunted, gave him an assessing stare, and then took Xerxes' reins. "Why don't you go into the house and get washed up? I heard Martha May ringing the dinner bell when you were riding in."

Gabe thought that sounded like a grand idea. He gave Henry a grateful nod and began walking toward the house. Holding his hand to the side that had taken the brunt of the fall, he berated himself the entire way for not paying more attention. He'd been working on this ranch for close to a year, and though he'd come a long way, he was still making stupid mistakes. He was just lucky it hadn't cost him his life.

Gabe was still feeling down when he entered the kitchen, but the mouthwatering aromas that greeted him took his mind off his troubles. "Evening, Martha May," he said. "Dinner sure smells good."

"Of course it does," the housekeeper replied, placing a large pot on the table. "I've got it all set out on the table."

Nodding his thanks, he made his way to the wet sink, trying his best not to show any signs of injury. If Martha May noticed he was in pain, she would coddle him and make sure he didn't leave his bed for days. Thankfully, she wasn't paying any attention to him.

Once Henry came in and cleaned up, they sat down at the table to eat the hearty beef stew served with thick slices of buttered bread, still warm from the oven. For a while, no one spoke, as they were more intent on filling their bellies, but finally, Martha May broke the silence.

“I went over to visit Sarah today, as you suggested, Henry,” she announced.

"Is that so?” he drawled.

“Well, she’s all in a dither getting the house ready for their cousin to arrive,” Martha May continued. “That poor dear looked so harried when she opened the door that I spent most of the time helping her with chores. She told me they planned to have a welcoming party at their place once their cousin had a chance to rest up from their long journey. I said we’d bring over some extra tables and chairs.” She turned to Gabe with a smile. “You don’t mind, do you?”

“No, that’s fine by me." He shrugged. “I don’t know if I’ll make it, though. Ashes is fixing to foal, so I’ll be sticking close to the ranch until she gives birth. She’s the best cutting horse we have.”

“What? But Gabriel, you *must* come,” Martha May wailed, hands flying to her cheeks.

Her distress caught him off guard. It wasn’t the first time he had skipped a community event or even Sunday services because of a problem with the herd. He looked over at Henry to see if he knew what was going on, but the foreman just shrugged and looked curiously at his wife.

“If it means that much to you, I’ll get Miguel or one of the other hands to watch over her when the time comes,” he said. “But I don’t aim to be gone for too long.”

Martha May sighed in relief and beamed at him. “Oh, good. Thank you, Gabriel. We must support our neighbors in any way we can.”

He nodded, still confused about why she was so insistent. There seemed to be quite a big fuss over just another family member moving in, but he’d said that he’d be there and was a man of his word. He turned his attention to his bowl of stew, and when he looked up again to speak, he saw Henry and Martha May exchange a look that he couldn’t puzzle out. He wanted to ask about it but decided it was none of his business.

The next morning, after having breakfast and clearing the dishes, Gabe asked Martha May and Henry to sit with him at the table so they could talk. The older couple looked concerned and took a seat at the table, holding hands.

"Gabriel, what's going on?" Martha May asked fearfully. "You're not planning to sell the ranch, are you?"

"No, of course not," he said, shaking his head. "But after I took a fall while I was riding fence with Miguel yesterday, it got me thinking about what would happen to this ranch if I died. In fact, I stayed up most of the night because of it. Uncle Telly worked so hard for the Lucky Strike, and I wouldn't want it taken by the government. I want to put you both in my will as my beneficiaries."

Martha May and Henry sat stunned for a while until Henry spoke up. "That's kind of you, Gabe, but I don't know if that's the best idea. What would happen if Martha May and I passed away before you? We aren't exactly young."

"Speak for yourself," Martha May said tartly, "and we'll come back to this bit about a fall in a minute, but Gabriel, what you need is a son to pass this place on to. Better yet, several sons. Daughters, too, for good measure." She sat up straighter in her chair and smiled. "I think it's time you looked for a wife. You're a tall, handsome young man. You shouldn't have any trouble attracting a woman."

"A wife!" Gabe let out a startled laugh. "Martha May, I just turned twenty-three in December. Besides, I'm too busy running this ranch to even have time for courting. I haven't even talked much with any of the women around, though you certainly tried your best to point out my availability to every eligible woman since I moved up here."

"You may be young now, Gabriel, but what happens when ten or twenty years pass, and you are out here all alone with only those cows for company? You own this ranch, which means you can make the time to go courting if you really want to, and no one can say a thing against you," Martha May said, a defiant look on her face.

Gabe turned to Henry for support, but the foreman held his hands up in front of him.

"Oh no. Don't come asking me for help. You came to us with a problem, and this is the best solution. We aren't saying you should go out and marry the first gal you set eyes on, but just think about it and see how you feel."

Being outnumbered and knowing better than to argue with Martha May, he threw his hands up in the air. "Fine. I'll think about it, but I'm not making any promises."

Martha May stood up and came around the table to kiss him on the cheek. "We just want you to be happy, Gabriel."

Though it wasn't what he'd wanted to hear, Gabe knew she was speaking the truth. The Rollings had taken him under their wing and been his biggest champions since he'd set foot on the ranch, but what they asked for seemed like too much right now. He still had so much he wanted to do to make this ranch his own, and taking a wife was not part of that plan.

Chapter 3

Emma and Mrs. Vance fell into a routine of needlework, reading, and taking their meals in the dining car. Occasionally, they would strike up a friendly conversation with other passengers, but mostly they chatted amongst themselves and looked out on the changing scenery in awe. They had still taken walks to stretch their legs during stops, but never again wandered far from the train. They had learned that lesson the hard way.

When she woke on the last day of her journey, a flurry of emotions stirred inside her: nervousness at what lay ahead, relief that the long days of uncertainty were nearly over, and a bit of eagerness at the prospect of being a part of a family again. She couldn't decide which held sway, and for the first time in months, the future felt less like a threat and more like a doorway—narrow, unfamiliar, but open.

She climbed down from her sleeping berth, careful not to wake Mrs. Vance, and slipped out to use the facilities and get dressed. When she returned, her chaperone was waiting for her with a small, encouraging smile.

"Shall we have some breakfast and fortify ourselves for the day?" Mrs. Vance asked.

Emma managed a small smile and agreed. She slowly sipped a cup of coffee while her chaperone ate eggs and toast, the familiar clink of silverware and the steady rocking of the train almost soothing. But as the miles slipped by, a knot in her stomach formed.

An hour later, when the clatter of the wheels softened and the train began to slow, Emma was glad she had chosen not to eat. Her stomach was already threatening to revolt, and the last thing she wanted was to step off the train and immediately lose her breakfast in front of her relatives. That was not the first impression she wanted to make.

She was fiddling with the pearl button on the cuff of her sleeve and staring out at the wide-open valley, nestled in the bowl of the mountains, when Mrs. Vance reached across the seat and squeezed her hands.

"You'll be fine, child," the chaperone said, while giving a supportive smile. "Just be yourself."

"I'll try," Emma promised, attempting a confident smile.

"Good. Now, collect your things. The train should pull into the station at any moment, and we don't want to keep your relatives waiting."

"You're coming with me?" she asked, surprised.

"Of course!" Mrs. Vance exclaimed. "I'd be failing in my chaperone duties if I let you go off on your own and some brigands abducted you!"

Emma laughed at the widow's dramatic comment and put her book and sewing supplies in her carpetbag, making sure that nothing was left behind. The train lurched to a stop a moment later, and when the doors of the Pullman car opened, passengers began filing out. Not wanting to fight their way through the crowd, she and Mrs. Vance waited for the crush of people to thin before disembarking.

The small wooden train station, located on the southern edge of Butte, was surrounded by a bustle of activity. The streets were lined with saloons, boarding houses, mercantiles, and the rough wooden buildings of a mining camp on the make. In the distance, smoke could be seen rising from the mine headframes, and the rhythmic thudding from the stamp mills could be heard in the distance.

Looking around as the other passengers milled about on the platform, Emma spotted a small but noticeable group standing to the right of the station platform.

"Look, Mrs. Vance." She nodded toward them. "Do you suppose those are my relatives?"

"Yes, I believe so," the widow agreed, craning her neck to see past a taller passenger. "Who else would be waiting with such a purposeful look?"

Emma raised a gloved hand in a tentative wave and started walking over, Mrs. Vance following close behind. As they drew nearer, certainty settled in her chest—this was her family. The older gentleman at the center had the same chestnut hair as her father, though streaked with more gray and worn longer under a wide-brimmed hat. He was taller, leaner, his face weathered by sun and wind, but the steady blue-gray eyes were unmistakably Barnes. This had to be Edward.

Beside him stood a pretty, trim woman of mid-height. Her deep brown hair, threaded with silver and showing her age, was pulled back in a practical bun. Her face was eager and open, the lines at her eyes crinkling with genuine welcome.

To Edward's right clustered three girls in simple cotton dresses and bonnets, two younger and one older. They favored their mother—dark, shiny hair neatly braided or pinned beneath their bonnets—and they watched her approach with open curiosity.

A step behind stood a handsome, broad-shouldered young man, arms folded, gaze steady as he leaned against the family wagon. He was the spitting image of his father, with his chestnut hair and lean build. Yet all of them, the girls and the young man alike, shared the same clear blue-gray eyes. It was a handsome group.

Even from this distance, their smiles were warm, if a little shy, and Emma felt her own lips curve in answer despite the sudden tightness in her throat.

"Are you Emma Barnes?" came the hesitant question from the older woman when they were a few feet apart.

"Yes," she smiled and extended her hand. "You must be Sarah."

"I am." Instead of shaking it, Sarah pulled her into a fierce hug. "Oh, I am so glad to meet you at last! We've been praying for your safe arrival."

The gesture was so unexpected that Emma froze for a moment. Not knowing what else to do, she returned the hug and gently patted the older woman on the back until the embrace ended.

"Dearest, let's give Emma a chance to meet us all first before you go smothering her," her husband said as he came near. He wrapped an arm around his wife's shoulder, lifted his hat in greeting, and extended his hand. "Hello there. I'm Edward, your father's cousin—which I guess makes us first cousins once removed! You can call us Aunt Sarah and Uncle Edward if that makes things easier."

"That's probably for the best," Emma agreed, his words instantly putting her at ease. "It might get tedious trying to explain the family connection every time I meet someone new."

"True." He gestured behind him and to the right. "These are some of our children. We had to leave the rest at home to tend to the farm. Micah, here is our oldest son, and these are our daughters, Mary, Esther, and Ruth."

They took turns welcoming Emma with polite nods and a respectful hat-tip, and she returned their greetings warmly.

"I know it might take a while to get everyone's names straight with their faces," Uncle Edward said, a wry smile forming. "But don't feel too bad. We still mix them up from time to time."

The comment made her smile. "Well, it's very nice to meet you all. Allow me to introduce my companion for the journey, Mrs. Vance. She's continuing to Missoula to stay with her son."

"Thank you so much for seeing Emma safely to us," Sarah said, wringing the older woman's hand. "We were worried about her being on her own for such a long trip."

"It was my pleasure. She's a delight to be around. Her father raised her well, and she's a testament to him." Turning to Emma and taking her by the hand, she sucked in a shaky breath. "Well, child. You're safe with your family now, so I shall let you go. Please write to me to let me know when you're settled. I'm going to miss you, you know."

"I'll miss you too," Emma said. "And I promise to keep in touch. You were the perfect traveling companion. I'll write to Mr. Chapman and thank him for finding you."

Mrs. Vance sniffed back some tears, waved goodbye once more before boarding the train, and disappeared inside.

Now alone with her new family, Emma turned and smiled at the assembled group, hoping that she didn't look as nervous as she felt.

"If you're ready, we should collect your things," Edward suggested gently.

"Of course," she replied, grateful for the gentle guidance. "I tied a blue ribbon around the handles of my trunks so they would be easier to identify. Oh—before I forget, Mr. Chapman gave me a letter for you."

She drew a sealed envelope from her bag and handed it to him. Edward nodded his thanks, tucked it into his coat pocket, and motioned to Micah.

"Let's get her trunks loaded."

Mary, the cousin who seemed to be around Emma's own age, came to stand next to her.

"I know that was undoubtedly an overwhelming greeting," she said with a tentative smile, "but we're so happy to have you here with us."

"Of course we are!" exclaimed Esther, skipping to join them. "We finally get to have another girl in the house! It's so unfair that the boys outnumber us."

"Well, we're still outnumbered, but at least it's better odds!" replied Ruth as she followed her sister.

"Better odds against what?" Emma asked, wondering what she was getting herself into.

The young teens exchanged glances, and Esther leaned in conspiratorially. "Against the boys winning every game of checkers and claiming the best spots by the stove in winter. You'll see."

Before she could reply, Sarah stepped closer and gently placed her hand on her shoulder. "Are you hungry at all? It will be a few hours before we dare back in Elk Ridge."

"No, I'll be fine," Emma said, still not sure if her stomach would rebel.

"Well, if you're sure..." Sarah looked as if she wanted to press the issue, but she gave Emma's shoulder a light squeeze and stepped back.

Across the platform, Edward and Micah worked quickly, lifting the burdensome trunks with practiced ease while the younger girls hovered nearby, offering suggestions which were largely ignored. Then, once the luggage was secured, everyone found their places in the wagon, and they set off down the dusty road toward Elk Ridge.

Throughout the long drive, Mary and her sisters filled the time by asking Emma eager questions while Micah sat quietly between his parents. The girls wanted to know all about her favorite books, fashion tastes, colors—anything that might help them know their new cousin better. Emma answered happily, grateful for their warmth and the way they accepted her so quickly. It seemed all her worrying on the train was for nothing.

Chapter 4

When they entered Elk Ridge, Emma got to her knees for a better vantage point and studied the town. Like most places she'd seen throughout her train journey, the businesses were wooden, with false fronts and large glass windows. The exceptions to this were a small, two-story hotel and a sheriff's office with an attached jailhouse, both made of sturdy red brick.

Most of the homes were simple wood-framed cottages with a front porch for shade, but here and there she spotted a few grander homes. The tall towers, bay windows, and decorative trim made them stand out against their neighbors, proclaiming the wealth of the owners. As Emma took it all in, her heart beat faster. This was her new home.

Noticing her interest in the town, her cousins began pointing out businesses they thought she might enjoy visiting, such as the dress shop, the milliner's, and the bookstore.

"A bookstore? Really?" she asked in excitement.

"Yes, it also functions as a subscription library, where they serve tea or coffee and pastries to customers at the book club," Mary replied.

"I'd love to join the book club!" Emma said excitedly. "Do you have to be a member of the library to attend?"

"Not at all," Aunt Sarah answered. "We don't meet as often as we'd like—everyone's busy working—but when we get the chance, we like to make the most of it. Last month, we discussed *Little Women* for most of the afternoon."

It sounded like something she would have done in Denver, if all of her time hadn't been dedicated to the Ladies Relief Society and her father's business pursuits. Though she'd just arrived, Emma sensed she would form fast friendships with her aunt and female cousins. They had many things in common, which was an immense relief, and she already felt comfortable in their presence. But what about her male cousins?

She glanced toward Micah, who was sitting silently on the bench ahead, reins loose in his hands as the horses plodded along. He hadn't said more than a few words to her. She supposed he might be shy, in which case it might be up to her to strike up a conversation. She hesitated for half a heartbeat before she asked, "What about you, Micah? Do you attend meetings at the library as well?"

Micah turned his head just enough to meet her eyes, an amused smile tugging at his mouth. "No, I'm not part of the *women's* book club. I do enjoy reading, though, as well as playing chess or cards."

Emma felt a small, pleased warmth bloom in her chest. He hadn't bristled or brushed her off; he'd answered easily and with a sincere tone. It was a tiny thing, but it eased something tight inside her, another quiet sign that she might not have to walk on eggshells here.

The road dipped and rose one final time, and as the wagon rolled into the farmyard, two sleek, lean black-and-white dogs bolted off the porch. Their tails whipped in wild circles as they unleashed happy, high-pitched barks. Uncle Edward pulled the team to a stop and set the brake, dust settling around the wheels.

A small boy—no more than twelve—came running from the barn, face flushed with excitement. "They're here!" he yelled, waving both arms. "Luke! Joseph! Come out—Emma's here!"

Two young men appeared from the barn door, wiping hands on their trousers—tall and broad like Micah, and close to his age. Behind them trailed another boy who looked to be in his late teens, then another, younger boy, hanging back a little, eyes wide with curiosity.

Edward climbed down first, then offered Emma his hand. "Easy now," he said to the dogs, who circled closer, tails thumping. He turned to her with a warm smile. "Welcome home. Let me introduce the rest of the family."

He gestured to each boy in turn, voice matter-of-fact. "This is Luke, Joseph, Benjamin and Isaac. And Matthew here," he drawled, rested a hand on the youngest's shoulder, the boy still bouncing on his toes, "is the one who just announced your arrival to the entire valley."

Emma watched them nod or offer shy smiles—Luke and Joseph with calm confidence, Benjamin with a quick grin, Isaac ducking his head slightly, and Matthew beaming as if he'd personally summoned her from Denver.

"I'm pleased to meet you all," she said, looking around at the new faces.

"Boys, will you help your Pa bring in Emma's trunks?" Sarah asked, her gaze resting briefly on her eldest sons. Then she turned to the two younger girls with a gentle but firm smile. "Esther, Ruth, come help me in the kitchen. Supper won't wait."

The three young men moved toward the wagon without hesitation, while Isaac—silent, watchful—slipped away toward the barn without a word. Esther and Ruth exchanged disappointed glances but followed obediently, their chatter fading toward the house.

"We'll have everything ready soon, Emma dear. Take a moment if you need it." Sarah gave her one last warm look before turning away and speaking quietly with Mary.

Matthew lingered nearby, watching Emma with bright eyes as the dogs circled his legs. She smiled and crouched to their level, pointing at the animals.

"Who do we have here?" she asked.

"This one is Sally. She's going to have pups any day now, and that's Jack. They're Border Collies," he said eagerly. "You can pet them. They won't bite."

Emma extended her hand toward Jack and waited. His wet nose brushed her palm, investigating the unfamiliar scent, then he began licking her fingers. She laughed softly at the ticklish sensation and stroked his silky head. When Sally trotted over and nudged her arm, Emma turned to her as well, scratching behind both dogs' ears. She lingered a few minutes longer, enjoying their companionship.

Edward and his sons were still wrestling her trunks down from the wagon, so she rose and stepped aside, taking a moment to drink in the farmyard. Standing front and center was a white, two-story home with a smaller addition next to it, forming an L. They were joined by a long, welcoming porch that stretched the full length between them. She could see at a glance how a person might walk from the main two-story house to the smaller wing without ever stepping into rain or snow—the thoughtful and practical design serving as a sheltered bridge.

Glancing around, Emma took in the rest of her surroundings: a large red barn with a tall, creaky windmill turning slowly in the breeze, flowerbeds lining the porch edges with bright spring blooms and herbs, and a neat patch of turned soil by the smaller wing where green shoots were already pushing up. She wasn't sure what half the little buildings that dotted the rest of the land were for, but the whole place felt sturdy, lived-in, and strangely comforting.

"Do you like it?" Mary asked, motioning to the house as she came to join her. "I know it must be a far cry from the houses in Denver."

"It's smaller," Emma said, giving her cousin a wry smile, "but I think it has a certain charm that houses in the city never quite managed."

"I'll have to take your word for it," her cousin laughed. "Come. Let me show you around while Pa and the boys take your things upstairs. You'll be sharing my room."

Emma had never shared a room before, but with Mary, it didn't seem like such a terrible prospect. She was more composed and mature than her sisters, though age played a role in that. At least, that's what she assumed. She'd never had the chance to watch her sister grow into adulthood.

Mary led the way inside, and they stepped into a central entry hall, where a steep staircase divided the space between two rooms. Aside from the empty coat rack in the corner, the hall held only a wooden bench set to one side, a few small pairs of shoes underneath, and a simple oval mirror hung above. Emma imagined that this space could be quite crowded with eleven—now twelve—people's belongings.

“To the left is the parlor,” Mary said, gesturing to the large room. “We spend most of our evenings in here.”

Emma could see why. The paraffin lamp suspended from the ceiling would cast a warm glow on the soft yellow walls once the sun had set. It was an inviting space for the family to gather for games, as Micah had mentioned, or conversation—especially with the open brick fireplace and tall, built-in bookshelves that stood on either side. Emma’s gaze lingered there, already imagining herself curled up with a good book.

Reading would have to wait, though, as Mary led her across the hall to the kitchen. The space was purely utilitarian: a large central table surrounded by mismatched chairs, freestanding cabinets, open shelves with jars and tins next to a cast-iron cookstove—but it still somehow felt welcoming.

Sarah was busy making dinner when the girls arrived, but she turned to greet them, a streak of flour lingering on her cheek and her dark hair falling in wisps about her face.

“Hello there!” she said cheerfully. “What are you girls up to?”

“Mary was just giving me a tour,” Emma replied, as she smiled at her cousin. “You have a beautiful home.”

“Why, thank you,” Sarah said with a pleased smile. “Edward modeled it after my childhood home. He wanted me to have a bit of the old place with me when we settled here.”

“What a lovely thought,” Emma said, touched by her uncle’s thoughtfulness. As the scent of cooking beef reached her nose, she sniffed in appreciation. “Dinner smells divine.”

“Thank you. I’m almost done making the biscuits, and the roast has been on the stove all day. I think all that we’re waiting for are the potatoes.” She wiped her hands on her apron and looked at her daughter. “Mary, why don’t you take Emma up to your room and get her things put away? I’ll call you down when dinner is ready.”

Mary nodded to her mother and led the way up the worn wooden treads. When they reached the landing, she explained the sleeping arrangements. “Micah and Luke are in this first room, Joseph and Benjamin are in the next, and Isaac and Matthew have the last. Over there’s Ma and Pa’s room, then Ruth and Esther’s, and then ours.”

As Mary led Emma to their room, she glanced back over her shoulder with a shy smile. “I used to share a room with Esther and Ruth, but I’m glad we get one to ourselves. Ma helped me decorate it for us.”

"I'm looking forward to it," Emma said, though when Mary opened the door, a tiny part of her wondered if she'd spoken too soon.

The amount of pink in the room was overwhelming. It was everywhere, from the walls to the curtains and even the rug. Only the handmade quilt spread over the bed, made up of white and red squares, broke up the monochromatic décor.

Aside from the color, it was a pleasant, cozy room, with a dresser and washstand to one side and a large wardrobe opposite. Two small wooden nightstands sat on either side of the bed, with Mary's holding a few books, a framed picture of the entire family, and an empty water glass, while the other stood empty.

"I see you've already made things ready for me," Emma said, gesturing to the bare nightstand. "I appreciate it."

"You're welcome," Mary said as she smiled brightly. "We'd better get a start on putting your things away before we have to go down to dinner. It looks like the boys finished bringing your trunks up and stacked them behind the door."

Emma turned and saw that her cousins had indeed moved her trunks—or at least the lighter ones—into their room. She was glad that the boys hadn't had to haul all the heavy chests up the stairs. They were filled to the brim with as many heirlooms and knick-knacks as she could fit from her old home before it sold.

"Oh, yes, so they are," she said, opening the top trunk. "I wonder how I missed that."

Mary shrugged and came over to help unpack her things, and she gushed over every piece she pulled out. "Look at this one! I just adore the satin with blue and white stripes," she said, and, "Oh, I love this! It's pink—my favorite color."

Emma glanced around the room. It was obvious to anyone who entered, but she just smiled, and Mary's commentary continued in a steady stream until the last piece of clothing was put away. As they shut the doors on the heavy oak wardrobe, they had to struggle to get them to close properly.

"I think I have too many dresses," Emma chuckled. "Some of these might need to go back in my trunk."

"Nonsense," Mary huffed, giving the door another push. "It just needs a bit of help. Come, push on it with me."

Emma obliged, and together they leant their weight against the latch until it snapped shut. How long it would stay closed was anyone's guess, but for now, their task was done.

When Sarah called the girls down to eat, Emma realized she was unprepared for the commotion of having eleven other people around the dining room table. For years, it had just been her and her father sitting together, eating meals that their cook prepared, and chatting about their day. The scene before her, with her younger cousins fighting over who got the place next to her, was a stark contrast.

"Quiet, please," Edward called out above the noise. "Everyone, find a place to sit; it's time for grace." The children, obviously knowing better than to disobey their father, stopped their arguing, and when everyone settled, he began the prayer. "Dear Lord, we come before you humbly in thanks for all the gifts you have bestowed upon us. Thank you, Lord, for the safe arrival of Emma into our home. We pray she can continue to know the reassurance of your love as she grieves her beloved father."

At this, Emma felt her throat tighten. She tried her best to hold back tears, taking a deep breath and slowly letting it out as the prayer concluded. How embarrassing would it be to be found sobbing before she even had her first meal here?

There was a chorus of "Amen," and bowls of mashed potatoes, gravy, and biscuits were passed around the table while Edward served up portions of roast. After not eating all day, it was exactly what she needed, and she served herself a larger portion than usual.

They ate quietly for a moment, forks scraping across plates, before Micah caught her eye and asked, "How was your train ride? I didn't get a chance to ask about it on the way home."

Emma smiled. Appreciating that he seemed to actually want to know her thoughts, she answered, "It was an adventure. This was my first time traveling by train. It was bumpy, but I imagine it is much more comfortable than a stagecoach."

There was a murmur of agreement around the table, and her cousins took turns asking her questions—some about her father, his business, or life in the city. When it was Benjamin's turn, he asked if she'd ever seen a baseball game, and the whole family leaned in, eyes wide as she described attending a Denver Brown Stockings game two years ago with her father and some of his associates. She could still hear the crack of the bat and the deafening roar of the crowd as the player slid home.

If she had any worries about getting along with her male cousins, this conversation put them to rest. Who knew that attending so many formal events, dinners, and sporting games with her father would help her connect with her new family?

Chapter 5

When Gabe rode into the stable yard on Tuesday evening, he was famished. After a long day in the saddle, he wanted nothing more than to have a hot meal and fall straight to sleep. Still sore from his fall down the gully, he carefully unsaddled Xerxes and fed him a sugar cube before heading inside to wash up. Martha May was setting plates of food on the table as he came in, and Gabe sniffed, his stomach grumbling in anticipation.

"That smells wonderful." Hanging his hat by the back door, he asked, "What do you have for us tonight?"

"I made roasted chicken, mashed potatoes, gravy, peas, and rolls. I would have made peach cobbler for dessert, but someone didn't go to town as he promised me." She paused and sent him a pointed look. "You'll just have to settle for apple pie."

"That sure is a hardship," Gabe quipped as he scrubbed the day's dirt from his hands. Then, more seriously, he said, "I'm sorry I haven't gotten to town yet. I promise I'll go tomorrow."

"Thank you," Martha May replied, sounding mollified. "Just for that, you can have an extra slice of pie."

"How come that boy gets an extra slice, and I don't?" sulked Henry, who'd come in silently while they had been bickering playfully.

"You can have an extra slice if you say grace," his wife consoled, patting his cheek tenderly.

Henry grinned, and after a quick wash-up, he joined Gabe and Martha May at the table. After saying grace, they passed the serving platters around, and Gabe put an extra scoop of mashed potatoes on his plate. It was one of his favorite foods, and Martha May always made a little extra for him to have seconds—or thirds.

"When you go into town tomorrow, you should buy a new shirt, Gabriel," Martha May suggested as she picked at her food.

Henry smirked at her while Gabe glanced down at the work shirt he wore under his leather vest. Dust streaked the blue chambray shirt he wore, but it had no holes or rips. "Why?" he asked. "This one is in fine shape."

"Of course it is. I meant a shirt to wear for church and special events. The one you have is getting a bit old, don't you think?"

"I guess so." Gabe squinted suspiciously at his housekeeper. "Is there a reason I need a new one?"

"Well, the Barneses are having folks over for a welcoming party on Sunday, remember? You want to look your best since you represent the ranch. No one wants to do business with a man who's dressed in rags."

"Now, dear," Henry cut in. "Gabe doesn't dress in rags—you wouldn't let him, for one—but I do agree he should spiff himself up a bit. If he looks like he's on hard times, then people might think the ranch is too."

"Fine," Gabe sighed. "If it will make you both happy, I'll pick a fresh shirt up when I stop at the general store for those canned peaches you asked for and whatever else is on your list."

Henry groaned. "Now don't go stepping and fetching every little thing for her, or you won't have any time to run cattle."

"Henry Rollings, you know I'll be too busy around here to go into town, what with all the baking I'll be doing for the party," Martha May huffed. "Besides, you told me Gabriel is going into town anyway to get hardware from Mr. Decker."

"Okay, you two," Gabe interrupted, his hands held up in surrender. These two could argue all night if he let them.

"Maybe I should give him your extra slice of pie," Martha May threatened her husband.

Gabe and Henry smirked at each other, knowing she wouldn't deprive her husband of dessert, and turned their focus to filling their empty bellies. A hard day's work on the ranch always built up a fierce appetite, and it didn't take them long to scrape their dinner plates clean. They offered to help Martha May clear the dishes, but she shooed them out of the kitchen and pressed a steaming cup of coffee and a large slice of pie into their hands.

"If you start doing my work for me, then I won't have anything to do," she said, grabbing a stack of dirty plates and taking them to the sink full of soapsuds. "Go sit down on the porch. I'll be out there in a minute."

Chuckling, Gabe and Henry settled into the sturdy wooden rocking chairs that rested on the front porch and looked out at the wide-open Montana sky. The sun was setting, painting the streaks of clouds hanging above the mountains with stunning hues of pink, orange, and red.

"I'll never get tired of these sunsets," Henry said, stabbing the pastry's flaky crust with his fork. "When Telly asked me to be foreman, I wasn't sure what to expect, but the first night Martha May and I arrived here, we watched the sun go down together and knew we'd never leave."

Gabe took a bite of his own pie and relaxed his head against the back of the chair, thinking. "You know, you never talk much about Uncle Telly. I don't even think I know how you met."

"That so? Must have been too busy training you up to give an ancient history lesson." Henry took a slow sip of coffee, eyes distant as he recalled, "We served in the same Union company together during the war, both being from Kentucky. Grew mighty close, too. I was there with him when he took that shot to the thigh. It missed anything vital, by the grace of God, but I had to drag his sorry backside over a mile to camp, bullets whizzin' past me the whole way."

Gabe's eyes widened. Henry spoke as if it were just another trek in the woods, but his actions were nothing short of heroic. It deepened his respect for the man considerably, but he knew if he said so, the gruff foreman would just brush it off. So he kept his thoughts to himself.

Henry shook his head, as if trying to dislodge a bad memory. "All he could talk about afterward was getting home to heal and marry his gal, but when he rejoined the regiment a few months later, all that talk turned to mining for gold. Not sure what changed his mind, to be honest. He asked me to come with him, but I just wanted to get back home to Martha May."

A smile crossed his face at the mention of his wife, brief but warm, before he continued, "After the war ended, Telly joined the first wagon train he could find going west. About eight months later, he sent me a telegram saying he had struck it rich in Montana and wanted to start a cattle ranch, with me as his foreman."

Henry took another bite of pie, chewing thoughtfully. "Course, gettin' the land was half the battle. Telly didn't have a clue about ranching, but he knew how to work the law. Started with preemption on the best valley spots, filed homesteads, used the Desert Land Act for the bigger parcels he could put water to, and whenever a settler gave up and walked away, he bought their claim cheap. That's how he pieced together the 5,000 acres you're sittin' on now."

Gabe laughed, feeling a bit better that he wasn't the only one who had been clueless about raising cattle at first. "He must not have been any better at ranching than I was. I wonder if he and Pa grew up in the city then."

"Land sakes, boy, do you know nothing of your family?" Henry asked incredulously.

"Pa never talked about his relatives when I was growing up, and I never thought to ask." He shrugged and looked into his mug of coffee. "Mostly, I just tried to avoid him, especially when he had been drinking."

"Ah, so it was like that, was it?" The old man asked, his face becoming an angry mask.

"Yeah," Gabe said, his tone not inviting any further discussion.

The two men sat in silence, eating their dessert as they slowly rocked in the chairs until Martha May finally appeared.

"Well. You two are a couple of chatterboxes," she said with a laugh.

"We're men," Henry pointed out. "We don't chat. Come sit down with me. You can tell Gabe all about our trip west."

Martha May beamed and settled onto her husband's lap. "Not much to tell. We joined one of the wagon trains—four and a half months of dust, short water, and hard days.

That's where we met Sarah and Edward, though. They were on the same train, heading west with his mother, Flora, and a few dairy cows to start a farm for the mining camps."

"Really?" Gabe said, leaning forward. "I knew you'd all known each other for years, but I hadn't realized you came here at the same time."

"Yes. Sarah and I became the best of friends. She already had Micah and Luke to care for and was pregnant with Joseph, so Flora and I helped watch the babies or cook whenever we could. I told them about Elk Ridge, and instead of going on to Oregon as they planned, they came here."

"Did you ever regret not coming out to mine with Telly right away?" Gabe asked Henry as he finished his generous slice of pie.

"Nope. I had more important things to see to." He squeezed Martha May's waist, making her blush like a young schoolgirl. "Now, don't go feeling too bad for me. Telly built our house on the ranch, and we have had a fine life here. We've got lots of friends, and there isn't a more beautiful place to live. Besides, after he passed, I found out Telly had put some of the money from his claim in the bank for me. Left me a letter saying it was his way of thanking me for making his ranch such a success."

Gabe grinned. No two people deserved it more than Henry and Martha May.

"Sounds like he was a good man."

"The best of men," uttered Henry solemnly.

The three of them sat together in silence, staring into the darkening evening as the sun sank behind the mountains, until Martha May stood up. "We'd best be getting home for bed," she said. "Daylight will be here before we know it."

Henry grunted in agreement and raised himself slowly out of the rocking chair, handing Gabe his coffee cup. "You heard my wife. To bed with you," he ordered playfully.

Gabe nodded, and as he watched the older couple walk home holding hands, he felt a pang of loneliness. Telly had left him this sturdy two-story home, and he had no one to share it with.

He realized that if he ever got married, he wanted his relationship to be like what the Rollings had. They argued and teased, but the deep love and affection they held for each other were plain to see. Unfortunately, with the ranch demanding his constant attention—branding in the spring, haying in the summer, and the ever-growing list of repairs to make before winter—he just didn't have the time to go courting.

Sighing, he collected the empty dishes and took them to the sink, which still held some soapy water, and cleaned them. Afterwards, he grabbed the lantern, locked up the house, and headed to bed. Tomorrow, he would buy a new shirt, and for some odd reason, the thought made him happy.

Chapter 6

Emma woke on her first full morning at the farm feeling gritty and sour, the residue of several days on the train clinging to her skin like a second layer of dust. She had never gone so long without a proper bath in her life. It just wouldn't do.

Glancing to her right, she saw she was alone in the bed. She reached out and touched the sheet on Mary's side, frowning. The cool cotton fabric confirmed what she suspected. Her cousin had been gone for a while.

Thinking that perhaps Mary had gone down for breakfast already, Emma quickly dressed and made her way to the kitchen. But instead of seeing the family gathered for the morning meal, she found her aunt kneading dough on the pine work table, the room empty but for the two of them.

"Where is everyone?" she asked. She was so surprised that she completely forgot her manners.

"Good morning, dear," Aunt Sarah said with an amused smile. "By now, they're either in the creamery making cheese or doing other chores. Dinner won't be ready for a few hours, but I can make you something to eat if you're hungry."

"No, thank you. I'm fine for the moment." She was disappointed that she'd missed out on having breakfast with her family, but she had more immediate concerns. "Would it be possible for me to take a bath this morning? I'm afraid the train left me... less than fresh."

"Of course." Sarah wiped her hands on her apron and gave her a kind, understanding smile. "We have a small bathing room off the summer kitchen. It's nothing fancy, but it's private. I'll heat a bucket of water on the stove if you'll fetch another from the pump. That should be plenty for a proper wash."

The pump. Of course. Mrs. Vance had warned her they wouldn't have indoor plumbing like her home in Denver, but that seemed like an easy enough chore to tackle on her first day.

"I'll go fetch it right now," Emma said.

The hand pump stood just outside the back door, a tall iron thing with a long handle. She had watched Sarah and the girls use it with effortless rhythm, but now that she stood in front of it, the mechanism looked foreign and intimidating. She gripped the handle with both hands and pushed down. Nothing. She pulled up. Still nothing. She tried again, harder, the iron cold and unyielding under her palms. The handle barely moved. After several frantic minutes of pushing and pulling, only a weak, sputtering trickle appeared, then died.

Her face burned as she heard whispers and giggles from behind her. She glanced over her shoulder and saw Mary hanging laundry while Ruth, Esther, and two of the younger boys were laughing at her expense.

"She doesn't know how to work the pump!" Matthew crowed, doubling over.

Mary shot her younger siblings a sharp look. "That's enough. Go on, finish your chores." She waited for them to scamper away and walked over calmly. "Would you like some help?"

"Yes, please." Emma said, trying to keep her voice light and unaffected, "I'm afraid I'm making a fool of myself."

Mary smiled, her voice gentle. "Come on, I'll show you. It's tricky the first time."

She walked Emma through the steps—priming the pump with a cup of water from the rain barrel and then the slow, steady rhythm of the handle. Within moments, clear, cold water gushed into the bucket.

"There," she said kindly. "You'll have it down in no time."

Emma wasn't so sure, but she thanked her cousin and, with her cheeks still burning, she carried the heavy bucket toward the addition.

After her flop at the pump, Emma had one bad turn after another as she attempted to help her cousin with their chores. She accidentally uprooted several young carrot tops while trying to pull weeds in the garden. And when she volunteered to help hang laundry, she fumbled with the pins and sent a large sheet into the mud. She'd tried to pick it up right away, but Esther, frustrated that she'd have to wash and wring out the fabric again, had snapped at her. It was a trying day, and even though her young cousin had apologized for her behavior later, Emma had taken to staying in her room during the day from then on.

She would wake at her usual Denver hour—eight or half past—when the house was already still. The family had risen hours earlier, gone to the creamery or the fields, and left the kitchen empty except for Aunt Sarah, who was preparing dinner. Emma ate alone, then retreated upstairs where she could hide behind a book or needlework until suppertime. That only gave her a few brief hours with her cousins before everyone retired early, ready to start again at dawn.

She knew she was choosing this distance, but it was safer than trying again and failing. She'd already exposed how ill-equipped she was for life on the frontier. No need to put herself through more embarrassment. Thankfully, no one commented on her absence from participating in household chores. They seemed to understand her need for solitude.

On Sunday, the family was just about to leave for services when Sarah met her at the foot of the stairs and laid a gentle hand on Emma's arm. "Rest today, dear. You've had a long journey and a heavy heart. There's no need to face the whole town just yet. We'll take you next week when you're feeling steadier."

Emma nodded, grateful for the reprieve, and watched from the parlor window as the wagon rolled away. Normally, she never missed going to church unless she was sick, but she was feeling so poorly about herself that she might as well have been. When the wind and the distant lowing of the cattle were the only sounds that remained, she wandered back upstairs.

As she sat on the edge of the bed, she thought back to her first day on the train, when she'd spun such tidy, comforting delusions to herself: You've worked hard. You've organized charity events and hosted dinner parties. A quaint farm, a few cousins—nothing you can't manage.

Emma scoffed. It was as if she thought she could step off the train and simply belong. She pressed her palms to her eyes, the sting building behind her eyelids. Not only had she lost her father and her home, but she'd also lost the invisible scaffolding that had held her life together—the people and systems that made everything effortless so she could remain ornamental. Pretty. Polished. Useless in any practical sense.

Planning a dinner for twenty was her forte, yet if you stuck her in the kitchen and handed her a spoon, she'd be helpless. She could help organize a gala for the largest investors in the city, but she'd struggle to roll carpets or wax the floors of the ballroom. It was like being the conductor of an orchestra: she set the music to be played and gave the cues for the musicians to join at just the right time, but the actual practice and performance were done by someone else.

Not that the things she'd done didn't require work. It had been stressful and tiring at times, but it was nothing compared to the backbreaking labor her family took on here at the farm. Every night, she listened as they talked about their day and the chores they'd done, and it made her realize just how privileged her life had been.

But that was over now. No matter how patient her aunt and uncle were, she'd still have to learn how to do those things herself eventually, and the sheer breadth of knowledge she lacked was overwhelming. The gap wasn't a single missing skill—it was an entire world of them. Every task she watched the family perform rested on layers and layers of hard-earned experience she had never needed to acquire. The thought of falling flat on her face again and proving to everyone, including herself, just how useless she was left her nauseous. So much so that she couldn't stand the thought of having supper with the family that night.

The heavy gray clouds and constant drizzle outside didn't help her mood, and Emma remained in her room as Sunday faded into Monday, then Tuesday. But by Wednesday morning, they had finally moved on, and golden sunlight was streaming in through her window to greet her when she woke.

Blinking at the unexpected brightness, she lay in bed, trying to find the motivation to get up. She wished she had someone to talk to about her troubles, but she was afraid she'd seem spoiled or ungrateful if she broached the subject with her aunt. She needed someone who could see the situation from the outside. Someone like… "Mrs. Vance!" Emma exclaimed, bolting upright. "Why didn't I think of it sooner?"

With sudden purpose pumping through her veins, she got up, changed into a clean dress, and carried her writing desk to the small table by the window. She sat, uncapped the ink, smoothed a sheet of paper, and, after a moment's hesitation, began to write.

Elk Ridge, Montana Territory

May 13, 1885

My dearest Mrs. Vance,

Greetings! I hope the rest of your journey to your son's house was as pleasant as mine was to the farm and that you found him and his family in good health and spirits.

Aunt Sarah and Uncle Edward have welcomed me with open arms, as have their children—all nine of them! I am settling in, though I confess my first few days here have been quite an adjustment.

We talked briefly about how different Montana might be from Denver, but I hadn't realized—not truly—how vast those differences would be, or how unprepared I was to face them. On my first day here, I struggled to do something as simple as drawing water from a pump. My dear cousin Mary was kind enough not to laugh at my blunder and offered her help, but her younger siblings had no such qualms. That, and a few other faux pas have kept me from trying anything new, for fear of making a fool of myself again and showing how much I don't belong here.

My entire life, I was cushioned by servants and streetcars and familiar routines. Schooled on how to set a formal table, plan menus for dinner parties, entertain guests politely, and pour tea gracefully. I studied literature, French, and scripture until my eyes crossed, but what use is that here? I have no practical skills. None at all.

Though my father let me help in the store when I was younger, I see now that it was more symbolic than necessary. He let me play at it by wrapping fancy parcels for society ladies, accepting payments, and tallying ledgers. Most likely, he wanted to instill some of his work ethic and teach me numbers, but I never truly labored.

I'm also the last one to rise, after the family has been hard at work for hours, and though no one complains, I feel guilty. Watching them go about their tasks with such purpose while I sit idle only deepens the feeling. Where do I even begin to catch up on a lifetime of knowledge when the list of things I have to learn feels endless?

What would you advise me to do, Mrs. Vance? I dearly appreciated the counsel you gave me on our little adventure, so I'm hoping I can rely on your wisdom once more. I'm eager to hear all about baby Jonathan and his parents in your reply.

Yours sincerely,

Emma Barnes

After three restarts, several crossed-out lines, and careful rereading, the letter was finally done. As Emma folded it neatly, slipped it into an envelope, and addressed the front, relief settled over her. She no longer carried the full weight of her feelings, and she felt lighter than she had in days. Rising from her chair, she quickly capped her ink bottle and stored away the rest of her things. If she hurried, she might be able to post the letter today.

Aunt Sarah was busy at the stove, adding chopped carrots to a large pot as she entered the kitchen. When her aunt didn't turn around, she announced herself with a soft "Good morning."

"Oh! Good morning to you, too," Sarah said, setting her knife down and turning to face Emma with a warm smile. "Are you hungry? I wasn't sure when you'd wake, but I have a plate saved for you."

"Thank you. I am rather hungry," she replied, taking a seat at the kitchen table. "Would it be possible to post a letter today?"

"I think so." Sarah took a plate of eggs and thick-cut bacon from the warmer under the stove and set it on the table. "Edward was talking about going into town for supplies soon, and I suppose today is as good a day as any." She looked at Emma, a flicker of worry crossing her face. "Are you writing to your attorney?"

"No, it's a letter to Mrs. Vance," she rushed to assure her aunt. "I promised to write to her."

"Oh, well, that's nice, dear," Sarah said, her face lifting in relief. "I'm sure she'll be pleased to hear from you. Just set your letter on the table, and I'll be sure Edward gets it."

Emma nodded, and once she'd finished her breakfast, she drew the sealed envelope from the pocket of her dress and set it next to her plate.

"I think I might go for a walk today," she announced, glancing out the window at the clear sky. "The clouds have finally cleared out."

"A walk is an excellent idea," Sarah said brightly.

Emma was already turning toward the stairs when she heard her aunt call, "It might be a little chilly out, so don't forget a wrap."

It was sound advice, and as she headed upstairs to collect her parasol, bonnet, and a light shawl, an eager anticipation grew within her. This was a perfect opportunity to clear her mind and get the exercise she had been missing over the past few days because of the rain. She'd been cooped up for too long.

The mid-morning sun was shining brightly as she descended the porch steps, and she could hear the birds in the treetops chirping their approval. While she tied her bonnet beneath her chin, she slowly surveyed the flat, green grassland that stretched northward for miles. From here, she could almost make out the shapes of the buildings in town. Behind the house stretched mostly cleared land, dotted with several outbuildings that gave way to a thick forest of evergreens climbing the rising mountain.

With no one around to direct her and no path to follow, Emma set off toward the tall pines. Their tops swayed gently in the crisp breeze, creaking softly as she moved deeper into the woods. Picking her way carefully through fallen branches and tangles of overgrown bushes, she thought about how strange it was not to be surrounded by the familiar clamor of the city—no street hawkers calling out their wares, no carriages rumbling past.

Here, there was only the steady rhythm of her feet on the needle-strewn ground and the faint rustle of leaves as the wind gusted past. With the trees closing in overhead, their needles filtered the sunlight into soft, dappled patches that danced across the forest floor, creating a muted, private shelter all her own. The quiet felt welcoming rather than confining.

As she wandered through the underbrush, several unfamiliar plants caught her eye—bushes with clumps of unripe berries, a feathery fern unfurling in the shade, and shrubs dotted with tiny white blossoms. Emma marveled at their beauty, wishing she knew their names. Perhaps she'd look for a botany book when she got back to the farmhouse.

Passing through a narrow spot between two thick bushes, she heard a loud rending sound and looked down to see a long tear in her dress near the hem. Frowning, she stooped to examine the damage and discovered several more snags and rips across her satin overskirt—some much larger and more jagged than the first.

"Oh, bother," she muttered, touching the tattered fabric.

There wasn't much she could do to fix it at the moment, and she didn't feel like turning back yet, so Emma pressed on, careful to keep the house in sight so she wouldn't lose her way. The sun climbed higher, warming her shoulders through the pines, and the forest gradually gave way to open patches where she paused to catch her breath or admire a bird flitting overhead. She walked for what felt like hours, cheeks flushed from the breeze and exertion, until hunger and thirst finally turned her steps toward home.

By the time she emerged from the trees, the yard was silent except for the rhythmic squeak of the windmill, and she found her cousins had already eaten their dinner and scattered back to their chores. Disappointed but not surprised, Emma slipped into the kitchen and found a heel of bread and a wedge of cheese on the sideboard. She carried them upstairs with a glass of water and ate her meal by the window, watching the distant shapes of the family moving across the fields, and then lay down on the bed, the morning's small adventures replaying pleasantly in her mind.

She must have dozed, because the next thing she knew, the light had softened to late-afternoon gold, and Mary was stepping into the room.

"Ma sent me up to collect you for supper," she announced.

"Oh, my!" Emma exclaimed, hurrying off the mattress. "I hope the meal wasn't held up for me."

"Not at all," Mary replied. "We just got back from milking for the evening."

Letting out a relieved breath, she followed her cousin down the narrow staircase to the dining room, where the warm scent of roasting meat and fresh bread drifted in from the kitchen. Ruth and Esther were just placing the last of the silverware on the table as the rest of the family filed in from the kitchen, and there was a bit of a shuffle as everyone found their seats. Luke pulled a chair out for her with a quick nod, and while they waited for everyone to settle, Uncle Edward turned to Emma with a friendly smile and asked, "How was your day?"

"It was pleasant. I took a long walk through the trees, just enjoying God's creation. I've lived near the mountains my whole life, but I've never actually spent any time in them."

"Well, there are plenty of mountains and trees here," he laughed. "Next time, take Jack with you. He'll protect you should a predator be wandering nearby."

Emma's face paled, and Sarah immediately chastised her husband. "Edward! Don't go scaring her like that."

"It wasn't my intention, dear," Edward said, softening his tone, "but she should know that there is always a risk of something like that happening if she wanders too far from home." He looked at Emma and said gently, "The boys and I are armed for a reason." He gestured to the gun slung low on his waist. "The dogs do their best to keep the farm and animals safe, but it's always best to be prepared."

She nodded, ashamed that she hadn't realized that there might be dangers in this untamed land that didn't exist in Denver. It was yet another example of her ignorance, and she was lucky that nothing had happened to her during her wanderings. Suddenly, she no longer had an appetite.

When Emma woke in the middle of the night and felt nature's call, she groaned softly. If there was one thing she missed the most from Denver, it was the indoor water closet. Huffing out a frustrated breath, she carefully pulled back the covers so as not to wake Mary and wrapped herself in the flannel dressing gown draped across the foot of the bed.

There was just enough soft moonlight streaming through the windows that she didn't need to light a lantern, so Emma set her hand against the wall and used it as a guide to make her way out of the house. As she stepped out onto the porch, she shivered at the sudden chill of the night air. Pulling the dressing gown tighter around her body, she hurried across the yard.

The stillness of the evening was punctuated with unfamiliar noises, and she couldn't help but recall her conversation earlier with Uncle Edward. She wondered if she should try to find Jack, but anything could happen to her as she was wandering the farmyard in the dark. Unable to shake off her apprehensive thoughts of wild predators silently sneaking up on her, Emma raced ahead.

She reached the outhouse in record time and quickly shut the heavy wooden door behind her, pressing an ear to the slats. Heart pounding, she listened for the growling of a predator, but she heard only the steady chirping of field crickets and the occasional lowing of the cattle in the field. Relieved that she wasn't being hunted, she went about her business.

When she was done, she opened the door of the outhouse, took a step out, and looked up to see an enormous figure coming toward her. The movement was so sudden and unexpected that she screamed at the top of her lungs, scrambling backward into the privy and fumbling to latch the door behind her.

Her scream had set Sally and Jack to barking somewhere in the yard, and Emma hoped that the racket would scare whatever it was away. Her entire body shook like a leaf, breath ragged, but when she heard the beast moving closer, another involuntary scream tore from her throat. She pressed herself against the back wall while praying for help. It felt like ages before she heard someone yell her name.

"Emma? Where are you?"

Uncle Edward's voice cut through the night air, and she sank to her knees in relief.

"I'm... I'm in the outhouse," she shouted, her breath still coming in short pants.

"Don't worry, I'm coming to get you," he called back. Then, in a harsher tone, he said, "Go on, you menace! Leave her alone."

Emma was sitting on her knees, taking long, slow breaths, when her uncle knocked on the wooden door.

"It's safe to come out now," he said.

Coming unsteadily to her feet, she opened the latch and slowly peered around the edge of the door. Edward was standing before her in trousers and a hastily tucked-in nightshirt, his graying chestnut hair sticking straight up on the side and a double-barreled shotgun draped across one arm. Though he looked disheveled, his steady gaze was calm and confident.

"Are you sure it's gone?" she asked in a small voice.

"I'm sure. It's just one of the cows—Darla. Looks like someone left the gate open. She probably got curious when you came outside and wanted to investigate."

"That was a cow?" Emma exclaimed as she felt her face flame with humiliation.

"Yes, but I'm sure it was frightening to encounter in the middle of the night," Edward said kindly. "Especially if you weren't expecting a visitor."

Stepping out of the outhouse, she could see light spilling out from the house and the silhouettes of people waiting on the porch. Emma groaned. She really didn't want to have to admit in front of the entire family that she had the daylights scared out of her by a cow. She'd already embarrassed herself enough with her ignorance of country ways, but there was no helping the situation.

Following Edward back to the house, she noticed it was just her three oldest male cousins waiting on the porch, each holding some sort of firearm. She felt marginally better that they would have been prepared to take on something much more dangerous for her, but humiliation still consumed her.

"Everything okay, Pa?" asked Micah.

"It's all been taken care of," Edward said, leaving out the details of the encounter. "Let's go back inside and get some rest."

Micah nodded and led the way inside, his brothers filing in behind him, one after the other, like ducklings, with Emma and her uncle bringing up the rear. As he took the firearms from his sons and began storing them away, she slipped upstairs and found Mary sitting on the bed, waiting for her with a concerned look, the warm glow of the lamp illuminating the room.

"Are you all right?" her cousin asked. "I heard screaming and noticed you weren't in bed. Ma told us all to stay in our rooms."

"Yes. I'm fine," Emma replied, and she sank onto the bed. "I'm so sorry for frightening everyone. Apparently, all the talk of wild animals at dinner tonight went straight to my head because as I was leaving the privy, I saw one of your cows and assumed I was about to be eaten by a giant beast."

"Oh, my," Mary said, holding her hand over her mouth. She was trying so hard to keep from laughing that her normally fair complexion turned red, and her slim shoulders shook before finally her laughter spilled forth.

Emma stared at her cousin, shocked that she would be so cruel as to laugh, but suddenly she saw the encounter through Mary's eyes and started chuckling as well. They laughed together until tears pricked their eyes, their breath became ragged, and they heard a stern "Shh" from down the hall. In that hushed aftermath, what had started as a deep embarrassment turned into a moment the two of them would carry for a lifetime.

Chapter 7

When Gabe went into town to pick up his order from the hardware store—along with the few things Martha May had requested—he had a hard time finding space to park his wagon. It seemed everyone in Elk Ridge had picked the same day to run their errands. Instead of waiting around for someone to leave, he pulled up in front of the livery and headed inside.

Cyrus Douglass, the owner of the stable, was sitting at a table in the back, mending some tack when Gabe came in. He was a large, broad-shouldered man with dark skin and the rough, steady hands of someone who'd spent years perfecting his craft with a forge and an anvil. He could make or repair just about anything.

As he approached, Cyrus looked up and held out his hand. "Howdy, stranger. It's been a spell. How are you?"

"I'm well, Cyrus," Gabe said, shaking his outstretched hand. "How are you and the missus?"

"Oh, we're doing fine! We're going to have a new child soon!" the blacksmith said, grinning from ear to ear. "She just told me! I'm bursting with happiness."

"Congratulations!" Gabe smiled, genuinely pleased for his friend. "Please give her my best wishes."

"Thank you. I'll be sure to pass it along." Cyrus clapped him on the shoulder. "Did you need something repaired?"

"Not today. I have some errands I need to run and want to store my wagon. The town's in full swing today."

"That it is, but don't you worry. I have plenty of space. You have your things sent over, and I'll make sure they're loaded up for you once you're ready to leave."

He thanked Cyrus, shaking hands with him once more, and headed to the hardware store. Mr. Decker was busy helping another customer when he came in, so Gabe made his way over to the buckets of hinges and nails to wait his turn. He quickly picked out what he needed, then grabbed some fence staples and a rubber curry comb. He added a new lantern to his armful of purchases, for good measure, and wandered around the store to see what new items had been stocked.

One thing that stood out was a clothes wringer, and he made a mental note to ask Martha May if she needed a new one. She worked hard to keep his clothes clean and mended, and he liked to make sure she had the best tools at her disposal. There were a few other odds and ends that caught his eye, but he passed them up, not wanting to haul home more items than necessary.

Mr. Decker returned to the counter and waved him over. "Hello, Gabe! What can I do for you today?"

"Hello," he smiled in greeting and set down the things he was purchasing. "I need a new wheelbarrow and forty pounds of barbed wire, along with these."

The squat, middle-aged proprietor noted the items in his ledger and rang up the goods on his new till. Instead of putting the purchases on a tab, as some folks did, Gabe paid with cash and asked for his items to be taken to the livery. Then he said farewell and walked across the street to the general store, where Mr. Harper greeted him as soon as he walked in the door, a wide grin on his face.

"Afternoon, Gabe. How's everything at the ranch?" he asked.

"Good, thank you. Just making some purchases for Martha May so she can do some baking," he said, putting the list on the counter.

"I see! Well, feel free to look around the store while I complete your order."

He hurried off to gather the goods, while Gabe leafed through a mail-order catalog, amazed at the things on offer. All someone needed to do was send in their order with the price of the item and freight costs, and a few weeks later, it arrived. He'd just found the page with rifles when Mr. Harper let him know his order was ready. Gabe returned the catalog to the shelf, paid what he owed, and left the store.

While striding down the boardwalk toward the livery, he suddenly remembered his promise to Martha May. She would skin him alive if he didn't come back home with a new shirt, so he dropped his purchases off at the livery and headed toward Mrs. Tandy's shop.

Stepping inside and glancing around the store, Gabe immediately felt out of place among the multitude of colors and fabric patterns stocked on the shelves. He'd never been in a store like this before, and he wasn't even sure what he wanted, aside from a nice shirt to wear for church and other special occasions.

Mrs. Tandy came out from behind the counter and smiled warmly when she spotted him. "Hello there, Gabe. It's nice to see you. How can I assist you today?"

He cleared his throat and looked around the store, suddenly overwhelmed by all the options. How was he supposed to know what to pick? He was a simple man with simple tastes. Most of the clothing he owned was in solid colors and only fit for work or church.

"Well," he began, shifting his weight from one foot to the other, "Martha May suggested I buy a new shirt to wear to services. I thought about getting one from the general store, but I heard you have things more in keeping with the times—getting all those magazines from back east and such."

"Indeed, I do!" She tapped her finger to her chin in thought as she studied Gabe. "Tell me, are you just in search of a shirt, or would you be needing some other things as well?"

"Um, well, I don't really know that I need much else."

"Well, that's fine, but I would hate for it to make your other clothes look worn in comparison." Mrs. Tandy tsked and stepped over to a mannequin that held a dark suit.

She touched the lapel of the jacket. "Take this suit right here, for instance. The sack coat is a black twill-weave wool lined with cotton sateen. I made this set with matching trousers, and I think it would look splendid on you. If you wanted to update your wardrobe, that is." She let the statement hang in the air and looked around innocently.

Gabe's mind had blanked when she'd started talking about twills and weaves. He did not know what they were, but the coat looked finely made. As if Mrs. Tandy could feel him considering it, she walked swiftly over to her rack of ready-made clothes, pulled out a few different waistcoats, ties, and neckcloths in one hand and a crisp white shirt in the other, and walked quickly back to him.

"Do you see how these waistcoats look with the jacket?" She asked, draping them over the mannequin's shoulder. "I have several colors and patterns to choose from. Let's take these to the back room, and you can see which ones you like best, shall we?"

Before he knew it, he was standing before a mirror in the small room where customers could try on clothing, quietly admiring the cut of the suit. The black coat had a small lapel, buttoning just under the necktie, and fell open on both sides in a smooth curve toward the bottom. It fit him well, as did the white cotton shirt she'd brought, but the trousers were too long. He also tried on several waistcoats but rejected most because they were too extravagant for his taste.

"Gabe, that's the point!" Mrs. Tandy huffed, hands on her hips. "You aren't purchasing these to wear when you work cattle. Don't you want to let all the single women in town see you looking handsome in a fancy new suit and waistcoat?" She began picking up discarded garments. "Mark my words—the next time we have a dance, you'll be begging me to sell you some fancy duds."

Pinching the bridge of his nose and cursing himself for a fool, he gave a resigned sigh. "All right, you win. I truly don't know what would look appealing to women, though. How about this: If you'll hem the trousers for me, I'll get the suit and let you pick out a waistcoat and tie or kerchief, as long as they're not in any flashy colors."

"It's a deal!" she grinned and shook his hand in a firm grip.

Gabe watched the seamstress flit around her store, pulling items from shelves and inspecting them. Some she draped over her arm, but others she shook her head over and folded them neatly before returning them to their proper place. It was like watching a hummingbird searching for nectar, he thought, smiling.

It took her several more minutes to finish curating the pieces, but in the end, Mrs. Tandy took pity on him and picked out a black and white pinstriped silk waistcoat and a silver paisley satin puff tie. She seemed rather pleased with her choices, but he picked out a black cotton waistcoat and tie and set them on the counter.

"Just to be safe," he said when she looked questioningly at him.

"That's a fine idea." She nodded. "Give me an hour, and I'll have those trousers hemmed for you. Or, if you'd rather, you can pick them up on Friday."

He didn't feel like making another trip back into town this week, so he said he'd be back in an hour and walked down to Jackson's, a small diner situated across the street from the hotel. As he walked in, the tinkling of the small bell signaled a new customer, and he was greeted by the mouthwatering scents of fresh-baked bread and cooked meat. Seconds later, a petite, harried-looking waitress met him at the door and gave him a quick, acknowledging smile.

"Afternoon, Gabe," she said, wiping her hands on her apron.

He returned the smile, polite but brief. "Afternoon, Rebecca. Busy day?"

"No more than usual." She shrugged, leading him to a small table by the front window. She set a tall glass of water on the red-checked tablecloth and hurried off to tend to other tables.

Normally, he would have spent some time looking over a menu, but since Jackson's was so small, he didn't bother. Pot pie, soup with fresh bread, meat sandwiches, or fried chicken with mashed potatoes and gravy were always on offer. It wasn't as good as Martha May's cooking in his opinion, but it would do while he waited for his purchases.

When Rebecca returned, he placed his order of fried chicken and settled back in his chair to wait, already half-resigned to an hour of people-watching and lukewarm coffee. But a few moments later, there was a tap on the window behind him, and he turned to see the three oldest Barnes brothers. Surprised but happy to see his friends, he motioned for them to join him and shook their hands as they came to sit at his table.

"It's so busy in here," Micah said as he sat down. "What are you doing in town today?"

"I had some errands to run for the ranch and Martha May," Gabe answered simply. He didn't feel like explaining his trip to Mrs. Tandy's.

"Lucky running into you then," Luke said. "I think you have the only table with empty seats."

"My waitress may not feel it's lucky," he chuckled. "It seems everyone decided to come to town at the same time. Did you escape the creamery for the day?"

"Just for dinner. Then it's back to work," Micah replied, looking around the busy restaurant. "I hope this won't take too long."

When Rebecca finally arrived with Gabe's food, she frowned at the new arrivals, quickly took their orders, and rushed off.

"Rebecca didn't look too happy to see us today," said Joseph as he intently watched the pretty brunette clear plates from an empty table. "Normally, she's as sweet as pie."

"Speaking of pie," Luke put in, rubbing his stomach, "I think I may get a slice. I saw they had blueberry pie when we walked in."

"You always want pie. It doesn't matter what kind," Joseph teased, tearing his eyes away from the waitress. "I'm surprised you aren't the size of a milking barn."

"I can't be when I'm working hard to pick up your slack," Luke shot back.

"Say, how did it go the other day picking up that cousin of yours? Martha May never said where he was from." Gabe asked the brothers to head off the conflict that was brewing.

The three brothers traded glances at each other, and Joseph's face split into a playful grin. "He's from Denver. Poor kid has never been away from the city before."

"Yeah, he's never even milked a cow before. I think he may be scared of them," Micah declared.

Luke nodded in agreement with his brothers. "It will be interesting to see how he acclimates to life on the farm."

Gabe couldn't help but feel a slight kinship with the newest member of the Barnes family. He'd also come here unprepared for life in an untamed territory and made a mental note to offer his assistance with the boy's acclimation process.

Mrs. Tandy was folding the trousers and setting them with the pile of his other clothes when Gabe walked into her shop after dinner, and she waved him over to the counter.

"What do I owe you?" he asked.

When Mrs. Tandy named the sum, he gave a low whistle. "You sure know how to spot an easy mark when they walk through that door."

“Oh, nonsense,” she chuckled as she wrapped up the clothes. “You’re a man of good taste, Gabe. You just needed a bit of sprucing up. I think you look right handsome in your new suit, and you can mix and match these pieces to keep your look fresh. Or, you could come back for different colors or a new necktie. You never know when you’ll need to be looking your best,” she added slyly as she tied a deft knot around the brown paper.

“You must be the best salesperson I have ever met. I came in for a shirt, and I’m leaving with that, plus a suit, two waistcoats, and two neckties. Reckon I’m missing anything else?”

“Well, I have these new scarf pins,” she said coaxingly as she pushed a velvet box toward him. “They just arrived from New York, and they’d finish your look nicely.”

Knowing he’d walked into that, he shook his head ruefully and picked a gold horse-shoe-shaped pin. When his items were paid for, he thanked Mrs. Tandy, quickly retrieved his wagon, and headed back to the ranch before he spent any more money.

As he pulled into the yard a half hour later, Gabe caught sight of Martha May hanging laundry on the clothesline. She waved, finished pinning the sheet up, and came to the side of the wagon.

“There you are! I thought you were just going for a couple of things. Looks like you made an extra stop.” She paused and looked at him squarely. “I hope you took my advice.”

“Of course I did,” Gabe said, leaning over the sideboard and picking up a crate of groceries. “I’m no fool.”

"Good." Martha May grinned in approval and followed him into the house. “Dinner will be ready in just a minute.”

“Actually,” he drawled, setting the box down on the table. “I already had dinner at the café with Micah, Luke, and Joseph. I hope you don’t mind.”

“Not at all,” she said cheerily as she began setting aside ingredients for dessert. “I’m glad they got a break from the farm for a while.”

Gabe smiled and left to finish unloading the wagon. He’d just brought in the last load when Henry came into the kitchen, ready for his own dinner.

“Back from your leisurely trip to town, I see,” the foreman teased. He kissed his wife on the cheek, glanced around at all the groceries, and picked up a few tin cans to check their contents. Then he spotted a wrapped package sitting on the table. “What do we have here?”

“It’s just the shirt I picked up,” Gabe said, and deftly snatched it away. “I promised Martha May I would get one today, remember? I’ll go put this away.”

Gabe bounded up the stairs, two at a time. In his rush to escape, he completely missed the conspiratorial smiles Martha May and Henry shared.

Chapter 8

It had been three days since Emma's frightening encounter with Darla, the inquisitive dairy cow. She still felt a twinge of embarrassment about it, but her most pressing problem was boredom. Since arriving in Elk Ridge, she'd embroidered two handkerchiefs, read through four books borrowed from the parlor shelves, and taken several walks—close to the house and always with Jack, as Uncle Edward had advised.

The only thing of real excitement that happened was Sally having her puppies. Emma had peeked into the barn the morning after, watching the wriggling bundle of ten black-and-white fur nursing at their mother's side while the children crowded around in delight. For a few minutes, she'd forgotten her own uselessness, smiling at the tiny paws batting the air and the soft, contented whimpers. But even that joy had faded quickly, leaving her with the same quiet ache.

While she enjoyed needlework and reading, it left her feeling more like a guest than a member of the family. Everyone else worked hard to keep the farm running, while she sat inside making pretty shapes with needle and thread, and the frustration of her idleness had begun to build. Of course, lying in bed and sulking wasn't helping, so she rose and went through her morning wash-up routine, slipping into a bottle-green checked walking suit.

Aunt Sarah was sweeping a pile of dirt and ash into a dustpan when Emma entered the kitchen. When her aunt spotted her, she straightened, reached into her apron, and pulled out an envelope. "You have a response from Mrs. Vance," she announced with a smile.

"Already?" Emma took the folded paper, her own smile breaking through. "That was fast."

"She must have posted her reply the same day she got your letter," Sarah said. "Why don't you go read it, and I'll fix you some food?"

She thanked her aunt and carried the letter to the parlor, her steps quickening with a flutter of anticipation. Then she settled onto the sofa, smoothed her skirts with a small, impatient motion, and tore open the envelope.

Missoula, Montana Territory

May 15, 1885

My dearest Miss Barnes,

I am overjoyed to have received your letter so soon after we had to part ways. The post must have flown on swift wings to bring your words to me in just one day.

The rest of my journey was uneventful, as I had only myself for company, but I had a joyous reunion with my son Rupert and his lovely wife Rose. Baby Jonathan is the spitting image of his father at that age and is such a delight to hold. I'd forgotten how tiny newborn babies are, although he is already three months old, so he's not so new anymore. I hold him every chance I get, and while my son says I'm spoiling him, I don't believe you can spoil a child by holding them too much.

Now, on to the request for advice you made in your letter. Don't let your lack of skill or experience stop you from growing where you're planted. You don't have to take on every chore at once. That would overwhelm anyone! Just find one small task to begin with and build from there. Perhaps start by asking your aunt to teach you the cooking and household duties you see her doing every day—preparing meals, washing dishes, and so on. Those are skills you can practice in the kitchen without fear of major mishap, and they'll give you a sense of usefulness right away. Once you feel steadier with those, milking the cows might come more naturally; it's a task many a wife on a homestead takes on, after all.

Remember, too, that the graces you worked so hard to acquire in Denver did not come to you overnight. You studied and practiced diligently to become the polished young lady you are. Why should farm skills be any different? They, too, require patient practice and gentle guidance, but they can be learned at any age. I have seen women far older than you take up new ways of life out here and thrive. You don't seem to be one to shy away from a challenge, so I know you can meet this one head-on.

Do write back and let me know if my advice was of any use. I keep you in my prayers and look forward to your next letter.

Yours sincerely,

Mrs. Vance

Emma set the letter aside, let out a slow breath, and let the words settle over her like a gentle but firm hand on her shoulder. She had let a few clumsy moments grow into something larger: a shield of excuses, a refusal to try again for fear of failing again.

Her father—a driven, self-made man who had built everything from nothing—would be disappointed to see her idling her days away rather than seizing the opportunity in front of her and using the move to Montana as a chance to grow.

The realization crushed Emma, and she couldn't stop the tears as they slid down her face, tracing silent tracks along her fair skin. She wished she could speak with him one more time and receive one of his rib-crushing hugs. No matter what troubles life brought, they always set her world to rights. But she knew what he would have said if he were here. Drawing a shaky breath, she whispered, "Onwards," the word a balm to her soul.

Resolved to make her father proud, she wiped her tears, placed her letter in the pocket of her dress, and went in search of her aunt. Thankfully, she didn't have to look far; Sarah was at the wide pine worktable in the kitchen, kneading a ball of dough with steady, practiced motions. She looked up and smiled when Emma entered the room.

"Hello, dear. How's Mrs. Vance doing?"

"She's doing well. She's been enjoying spending time with her grandson." Emma paused, unsure how to phrase her request. "Aunt Sarah, would you teach me how to cook? And.. and do other things around the house? I know you've been kind enough to give me time to settle in, but I see now how much work there is, and I want to help. I don't want to sit by anymore." She swallowed, her voice dropping a little. "Mrs. Vance wrote I should start small, and well, I think she's right. I want to learn."

A wide smile bloomed on Sarah's face. "Of course I'll teach you! I suppose I should have thought of offering sooner, but I didn't want to rush you while you were finding your feet. We'll speak to Edward tonight after dinner, and you can discuss when you'd like to start milking. In the meantime, you can help me make dinner. There's an extra apron hanging by the door there. Put it on so your dress doesn't get dirty, and we'll get to work."

When Emma came into the kitchen the next morning, she saw Aunt Sarah standing in her usual spot before the stove, vigorously mixing batter in a bowl with a wooden spoon. Wonderful aromas, both sweet and savory, already filled the kitchen. She watched her aunt for a minute before walking closer to inspect a line of pies that were cooling on the table.

"Good morning, Aunt Sarah. It seems you've been baking up a storm."

"I have, though I'm not finished yet." Sarah set down the bowl and pulled out a tray of cookies from the oven. "The party tomorrow has me in a bit of a whirlwind."

Emma paused, her hand stilling on the worktable. "The... party?"

Her aunt chuckled softly and wiped her hands on the towel slung over her shoulder. "Yes, dear. We're having a welcoming party for you tomorrow after services. We invited our friends and neighbors, and they'll each bring a dish to share, so there will be plenty of food to go around. My dear friend Martha May is coming too—she lives on the ranch next door. Her husband, Henry, is the foreman, and she works as the owner's cook and housekeeper. You'll get to meet them both."

"A party... for me?" she parroted, her mind still catching up. Tomorrow? She'd only just started helping in the kitchen yesterday. She barely knew how to scramble an egg, and now the whole town would be here. The thought didn't frighten her exactly. She knew how to smile through a crowded ballroom, but it caught her off guard. It was like stepping onto a stage without knowing her lines.

"Of course, for you," Sarah smiled, warm and steady. She stepped closer and rested a hand lightly on Emma's arm. "I didn't tell you sooner because I didn't want to worry you about it all week. You've had enough to adjust to—grief, the travel, finding your way around the house—and I thought it best to wait until tomorrow was close."

Her aunt was right, of course. If Emma had known about it sooner, she would have worried herself sick. "How many people will we be expecting?" she asked.

"I'd say about a hundred or so, including children, but word spreads. Some will have to leave early to take care of their farm chores, so not everyone will be here at once. I think it will be a nice chance for you to meet some more folks your own age. And we have several very handsome single men in town who will definitely want to meet you."

"They will?" She asked faintly, sinking into a chair at the kitchen table.

"Of course, they will. You're a very beautiful young woman. Surely, you've been told that before?" Sarah waited for Emma's shy nod of acknowledgement before she said, "Out here, the men outnumber the women almost nine to one, so there is a lot of competition among them for a wife. In Elk Ridge, most of the single men have known all the eligible young women since they were in school, so having someone new in town will draw them like bees to a honeypot."

Emma could handle crowds and polite conversation, even sidelong glances. She'd spent countless hours in etiquette class perfecting that—but the casual mention of "handsome single men" and "nine to one" made her feel slightly queasy.

As if she could sense Emma's unease, Sarah set her bowl down and patted her shoulder in comfort. "Everything will work out, dear, so don't worry too much. Why don't you grab your apron and help me roll out some sugar cookies?"

Emma still felt a knot of worry about the party tomorrow, but sitting here with the family, surrounded by the scrape of forks and the soft clatter of plates as they ate, it loosened just a fraction.

The house felt truly alive with them all present. She would listen to their stories, watch their familiar teasing, and slowly piece together who each of them was—like reading a novel where each new day revealed another chapter, drawing her closer. She smiled to herself at the thought and turned her attention back to the conversation around her as Micah leaned back in his chair and said, "We had dinner with Gabe."

"You saw Gabe in town?" Aunt Sarah asked, seeming rather interested in this information.

"Yep," Luke answered and shrugged. "He was picking up stuff for the ranch."

"Gabe is the owner of the ranch next to ours," Sarah explained. "He inherited it after his uncle passed away."

"Oh! How very sad. Were they close?" Emma asked, knowing how painful loss could be.

"No, they had never even met before," Benjamin put in.

"Let's not go spreading around other people's business," Uncle Edward interrupted.

The conversation stopped after the gentle chastisement, and for a while, all that could be heard was the scrape of utensils against the plates. No one seemed eager to be the first to speak, so Emma decided to fill the quiet.

"Aunt Sarah told me there'll be a party here tomorrow. Are there many such activities in the community?"

"It depends on the season, but we see folks a fair bit," Edward answered. "Anything from a barn raising to corn husking can become a social event once the work is done. We also have events in town for things like Independence Day or Founders' Day, and every Christmas, the children put on a nativity play at church."

"How wonderful!" Emma said excitedly. "I bet they enjoy doing that."

"Not always. Last year, I was a sheep, and Pastor Langley kept getting mad when I was bleating," Matthew complained.

"That's because you kept making noises when the wise men were reciting their lines and distracted them," Esther stated.

"Well, that's what sheep do! They make noises all the time, and they don't care if someone is talking," he retorted.

"How would you know? You've never even been around sheep before," Ruth pointed out.

"Enough children," Edward broke in. He gave each of the bickering children a pointed look and then cleared his throat. "Ma made a lemon custard pie, and I, for one, plan on finishing all my dinner so I can have a slice."

The promise of a sweet reward put the children on their best behavior, and once everyone had finished, the pie was dished up and passed around the table. Emma thought about refusing after such a filling meal, but the lure of a sugary treat won out. The lemon pie was wonderfully tart, and the light and airy meringue kept it from being too sour. As she set her fork down on the empty plate, she felt her stomach press painfully against the rigid boning of her corset. She would have to watch herself, or she'd no longer be able to fit into any of her dresses.

Once the plates had been cleared away, Sarah declared an early bedtime for the family. "We've tasks for the party that need finishing before we leave for church in the morning."

The younger children erupted in loud protest—groans, whines, one dramatic flop onto the table—but a single quelling look from their father had them sighing in resignation and pushing back their chairs.

"I wish you were sharing my room, Emma," Esther declared sullenly as they got up from the table. "Ruth snores and always hogs the covers."

"I do not!" Ruth protested.

"You do too!"

"How do you know I don't snore?" Emma asked, trying to stop their argument before it got out of hand. "I could be just as bad, if not worse than Ruth. I think I should share with Mary. Then I can annoy her with all of my dreadful sleeping habits, and instead of you."

Esther looked as if she hadn't thought of the possibility and took a moment to think it over before nodding. "I suppose you're right. Come on, Ruth, let's go."

Emma smiled as she watched the sisters grab hands and race up the stairs. They might fight like cats and dogs, but she was coming to see how deeply bonded the two girls were. Mary touched her elbow gently. "We should get ready for bed, too."

Together they climbed the narrow staircase and got ready for bed, using the soft glow of the lamp to guide them as they washed up and changed into their nightgowns.

Long after her cousin had drifted off to sleep, Emma lay awake in the darkened room, listening to the soft hooting of owls and the wind rattling through the trees as it floated through the open window. She'd tried to silence her whirling thoughts, but Sarah's comments about single men wanting wives kept returning, insistent and unsettling. It had been almost eight months since she ended things with Michael, and while part of her felt like she was ready to move on, her ability to trust was still fragile.

Knowing there was only one solution, she carefully slid out of the bed and knelt beside it to pray.

"Lord, please help me find my place here. Guide me on the path you have set out for me. I trust you, and I promise to remember that when I'm feeling afraid. Amen."

She stayed on her knees a moment longer, as a quiet peace settled over her. It was in His hands now. Emma crawled back into bed and closed her eyes, imagining a future full of friendship, laughter, and love.

Chapter 9

When Emma woke on Sunday morning, Mary was gently shaking her shoulder and softly whispering that it was time to get up. Rubbing the sleep from her eyes, she looked at her cousin, who'd already donned a cream-colored dress with pink roses printed on the fabric and matching ribbon adorning the cuffs and collar. It suited Mary well, reflecting how sweet and cheerful she was, without making her look like a child.

"You look beautiful," Emma mumbled groggily.

"Thank you," Mary said, a slight smile touching her lips. "We'll be leaving for church in an hour. Do you need any help to get ready?"

"No," she said, rising from the bed and putting on her dressing gown. "I'll be fine. I know exactly what I want to wear."

As her cousin left the room, Emma padded across chilly floorboards that creaked softly underfoot and opened the wardrobe. Pushing garments aside, she rifled through the clothing until she found her favorite dress—a gorgeous cobalt silk with white lace adorning the cuffs and collar. Her father always said it brought out the color of her eyes. *If I'm going to be on display,* she thought wryly, *I might as well look my best.*

Chuckling to herself, she began donning the multitude of layers: chemise, stockings, corset, bustle cage, three starched petticoats, and finally the overskirt and bodice. By the time she was done, her cheeks were flushed, and there was a sheen of sweat on her forehead and upper lip that she quickly wiped away. Then she carefully styled her burnished auburn hair using the mirror above the washbasin, smoothed her hands over the silk of her dress one last time, and went downstairs.

When she entered the dining room, she found the rest of the family had already gathered and were anxiously awaiting her arrival.

"Take a seat, dear," Aunt Sarah said, gesturing to the only open chair. "We're running a bit late this morning."

Murmuring apologies for taking so long to dress, Emma hurried to the chair. Luke pulled it out for her, and once she was settled, Uncle Edward blessed the cold spread: sliced bread and preserves, hard-boiled eggs, pickled beets, and leftover boiled ham from yesterday's dinner. As soon as the prayer closed, everyone bolted to fill their plates, and the usual boisterous chatter at mealtimes was reduced to a few hushed words as they ate.

"I'll go hitch up the wagon," Luke said a few minutes later, stuffing his last bite of bread into his mouth.

"Right behind you," Micah called out, and he and Joseph followed their brother out the door.

One by one, the rest of the family finished eating and left the table, until only Emma remained. She wasn't used to eating with such speed, having been instructed to eat slowly and take small, delicate bites, but she did her best to finish her food quickly. After taking her plate to the sink, she hurriedly pinned on her white straw hat with blue silk flowers, slid on her gloves, and checked her appearance in the hall mirror. The cobalt silk really did make her eyes stand out, and after assuring herself that she was ready to make her first impression on the folks in town, she took a steadying breath and stepped outside.

Micah, Luke, and Joseph had ridden ahead, so once everyone else was settled in the wagon, Edward flicked the reins, and they rolled toward town. As the wheels creaked over the rutted road, Emma felt every bump in her stomach. Somehow it felt like her nerves were worse than when she was about to disembark the train, though surely that was impossible.

Sarah, who sat on the bench next to her husband, was twisting the fabric of her green cotton dress in her hand.

"I hope we aren't too late," she said.

"We'll make it in time, dear," Edward comforted her as he gave the horses a quick snap of their reins and urged them faster.

Though they had to wait behind the line of people wanting to park their wagons in front of the church, Edward guided his team to a halt just before services started, and Sarah's relief was palpable. She hurried out of the wagon, sending the youngest children scurrying ahead to claim seats as a plump older woman in a light blue floral dress came rushing up and pulled her aside. Emma watched as the two women spoke quietly, their heads close together, wondering what was so urgent. She turned to ask Mary what it was about, but her uncle ushered them inside before she could get the words out.

The humble wooden building, so different from the soaring revival-style buildings adorned with their tall spires and stained glass she'd seen in Denver, was packed to the brim. If Sarah hadn't sent the children ahead to save them seats, they might have spent the entire sermon standing in the vestibule. As it was, they had barely sat down before Pastor Langley, an elderly man with hair gone white and warm brown eyes, made his way to the podium to give a sermon on marriage.

Emma shifted in her seat uncomfortably, wanting to avoid listening, but found herself drawn in once she truly began paying attention. The pastor made some sound arguments for entering into marriage, and she wondered—not without unease—if her own reluctance to embrace the possibility of getting married was unfounded. After all, not every man was a snake. Her father, uncle, and cousins were all proof of that.

As the service ended and the congregation joined in song, Emma sat in silent reflection. The sermon had given her a lot to think and pray about. Marriage wasn't something she could simply dismiss after hearing the pastor speak of it as companionship, partnership, a shared path through life's difficulties. But she wasn't ready to rush toward it. Not after Michael. She also couldn't close the door on it forever. She would have to allow herself to meet people and see where trust might grow again without promises she wasn't prepared to make.

A feeling of rightness settled in her chest as she followed her family down the aisle to exit the church. She could do this. When they reached the doors, Sarah gently guided Emma over to Pastor Langley, who'd positioned himself at the door to speak to his congregants, and offered an introduction.

"Miss Barnes!" he exclaimed, clasping her hand warmly with both of his. "I am so pleased to have you here with us in Elk Ridge. How are you finding our growing little town?"

"Well, thank you," Emma answered, an involuntary smile tugging at her lips at his delight in meeting her. "I haven't been here long, but I'm looking forward to being part of the community."

"We're excited to have you with us," he beamed. "I'll be attending your welcoming party this afternoon, and I look forward to introducing you to my wife."

"I look forward to that as well," she said, nodding farewell to the pastor and moving down the steps to allow him to speak with the next person in line.

She let out a small exhale as her aunt shepherded the family to a more secluded spot in the churchyard, where a large cottonwood tree offered its leaves for shade from the midday sun. *That's one introduction done*, she thought, *and only about a hundred more where someone might ask if I'm looking for a husband.* The thought was half-joking, half-weary, but it steadied her. She had survived the pastor's warm clasp and kind words; she could survive the rest.

Micah, Luke, and Joseph began arguing quietly among themselves, but the squabble barely registered anymore. It was just background noise, having become as familiar as the creak of wagon wheels, and Emma took a moment to admire the church building from the outside. A fresh coat of whitewash covered the clapboard siding, and the bell tower rising from the front held a shiny new bronze bell. It caught the sun and sent a small flash across the yard.

"Dear, did you hear me?" came her aunt's soft voice.

Emma turned to see that a large group of people had gathered around her in a circle. She was a bit surprised by how quickly they'd appeared, but put on her best Denver hostess smile and nodded courteously.

"Allow me to introduce you all to my husband's cousin, Miss Emma Barnes. She recently moved here from Denver," Sarah announced to the group.

As Emma looked around, she noticed that the group of well-wishers consisted mostly of young men, though there were several older ladies with them she assumed were their mothers. They were all fine-looking men, dressed in their Sunday best, and eagerly waiting for their introduction.

"This is Timothy Shelton and his mother, Mrs. Maria Shelton. Mr. Shelton owns the druggist's shop," Sarah said.

Emma smiled at them and held out her hand for Mrs. Shelton to shake, followed by Timothy, who tipped his hat politely. She returned the greeting warmly, and her aunt turned to the next person in the circle.

"This is Alexander Payne and his mother, Mrs. Tabitha Payne. Alexander works as a legal assistant and is studying law."

Emma gritted her teeth, her smile never slipping, and extended her hand for Mrs. Payne to shake, then for Alexander, who tipped his hat in a courteous nod. He was a good-looking young man, but his chosen profession slightly soured her opinion of him. It wasn't fair, she knew, but there it was—and all thanks to Michael.

The pattern of introductions continued until Sarah gestured to a man who stood alone. "And this is Gregory Callaway. He's the bank manager here in town."

She held out her hand again, but instead of just tipping his hat as the others did, he held it briefly over his heart and pressed a kiss to her gloved hand. Emma was surprised by the flourish, but gave the same generic greeting she had offered the other men.

Gregory could barely get two words out before Sarah said, "Well, now that we all know each other, we should be going. Ah, yes. I see Edward waiting for us in the wagon. Please excuse us. Good day."

After cutting the conversation short, her aunt propelled Emma forward toward the wagon by taking her by the elbow. The forced movement and furious pace that her aunt had set caught her off guard, and she quickly raised her skirts so she wouldn't trip. Once they were a few feet from the wagon, where her uncle was indeed waiting with Mary and the younger children, her pace slowed. Edward seemed to have noticed their labored breathing, and he waited for them to catch their breath before helping them climb up.

The entire trip back to the farm, Sarah looked annoyed, and Emma wondered if she had done something wrong. She replayed the day's events in her head—the introductions, the hand kiss, the smiles—but couldn't pinpoint anything that would have offended or embarrassed her family. She wanted to ask her aunt about it, but the sound of hooves announced the arrival of her cousins, drawing everyone's focus.

"Where were you?" asked Edward.

"I was talking with Gabe," Joseph replied with a breezy grin. "These two insisted on riding with me. I guess they didn't trust their baby brother to find the way home on his own." He flashed a self-deprecating smile and urged his horse into a gallop, disappearing into the farmyard ahead of them.

The wagon rolled in a minute later, wheels crunching over the gravel as her uncle pulled the team to a stop near the barn. The younger children scrambled down almost before it fully halted, laughing and calling to each other, while Sarah began directing everyone with calm efficiency.

Since a group of local laborers had come by while they were at church to do most of the major preparations before guests started arriving, she assigned tasks to each of the family members, and they all set off in separate directions to carry them out. Tables and chairs were quickly brought from the house and placed in the shade, along with the food prepared in advance. Extra buckets of water were hauled from the well, pitchers filled for lemonade, and a fire started in the pit to keep coffee hot. Canvas sheets were strung between posts for more shade, and the privy was given a quick tidy. With the whole family working together, the setup went smoothly, and by mid-afternoon, guests began rumbling up the drive.

The first wave of arrivals was families with young children, then older couples, and finally, young men began drifting in, hats in hand and eyes bright with interest. Emma seamlessly stepped back into her role as the polished young lady she'd been raised to be, emerging as naturally as breathing. She smiled, offered her hand, returned greetings with warm courtesy, and asked the right questions about farms and families. To everyone watching, she was grace itself.

Inside, though, the constant stream of unfamiliar faces and appreciative glances was wearing on her. She could keep the smile fixed, the voice steady, the posture perfect—that part was second nature—but being the center of attention felt different here. In Denver, people came, said the polite things, exchanged a few words, and moved on to the next conversation; the interactions were light, superficial, and fleeting. Here, everyone lingered. They wanted to know *her*—her story, her impressions of the town, her plans. Some of the young men especially watched her with open interest, their eyes lingering a moment too long, their questions carrying a hopeful edge. It wasn't hostile, but it was relentless, and the romantic undercurrent made her feel more exposed than any crowded ballroom ever had.

Eventually, there was a lull in the guests' arrivals, and she leaned close to her aunt. "Aunt Sarah," she murmured, keeping her smile in place for anyone watching, "could you make my excuses for a few minutes? I need a short break."

"Of course, dear! How thoughtless of me! Why don't you go inside? I think there are still some cookies in the kitchen you can enjoy," her aunt said, giving her a conspiratorial wink and sending her on her way.

Inside, the kitchen was blessedly free of people. After the noisy chatter of the farmyard, the silence felt like a weight lifted from her shoulders. Emma stood near the stove for a moment, taking a deep breath. When she felt steadier, she took two sugar cookies from the jar on the counter, carried them to the parlor, and sank onto the sofa. With her eyes closed, she slowly chewed her cookie, the sweetness acting as a small comfort against the day's whirl.

She tried to place names with the faces of people she'd met, but it was impossible. They all blurred together in her mind, and she hoped the townsfolk would give her some grace if she misspoke or forgot a name the next time they met. She had just taken a large bite of cookie to console herself when the woman who had been in such a rush to talk to her aunt this morning came into the parlor.

"Hello there," she said cheerfully, eyes twinkling. "You must be Emma! I'm Martha May. Sarah told me I could find you here."

Emma hopped off the couch and put her hand over her mouth, cheeks flushing as she realized how full it was. Unable to answer without being deeply improper, she nodded vigorously. Martha May seemed to understand her distress and laughed, coming over to sit down on the sofa.

"It's all right, dear. I've been known to sneak a cookie or three when I'm overwhelmed, too."

Emma swallowed her food as she retook her seat, and when she was finally able to speak, she said, "It is nice to meet you, Mrs. Rollings. Aunt Sarah has told me what a wonderful baker you are."

"Why, thank you, dear," the older woman responded with a widening smile. "But please, call me Martha May. You know, Sarah is also very accomplished in the kitchen. We swap recipes all the time. Now tell me, are you enjoying Elk Ridge so far?"

"Well, I've only been here for a little while, but it is very beautiful. I do miss certain things about Colorado, though. I used to be part of a charity organization that supported the Denver Orphans' Home, and I volunteered there several days a week to read books to the children." Emma frowned, worrying her lower lip with her teeth. "I hope they find someone else to fill in soon. It was the children's favorite part of the day."

Martha May patted her hand. "I'm sure they will," she consoled, then stood and shook out her skirt. "I need to go make sure everything's been brought in from my wagon. Would you like to come with me?"

"Yes, I'd like that. I've spent far too long in here hiding. I'm sure the guests are wondering where I am."

"Hiding?" Martha May stopped and turned to her, face lined with concern. "Has someone been unkind to you?" The older woman looked ready to play the avenging angel if she'd been slighted.

"Oh no, of course not. I misspoke. Everyone has been very kind and welcoming, but I can't help but feel like I've landed in shark-infested waters. I've never had so many single men vying for my attention all at once. I was admiring the church one moment, and the next I was surrounded."

Martha May hooted with laughter at her exasperated expression. "I bet those boys took one look at you and were begging their mothers to ask Sarah for an introduction. They're the smart ones, trying to make their mark before anyone else. Who were they?"

"Well, let me try to remember." Emma closed her eyes for a brief second and said, "Alexander Payne, Timothy Shelton, and Gregory Callaway. There were others as well, but I can't recall their names."

"I see," the older woman drawled as they exited the house. "Well, they are all nice men, have good jobs, and regularly attend services. I suppose they would do all right as a husband."

"Aunt Sarah didn't seem to think so. When she introduced Gregory to me, instead of just shaking my hand like the others, he kissed it, and suddenly she said we had to leave."

"Well, I should think so!" squawked Martha May.

"I've had a gentleman kiss my hand in greeting before—though it was infrequent," Emma said. "Nothing I learned in my etiquette classes stated it was forbidden."

She paused at the foot of the porch steps and turned to Martha May, her eyes wide in dawning horror. "Is that not how things are done out west? Oh, no wonder Aunt Sarah seemed so upset on the ride home." Her hands flew to her flaming cheeks in dismay. "My goodness! I've embarrassed my aunt!"

Martha May took her hands from her face and held them gently. "It's all right, dear. You did nothing wrong, and Sarah isn't upset with you. She may be miffed at Gregory for being presumptuous and a bit forward, but never at you."

Her calm and caring voice helped bring Emma back from her spiral of anxiety, and she felt herself sag in relief.

"Thank you, Martha May," she said as she squeezed the older woman's hands.

"You're welcome, dear. Now, stand up straight and come along; I think I see someone I know. Yes, there he is. Gabriel!" Martha May shouted.

Emma followed her gaze and blinked several times, making sure that her eyes weren't playing tricks on her, because the most handsome-looking man had just turned their way.

Chapter 10

Earlier that morning

Gabe woke late, having spent most of the night in the stable, waiting for the birth of a foal. It was the first one born since he'd taken over as owner of the ranch, and he'd wanted to make sure nothing went wrong. As the hours had dragged on with no sign of labor from the mare, his eyes had grown heavier and heavier until Miguel came in a little after two and sat with him in the straw.

"You should get some rest. It does no good to miss sleep. That's when mistakes happen," he'd said pointedly. "Go. I'll stay and watch over her."

Gabe had understood the gentle rebuke. He made his way to bed and slept deeply, waking to sunlight streaming through his window. Scrambling up, he washed quickly at the basin in the corner of his room and headed straight for the stable. When he reached the stall with the pregnant mare, he heard someone crooning softly to her in Spanish. He looked slowly over the door and saw a new foal wobbling on fresh legs—a beautiful gray coat like his mother's.

"You see," Miguel whispered, coming to stand next to him. "Sleep can bring good things."

"You're right." Gabe watched as the foal picked its way toward its mother and nursed. "How'd Ashes fare during the birthing?"

"Fine. She's a strong one," the hand said admiringly.

The gray mare looked over at the two men peering over her stall door—as if knowing they were talking about her—but when they didn't move, or show any sign of threat to her newborn, she flicked her tail in the air and went back to munching on hay.

"I'll hook the wagon up for you," Miguel offered. "Martha May will want to head to church soon."

Gabe thanked him and returned to the house for breakfast. A plate was already sitting at the table when he entered, and he was filling up a fresh cup of coffee when Martha May turned and caught a look at him. Putting the enameled pot on the table, she sighed.

"Gabriel, I know you wanted to check on the new foal Henry told me about, but could you at least brush your hair before we leave?"

He reached up and felt his wavy brown hair. It was sticking up at odd angles. He gave Martha May a sheepish look and headed back upstairs to make himself presentable, with his housekeeper's voice calling after him, "Don't forget to wear your new shirt!"

Gabe wet his brush in the washbasin and looked in the mirror as he tried to comb his wild hair into submission. It was getting a bit too long—the dark locks curling at the nape of his neck and at his ears—but there wasn't time for a proper trim today; he'd have to make do.

Then he lathered his face, scraping the razor carefully against his jaw, and dressed. The crisp white shirt he'd purchased from Mrs. Tandy looked presentable enough, so he decided not to wear the new suit just yet and instead put on his pair of gray wool trousers and matching waistcoat. He knotted his black tie, slipped his Uncle Telly's gold watch into his pocket, and returned to the table to scarf down his food.

"There now! You look so handsome!" Martha May exclaimed, her eyes twinkling in delight. "I just knew that with a little effort, we could make you shine."

"Thank you," Gabe said between bites. He was in a hurry to eat, but he still had manners. When he finished his cup of coffee, he stood. "Are you ready to go?"

"She's been ready to go for an hour," Henry said as he swaggered in and gave his wife a right smacker on the mouth. She blushed at such overt physical affection, but the foreman just laughed. He tossed Gabe his hat and gestured to the door. "Let's go. The surrey's ready, and you know how my wife likes to get there early and spin yarn with the ladies."

Martha May swatted playfully at her husband as they walked to the fringe-topped wagon, but accepted his help into it and fussed over her green, flowered, patterned dress, making sure it fell just right to prevent wrinkles. Henry rolled his eyes and hauled himself into the driver's seat, and Gabe climbed in on the other side.

A sharp snap of the reins set the horses moving, and as the surrey rumbled down the drive, Martha May began straightening Henry's clothes. She pulled down the back of his waistcoat and was brushing some minuscule piece of dirt from his black trousers when he grabbed her hand. "I'm fine, woman. Just sit back and enjoy the ride."

By the time they arrived at the church, there were already several wagons parked haphazardly in the yard. It was a clear signal it was going to be a full house, and once Martha May descended from the wagon, she took off toward the church without waiting for her husband.

Gabe frowned, wondering what had lit such a fire under her skirt. He shot a questioning look at Henry, but the foreman just shrugged and released the horses from their traces with swift, practiced movements before tying them to the hitching post in front of the churchyard.

After helping maneuver the surrey to an open spot in the yard, he glanced around the churchyard for his friends, but the Barnes brothers were nowhere in sight. It wasn't unusual for them to be late, and since he'd see them later at the welcoming party, he joined Henry as he spoke with some of their neighbors—mostly about cattle prices or this year's hay crop, the same conversation they'd had last Sunday and the Sunday before. He listened with half an ear until Pastor Langley's wife began playing the prelude. Martha May was still nowhere in sight, so they made their way inside the church to grab a pew.

As they entered the vestibule, Gabe could see that his earlier assessment was correct. The chapel was already crowded with congregants—some he hadn't seen attend a service in months—and their choice of seating was limited. Henry nudged his elbow and nodded to an empty pew near the front. It wasn't their preferred place to sit, but since they weren't spoiled for choice, they moved to claim it before anyone else could. It wasn't until the last notes of the prelude were fading away that Martha May slid into the pew. Her husband gave her a questioning look, but she just stared straight ahead, giving the pastor her rapt attention.

Lack of sleep and the overly warm chapel made it hard to stay focused, and Gabe felt his attention wander shortly after the sermon began. He was just turning his head to look out at the congregation behind him—hoping to see if his friends had arrived—when Martha May gave him a swift jab to his still-sore ribs with her elbow. He grunted in pain and turned back to the pulpit, but after listening for a few minutes, he glanced suspiciously at his housekeeper. When she caught him, she leaned close and whispered, "What is it, Gabriel?"

He looked at the pastor and then back at her. "If I didn't know any better, I'd have said you asked him to preach on this topic. Didn't you just tell me the other day I need to get married?"

She huffed quietly. "Gabriel Lucien Moreau, how dare you! I would never try to influence a man of God for my own purposes."

Someone in the pew behind let out a soft but pointed "shhh," and they straightened in their seats. Martha May, obviously still furious, reached over and gave a sharp pinch to the underside of his bicep, and he had to bite down hard on the inside of his cheek to keep himself silent. Henry cleared his throat and gave both of them a stern look before settling back to listen to the sermon.

When the service finally ended, he let out a silent sigh of relief and slowly followed the mass of people leaving the chapel. Martha May slipped ahead of their little group, weaving through the crowd as if on a mission, leaving the two men to trail behind. That suited him just fine, though. He was still annoyed with his housekeeper.

Once they'd finally made it outside, Henry left to get the horses while Gabe lingered for a moment in the churchyard. He was wondering what to do with himself when he spied his friends taking refuge from the noonday sun under the cottonwood tree. The brothers were talking animatedly to each other, but Luke was the first one to notice him and nodded in his direction. There was another brief discussion between them, and then Joseph came trotting over.

"Howdy!" Putting his arm around Gabe's shoulder, he turned him in the opposite direction. "Come with me. I want to show you something," he said. He gave a quick look behind him toward his family and then steered them to the hitching posts.

"What is it?" Gabe tried to turn around and see what Joseph had been looking at, but a passing couple blocked his view.

"It's a little trinket I picked up at the general store the other day. It's over here in my saddlebag."

When they reached the hitching post where Joseph's sorrel Quarter Horse, Honey, was waiting, Gabe scratched her neck in greeting. The mare nickered softly, her long tail swishing while Joseph dug in the saddlebags. After a few minutes, he became impatient.

"Well? Did you find whatever it is?" he asked his friend.

"No," Joseph replied, still fishing around, "not yet."

"Why don't you show it to me later?" Gabe asked. "I'm sure the surrey is hitched up by now."

Joseph glanced across the yard and turned, giving him an apologetic smile. "Sure. I'll try to find it by the time you come for the party." Then he mounted his horse, touched two fingers to the brim of his hat in a salute, and rode off.

Shaking his head in exasperation, Gabe made his way toward the fringed wagon where Henry and Martha May were waiting and climbed into the seat.

"I told Sarah we would bring a few extra chairs to the party. Could you and Henry take care of that when we get home?" she asked, apparently having forgiven him for his comment in church.

"Sure," Gabe said, glad that their earlier dust-up was settled.

The surrey rattled up the familiar lane leading to the ranch, dust kicking up behind them in the warm afternoon sun, and as soon as Henry pulled the team to a stop near the kitchen door, Martha May hopped down. "I'll fetch the last of the pies from the cooling rack while you get the wagon," she said, calling back over her shoulder for them to hurry as she disappeared inside.

Henry nodded dutifully, and he and Gabe made quick work of putting up the surrey before hitching up the flatbed wagon, which waited, already half-loaded with covered dishes from earlier preparations. Together they carried out the extra chairs—sturdy oak ones that had seen better days but still held strong—and stacked them carefully alongside crocks of potato salad, jars of pickled beets, and Martha May's famous apple dumplings wrapped in clean cloths. Gabe secured the load with ropes, double-knotting the corners so nothing would shift on the rough path, then gave the taut line a firm tug in satisfaction.

Martha May emerged last, carrying two pies in one arm and a tray of molasses cookies under a checked cloth in the other. "Everything tied down?" she asked, eyeing their work as she set the food in the wagon.

"Should hold," Henry grunted, wiping sweat from his brow with a sleeve.

With the wagon hitched and the team rested just enough, they set off down a narrow, rutted trail that cut through the back pasture between the Lucky Strike and the Barneses' farm. Shaded by cottonwoods and lined by bushes filled with wild blackberries, still green on their woody stems, the wagon swayed and creaked over roots and dips, forcing them to go slow to keep the food from spilling. The shortcut saved them the long loop to the main road, but they were still late to the party.

As the farm came into view, they could see smoke curling from the fire pit, colorful quilts spread out in the yard with families picnicking, and hear the first strains of laughter carrying on the breeze. Gabe looked around as the wagon came to a stop and smiled. There were folks all around, chatting with friends and laughing while children raced through the yard. He loved events like these, where it felt like a giant family all gathered together.

Martha May wasted no time, grabbing a tray of cookies and taking off toward the house, while Henry and Gabe unloaded the chairs. It didn't take them long to get set up at an empty table, and he was just about to seek his friends when he heard, "Gabriel!"

He looked up at the sound of his name and searched the crowd for Martha May, for it was unmistakable who was calling for him. When he spotted her standing by the back porch steps with a tall, sophisticated, and well-dressed woman, he sucked in a breath. With dark reddish-brown hair piled up under a fancy hat, fair skin, and a trim figure, he could tell that she was a beauty, but when she smiled at him, it made Gabe feel a little dizzy. He stood in the same spot, probably looking like a trout with his mouth wide open for a full thirty seconds before he could move. As he neared the porch, he wiped his suddenly sweaty palms against his trousers.

"Gabriel, let me introduce you to Edward's cousin, Emma Barnes," his housekeeper said with a wide smile. "She came to live here after her father's passing. Emma, this is Gabriel Moreau, my boss and your new neighbor."

He was so mesmerized by the young woman standing before him that he almost didn't hear the introduction, but when his mind finally caught up, he looked at Martha May in shock and blurted, "*This* is their cousin?"

"Gabriel!" came the immediate rebuke, along with hearty laughter from nearby.

He turned slightly and saw the three eldest Barnes brothers standing a few feet away, holding their stomachs and wiping away tears of mirth. Suddenly, Joseph's strange behavior at the church made sense, and Gabe felt his face flush.

When he turned back to the women, Martha May was glowering at him, but Emma seemed amused rather than insulted.

"I apologize for my confusion, Miss Barnes," he said, lifting his wide-brimmed hat a few inches off his head before replacing it. "It's a pleasure to meet you."

Emma offered her hand for him to shake, her captivating blue eyes twinkling as she replied, "It's a pleasure to meet you as well, Mr. Moreau. I can see you're familiar with my cousins."

"I am."

For a moment, he couldn't look away from her, and they stood locked in each other's gaze until he heard Martha May clear her throat. He brought his attention back to where it was supposed to be and saw that Sarah Barnes now stood on the porch with them. She gave Gabe a knowing smile, and he felt the tips of his ears heat up.

Taking a step forward and tilting her face up to the sky, Sarah sighed contentedly. "I'm so glad the weather cooperated with us. It's been raining on and off for days." Then she paused and looked over at Gabe. "A perfect day for a walk, wouldn't you say?"

"I would," he agreed, picking up on her hint. Then, heart pounding at the thought she might decline, he looked at Emma and asked, "Would you like to take a turn around the house with me, Miss Barnes?"

"I'd be delighted to, Mr. Moreau," Emma replied in a soft, refined voice.

Relieved that she'd accepted, he held his arm out as a gentleman should, and she threaded her slim arm through his. A warm thrill coursed through his body at the contact, and the slight catch of breath that he heard from Emma told him she felt it too. For a moment, neither spoke as they descended the porch stairs, but they exchanged a tentative smile.

"Have a nice time, you two!" Sarah called as they walked away.

As they made their way around the house, their boots scuffing softly on the grass, Gabe was suddenly overcome with shyness. He didn't have much experience with the opposite sex, and he said out the first thing that came to his mind, which was, "You look mighty fine in that dress, Miss Barnes."

Though he wished he'd come up with something better to say, she really did look beautiful. The dark blue dress fit her slender figure to perfection, and the full skirt swayed gracefully as they walked. It was definitely an expensive gown, made from richer, lusher fabrics than anything worn by the other ladies attending today. Even in their Sunday best, Emma still outshone them.

She blushed becomingly and ducked her head, murmuring, "Thank you, that's kind of you to say. Everyone here has been so pleasant and welcoming."

Gabe nodded. "There's a lot of good, honest folk here."

As they picked their way across the uneven ground, he prayed he wouldn't look like a fool to a woman so refined and polished.

Chapter 11

Emma was still in disbelief that she was on a walk with someone like Gabriel. When she'd seen Martha May beckon over the most dazzlingly handsome man she had ever laid eyes on, she'd wondered if she was still sitting on the sofa in the parlor, dreaming. It was no wonder he'd been named after the archangel. His shiny, chocolate-brown hair was neatly combed beneath his hat, but she could tell it had a natural wave to it, with one rebellious lock of hair at his forehead falling over his dark, expressive eyebrows.

Up close, he was even more striking with a strong, clean-shaven jaw and a perfectly straight nose. His hazel eyes were spellbinding, and when they'd shaken hands, Emma could feel the heat from his palm radiating up her arm. She had never felt like this around a man before and struggled to bring her scattered thoughts back to the situation at hand

and reminded herself not to stare. This was her first time alone with a single man that wasn't Michael or a relation, and here she was, gazing at him quite improperly.

Fighting the blush creeping up her cheeks, she said, "I hear you're also new to Elk Ridge. Where are you from, Mr. Moreau?"

"Call me Gabe, please. We don't stand on ceremony around here, and the only one who calls me Gabriel is Martha May."

Emma hesitated, then gave a small, polite smile. "Perhaps in time. For now, Mr. Moreau will do nicely."

"If you wish, and to answer your question, I was born in a small town in Texas called Jefferson, but I moved around the state a lot."

"Oh! That is quite a long way from Montana."

Gabe laughed, rich and deep. "That it is. It was a long train ride, too."

Emma smiled, amused that he'd found so much humor in her innocent remark. "My ride from Denver took five days. I can only imagine how long it took you to come from Texas."

"It took almost two weeks. I lost count of all the transfers and layovers I went through after the first few days, but I saw some beautiful country along the way. Met some mighty kind people, too."

"That sounds like an interesting journey," she said, glad that her trip hadn't taken that long. "Did you leave any family behind in Texas?"

Emma saw him turn his face away slightly before he answered, "No. What about you? Was it just you and your father in Denver?"

"Yes. My mother and sister died when I was young, and it was just the two of us for almost a decade. I was almost—" Emma stopped abruptly before she divulged too much about her messy past. "Do you like it here in Montana?" she asked instead.

"I do," Gabe replied, a flicker of relief crossing his face as the subject changed to more neutral ground. "It's a lot different from Texas. For one, the air here is so fresh, not thick and humid like back home. And the mountains!" He looked to the south, where the slope of the foothills began to climb in elevation, and grinned. "When I was on the train, I was glued to the window, just staring in awe at how big the mountains are. The trees are different as well."

She looked up at his handsome face and smiled. "They don't have pine trees in Texas?"

"They do, but they look a little different, and there aren't as many. In Montana, they're everywhere, and they grow so tall. I love it, though," he admitted, and gave her a charming grin that set her heart fluttering.

"It is so interesting that the land and vegetation can vary so much depending on where one is in the country," she said, trying to focus on something mundane rather than the effect he was having on her. "Was the landscape the biggest change for you when you moved here?"

"Not even close," Gabe chuckled. "I'd never worked on a cattle ranch before, or had employees to manage. Henry, my foreman, had to teach me everything—and I do mean everything—about running a ranch. I always considered myself fairly intelligent, but coming here and seeing how little I knew was a disheartening experience."

"I know exactly what you mean," Emma murmured, thinking of all the things she'd taken for granted in Denver that were common knowledge here.

When they'd made one full circle around the house, they stopped at the food table to get a refreshment from Mrs. Langley, who was passing out glasses of lemonade. Then, with their drinks in hand, they continued their leisurely walk.

"What about you?" he asked. "What's been your biggest change?"

"Well, I've only been here a few days, and there have been so many changes, but living with people I've just met is a big adjustment. As I said, for the past few years, it was just my father and me. I'd never even met Aunt Sarah and Uncle Edward or their children until I came here, but I enjoy their company ever so much."

"If it makes you feel any better," he began, his lovely hazel eyes steady on her, "I didn't know my Uncle Telly existed until his attorney contacted me. It was shocking to find out I had other family members."

"I would imagine so. I've been meaning to ask Uncle Edward why he and my father had grown distant, but he's always so busy. It's hard to catch a moment alone with him. Whatever the case, I'm glad that I know them now. We spend the evenings together as a family in the parlor, talking and reading aloud or playing games. I've recently learned to play Brag, though I'm terrible at it."

Emma leaned in and said conspiratorially, "I found a book in the parlor called *The American Hoyle,* which gives instructions and strategies on several games. I plan to read it and try to gain an advantage over Joseph. I'm convinced he's cheating."

Gabe laughed. "That wouldn't surprise me," he said, still grinning. "Joseph is a prankster, but it's all in good fun. He would never actually swindle anyone. He reminds me a bit of a character from a book I'm reading, *Tom Sawyer*. Have you read it?"

"I have! Reading is one of my favorite pastimes. Too often, I get lost in the pages of a book, and when I stop reading, I have no idea what time of day it is." Emma stopped herself before she began to ramble and delicately took a sip of her drink. "I believe you're correct, though, as he does resemble Tom a bit in his love for a good laugh and his irreverence."

"Don't I know it. He misled me into believing that you were a man—and his brothers went along with it."

"So that's what they found so funny," Emma said, more surprised that Luke and Micah had been in on the deception than that Joseph was making up stories. "What a rude trick to play on their friend! I trust you'll give them a piece of your mind."

"I will, along with some sort of retaliation, so they'll learn their lesson." He chuckled to himself for a moment. "You could have pushed me over with a feather when I realized that you were their cousin."

"I can see how it would have been quite a shock," she said with a light laugh. "Were you disappointed?"

"Not in the slightest," he said, and a slow grin formed as his hazel eyes roved over her face.

Emma blushed at his evident evaluation of her looks and took another sip from her glass. It wasn't the first time a man had looked at her like that, but for some reason, she found herself rather pleased by it. She was about to ask Gabe about his favorite books when a leather ball came hurtling out of nowhere, bouncing against her hand, and making lemonade spill all over her and the beloved silk dress.

"Oh, no!" she cried out, stopping dead in her tracks and taking her arm from Gabe's so she could try to get as much liquid off her dress as possible. "Please, no."

The children who'd thrown the ball came running toward them, and the oldest boy of the bunch began speaking. "I'm so sorry, Miss! We didn't mean for the ball to come your way. Robby tripped and couldn't catch it in time." He looked scared—likely waiting to be yelled at.

"I understand," Emma said. Her voice quavered, and she tried to sound calm when inside she was falling apart. "Accidents do happen. Perhaps you might take your game a little further from the guests?"

The children all promised to move their game to the other side of the house, and Gabe tossed them their ball. "Are you all right?" he asked her, looking at her dress and then up at her hair.

Emma reached up and found that her hair, which she had spent an inordinate amount of time on, was wet as well and rapidly coming loose from its pins. She couldn't believe that an afternoon that had started so promisingly was now a disaster. Tears threatened, and she turned from Gabe, not wanting him to see her cry and think it was over something so trivial as her appearance.

"Yes, I'm fine. If you will excuse me, Mr. Moreau, I need to freshen up."

Then she practically ran toward the house, holding her sodden skirt up so she wouldn't humiliate herself further by tripping. Feeling hot tears spill down her cheeks, Emma raised a hand to hide her face, and thankfully, she was able to make it inside and all the way up to the room she shared with Mary before collapsing to the ground in loud, full-blown sobs.

"It's ruined!" she cried, slamming her fist down on her knee. "Father's dress, my time with Gabe, the party! Oh, why did those children have to be playing so close?"

A loud knocking interrupted her self-pitying tirade, and she took in some deep breaths before calling out, "Who is it?"

"It's Aunt Sarah, dear. Can I please come in? I'm worried about you."

With a resigned sigh, she dried her tears with the back of her hand and moved away from the door so it could be opened. When her aunt came in and saw her on the floor, eyes rimmed red from crying, she knelt and wrapped Emma in a hug.

"Oh, my! What on earth happened? Are you hurt?"

"No," Emma sniffed. "Not physically, at least." Taking a deep breath, she told her aunt what had transpired and shook her head. "I'm afraid my dress is destroyed now, and it was the very last thing my father gifted to me before he died. He was so proud when I wore it."

When her tears came again, Sarah shushed her while rubbing her back. "I'm so sorry, dear. It will be all right, though. I'm sure I can clean it, so let's get you out of these wet things."

"But what about the party?" Emma asked.

"Most of the guests have gone home now," her aunt consoled. "I'm surprised you didn't notice. Why don't you stay up here, and I'll make your excuses to whoever's left?"

"I'm sure by now Gabe probably thinks I'm terribly self-centered and rude for leaving him standing there all alone," she said morosely, while she stood and let Sarah tend to her.

"Let's not worry about that right now. We can get everything sorted out later, but for today, I just want to take care of you. Wash up as best you can and then rest."

When her aunt had left the room, Emma cleaned herself up at the washbasin in the corner and changed into a clean nightgown before crawling into bed. She could still hear the distant chatter of the remaining guests outside the house as she lay there, and although she felt she should return to the party, she simply couldn't.

The thought of going back downstairs and trying to socialize while pretending she didn't just hightail it into the house like her dress was on fire felt impossible. She knew she owed Gabe an explanation for her behavior, but it would have to wait. Emma pulled the covers over her head, trying to hide from the world, and fell asleep, exhausted from the events of the day.

Chapter 12

Gabe stood in the spot where Emma had left him, wondering what on earth had just happened. He was still trying to make sense of why she would flee from him when Martha May found him.

"Gabriel, what happened to Emma? I saw her running into the house."

A second later, Micah showed up, asking the same question. Gabe explained about the rogue ball, the lemonade spill, and Emma's sudden exit. Then he shrugged. "I don't get what she's so upset about," he said. "I'm sure it can be cleaned."

"Really, Gabriel? That's *silk*!" Martha May shook her head. "No wonder you aren't married yet."

It was then that he noticed that every guest who'd been in the vicinity was staring at him. Furtive glances and hushed words were exchanged behind hands, and Gabe began to feel extremely uncomfortable. He was never one who sought to be the center of attention, and this was a bad time to take on that role.

"I think I should just head home." Turning to Martha May, he said, "Tell Henry he'll have to load up the chairs without me. I'm gonna walk." Then to Micah he said, "Give my excuses to your parents, please."

Before either of them could stop him, Gabe made his way to the worn path they'd followed to the farm and set off toward the ranch. He arrived home much sooner than he'd expected, and since there was still daylight left, he headed to the stable to get some work done. He entered the large wooden building, intending to climb the ladder to the haymow, but a soft nicker drew his attention. The gentle sound came again, so he stepped over to the birthing stall and saw that the new foal was up and walking around, much steadier than it had been hours ago. He was curiously exploring his new surroundings, but when his mother spotted a visitor and came to say hello, he followed close behind.

Reaching over to the sack that held sugar cubes, Gabe pulled one out and gave it to the mare while he scratched her neck. Some of the tension he'd been feeling in his shoulders eased as he stood there in the quiet barn. There was something about the warm, dusty smell of horses and the simple trust in their dark eyes that always steadied him. When he pulled his hand back, Ashes gave an appreciative flick of her tail and ambled away, but the foal stayed behind.

"None for you yet, little one," he said to the newborn with a wry half-smile before turning away.

He climbed to the loft, grabbed the pitchfork from its place against the wall, and began tossing forkfuls of sweet-smelling hay down to the stalls below. The familiar task was comforting, and he let his mind wander as he worked.

Today had started so well. When Martha May had introduced him to Emma, a small spark of hope had kindled in his chest. A beautiful woman had agreed to go for a walk with him, and surprisingly, their conversation had flowed nicely. She seemed interested in getting to know him, too, though perhaps she was simply being polite to her new neighbor.

He certainly hadn't expected her to flee over a bit of spilled lemonade. But he supposed he should have. A woman who was that refined, dressed in fabrics that probably cost more than one of his ranch hands made in a month, would naturally be more concerned about her gown than a common rancher's feelings. Sighing at the disheartening thought, he finished his work and left the stable.

As he trudged down the dusty path that led toward the ranch house, Gabe heard the low rumble of a wagon coming up the drive. He looked to the left and was surprised to see Henry sitting by himself on the high bench.

"Where's Martha May?" he asked as he met his foreman in front of the house.

"She stayed behind to help Sarah clean up." Henry set the brake and climbed down from the wagon. "Edward, or one of his boys, will bring her home later. Give me a hand with these chairs."

Gabe came around the back of the wagon and picked up the chair closest to him. As he hauled it up the porch steps, he asked, "How'd things go after I left?"

"Fine. Folks hung around for a little while, but they all had chores and livestock to get back to." The gruff older man paused for a moment before he said, "Edward was sorry he didn't have time to say goodbye to you, but I told him you were eager to check on that colt."

"Thanks," Gabe said, feeling relieved that his neighbor hadn't held this afternoon's upset against him.

Henry nodded, but then, as if he couldn't help himself, he asked, "What did you make of her, though? Emma? It sounds like you two were gettin' on fairly well before things went sideways."

Gabe let out a frustrated chuckle. "She's the most gorgeous woman I've ever laid eyes on, no question, but what if that's all there is to her?"

The older man's bushy eyebrows raised. "Hmm. Well, I haven't had the chance to meet her, so I can't say one way or the other, but Martha May sure seems to think Emma is a fine woman."

He shook his head. "I'm sure she is, but I'll be keeping my distance in the future. I don't think we'd suit."

Henry gave a slow nod. "Let's finish unloading the wagon so I can go home."

After the dust-up at the party, Gabe was determined to turn his focus back to where it belonged, so bright and early Monday morning, he headed off in search of Henry. It was time to stop avoiding the future of the ranch. Telly had run things well enough in his own way, but it was time for Gabe to truly make it his own.

When he spotted his foreman on his way up to the house, he hurried to meet him. As they fell into step, Gabe said, "Before we get started for the day, I'd like to talk to you about something that's been on my mind."

"Sure," Henry replied easily, though he gave a curious look. "Let's go grab a cup of coffee and sit out on the porch. I bet my wife's made us a nice big breakfast."

Gabe's stomach rumbled at the thought, and they quickened their pace. They had just finished climbing the steps when Martha May met them on the porch with two steaming mugs in hand. She must have spotted them from the window and anticipated exactly what they needed.

"Why, thank you!" Henry exclaimed in delight as he took a mug. "That's some good service. I'll even tip ya." He bent down and pecked his wife on the cheek.

"You silly old man, you," she said with a blush and slapped him playfully on the shoulder before going back inside the house.

The men settled into the rocking chairs, and after taking a sip of his steaming brew, Henry asked, "What's on your mind, son?"

"Well," Gabe began. "I've been thinking about buying a small herd of sheep. Only about thirty or so to start with."

"Sheep!?" The grizzled foreman choked on the sip of coffee he'd been taking, and when he caught his breath, he said, "Those hoofed locusts don't belong on a cattle ranch."

Gabe huffed out a frustrated breath. He knew Henry wouldn't like the idea, but this was his ranch, wasn't it? "Yes, sheep. Their wool will be another source of income."

Henry still looked irritable, but his eyes held a trace of admiration. "Seems you've given this a great deal of thought. How long have you been waiting to bring this up with me?"

"A few months," Gabe admitted. "I held off until I had a plan in place."

"Hmm." The older man raised a bushy gray eyebrow at him and asked, "What made you want to add sheep to your spread?"

"I wanted to do more with the land," he replied. "I can't add more cattle without overgrazing, but the sheep can graze on areas that the cattle have a hard time getting to."

Stroking his mustache, Henry looked off to the east where the sun was rising. "I suppose it might work, but you might need more feed for them if we have a harsh winter and they aren't able to graze. Right now, you have enough land to grow what you need for your current herd size."

"I thought of that. I can use the Desert Land Act like Telly did to get another 640 acres and expand our fields. There's no one to the east of us, and it's all good flat land," Gabe said. He was getting excited now.

"You know," Henry drawled with an innocent look as he took another sip of coffee, "if you were married, you and your wife could both file a claim. Then you'd add almost 2000 acres for all your cows and sheep to graze to their hearts' content."

"Drop it, Henry," he said, his voice hard. "We've already talked about this."

"All I'm asking is that you think on it," the foreman cajoled and left Gabe to sit in his rocking chair with visions of a certain auburn-haired beauty who loved books running through his mind.

Chapter 13

Almost three weeks had passed since 'the fiasco,' as Emma had privately labeled that dreadful afternoon, and she'd neither seen nor heard from Gabe at all. She'd looked for him at Sunday services, but he was nowhere to be found. While he might have been busy on his ranch, she suspected he was deliberately avoiding her, which made any chance of offering an apology impossible.

Though it was frustrating that she couldn't resolve the situation, she did her best to focus on what she could control by learning household tasks. Every day, she trailed Aunt Sarah wherever she went, watching her closely as she demonstrated her tasks while explaining every motion. Only then would Sarah step back and let Emma take over.

This technique worked especially well with simple tasks, such as preparing the bunkhouse for the temporary workers who'd be arriving for haying—sweeping the floors, scrubbing them clean, and changing the linens. Work in the kitchen, however, was more humbling.

Since there was no accurate way to gauge the temperature on the cookstove, she constantly had to add more fuel, adjust the dampers for airflow, and monitor the fire. It was quite the balancing act, and the family had endured several batches of blackened, rock-hard biscuits as she struggled to master the temperamental range. Despite her mishaps, Sarah was pleased with her progress, and so was Uncle Edward.

"If you feel up to it, Emma, you can start helping in the milking barn," he suggested one evening as the family gathered in the parlor after dinner.

"Oh, well, I suppose it is probably time for me to learn," she said. "Should we start tomorrow?"

It had seemed like a perfectly logical next step in learning the ways of living on the frontier, but the idea of rising at the crack of dawn and the practice of it were two different things.

Emma had been enjoying a dreamless sleep when she felt someone nudging her shoulder the next morning. She groaned and tried to swat the insistent hand away, but it just kept shaking her. With a resigned sigh, she cracked one eye open and saw Mary sitting at the edge of the bed.

The sun hadn't even risen, yet her cousin was already dressed in a light brown calico dress with a white apron tied over it, ready for the day's chores.

"Sorry to wake you," she said softly, pinning up her brunette locks, "but you said you wanted to learn to do the milking."

"I did say that, didn't I?" Emma yawned. "How vexing."

"Come on," Mary laughed, putting a hand out to help her get out of bed. "Let's get you dressed and down to breakfast. You'll feel more awake once you start moving."

With her cousin's help, she rose from the bed and slipped on her flannel dressing gown against the morning chill. Swiftly, she padded across the cold floorboards to the wardrobe and opened the door, her eyes scanning the row of dresses hanging on the wooden rod.

None of them seemed right for dairy chores.

She'd been wearing her morning dresses of velveteen and cashmere while working with her aunt around the house, but those fine fabrics would be ruined by the day's end if she wore them while doing any real physical work. Glancing at the dress Mary was wearing and back at her things hanging before her, she asked, "Which dress do you think I should wear today?"

Her cousin came to stand beside her and, with a slight wince, looked at the selection. She bit her lip and looked over shyly as heat rose on her cheeks. "Well, I do truly think they are all beautiful, but not very practical."

Emma reached out to stroke her arm in comfort, letting her know she took no offense. "I see what you mean." She crossed her arms over her chest and tapped her finger on her cheek while she thought.

"Why don't you try on one of my dresses to see if it will fit?" Mary suggested as she pulled a dark blue gingham dress from the wardrobe.

"Alright," Emma said, glancing at the garment skeptically.

She was a few inches taller than her cousin, and the dress was already hemmed higher for doing chores, but she dutifully tried it on. As she slipped the fabric over her head, she turned and looked at herself in the mirror above the washbasin and burst into laughter.

"Oh, goodness! This won't do at all." The hem of the dress ended just below her knees, making her look like a child who'd outgrown her clothes. "It's much too short, and I feel as if I'll rip the bodice if I breathe too deeply."

Mary chuckled while helping her out of the dress. "I didn't realize you were so much wider in the chest and shoulder than I am."

"I think I shall have to choose one of my own dresses and offer it up as a sacrifice," she sighed as she grabbed a white chintz day dress printed with small pink flowers, embellished with ribbon and ruffles on the cuffs and hems. It was her least favorite pattern, so she didn't mind the loss.

"Mary," she said, as a sudden thought struck her, "if we picked up some fabric at the general store, do you think your mother would help me make some new dresses? I mean, ones suited to doing chores rather than taking tea with society matrons?"

Mary grinned, her blue-gray eyes sparkling with excitement. "Yes, and my sisters and I can help! We should check the seamstress's shop first, though. She has a wider variety of materials to choose from than the general store. Ma has a sewing machine we can use, and if we work on them at night after the last milking is done, it should only take a few days."

With a plan in place, Mary left to speak to her mother, and once Emma had dressed, she made her way downstairs. Everyone else in the family had already left to attend to their daily chores when she arrived, except for Joseph, who was warming himself by the stove.

"Morning, sleepyhead," he greeted. "Best be quick, or there'll be no cows left for you to milk."

"Don't listen to him, dear," Sarah said as she began flouring the work table. "You have plenty of time if you want a cup of coffee before you go."

"Oh, Ma, you're no fun," Joseph pouted playfully.

Sarah scowled and tried to swat her son's arm, but he moved out of the way at the last second, smiled at her with an impish grin, and strode out the door.

"Oh, that boy," she sighed in exasperation, though a small smile played briefly on her lips.

Emma smiled too. She enjoyed watching their familiar teasing. It showed the ease and contentment of the family despite the hardships of frontier life and the daily grind of chores.

Deciding to skip coffee, she bid her aunt farewell, headed out the back door, and stepped out into the chilly May morning. It was still dark as she carefully picked her way through the damp grass, hundreds of stars twinkling above in the vast sky, but the soft lamplight spilling from the open doors of the milking barn helped guide her.

As she stepped inside for the first time, a wave of cool, moist air washed over her. Sweet, dusty hay was being tossed down from the mow overhead by Isaac, but it could not quite mask the stronger, richer pungency of manure that rose from the stalls below. She had caught whiffs of it around the farmyard, of course, yet here the smell was deeper, more concentrated.

Wrinkling her nose at the aroma, she walked down the central aisle, glancing at the cows lazily flicking their tails as they ate. She was nearly at the end of the row when Uncle Edward peeked his head out from a stall and waved her over to him.

"Are you ready to learn how to milk Daisy?" he asked.

"I think so," she said tentatively, eyeing the animal. "As long as Daisy doesn't mind."

Edward smiled as he patted the black and white cow's rump. His blue-gray eyes, which were almost identical to her father's, crinkled at the edges where age and the elements had weathered his kind face. "I promise she doesn't. In fact, she's eager to be milked."

Emma was skeptical about that statement, but she watched closely as her uncle showed her how to use a clean rag to wipe off any dirt from the udder and position a pail under the cow. Then he sat down on the short-legged milking stool to demonstrate the correct hand positioning for her.

"Now, we want to talk calmly around the cows. If she feels stressed or afraid, she won't let any milk down." He waited for her to nod her understanding and continued. "Before we put anything in the pail, we squeeze a few times on each teat to make sure the milk is flowing and that there aren't any problems."

"Does it hurt them?" she asked, wincing as she imagined someone yanking on her twice a day. She certainly wouldn't take kindly to it.

Edward let out a soft chuckle as he stood from the low stool, brushing straw from his knees, and moved aside. "No, it doesn't hurt. Truth is, they know what time we come to do chores, and once they hear the milk pails clanging, they come running. Sometimes, though, we get stragglers who are being lazy, and we have to round them up. Now, come sit down and give it a try."

Emma came closer, bent at the knees, and confidently lowered herself onto the short wooden seat. Unfortunately, the stool was much lower than a sofa, and she felt herself lose balance. If it weren't for the quick action of her uncle, who'd caught her under the arms, she'd have fallen flat on her back.

"Oh, bother," she said once she'd gotten to her feet. "Let me try this again."

Instead of standing in front of the stool, she set herself to one side and tried to settle sideways on the seat, but that put too much of her weight to one side, and the stool tipped over. Edward grabbed her by the elbow, once again saving her from landing in the dirt, straw, and manure that littered the floor, and gave her a patient smile.

"You are trying to sit like a lady, and that won't work. Sit like a man," he suggested. "Place the pail between your knees, feet spread apart."

Emma had never in her life been told to sit like a man. She could imagine her old etiquette teacher, Mrs. Ballard, clutching her high lace collar in horror at such an indelicate suggestion. The absurdity of it all made her burst into laughter, but she did as her uncle suggested.

Though the technique proved successful, and she'd settled onto the stool, she faced another problem. The cramped confines of the stall had caused the stiff wire cage of her bustle to dig into her back and push her shoulder forward into the side of the cow. With a huff of annoyance, she grumbled something decidedly unladylike as she tried to wrestle the bustle to the side so it wouldn't be in the way. She could hear the snickers of her male cousins from the opposite stalls, and her cheeks warmed with embarrassment.

"Don't pay them any mind, Emma," hollered Mary from somewhere further down the stalls. "I'm sure you're doing just fine."

"If she started milking, she would be," muttered Matthew as he walked by with his own pail full of the frothy white liquid. His father gave him a warning look, and the youngster hung his head as he hurried away.

"It's all right, dear," Edward said. "Take your time. No one expects you to be perfect. We were all beginners once. Try to strip a few squirts of milk out so we can check its quality."

Emma took a deep breath and nervously reached out to grab the two teats closest to her. She pointed them away from the bucket as he'd shown her, but when she squeezed, nothing came out. Frowning, she tried again, but to no avail. Her uncle squatted down beside her and showed her the proper technique again. This time, when she squeezed, a stream of milk came shooting out.

"I did it!" she exclaimed. "It worked!"

"Very good," he said, a pleased expression on his face. "Now do the next two, and if everything looks all right, you can start aiming into the pail."

He stood nearby, watching her work for a few minutes until he felt that she'd gotten the hang of it. "I'll leave you to it, then. If you need any help, just call out."

Nodding in acknowledgment, she settled into a rhythm, squeezing gently with one hand and then the other. The steady ping-ping-ping of milk striking the side of the tin bucket soon filled her ears, and she lost herself in the sound and the warmth of the cow's flank against her cheek until her fingers began to cramp and burn with fatigue.

Emma straightened, flexing her aching hands and rubbing the sore muscles. When she glanced up, she saw her cousins working with practiced speed as milk streamed into foaming pails, which were swiftly poured into waiting jugs. Her own bucket was still only half full.

"You doing okay?" Micah asked when he walked past her stall and saw her looking around.

"Yes, but how do I know when to stop? Milk just keeps coming out, and I've been working for quite a while."

"Let's see." He squatted next to her and tested the teats, sending a powerful stream of milk into the bucket.

Emma frowned. There hadn't been nearly the same amount coming out when she'd been doing it.

Micha must have sensed her upset because he patted her arm. "It's all right. I've been doing this since I was little. The more you do it, the better and faster you become. You did really well for your first time."

"Thank you for saying so." She sighed and leaned her aching back against the wall of the stall. "I just want to feel useful."

"You are," he said earnestly. "Just remember that we were all beginners once."

She looked at her cousin's handsome face and smiled ruefully. "That's exactly what your Pa told me earlier."

"Oh, no!" he groaned, closing his eyes and putting his hand over his face, as if to ward off the prospect. "Don't tell me I'm turning into my father already! I'm only twenty-two."

She laughed at his dramatic display, and Micah helped her up off the stool.

"Let me finish up with Daisy," he said. "You can head into the house. I'm sure Ma is waiting for you."

Grateful for the reprieve, she thanked her cousin and headed back to the house, eager to ask her aunt for some liniment for her aching hands.

The next morning, as Emma was coming back into the house after another poor attempt at milking Daisy, she heard low voices drifting out from an open window in the kitchen. She couldn't initially discern the words, but as she got closer, she clearly heard, "I haven't heard from him since, have you?"

Micah's voice was recognizable, and so was Aunt Sarah's when she answered, "No, I haven't. I thought by now he would have come around. Do you think I should talk to Martha May?"

"No," he replied. "I think I should talk to him. We're friends. At least I hope we still are." There was a pause before he said, "I think I might head over to Gabe's tomorrow and see if he can spare a minute to talk."

Feeling guilty for having caused the situation, Emma strode inside. Sarah and Micah were standing by the stove, holding steaming mugs of coffee, and they looked shocked to see her.

"I didn't mean to eavesdrop, but I was coming in for my lessons and couldn't help hearing what you said to your Ma." She came closer to them and set her hand on Micah's arm. "I'm sorry I reacted so poorly and caused trouble between you and your friend. The truth is, I ran from Gabe, even though he had nothing to do with what happened. In fact, he was concerned about me and asked if I was all right. I'm sure if I had stayed, I could have explained it all to him and made sure he understood why I was upset."

"I'm sure, but he could at least give you the chance to explain it now," Micah insisted.

"I'm afraid he might not take it kindly to seeing me at the moment," she said as she smiled ruefully at her cousin to lighten the mood.

"Might not," he agreed, and then he sighed and pulled her into a hug. "I know you haven't been here long, but you already feel like one of my sisters," he said. "I just want you to be happy."

Sarah sniffed, beaming at them, and Emma saw Micah roll his eyes. "Oh, Ma. There's no need to get all tearful." He released her, giving her a pat on the shoulder, and stepped back. "Well, I reckon I've had my fill of soft feelings for the day. I should get back to work. The cheese won't make itself."

He turned on his heel and quickly strode out of the house, as if wanting to put distance between himself and the emotionally charged atmosphere, and Emma looked to her aunt.

"I hope this hasn't affected your relationship with Martha May."

"Not at all, so please don't try to add that to your conscience." Sarah reached out and squeezed her hand. "Are you ready to do some cooking now? I think, in light of everything, we should make something to cheer us up. How about we start with cookies?"

Emma agreed, and the two women spent the morning making thick, soft molasses cookies, which did, miraculously, cheer her up quite a bit.

Chapter 14

Gabe was getting tired of avoiding the Barnes family. For weeks he'd been riding to church on Xerxes instead of in the surrey with Henry and Martha May, like he usually did. He'd arrive just in time for services and slip out right after. While this worked well to avoid a public confrontation, he missed the company of his friends.

He was ruminating on the situation as he worked to replace a rotting fence post when he felt his handkerchief pulled from his pocket. Swinging around to see who had taken it, he saw his gelding happily nibbling on the linen fabric. He stared, mystified that a twelve-hundred-pound horse had snuck up on him.

"Hey! Give that back," he shouted, dropping his hammer and taking a swipe at the cloth.

Xerxes shook his head with a huff and pranced a few feet away, the handkerchief still hanging from his lips.

"Come on, I need to get back to work." He stepped toward the horse, but it shied away. "Stop that! I don't have time to play games."

When he started walking forward once again, Xerxes took off, circling Gabe in a wide loop and kicking his hind legs up in the air as his high-pitched whinny split the air. When the gelding stopped, he bobbed his head, which sent the cloth waving in the spring breeze like a banner.

Putting his hands on his hips, Gabe scowled at his horse. "Fine!" he yelled as Xerxes took off toward the stable with his prize. "Keep the thing for all I care."

He turned, intending to get back to work on the fence line, but stopped dead in his tracks as he caught sight of Micah riding down the front drive toward him. He watched as his friend dismounted, and they stood facing each other awkwardly for a minute, neither seeming to know what to say.

"What are you doing here?" he finally asked, breaking the silence.

"I came to make sure things were okay between us," Micah stated. He took off his hat and began twisting the felt brim around in his hands. "Haven't seen you since the party, and aside from my brothers, you're the closest friend I have. If there's an issue, I'd rather fix it than let it fester."

"I've got no issue with you," Gabe said, and then he added, "or the rest of your family."

"You sure?" Micah asked. "You know, I talked with Emma the other morning. She told me she's responsible for the situation and that you were nothing but kind. She says she owes you an apology, too, but she doesn't think you want to see her."

Gabe sighed and ran his hand through his dark, unruly hair. "I don't know if I can handle any more apologies. But she shouldn't take all the blame. I should've stuck around to talk through things. But right now, I want to move past this and have everything back to normal. Let's forgive and forget."

Micah nodded, and they clasped hands—firm, brief, and without too much soft emotion, though he looked disappointed. "I understand. Well, I'd better get back to work then. See you around."

"Yeah, see ya."

He waved to his friend and watched him ride off down the dusty road toward home, feeling glad that they had talked.

"Well, now," a voice drawled. "Seems like you've been doing more than one kind of fence mending out here today."

Gabe turned to see Henry leaning his shoulder against a nearby tree, his hat tipped back from his face.

"You could say that. How much did you hear?"

"Not all of it," the foreman admitted, "but enough to know his cousin wants to get back into your good graces."

Letting out a deep sigh, Gabe shook his head. "We're too different."

"I think you are judging her too harshly," Henry warned. "You've only had one interaction with her."

"One was quite enough; just look at all the trouble it caused," he retorted.

"Fine," the older man groused. "But don't come crying to me when you realize you've made a mistake by letting your wounded pride get in the way and she's engaged to some other fella."

As Gabe watched him storm away, a sinking feeling settled into his gut. Was Henry right? Had he been too quick to rush to judgment? He supposed it was possible. What happened during their picnic *had* skewed his impression of her negatively. Sighing, he picked up the discarded hammer and went back to work, promising himself that he'd at least try to see Emma through everyone else's eyes. After all, if he wanted others to trust him, he needed to extend them the same courtesy.

As he sat in the wooden pew, listening to Pastor Langley draw his sermon to a close, Gabe felt tension coiling tight across his shoulders. He'd meant to speak with the Barnes family before services began, when fewer eyes would be watching should the conversation turn difficult, but their late arrival had ruined that chance. Now he'd have to face them, or rather Emma, with half the congregation looking on.

Trying not to draw attention, he shifted in the pew to ease his aching muscles. The hard, cramped seat made it nearly impossible, and Martha May's sharp look of reproof told him he had failed. He offered her a small, apologetic smile and sat up straight once more, eyes fixed dutifully on the pulpit.

When at last the final hymn came to a close, he sent up a silent prayer of thanks and rose with the rest of the congregation as they began filing slowly down the narrow aisle. Neighbors paused to exchange greetings as they went, and while he ordinarily enjoyed these brief, friendly exchanges, today the delay only sharpened his tension. He regretted not choosing a seat nearer the back.

Finally, after what felt like an eternity inching down the aisle, Gabe made it out into the warm, sunlit churchyard. The bright golden rays were a stark contrast to the dim chapel, and he paused to put on his hat, glancing around the area for the Barnes family. With such a large family, they should have been easy to spot, but the increase in church attendance over the past few weeks was making things more challenging.

Still, it didn't take long before he caught sight of them amidst a large cluster of people about forty yards away, under the shade of a tall cottonwood tree. In the center of the group was Emma, wearing a frilly, expensive-looking blue-and-white striped dress and a hat with long feathers stuck into a ribbon band. Sarah and Edward were flanking her on either side, while Micah, Luke, and Joseph stood off to the right. The younger children weren't anywhere in evidence, but he supposed they must be off playing with friends.

Gabe couldn't help noticing that she looked just as lovely as the first time he had seen her. She might have stepped straight from the pages of one of the fashion magazines Mrs. Tandy kept in her shop. Poised, graceful, and far too refined for this raw, untamed country.

Henry and Martha May, who'd exited just behind him, excused themselves to go visit with friends. Before they left, they promised to meet him at the wagon, but Gabe scarcely heard them. He rolled his shoulders, and while the knots in his back eased, the fresh air did little to slow his racing heart. He couldn't exactly say why he felt so uneasy, only that he had never cared for confrontation.

Taking a bolstering breath, he strode forward, trying not to appear too nervous as he crossed the churchyard. As he joined the crowd, he looked around and realized Henry was right. Most of the men standing there were single, and the looks they were giving Emma made it plain that she could be spoken for before the year was out. This, of course, didn't bother him in the slightest. He didn't want to marry someone so high-maintenance.

At least, that's what he told himself, though even in his own thoughts the statement rang hollow. Who wouldn't want to be married to a beautiful woman who could make him speechless with just one look? He was still concerned that she was just a pretty face in nice clothes, but he'd promised himself that he would give her the chance to prove him wrong, and this seemed to be a good opportunity.

"Gabe! It's so nice to see you," Sarah said warmly as he joined the group. Edward nodded beside her, his smile equally genuine.

"Thank you. It's good to see you all as well." His gaze shifted to Emma. For a moment, their eyes met and held. A sharp thrill ran through him, warm and unexpected, raising gooseflesh along his arms. She must have felt something, too, for a delicate blush rose to her cheeks.

"As I was saying," said an unctuous voice. "My aunt would love to meet you. She attends a different church, so I'm not able to introduce her to you right now, but I think you would get along splendidly."

It was a heroic feat not to roll his eyes at Gregory Callaway and his attempt to steer the conversation away from Gabe with flattery.

"I'm sure we would," Emma said diplomatically. "I've met so many people recently, and they have all been very welcoming."

"Yes. Elk Ridge is a quaint little town," Gregory crooned, his voice thick with false sympathy, "but nothing like where you're from. You must miss the bustle of Denver terribly."

Gabe thought the remark rather callous, given that Emma had only come here because of her father's death, but he held his tongue.

"There are certain things I will miss," Emma said softly, glancing down for a moment. "But I find I'm adjusting here quite well." She looked at Sarah and Edward and smiled. "I'm blessed to be surrounded by my family and all the new friends I've made... like Mr. Moreau."

Her eyes met Gabe's hopefully, and he couldn't help but smile—especially when several of the surrounding men scowled at him for being singled out.

"Yes, and we're blessed to have you here, Miss Barnes," he replied steadily, knowing that she preferred to stick with formality.

"Of course we are," Gregory cut in. "The men in Denver must be pining away since your departure."

"Oh, I doubt that very much," she said, giving a tight smile.

"Gentlemen, I hate to interrupt," Sarah said, not looking the least bit distressed at the disruption, "but we need to be going now. We'll see you all next Sunday."

Despite the crestfallen looks on the men's faces, the Barnes family offered their polite farewells and turned to leave. As they walked away, Emma glanced once more over her shoulder—directly at Gabe. The look was brief but unmistakable. His heart lifted at the quiet certainty that she had looked back for him, and he replayed the moment all the way back to the surrey, where Martha May and Henry were waiting for him.

"Well?" Martha May finally asked, looking expectantly at him.

"Well, what?" he replied evenly. The back of his neck heated, and he tried not to look directly at them as they drove off.

"Oh, Gabriel, you know exactly what I'm asking. Did you get a chance to talk with Emma?"

"As much as I could with Gregory and every other single man from the church standing beside me."

She scoffed and folded her arms under her ample chest. "That boy is such a sycophant. Even I could see that Emma was uncomfortable with his fawning, the poor dear." She looked at Gabe inquisitively and asked, "Has your opinion of her changed at all?"

"I don't know yet. Time will tell, I suppose."

Henry grunted and shook his head. "Don't let too much time pass, or those vultures circling her today will pick her off before you make up your mind."

Before today, he would have said that Henry was exaggerating the situation, but after having seen for himself, he knew it to be true. There had never been a girl in Elk Ridge to strike his fancy before, though they were all very nice and pretty, and Martha May had done her best to sing their praises. It was just his luck that the one woman he felt this inexplicable pull toward was the same one every red-blooded male also wanted. Now he just had to figure out what to do about it.

Chapter 15

Emma's days, once full of charity meetings, high-class social events, and dinner parties, now involved daily farm chores and lessons in domestic duties. And with the haying in full swing, she was helping her Aunt Sarah and cousins prepare meals for the workers. It wasn't the life she had envisioned for herself just a few months before, but it was growing on her.

She was growing more skilled each day with Daisy, her assigned cow, and she could now finish milking in under an hour, which was a vast improvement in her mind. She'd also taken on the task of gathering eggs, which had proved far more hazardous than she had expected. Several of the hens resented her intrusions and expressed their displeasure with sharp beaks.

One morning in the coop, a particularly ill-tempered hen named Bertha delivered a vicious peck to her arm, drawing blood.

"You wretched little beast," Emma scolded, examining the small wound. "If you don't mend your ways, I'll inform Aunt Sarah that you have stopped laying, and we shall have you for Sunday dinner."

The chicken stared at her with its black, beady little eyes, fluffing up its feathers and letting out a growl.

"Don't test me, Bertha," she threatened, putting her hands on her hips. "I happen to enjoy fried chicken, and I'm feeling rather hungry at the moment."

Looking around the coop for something to aid her, she spotted an empty tin bucket sitting by the fence and picked it up—an idea forming in her mind. Cautiously, she used the lip of the bucket to scoop Bertha up just high enough so she could safely grab the eggs while the hen took her anger out on the metal instead of flesh.

"Ha! It worked!"

Emma placed her prizes into the collection basket and grinned happily to herself. Every day she spent on the farm, working to contribute toward the success of the family, brought her self-confidence that she hadn't known she was lacking. Her father had believed that making her a refined young woman was the best path to a successful future, but all it had led to was a disaster with a faithless suitor. It had also deprived her of the satisfaction one has when they work with their hands to accomplish a task.

She thought back to the morning when she was being taught how to milk by Uncle Edward and how pride had swelled in her when she'd seen that first stream of liquid pinging into the bucket. It was a feeling she wanted to flourish, and she'd promised herself that she would keep working for it.

As she exited the chicken coop, Esther rushed up, grabbed her by the hand, and shouted, "Emma! Let's go!"

The fifteen-year-old girl was a whirlwind, always in a hurry to get where she was going. Today was no different. "Ma says since the chores are done, the boys can handle the creamery by themselves while we go into town. We can show you our favorite shops, and you can get the fabric you've been wanting for your new dresses. Isn't that exciting!" She gave a little jump and beamed a wide smile as her chestnut locks, which had once been in a simple bun, tumbled down around her shoulders.

"It is! First things first, though. We must tidy ourselves a bit."

She held Esther's small hand—mostly to keep her from racing ahead—and they walked back to the house at a pleasantly sedate pace. Mary met them on the porch, and they all entered the house together.

"Are you girls ready to leave?" Aunt Sarah asked, untying her apron as they came into the kitchen. "I want to get to the general store as soon as we can."

"Almost," Emma replied, setting her basket of eggs on the table. "I was thinking I might try my hand at styling hair if Esther would let me."

The younger girl let out a loud squeal, dancing around with glee. "Will you really do my hair? I would love that so much!"

"What about my hair?" Ruth asked when she came into the house, panting. She'd obviously run full tilt to catch up with her sister.

"Of course! Mary, would you like to enlist my services as a lady's maid as well?"

"Not today," Mary laughed, already untying her work apron. "I just need to take off this apron and find my bonnet."

"Then I shall hurry with my ladies' hair," Emma declared, dropping into a low, exaggerated curtsey like a proper lady's maid.

Esther and Ruth burst into delighted giggles, and she herded them upstairs, continuing the charade as she arranged their hair into graceful high coils. She'd left several strands of soft curls to frame their faces, and the style made them look delightfully grown-up. The girls seemed to agree, and they dashed downstairs to show their new coiffure to their mother.

Now alone, Emma turned her attention to her own hair. Working quickly, she braided her long, dark, coppery tresses, coiled the braid into a neat bun, and pinned it securely. It wasn't perfect, but for a quick trip into town, it would do. Satisfied that it would withstand any wind, she collected her purse and hurried downstairs, where her aunt and cousins were waiting.

"The Independence Day picnic is coming up soon. Do you think we should get something to put in our bonnets?" Mary asked as they strolled down the main street of Elk Ridge after parting from Aunt Sarah in front of the general store. "Mine could use a new ribbon."

"Oh yes! Mine too!" Esther put in. Ruth, of course, agreed with her sister.

"I think that's a perfect idea," Emma said. "We can all get something and redesign our hats."

"Then let's go visit Mrs. Tandy!" Esther exclaimed, taking her by the arm and nearly dragging her down the street. All the while, she gushed over a new dress that had been put on display.

As they stepped onto the wooden boardwalk in front of the shop, Emma could see why her cousin was so enamored. Standing behind the thick glass window were a handful of mannequins showcasing finely crafted, highly fashionable clothing designs for men and women. The attention to detail that went into each piece was obvious. She could have stood there for ages just admiring the craftsmanship, but the girls were eager to go inside.

The cheerful tinkling of a bell announced their arrival, and a moment later, a soft, feminine voice from a back room called out, "I'll be with you in just a moment! Have a look around, won't you?"

The younger girls didn't need to be asked twice. They rushed off eagerly, with Mary trailing behind them. Emma lingered near the entrance, taking everything in. Wooden shelves lined the walls, filled with a dazzling array of fabrics in every shade imaginable. Patterns and prints spilled across the counters, while a corner devoted to trimmings overflowed with lace, ribbon, beads, feathers, embroidery thread, and tassels. Nearby, a rack held several ready-made dresses and suits. It reminded her strongly of the elegant dressmaker's shop she used to frequent in Denver. This one was much smaller, of course, yet still surprisingly impressive for such a modest frontier town.

She was still standing near the entrance when Mrs. Tandy emerged from the back room. The petite seamstress was in her thirties, with golden-blonde hair and sparkling azure eyes. Emma had met her at church shortly after arriving in Elk Ridge and had taken an instant liking to the woman.

"Afternoon, dears!" Mrs. Tandy said brightly, bustling around the front counter with a warm smile. "It's wonderful to see you all. And you brought in your cousin! Hello again, Miss Barnes."

"Hello, Mrs. Tandy," Emma replied, dipping a polite curtsy. "Esther has told me how much she adores the dress you put up in your store window, and I just had to see for myself. I believe it's that one over there."

She pointed to the striking silk gown: white with bold forest-green stripes, embroidered with delicate floral garlands along the collar and cuffs. The pleated underskirt was trimmed with ruffles at the hem, while a rich green overskirt draped elegantly over the large bustle.

"Oh, yes. That's my latest creation," the seamstress said, her voice brimming with pride. "Isn't it lovely?"

"It is! Just look at it!" Esther said as she stood near the dress and gazed at it in adoration.

"It's a stunning creation," Emma agreed. "I love the embroidery."

"You should try it on, Emma," Ruth suggested.

"Oh, Emma, please! Please try it on. Please? You will look so beautiful in it," Esther chimed in, hopping from one foot to the other.

"Maybe another time," Emma laughed. "We came to buy new fabric so I can have some dresses to wear while working on the farm, remember? Besides, your mother is still waiting for us at the general store, so we shouldn't take too long."

"I never get to do what I want," Esther pouted, stomping away, leaving Mary and Ruth to trail after her.

Emma knew she was disappointing the girl, but she did not need another fashionable outfit. In fact, she could stand to part with half the ones she already owned. She released a deep sigh before turning to Mrs. Tandy and putting on a smile.

"As you can see," she said, gesturing to her own dress, "the clothes I brought with me from Denver aren't exactly suited for farm chores."

The seamstress chuckled as her gaze dropped to the printed white muslin, its hem already stained with dust and grass. "You're quite right about that. Come, let's step over here."

Emma followed her to the section of sturdy fabrics and began sorting through the bolts. The wide assortment of printed cotton calicos felt far more practical for her new life on the ranch, and she quickly made her selections.

Mrs. Tandy complimented her choices warmly as they walked toward the counter. Then, with a meaningful glance at Emma's already-stained muslin dress, she asked, "Would you like to look at some of the ready-made dresses while you're here? It'll take a few days to sew anything new, and I'd hate for you to ruin a good gown in the meantime."

Without waiting for an answer, she turned and headed toward the clothing rack.

Smiling ruefully, Emma beckoned her cousins over. "Would you girls come and help me choose a dress, please? Mrs. Tandy has wisely pointed out that I require it sooner than we can sew it ourselves."

Esther looked instantly mollified by the request, and as the girls gathered around her, she inclined her head to Mrs. Tandy in quiet acknowledgment. The woman would have made a fortune in Denver with salesmanship like that.

With her cousins' help, Emma chose a pretty pine-green calico sprinkled with delicate floral swirls. Then they each selected a roll of ribbon—light pink for Mary, leaf green for Esther, pale yellow for Ruth, and a deep indigo for her—and left the shop with bright, cheerful smiles, thoroughly pleased with their successful morning of shopping.

They had just crossed the street when a loud, screeching voice pierced the air, making everyone within hearing distance stop and turn toward the disturbance.

"You stupid child! How many times do I have to tell you? I wanted a ten-pound sack of flour! Why your father lets you anywhere near his customers is beyond me."

Emma gasped in shock, horrified that someone would speak to another person that way. As the shrill voice continued to reverberate through the town, she shoved her packages at Mary. Completely disregarding all the etiquette lessons she had learned, she gathered her skirts in her hands and raced forward down the boardwalk.

The raised voices were coming from the general store, and when she entered, she saw a young girl around Ruth's age with braided brown hair and a simple calico dress standing behind the counter, crying and stuttering. A pinch-faced older woman was leaning over the surface, still berating the child. Though several other customers in the store were trying to intercede on the girl's behalf, including her aunt, the banshee wasn't paying them any mind.

Fury filled Emma's veins. She thrust two fingers into her mouth, took a deep breath, and let out a shrill whistle she had learned to do at a baseball game. The store fell silent as the ear-splitting sound cut through the din, and every head swiveled in her direction.

"How dare you, madam?" she asked as she stepped forward. Righteous anger was fueling her actions, but her voice remained calm and measured. "No one should be spoken to that way. She's just a young girl. I insist you apologize."

Everyone in the store gawked at her in stunned disbelief, but Emma didn't care. If no one else would stand up to this woman, then she would. From behind, someone whispered, "Did she just tell Mrs. Callaway to apologize?"

The sharp-tongued matron sputtered as she grasped for words. "Excuse me? Do you want me to apologize? To this halfwit? Just who do you think you are, young lady?"

"My name is Emma Barnes, and yes, I believe you should apologize. As a Christian woman—which I assume you are—you should be familiar with the verse in Matthew 7:12. 'Therefore, all things whatsoever ye would that men should do to you, do ye even so to them: for this is the law and the prophets.'"

She paused slightly for effect, letting her words settle over the hushed silence. "How silly of me. Of course you are, so I ask—would you wish someone to speak to you in the same manner?"

"Well, I—" the woman faltered, grasping for words.

"I was taught that politeness begets politeness," she pressed on, "and that ridicule is coarse, unladylike, and unfeeling."

"What! How dare you speak to me like that? You should respect your elders."

Emma smiled faintly. "Ah, yes, I see. If you'd like to continue to quote from the Bible, let's use Titus 2:1-3." Her voice remained steady as she recited, "But speak thou the things which become sound doctrine: that the aged men be sober, grave, temperate, sound in faith, in charity, and in patience. The aged women, likewise, that they be in behavior as becometh holiness, not false accusers, not given to much wine, and teachers of good things."

She placed a gentle, yet unmistakable, stress on the word "holiness," bringing even more murmurs from the crowd.

Mrs. Callaway, as Emma assumed she was called, flushed a deep crimson. The thought that this could be Gregory's aunt briefly crossed her mind, so she softened her voice and tried a more diplomatic approach.

"I agree that respecting your elders is important. However, your actions here today have not earned you such respect. Now, should you choose to apologize to Miss...," she stopped speaking and looked at the young girl who had been the catalyst of the exchange.

"Eunice Harper," her aunt supplied instead, a proud smile shining on her face.

"Thank you, Aunt Sarah." She turned back to the nasty old woman. "As I was saying, should you choose to apologize to Miss Harper, my respect and admiration for you would increase dramatically. It takes good breeding and a godly, virtuous heart to seek forgiveness for one's mistakes."

With those final words, Mrs. Callaway's fate was sealed. No matter her personal feelings, she would have to apologize if she wanted to save her reputation as a Christian woman. Emma met her eyes steadily, and a silent battle of wills unfolded until she cocked an eyebrow in a silent challenge.

"I apologize for my harsh words," the matron said begrudgingly. "I'll take my order now, Miss Harper."

Eunice hesitated, then slowly slid the crate across the counter and took a cautious step back—clearly afraid she would be yelled at again. Without a word, Mrs. Callaway gave a stiff nod, snatched up the crate, and marched out of the store with her head held high in defiance.

As soon as she was out of sight, Emma let out a long breath and closed her eyes as she regained her composure. She hadn't meant to charge in like a wrathful Valkyrie, but when she saw Eunice behind the counter—her upward-canted brown eyes wide with fear, tears running down her cheeks—she couldn't stop herself. A vision of Abbey standing in Eunice's place had come to mind when Mrs. Callaway had spat the word "half-wit." It was enough to push her over the edge.

Tentatively opening her eyes, she was surprised to find herself surrounded by smiling faces.

"You were amazing, dear!" Sarah declared, pulling her in for a tight hug.

"Oh, I don't know about that," Emma said, a bit uncomfortable with the praise.

"No, Ma's right. I've never seen anyone stand up to Mrs. Callaway before!" Mary said in awe.

"I wish I had been the one to do it," a middle-aged woman put in, patting Emma on the back. "You sure showed her!"

Several other patrons came forward to thank her for her bravery, and all Emma could do was smile and nod politely until the crowd finally dispersed. When the low hum of conversation filled the store once again, she noticed Eunice still standing shyly behind the counter and moved closer to speak with her.

"Hello, sweeting. My name's Emma." Trying to be calm and comforting, she slowly held out her hands in front of her.

"He- hello. I'm Eunice," the girl replied, her words soft and deliberate as she reached for Emma's hands.

"So I heard. I'm very pleased to meet you." She stroked the back of Eunice's hands with her thumbs in what she hoped was a calming gesture. "How long have you been helping in the store?"

"Since I was little. My Pa owns the store. He left me in charge so he could help Mr. Decker for a bit. He lets me fill orders, but people have to tell me what they want because reading is hard for me," she confessed.

"That's all right. I'm sure your pa appreciates your help. My father used to own a general store just like this one, and he used to let me help, too."

At this, Eunice's head came up, and her eyes grew wide. "You did?" A broad smile grew on her face. "So, you're like me!"

Emma smiled and gave a soft laugh. "Yes! Exactly like you. Would you like me to help you fill orders until your Pa comes back?"

"Would you? Then you could read the lists to me while I get everything from the shelves."

Eunice was looking at her with such adoration that it made tears come to her eyes, but she quickly blinked them away.

"Of course! Do you have an extra work apron I can borrow?"

Eunice hurried away, and Emma turned to her aunt and cousins. "Do you mind terribly if we stay a bit longer?"

"Not at all, dear," Sarah replied, reaching out to rub her arm affectionately. "We can stay until Mr. Harper returns. Eunice seems eager to have you help her. I'll do some more browsing in the store while we wait."

When Eunice returned with a crisp white work apron, Emma slipped it on and stepped behind the counter. A pile of handwritten lists sat near the cash register, so she picked up the top sheet and began calling out items for Eunice to gather.

Despite the girl's admitted difficulties with reading, she had no trouble identifying the necessary goods by the pictures on the labels or by peering into sacks and containers with quick, practiced glances. They worked together to fulfill every order by the time her father came back, and Emma pulled him aside and introduced herself. She explained the situation with Mrs. Callaway as tactfully as she could, but instead of being upset at possibly losing a customer, Mr. Harper smiled and tearfully shook her hand.

"Thank you so much, Miss Barnes. Few people would stand up to that bully, and if I didn't need all the money I could get since my wife's passing, I would refuse to sell to her. People see my little girl as different, but she's the light of my life and the only one who can make me smile when I'm feeling down. The Lord truly blessed me when he made me her Pa."

He looked lovingly at his young daughter, and Emma felt her throat tighten as she remembered her own father looking at her like that.

"I understand, Mr. Harper. Eunice is truly a delight to be around, and I'm glad to have been here in her time of need."

Emma took off the work apron she had borrowed, returned it to Mr. Harper, and waved goodbye to Eunice before following her aunt out of the store. When they got to the wagon, she looked at her aunt and was surprised to see that there were tears shining in her eyes.

"Are you all right?" Emma asked, slightly alarmed.

"Yes. It's just... that was the nicest thing anyone has ever done for Eunice," Sarah said, her voice thick with emotion. "Everyone in town—excluding Mrs. Callaway—is kind and polite, but you saw her as a person deserving of more than just niceties. You saw her as she is: a precious child of God."

Emma was humbled by the comment. "I think it's time I told you about Abbey," she said softly, settling into the wagon. She wasn't ashamed of her sister—only protective of her memory.

Chapter 16

For weeks, Gabe had been putting all of his focus on learning the best breeding, housing, and feeding recommendations for sheep. Anytime he wasn't working, he was reading livestock journals and making lists of materials he needed to purchase. He planned to build sheds for his sheep to bed down in during inclement weather and add extra rails to his fencing before sending off for the animals, which meant he needed to take a trip to town for building supplies.

After saying hello to Cyrus and stabling Xerxes at the livery, Gabe stopped by the sawmill and placed his lumber order. He arranged for delivery within the week and then headed to the hardware store for more nails and some other odds and ends. His last errand before leaving town was to purchase the things on Martha May's list from the general store, so he stowed his goods in the livery saddlebags and went across the street.

Mr. Harper was nowhere in sight when he entered the store, but his daughter, Eunice, was behind the counter helping a customer. She looked up at the sound of the bell, and Gabe smiled and waved to her. Since she was busy, he decided to thumb through the catalogs in the back of the shop, picking up one from Montgomery Ward.

Gabe had lost track of time as he studied the illustrations in the catalogue, but his head snapped up when he heard Mrs. Callaway begin to tear into Eunice. Frowning, he set the catalogue down and started forward, unwilling to stand by while the woman berated the shy girl.

Then came an ear-splitting whistle, and an unnatural hush descended on the store.

He walked toward the front of the store to see who the sound had come from, but stopped short when he saw Emma. She stood tall and dignified as she gave Mrs. Callaway an extremely civil dressing-down. She hadn't yelled or spoken overly harsh words to the older woman, but even he could tell it was a rebuke of the woman's crass behavior.

As soon as Mrs. Callaway left the store, a swarm of ladies surrounded Emma, each of them excitedly congratulating her for standing up for Eunice. He had meant to step forward too, but something held him back. He watched as Emma calmly tied on a white apron and moved behind the counter with Eunice. She accepted a customer's list without hesitation and began calling out items in a clear, patient voice.

Suddenly, Gabe felt a strange tightness in his chest. He had thought Emma was delicate and perhaps a little vain. A city girl, who'd never worked a day in her life. But here she was, helping the girl who had just been humiliated in front of half the town. He stayed where he was a while longer, quietly observing, unsure what to make of this new side of her.

When he heard a sharp clearing of the throat, he turned and realized he was in the way of other customers. Offering a quiet apology, he waited for Emma's attention to be drawn away before he slipped outside and hurried across the street to collect Xerxes from the livery. In his hurry to get out of the store, he'd completely forgotten to purchase the things on Martha May's list. She'd be hopping mad, but there was no way he was going back now. Not with all the new thoughts and emotions swirling inside him.

What he needed to do was talk to Henry. His foreman repeatedly told him not to judge Emma too harshly. Had he known something that Gabe hadn't? Or was it his years of tough living that had given him a sense about people? Sending his gelding into a gallop, he raced back home, determined to talk with the older man, but annoyingly, he couldn't find Henry anywhere.

After searching the obvious spots around the ranch, he tracked down Tommy, his youngest ranch hand. The tall, gangly seventeen-year-old was mucking out stalls in the stable, and when Gabe asked him if he'd seen Henry, the kid nodded.

"He's out with Riley, counting cattle. They won't be back until dinner."

Gabe growled in frustration. He needed Henry's no-nonsense wisdom *now*, not in six hours.

He stomped out of the stable and began pacing the yard, his boots scraping the soft dirt and kicking up little clouds of dust. Who else could he talk to? Definitely not Edward. He was Emma's uncle, and it would be too awkward to tell him about his feelings toward her. Gabe needed someone impartial who could see the situation from the outside and give an unbiased opinion, and the only other person he could think of was Miguel.

When he returned to the stable, he asked Tommy, "Do you know where Miguel is?"

"Sure," the young ranch hand answered. "He's in the bunkhouse with Stew."

Gabe let out a relieved breath, thanked Tommy, and strode across the yard to the bunkhouse. As he entered, the familiar smell of cooked beans and fried bacon greeted him, and two pairs of eyes met his. Stew, the balding, grizzled old cook, was at the stove, slowly stirring a pot while Miguel reclined in his seat at the table, a halter half-mended in his lap.

"Stew, would you mind if I had a private word with Miguel?" Gabe asked.

The cook quirked an eyebrow, looking between the two men, but shrugged. "I'll step outside for a smoke," he said. He pushed the pot to the back of the stove and collected his cigar and matches, stepping out the door.

When they were alone, Miguel looked curiously at him. "Jefe, what brings you here? Has Martha May stopped feeding you?"

"I need someone to talk to about a situation that I messed up," Gabe said as he paced around the room. "At least, I think I did. At the time I-"

"Ah," the older man said with a knowing smile. "It is about a woman, sí?"

"Sí," he said as he sank onto a bunk and ran his fingers through his dark brown hair, thoroughly mussing it.

Miguel got up and sat on the opposite bunk as Gabe explained the details of what happened at the party. Or, at least, what he *thought* had happened. He was sick of repeating the story, but it needed to be laid out in full. "You see why I wanted to stay away from Emma, don't you?"

Miguel looked thoughtful as he nodded. "A woman like that would not do well as the wife of a rancher. She would not be happy living so far from the finer things they have in big cities."

"That's what I thought too," Gabe agreed, rubbing the back of his neck. "But something happened when I was in the general store that makes me think I had her all wrong."

The older man raised his eyebrows, waiting.

"Mrs. Callaway was in the store, raising hell and hollering at Eunice Harper, just for mixing up her order."

"That evil witch," Miguel spat. "She treats everyone like dogs—except for her precious nephew."

Gabe rolled his eyes at the mention of Gregory and nodded in agreement. Though he wasn't malicious like his aunt, he was arrogant as all get out and twice as full of himself.

"I was about to get involved when Emma came storming in and demanded that Mrs. Callaway apologize to Eunice."

Miguel sat forward, a look of surprise in his dark eyes. "She did? What did Mrs. Callaway do?"

Gabe grinned. "She was so surprised Emma had the gumption to stand up to her, she was struck dumb for once. I wish you could have been there, Miguel. Emma was so calm and composed. She quoted Scripture and put that she-devil square in her place. Then she let drop that if Mrs. Callaway didn't make amends right quick, she wasn't the fine, upstanding Christian lady she made herself out to be."

Miguel hooted with laughter, and he slapped his knee in delight. "Oh, this is too good to be true! Did she truly apologize?"

He gave a quick nod, which only made Miguel laugh harder. "I must meet this woman. To put that witch in her place with just words? That's divine justice for somebody who cuts folks down whenever she speaks."

"It was downright satisfying to watch Mrs. Callaway get her comeuppance," Gabe agreed. "But what really got me was seeing Emma comforting Eunice afterward. The way she spoke to her was so calm and caring. She asked her about her Pa and the store, and when Emma learned Eunice couldn't read, she stepped in and read off the lists herself, helping fill the orders like it was nothing."

He shook his head and leaned forward, placing his elbows on his knees. "She isn't the woman I thought she was. No one self-centered and wrapped up in their finery would become a champion for someone like Eunice. She cares about more than dresses and looking pretty. I think she's got a real heart."

"More than some around here," Miguel said simply.

Groaning, Gabe dropped his head into his hands. "So, what should I do now? I tried to talk with her on Sunday and could barely get a word in edgewise with Gregory and all of her other admirers crowding around."

Miguel studied him thoughtfully for a moment. "You need to catch her alone somehow. There are too many prying eyes in the churchyard. Maybe talk to your friends. They're her cousins; they might help you find a quiet moment."

"That's smart. Thanks. I know this isn't part of your job, but I needed someone to help me see straight on this."

Miguel stood up and gave him a friendly clap on the back. "I'm just an old vaquero who has lived a lot of life," he said, with a faint, crooked grin. "Take what I said with a grain of salt, but I think this Emma may be worth the rough trail you've been on."

"I think you may be right. I just hope it didn't take me too long to figure that out."

Gabe said farewell and stepped out into the warm afternoon sunshine, feeling renewed. With the ranch hands' counsel still ringing in his ears, he knew he needed to speak to his friends as soon as he could. No sense letting the grass grow under his feet. He checked his pocket watch and saw that it was just before dinner. If he hurried, he could catch Micah or one of his brothers before they went home to eat.

Gabe had taken the shortcut between his spread and the Barneses' farm, which brought him out about fifteen feet away from the creamery building. He didn't want to draw the attention of the entire family by riding up to the front door, so he swung down from Xerxes, looped his reins over a low branch, and slipped the gelding a sugar cube. Walking as quietly as he could through the brush, he found a shady spot out of sight from the house and waited for one of his friends to exit the building.

It didn't take long before Micah walked into view, and when he got close enough, Gabe tossed a rock to grab his attention. "Psst! Over here," he called softly as his friend turned around.

"Gabe?" Micah asked as he squinted through the trees. "What are you doing out here?"

"I need to talk to you and your brothers, but I didn't want anyone else to overhear. Can you get Luke and Joseph?"

"Sure, but are you all right? You look like you're waiting to rob a stagecoach."

"I'm fine," Gabe replied. "I just need help with something, and it might take more than one person."

"Okay, I'll go get them and be right back."

Micah was only gone a few minutes before he emerged from the creamery with his brothers in tow, each wearing the same concerned expression.

"What's the problem?" asked Luke as soon as they were all concealed in the trees.

"It must be something big if Gabe's going through all this work for secrecy," Joseph guessed.

"I wanted to ask you all to help me find a way to speak to Emma. When I saw her on Sunday and could only get a few words in with all the other men flocking around her."

Micah looked puzzled. "Really? What changed your mind? You've been sidestepping her like the plague these past few weeks."

"I saw her at the general store this morning," Gabe said, grinning as he remembered the incident.

Joseph smirked. "We heard all about it from Ma and the girls the second they got home. I'm glad that old biddy finally got what was coming to her. Ma never mentioned seeing you in there, though."

Gabe shrugged, and he could feel his ears heat. "I was in the back looking at the catalogs when I heard all the yelling. When it was all over, I didn't know what to say to her, so I left when no one was looking."

"I can understand that," Luke said. "I doubt I would have reacted any differently. But aside from knowing that she can hold her own in a verbal boxing match, what's with the sudden change of heart?"

"When I saw her with Eunice, I knew I'd misjudged her," he admitted. "I know she must have had some reason for running off that day. I just haven't figured out what that is yet, which is why I need your help." He looked at Micah and his brothers a bit self-consciously and cleared his throat. "So, any ideas on how to make this happen?"

"I'm not sure," Micah said, "but you'd better hurry. Pa said he's already had three men ask to court Emma. He turned them all down flat. One was pushin' forty, with four kids that needed a new Ma."

"I wish I could go back to the day of the party." Gabe kicked at a rock in frustration and shook his head. "I'd do it differently—every last bit."

Suddenly, Joseph's eyes narrowed mischievously, and he grinned. "I think I have the perfect idea. It even involves a party of sorts."

"Really?" Micah asked, sounding suspicious. "What is it?"

"The Independence Day picnic, of course. We just need to convince Emma to enter a basket into the box social so Gabe can bid on it. That shouldn't be too hard. Then they can have the privacy they need to talk."

"But how will he know which basket to bid on?" Luke asked. "It's supposed to be a secret."

"We can tell him what the basket looks like," Joseph said. "Emma will have to decorate it, so we will know which one is hers."

"That's cheating," Micah pointed out.

"All is fair in love and war," Joseph shrugged.

While Gabe agreed it was technically cheating, he had to admit it was still a solid plan. The brothers promised to run interference with any men who tried to monopolize conversation after services, and by the time they parted ways, he felt hopeful for the first time in weeks.

Chapter 17

The churchyard was teeming with people when Emma and her family arrived for services a few days after the confrontation in the general store. Wagons parked haphazardly on the lawn filled every available space, and only a few empty spots remained at the hitching post. The last time it had been this full was the day of her welcoming party, which Emma should have taken as a warning sign.

As soon as she had both feet on the ground, a crowd gathered around her, pressing in on her from every side. Apparently, word of her good deed had spread like wildfire through the town, and they all wanted to shake her hand and commend her for standing up for Eunice. But she hadn't done it for recognition or acclaim from the members of the community. In fact, she hadn't really been thinking at all, but rather acting on instinct.

Smiling politely, she thanked everyone for their kind words and excused herself to follow her family inside the church. They were late enough as it was.

The reverent hush of the chapel was a welcome respite from the noise of the gathering she'd just escaped, and Emma took a deep, steadying breath. There were still whispered words exchanged between friends and the rustling of fabric as folks found their seats, but it was peaceful.

Once the final tender notes of the prelude drifted into the rafters overhead, Pastor Langley took his place at the pulpit and began his sermon. As he spoke on the importance of "serving the least of these," Emma felt the tension uncoil from her shoulders. By the time the closing hymn faded, she felt almost like herself again, and she rose to follow her family toward the exit.

"Miss Barnes!" Pastor Langley greeted her jovially as she passed him on the steps of the church. "I am so pleased you could be here today. My wife was in the store the other day and told me what happened. She said Eunice was smiling from ear to ear when you left with your family after spending time with her."

"Eunice is a pleasure to be around, Pastor Langley. It was no hardship on my part," Emma replied honestly.

"You're so gracious. Maybe you should change your name to Beatrice. You've shown that you exemplify many of the beatitudes," the pastor chuckled. "I must say, though, I admire your knowledge of the Bible and how you handled Mrs. Callaway. While she isn't one of my congregants, I've tried to speak with the lady about her behavior toward others. Unfortunately, it just goes in one ear and out the other. Hopefully, now she'll see fit to repent."

"I hope so as well," Emma said earnestly. It must be tiring to be so mean all the time.

"I should write to my grandson to forewarn him about her. He is finishing his seminary training at Nyack College in New York and will take over for me when I retire in a few years. You should come to dinner and meet him when he arrives in the fall."

Pastor Hinkey looked expectantly at her, and Emma—understanding what he was hinting at—promised to greet him when the time came. She prayed that her statement was ambiguous enough not to get his hopes up and bid farewell to the pastor. She had just joined Mary, who had been waiting for her in the churchyard, when Aunt Sarah approached with two men in tow.

"Hello, girls," she said happily. "Emma, I'd like to introduce some of our friends who weren't able to attend your welcoming party. This is Peter McCoy, one of our local deputies, who's been away visiting family in Nebraska, and Walter Robins, who owns a hog farm about fifteen miles from here. We don't get to see him often, but we're sure glad he's here today. Peter, Walter, this is Edward's niece, Emma Barnes."

Emma smiled warmly, extending her hand first to the deputy and then to Walter. "Pleased to meet you both."

"Pleasure's all ours, Miss Barnes," Peter said, tipping his hat, though he glanced not at Emma, but at Mary.

From the rosy tint on Mary's cheeks, it was obvious that there was an attraction between the two, and Emma moved subtly nearer to Walter. She watched as the deputy shuffled closer to her cousin and offered a shy smile. It seemed she wasn't the only one in the family drawing the attention of the single men in Elk Ridge.

Emma was glad that her cousin had an admirer. Mary was kind, sweet, and patient. All traits that any man would look for. And she was beautiful to boot.

The small group stood exchanging pleasantries for a few minutes, the churchyard chatter light and easy, until Gregory Callaway stepped up to join them. He was smiling brightly at Emma as he came to stand next to her—close enough that she caught the sharp burst of citrus cologne mingled with tobacco on his coat. It was stronger than she expected at such proximity. The mixture tickled her nose and made her want to sneeze, so she took a small step back.

"Hello, Emma. How are you on this fine Sunday afternoon?" he asked smoothly, placing his hat over his heart.

"I'm doing very well, Mr. Callaway," Emma replied, deliberately using his surname. She had no intention of encouraging familiarity. Frankly, she was surprised that he was talking to her; she had very publicly shamed his aunt just a few days ago.

"Spectacular now that I'm here with you," he said, his tone fawning.

"Oh, that's kind of you to say," Emma replied, though she was a bit distracted as she noticed Micah fast approaching as she glanced over Gregory's shoulder.

"I hope you won't hold my aunt's actions against me," Gregory said apologetically. "The poor dear is the only family I have left, so I'm forced to put up with her little foibles now and then."

The nonchalant way he referred to his aunt's atrocious treatment of Eunice as a 'foible' snapped Emma back to attention. She was about to set him straight when Micah arrived, pushing past Gregory to stand next to Emma, positioning himself between them.

"I've got the wagon all ready," he said, gently taking her by the elbow. "Come on."

Emma gave him a grateful smile, relieved to be saved from starting another scene with one of the Callaways. She had no desire to be seen as someone who was contentious, but they didn't seem to make it easy for her.

"That's a shame. Hopefully, we can speak more next week," Gregory suggested.

"Perhaps," Micah said, a slight edge to his voice.

"Well, until next time, then." Gregory gave her cousin a tight smile and then a more genuine one to Emma, Mary, and finally her aunt before striding off.

When he was out of earshot, she heard Micah mutter, "Good riddance," before leading the way to the wagon.

With the Independence Day picnic coming up next week, the conversation at supper that evening was lively, and the children took great delight in explaining the activities the town put on for Emma.

"There's a parade," Matthew said, his bright blue eyes shining with excitement. "All the businesses in town get to decorate their wagons and drive them down Main Street!"

"There are lots of games to play too, like sack races, ninepins, and musical chairs," Ruth chimed in.

"Oh, well, that sounds rather exciting," Emma said, intrigued by the idea of having the whole town gather in one place.

"Sometimes folks set up chessboards and play each other for pennies," Isaac said, breaking his usual reticence, "and they have contests for who makes the best pies, cookies, and cakes."

"Don't forget the box social!" Esther exclaimed. "I would enter, but I'm not old enough yet."

Then she let out a long, theatrical sigh and stared mournfully at her plate. Emma caught her cousins exchanging eye-rolls, though a couple of the younger ones bit back grins at the performance.

"I used to attend box socials quite often back in Denver," Emma said with a small smile. "Though I confess I'm a bit out of practice."

"Well, you should enter a basket then," Joseph said with a wide grin, "for old time's sake. All the money goes to a worthy cause for the community. Last year, we made enough to put up a new church bell."

"Who gets to decide what the money goes to?" Emma asked curiously.

"The Mayor and town council take a vote amongst themselves," Uncle Edward answered.

"Mary, were you planning on putting one up for auction?" Emma inquired.

"Yes," Mary said, a bright smile on her face. "It's my first year being able to do so. The church committee made it a rule that you have to be at least eighteen. Would you like to make one too?"

"Absolutely! Do you think we'll have enough time to decorate our baskets?"

"I do," Mary replied. "Tomorrow, may we go into town to get some ribbon or fabric? Please, Ma?"

Aunt Sarah smiled at her daughter. "Yes. But it will have to be a quick trip to the general store and then straight home. If we go to Mrs. Tandy, none of us will be leaving without empty pockets."

"Wonderful!" Emma said, beaming at her aunt. "I'll be able to see Eunice too!"

After supper, she spent the rest of the evening in the parlor with Mary, discussing how they should decorate their baskets.

Chapter 18

The next morning, Emma donned the green floral ready-made dress that she'd purchased from Mrs. Tandy and headed downstairs, the lighter fabric swishing softly against her legs. She liked that the hem, raised a few inches higher than the current city fashion, prevented her from tripping over skirts as she moved through the farmyard doing chores.

She'd made other, more subtle modifications to her clothing too: shorter corsets that ended at the waist, loosening her laces for easier breathing, and reserving the stiff bustle for Sundays and special occasions. She had begun seriously contemplating abandoning the bustle altogether, but her dresses would hang oddly without it. Still, practicality was winning out over style on the farm.

With the prospect of a trip to town once all the morning chores were done, she headed out of the house to do her milking and egg collection. She was getting better and better at her tasks every day, and it gave her a new and growing confidence.

With her wicker basket brimming with fresh eggs, Emma entered the kitchen to drop it off in the larder and greeted Mary, who was hanging her work apron on a peg by the door.

"Ma's getting the wagon brought around, so we should hurry. Would you like me to grab your purse from the room?" her cousin asked.

"Yes, please. I'll put these away and wash up while you do that."

Mary nodded, disappearing upstairs, and was back by the time she'd finished cleaning up. Emma took her purse from her cousin, and together they left the house just as Aunt Sarah pulled up in the wagon.

"Come along, girls! I want to be back in time to make dinner."

Sarah held out her hand, assisted both young women up into the bench seat, and then set off toward town. It was still early when they arrived, but Mr. Harper had the door to his store open and was busy sweeping off the wooden boardwalk when the wagon pulled to a stop beside him. When he looked up and saw who the occupants were, a wide smile grew on his face.

"Good morning, Sarah. And to you, too, Mary and Emma. What brings you into town first thing?"

"The girls wanted to find some items to decorate their box social baskets with, and I needed a few supplies," Sarah explained as she set the brake and let the girls climb down.

"I see. Well, you girls go on inside and pick out what you need. Eunice is stocking some shelves right now, and I know she'll want to see you."

Emma smiled broadly at Mr. Harper and followed Mary into the store. They had only walked a few feet when a squeal sounded.

"Emma! You came back!" Eunice shouted as she rushed forward, her long brown braids steaming out behind her as she ran.

"Of course I did. I'll always stop by to say hello to you if I'm in town."

Eunice threw herself against Emma and gave her a tight hug. "I'm glad you are my friend."

"I'm glad too, sweeting." Emma felt her throat tighten, and tears threatened, so she bit her lip to distract herself enough to regain her composure before she hugged her back.

"Do you think you could help Mary and me pick out some things to decorate a basket with? Maybe some ribbon or lace?"

Eunice stepped back, her soft, rounded features lighting up with happiness. "Yes! I'll show you my favorite ones."

She grasped Emma's hand tightly. Then, shyly, as if unsure the gesture would be reciprocated, she extended the other to Mary, who took it immediately. The young girl grinned happily and guided them to a section of the store stocked with fabric and accessories. Working carefully, she brought out several varieties of ribbons and laid them on the counter, pointing out her favorites and even suggesting a few that Emma and Mary might like. When they finished making their selections, Eunice led the way back to the front counter, where Sarah was waiting, having finished her shopping.

"Did you find everything you needed?" Mr. Harper asked them.

"We did. Eunice helped us pick out some beautiful things, and I believe we'll have the best decorated baskets in the box social."

"I think you're right, and to show my appreciation for all you have done for my daughter, I insist you have these," Mr. Harper nodded to their pile of goods, "for free."

"That is so generous of you. Are you certain? I am more than willing to pay for them," Emma replied.

"Consider it payment for the work you did in the store," he said, winking at her as he wrapped the materials and slid the package across the counter.

She smiled and gratefully accepted the parcel.

"Will you both come back and see me soon?" Eunice asked as they prepared to leave the store.

"Of course we will," Emma said, rubbing the girl's shoulder.

"Pinky swear?"

Emma and Mary exchanged a glance—amused, touched—and nodded in unison as they extended their little fingers. Eunice beamed, hooking her small finger around Emma's, then Mary's, her grip surprisingly firm, sealing the promise.

After another round of hugs, they bid the Harpers farewell and followed Sarah out to the wagon. Emma had just handed the parcel of goods to Mary when someone shouted her name. She paused and searched in the direction the voice came from, and saw Gregory Callaway hurrying down the street.

"Emma! Good day!" he said as he bowed before her. He was dressed well today in a charcoal sack suit that cut neatly to his frame with a bright red paisley vest that added a pop of color against his black tie and bowler hat. For a working man, it would have been odd attire, but he was the bank manager—appearances mattered in that line of work.

"Good day, Mr. Callaway," she replied. "Are you purchasing something from the general store? We've just come from there."

He noticed her choice of words and looked up to see Mary and Sarah patiently waiting for him to acknowledge them. "Oh, hello, Mrs. Barnes. Hello, Mary," he greeted, well-mannered but brief, before turning back to Emma. "I saw from the window at the bank that you were in town, and I just had to come speak with you."

"I see. How kind of you," Emma answered with a polite smile. "Was there something in particular you wanted to say, or just a general hello? I only ask because we need to be getting back soon. There are still quite a few chores to finish before dinner."

"Of course." He nodded. "I wanted to ask if you'll be making an entry to the box social," he asked eagerly.

"Yes, I will. In fact, we came into town today for that very purpose," she answered.

"Ah, then I look forward to bidding on it. Good day, ladies." Gregory doffed his hat to them in farewell and left, striding confidently back down the street toward the bank.

"My word, he's persistent!" Mary groused as she helped Emma into the wagon.

Her cousin's disgruntled tone shocked Emma. Mary was never cross, yet today, as she watched Gregory walk away from them, her features were disapproving. "Your family doesn't seem to like him much. Is it because of his aunt?" she asked quietly as Sarah drove them home.

"No, but she is terrible," her cousin said. "But before you came to town, he never gave any of the eligible women the time of day. And now that you're here, he is suddenly very interested in a relationship. It's as if the women of this town aren't good enough for him."

"That's nonsense. And if he can't see that, then he's a fool," Emma proclaimed.

"Don't worry on my behalf," Mary consoled. "I've never held those types of feelings for Gregory, but I have friends who do."

Emma could see why. Gregory was a good-looking man, and he had a good job, but in her eyes, he couldn't hold a candle to Gabe. "Well, I have no interest in him. I'm sure once more time passes, he'll move on."

"Maybe," Mary said skeptically, and they spent the rest of the ride home lost in their own thoughts.

Emma and her aunt dedicated an entire day to baking for the Independence Day picnic. They'd done most of the prep work the day before, so as soon as she came in from her chores, they dove straight in. With so much to bake and only so much room in the cast-iron stoves, they divided the work. Emma worked in the house, where the oven ran steadier and cooler, while her aunt claimed the summer kitchen, whose stove blazed hotter and suited her surer hand. Since she still scorched the occasional batch of biscuits, the arrangement worked perfectly.

Together they produced six pies—all different fruit varieties—two dozen molasses cookies, two dozen snickerdoodles, three cakes, plus a few small hand pies to go in the girls' picnic baskets. It had been nothing short of a miracle that Emma had found room to fit them in the oven amongst all the pies and cakes, but she'd managed the trick on the last tray as the oven's heat finally began to fade.

Emma and Mary packed fried chicken and potato salad into their baskets for the box social as well as a drink. Mary planned to include a jar of lemonade, but Emma chose sweetened black tea instead.

That evening, when the family gathered in the parlor after their supper of cold sandwiches and salad, everyone was buzzing with excitement for the festivities the next day. While Emma and Mary worked on the finishing touches for their baskets, adding bits of lace or flowers to make them stand out, Esther asked them which man they wanted to win the bidding on it. Mary blushed prettily and confessed she hoped Deputy McCoy would win her basket, but when it was Emma's turn to answer the same question, she hesitated.

Deep down, she knew her first answer would have been Gabe. He was a strikingly attractive man, and when she had been close to him, her heart went wild, but she was afraid her chance with him had passed.

Instead, she shrugged and said, "It won't matter much to me who wins. I'm still getting to know people, and this will be a good opportunity to do just that."

She could feel her aunt's gaze on her as she tied a bow onto the handle of the basket, and she tried not to look too guilty. If anyone could spot her lie, it would be Sarah. She had been there with Emma while she sobbed out the events of the party and knew her feelings about Gabe. At least, the fledgling ones she'd begun to have. She didn't quite know what to feel anymore.

Chapter 19

The morning of the Fourth was a hectic one. The family rushed through chores in the farmyard while Esther and Ruth dogged Emma's every step, begging to be the ones who picked the outfit she wore. She was hesitant to let the girls have their way, knowing they could eat up the minutes with their bickering, but eventually gave in. Her only condition was that it had to be something breathable, as the day was already hot, with no end to the soaring temperature in sight.

Thankfully, the girls were able to agree on an outfit without too much quarreling, and they laid out a beige and burgundy pinstriped muslin dress with a matching burgundy overskirt. It was a good choice. The color of the dress brought out the subtle red tones in her hair, and the fabric wouldn't have her drowning in sweat.

After dressing, Emma took one last look in the hall mirror, and she almost didn't recognize the woman staring back at her. Her pale skin had become tanned from her time in the sun, and a smattering of freckles showed on her cheeks and the bridge of her nose. If her father were to see her now, he'd be horrified. Chuckling to herself at the thought, she left the house.

By the time they rumbled into town, the streets were crowded with excited townsfolk, happily chatting with one another as children ran back and forth across the street. Emma was amazed. She was used to crowds in Denver, but she had never seen so many people in Elk Ridge at one time. She wondered how far they had traveled to be here today.

With his face set in concentration, Uncle Edward carefully guided the wagon through the throng of people and stopped in front of the long tables lining the main street, each heavily laden with food.

"I'll let you all out here and go find somewhere to park the wagon," he told his wife, holding onto a plate of cookies while she hopped down from the front seat. "Hopefully, Cyrus still has a spot available at the livery."

Aunt Sarah nodded, and once everyone had climbed down from the wagon and all the food had been taken out, he drove off. Then, clapping her hands to get her children's attention, Sarah gathered everyone around her and supervised the placement of the dishes being entered in the food competition, while the rest of the food went to the communal tables. When they were done, she herded her younger children down the street while Emma and Mary left to drop off their baskets.

It wasn't hard to find the middle-aged woman who was coordinating the box social, and as she saw the cousins' approach, she gave them a wide smile. "Hello! Names, please?"

"Emma and Mary Barnes," Emma supplied.

"Wonderful." She quickly wrote them down in a small ledger book and reached out to collect their baskets, setting them on the table's edge, next to the others. "It looks like we have a record turnout this year," the woman said happily. "Enjoy your picnics!"

Waving goodbye, the girls began making their way slowly through the crowd. Though they were stopped several times by friends and neighbors who wanted to chat, they made it back to their family just in time for the parade to start. Excited murmurs rippled through the crowd, and townsfolk parted to each side of the street to allow the procession a clear path.

Through the surrounding conversation, Emma could hear the thunderous sound of dozens of wagons rumbling down the dirt road. As the crowd turned in that direction, a jaunty tune rang out from a small band of local musicians as the first few participants of the parade came into view. They saw Mr. Decker, who had a giant wooden hammer propped up in the bed of his wagon, and Mrs. Tandy had mannequins dressed in her best creations displayed in hers. Though each business had a display that represented its store, one thing they all had in common was an abundance of red, white, and blue bunting and American flags.

Emma was enjoying herself immensely, and when she saw Mr. Harper drive past with Eunice sitting proudly in the back of the wagon, she grinned. The young girl was waving her thin arm furiously at the crowd, a wide, radiant smile on her face. She seemed to have forgotten to hold up the sign with "Harper's General Store" written on it, but at least she was having fun.

As the last wagon in the parade trundled past, the townsfolk reclaimed the street. Some darted off to get in line for games, while others found their way to the food tables. Emma stayed close to her family, enjoying the lively chaos until the sheriff's booming voice rang out.

"The box social will begin in ten minutes!" he announced. "All participating ladies, please make your way to the stage at the edge of town. Mayor Marlow will serve as auctioneer today."

A buzz of nervousness went through Emma when she heard the announcement, and she gripped Mary's hand tightly as they walked toward the stage. What if she didn't like the man who bid on her basket? She knew she could be polite and endure even the most boring conversations—she'd had enough practice at it—but it would be a shame to spend all that time with someone she disliked. Frowning, she reasoned that she didn't have much choice in the matter. This was what she'd signed up for when entering the box social, after all.

When Emma and Mary joined the other participants on the stage, she noticed a handful of men already milling about in front of it. She recognized Gregory and several other young men from church, but the crowd continued to grow as the mayor made his way to the podium. He waited a few more minutes, clearly wanting a good-sized audience, then gave a loud whistle to quiet the crowd.

"Thank you all for coming to the box social. These baskets here to my right represent the hard work and kindness of our fine young women, and I expect every one of them will be gone by the end of this. Remember, your bid will go toward the funding of a schoolhouse, so loosen those purse strings and let's begin!"

Mr. Marlow picked up a gavel, banged it on the wooden podium, and looked into the first basket. He sniffed its contents, grinned, and began describing them in great detail. The men who had gathered at the front of the stage jostled one another as they craned their necks to see for themselves, and the mayor started the bidding at twenty-five cents. Hands shot up into the air, and the bidding price began to rise, finally closing at fifty-five cents.

"Well, gentlemen, that was a wonderful start!" he declared as the man who had won the bid came forward to meet his picnic partner. "I hope you keep up this same spirit of generosity as we move forward."

The next basket was brought up, and the bidding process started all over again, with Mr. Marlow giving a glowing review of its contents while men raised their hands or called out their bids. The pattern continued like this six more times until Mary's basket was brought out, and she clutched Emma's arm anxiously as the bidding began.

Emma patted her hand, and together they watched as the men in the crowd vied for the top bid. It seemed that there was a lot of interest in it. The price continued to climb, but after some competitive bidding, it was won by Deputy McCoy for a dollar, and he was smiling ear to ear.

"Oh, my!" Mary exclaimed, looking as if she might be about to faint. "He won!"

Emma grinned and hugged her cousin. "How wonderful! Now, go have fun. I expect to hear all about it tonight."

Mary squealed, gave a little hop of excitement, and then hurried off to meet the deputy, her face almost the same color of pink as her dress. Emma chuckled at her cousin's antics and then turned her attention back to the auction, which had already resumed. As basket after basket drew spirited bids, she felt her anxiety rise, and by the time it was finally her turn, she felt almost faint.

Before Mr. Marlow could even open her basket and start to call out its contents, Gregory came forward from the back of the crowd where he'd been lingering, a self-satisfied smile on his face. "I bid two dollars!" he shouted.

Surprise and displeasure could be heard from the men surrounding the stage, but the mayor was extremely pleased by the bid. He called out to any challengers, but since two dollars was more than some of the men made for a day's work, it was answered with silence. Emma stood still, waiting for Mr. Marlow to name Gregory the winner when a loud, powerful voice rang through the crowd and shouted, "Three dollars!"

Murmurs rippled through the gathering, and Emma gasped as she saw Gabe walking confidently toward her, a spark of fiery intensity in his hazel eyes.

Chapter 20

Today was not going the way Gabe had planned. He had been on his way to town when Xerxes threw a shoe. Not wanting the gelding to injure himself further, he had to walk the rest of the way. Thankfully, it wasn't too long a distance. He settled Xerxes at the livery, getting Cyrus's promise that the horse would have a new shoe fitted by the time he returned.

Gabe thanked the big man and exited the building, expecting to have to search for his friends, but they were waiting for him just outside the sliding doors. Before he could even say hello, Micah dug into his pocket and plopped a bundle of bills into his hand.

"What's this for?" he asked.

"The box social," Joseph said quickly. "Benjamin saw Gregory trying to bribe the woman running the auction so she'd point out Emma's basket. We're chipping in to make sure you get the winning bid." He nodded at the money in Gabe's hand. "You've got about five dollars there, but we have to hurry. The auction's already started."

Joseph pointed toward the large stage that had been erected at the north end of the field, and without another word, Gabe stuffed the bills into his pocket and sprinted down the dusty street. He dodged between clusters of townsfolk strolling down the boardwalk, while Micah and his brothers pounded along behind. As he ran, a silent prayer looped in his mind: *Not too late, Lord, please—not too late.*

He skidded to a halt at the rear of the crowd just as Gregory's bid rang out, clear and sharp. There was no way in hell Gabe was going to let that smug snake win Emma's basket. He sucked in a deep breath and bellowed, "Three dollars!"

The men closest to him turned to see who was challenging Gregory, parting for Gabe as he strode forward toward the podium. He could see Emma's shocked expression as he got closer, and their eyes met and held for a moment until they were interrupted by another shout.

"Three dollars and fifty cents," Gregory countered, jaw clenched, and looking mad enough to spit nails.

"Four dollars," Gabe shot back, glaring daggers across the crowd.

Gregory called out another bid, and with each increase, the surrounding crowd grew larger, and Mr. Marlow became more gleeful. Everyone was riveted to the scene before them, and as the men glowered at each other, Gregory raised the bid to six dollars.

"Seven dollars," Gabe responded instantly, his voice carrying clearly in the hushed anticipation.

Gregory's face purpled in rage. He rummaged in the pockets of his fine wool trousers for a moment and brought out a fistful of coins, counting the loose change. After a moment, he shouted, "Seven dollars and twenty cents."

"Eight dollars," Gabe called out, folding his muscled arms across his chest, and a slow, triumphant smile spread across his face—the smile of a man who'd known he'd won before the gavel even fell.

Visibly shaking, Gregory spun on his heel and stalked off, his boots kicking up dust, his dignity in ruins. Gabe watched him go for a moment, a flicker of satisfaction running through him. It would have been tempting to watch the man squirm a little longer, but Gregory had been humiliated enough for one day.

Mr. Marlow called for a counter, but when no further bids rose, the mayor lifted his gavel with a wide grin. "Sold to the rancher for eight dollars!" he said as he smacked the wooden mallet on the podium.

A roar of cheers erupted around Gabe, but he barely noticed it. His mind was focused on a single purpose: Emma.

He forced his way through the admiring masses, all looking to clap him on the back and congratulate him, until he got to the front of the stage. And there, just off to the side, stood Emma. She looked every bit as beautiful as the last time he'd seen her. The pleased expression she wore was open, unguarded, and it made his chest expand until breathing felt like a minor miracle. This wasn't polite courtesy, like she'd shown other men; this was joy, bright and real, meant for him alone.

He started toward her, but Mr. Marlow's voice cut through the din. "Mr. Moreau! Over here—time to settle up."

Reluctantly, Gabe made his way to the podium, fished the crumpled bills from his pocket, and counted out the eight dollars he owed. The mayor beamed as he accepted the money, thanking him profusely for his generous bid. He shook Gabe's hand with enough force to rattle his teeth, then handed him a neatly folded patchwork quilt along with the picnic basket.

When he turned around, Emma was right there, a bright smile on her stunning face. "I'm so glad that you're here," she said breathlessly. "I was afraid you might never want to spend time with me again after..." She blushed and looked down for a moment. "Well, after last time."

"I was hoping we could start again," he said, holding out his arm to escort her away so that the next round of bidding could start.

"I would like that very much," Emma said, taking his arm with a smile.

As they left behind the noise of the auction, he scanned the road before them and saw a flat, open spot under a large black cottonwood tree. It was still in public view, but secluded enough for them to talk freely. "Would you care to sit over there?" he asked. "It looks like a nice, shady spot."

"Oh yes. It will be nice to take a break from the sun for a while."

They took their time strolling down the dirt road, their conversation light and friendly, and when they reached the shelter of the cottonwood's wide canopy, Gabe carefully spread the quilt. He made sure that there were no wrinkles in the faded blanket, and when it was laid out to his satisfaction, he offered Emma his hand. She took it without hesitation, lowering herself gracefully to the ground, and he sat opposite her.

"I hope you enjoy what I've packed," Emma said, opening the wicker basket. "Aunt Sarah has been giving me cooking lessons every day, and she says I have improved quite a bit. I only burned three batches of cookies yesterday."

When Gabe saw her teasing smile, he grinned. Inside, however, surprise flickered through him. It was hard to believe this was the same girl he had met at the welcoming party. The refined young lady from Denver was now toiling away in a frontier kitchen day after day. Yet he'd seen her in the general store working with Eunice, and she'd taken to it like a duck to water, without a word of complaint.

A realization settled warmly in his chest, pulling his admiration deeper. She wasn't just polite or pretty; she was willing to change, to dig in and learn what mattered out here. That made her more intriguing to him than ever—more real.

"You're full of surprises, Miss Barnes," he said, voice low and warm with genuine appreciation. "Do you enjoy these lessons?"

"I do. My mother passed away when I was young, so I never had the chance to learn from her as my cousins have from their mother. I'm very grateful that my aunt agreed to teach me."

"If you enjoy cooking, I could ask Martha May if she could show you some of her recipes," Gabe offered. "She's an excellent baker."

"Oh! I met her at the party. I liked her very much. If you think she would be willing, I'd love to learn from her."

"I'm sure she would. She doesn't get much female company unless we come in for services or Sarah comes to tea."

"Wonderful. I'll ask Aunt Sarah to arrange a schedule," she said, her sapphire eyes sparkling with excitement.

They ate in comfortable silence, just enjoying being in each other's presence on a fine summer's day. The shade from the tree and a slight breeze kept them cool as silverware scraped across their plates. Emma was the first to finish her food, and she set down her plate and faced him squarely.

"I'd like to talk about what happened at the welcoming party," she said, her tone serious.

He set down his plate as well and turned to give her his full attention. This was a conversation he had wanted to have today, but he hadn't known how to bring up the subject. A part of him was worried about what she would have to say. The afternoon was going well, and he was enjoying the easy camaraderie they were developing, but that could all change.

"I want you to know that I feel terrible about running away from you." She took a deep breath, as if bolstering herself for what was to come, and continued. "The dress I wore that day is special to me. It is the last gift my father purchased for me before he died, and the thought of the dress possibly being destroyed felt like having my father taken from me all over again."

Tears began spilling down her soft cheeks unchecked, and Gabe handed her a clean napkin so she could wipe them away. As she dabbed her eyes dry, he thought about what she had revealed. His Ma had been gone for years now, but if someone had ripped pages out of her Bible—something he treasured beyond almost anything—he'd probably cry, too. It was the only thing he had of hers.

"So, you see, it was never about the actual dress, but the symbolism I had placed on it. He's only been gone for six months, and my grief is still strong." She gave him a watery smile. "I was truly enjoying our time getting to know one another and didn't want it to end, but when my drink spilled..." She paused, toying with the napkin, her eyes downcast. "I didn't want you to see me cry and think it was over some fabric and ribbons, so I fled. Regrettably, I think that is exactly the impression I left you with."

Gabe sighed and rested his elbow on his raised knee. "It was, at first, but I talked to Henry and my ranch hand, Miguel, about it. They both agreed that there was something more going on, and that I should speak to you about it."

"I do appreciate beautiful clothing; I am a woman after all," Emma joked lightly, her lips lifting at the corners. "But I'm just as happy in my new work dresses. Most of the things I own are fashionable and sophisticated because I needed them to be—and until recently, they were all I owned. After my mother passed away, my father needed someone to act as hostess when he invited business associates to our home for dinner or drinks. He frequently met with investors at places like sporting events or business conferences, and he always brought me along. I had to 'look the part,' so to speak."

"Martha May said something similar to me recently about dressing to show your success." Gabe gave a little shrug. "I've never had to think about what my clothing said about me before."

"It was something my father was very sensitive about. He wanted to be taken seriously as a businessman, not the son of a dairy farmer." Emma stopped and let out a laugh. "I guess I've come right back around to it."

Gabe grinned. "Yes, and what a charming milkmaid you are."

She snickered and slapped his arm with her napkin. "I might be a milkmaid now, but my father wanted me to be seen as a high-society lady. He sent me to an all-girls school and hired an etiquette teacher. I was encouraged to take part in local charities, where I could meet other women of standing, and I joined the Ladies' Relief Society. It allowed me to meet many affluent people, and through that, my father met more prosperous investors and business contacts."

"What did this Relief Society do?" he asked, curious to hear how she had occupied her time before she came to Elk Ridge.

"They supported an orphans' home, among many other projects." She placed the napkin on her lap now that her tears had dried and gave a small, wistful smile. "A new building was built a few years ago, and I would visit there a few days a week to read stories to the children."

"Sounds like a worthy cause to invest your time in," he said, touched that she chose to spend it with children who had no home of their own. "I haven't had a story read to me since my Ma died."

"Was your Pa unable to read?" she asked, without a trace of condescension in her tone.

"He could read," Gabe said. "He just... didn't want to read to me."

Emma's nose wrinkled in confusion, and he felt a pang of regret—he hadn't meant to open that door so soon. But the words were already out.

"When I was twelve, I caught yellow fever. My Ma stayed with me the whole time and nursed me through it... but she caught it too." He swallowed hard. "She didn't survive."

"Oh, how terrible!"

"It was," he agreed quietly. "My Pa changed after that. Started drinking, missing shifts at the iron foundry. I had to find work young just to help keep food on the table. Then one day, he was just gone."

Emma's hand gently rested on his forearm. "You had no one else to care for you?"

"I didn't know about any other family back then. I thought I'd at least have the house, but the bank took it not long after. I ended up moving around, doing whatever work I could find. Eventually, I took a job with an undertaker in Dallas digging graves and stayed with him until I got the letter about Uncle Telly leaving me the ranch."

"Well, from what I understand, you've worked hard to make a name for yourself here," Emma said softly. "Uncle Edward speaks very highly of you. You should be proud of what you've accomplished." She reached into the picnic basket with a small, hopeful smile. "In celebration of that, we should have some dessert. I made cherry hand pies for the first time, so I hope they turned out well."

"They look tasty to me," Gabe said, accepting one and taking a large bite. The tartness of the cherries was tempered by just the right amount of sugar in the filling, and he had to restrain himself from shoving the whole pastry into his mouth. When he was finished, he used a napkin to make sure he didn't have any filling on his face and said, "I was right."

"Thank you," she said, her face flushed with pleasure from his compliment. "Pie crust has been tricky for me to master. I'm glad you enjoyed it."

He had. In fact, he secretly hoped she had another one tucked away in the basket, but when she began packing away the dirty dishes, he knew that their picnic was over. Only, he wasn't ready to part company yet. He glanced around, searching for an excuse to prolong their time together, and saw games being arranged on the main street, and an idea sparked in his mind. "Would you care to take a walk around town now that we're done eating?"

"Yes, that sounds lovely," she said enthusiastically. "I'll just clean up, and then we can go."

"Let me help you," Gabe offered, happy that she wasn't objecting to spending more time with him.

When they were finished, he helped Emma to her feet and quickly folded the blanket before offering his arm again. As they walked back toward the stage, they saw that a sack race was about to begin, and they stopped on the sidelines to watch as the children readied themselves.

"Oh, look!" she shouted to him over the noise of the crowd. "Matthew and Isaac are in the race!"

Gabe spotted the boys lined up with their peers, their young faces set in determination, and he guided Emma forward so they could cheer on her cousins. Seconds later, the starter's pistol cracked, and the children began hopping forward in their cloth sacks.

Despite their best efforts, one or two of the children would fall now and then, but when they got back up, there was a roar of applause from the crowd. As the race progressed, he shouted encouraging words to the boys, while she let out that same ear-splitting whistle she had used in the general store, jumping up and down with excitement.

It was a good time all around, and whether it was because of Gabe and Emma's enthusiastic support, or the raw athleticism of youth, Isaac and Matthew managed the finish line in first and second place, respectively. As the crowd dispersed, he looked down to see Emma grinning widely. All the jumping she'd done had shaken loose some of her deep reddish-brown locks, and he reflexively brought his hand up to tuck the strands behind her ear. At his touch, she blushed and turned away slightly, bringing even more color into her already flushed cheeks.

"I must have made a mess of my hair," she said, reaching her own hand up to her head.

"You could never look a mess, Miss Barnes," he said quietly. "Not even for a moment."

Emma quirked an eyebrow at him, obviously not believing his statement, and quickly tucked the unruly strands of hair back into place, securing them with a pin. "Well, it's fixed now," she said cheerily, retaking his arm. "Shall we continue?"

They spent the next hour strolling down the street, watching the children of the town play games and sampling the food that was for sale. While they walked, they talked more about their childhoods—the better aspects of them, at least—favorite pastimes, and how she'd been adjusting to her life on the farm. The more he got to know her, the more he was struck by how level-headed she was, despite her privileged upbringing.

They were just walking past the livery when Micah and his father approached them. Gabe stopped and held out his hand for Edward to shake.

"Afternoon, Edward, Micah. I was just about to ask Miss Barnes to play a game of dominoes with me. Would you care to join us?" He definitely did *not* want Emma's family to join them, but he felt that offering was the polite thing to do.

"No, thank you, Gabe. We just came to let Emma know we're going to head home soon." Edward glanced between the two of them, standing arm in arm, and smiled. "I'll let you two say goodbye. Emma, meet us at the wagon when you're done. We're parked just down the street."

"Of course. I'll be there in just a moment," she said sweetly to her uncle.

When her uncle and cousin were out of earshot, she turned and looked earnestly up at him. "I'm glad you won the bid on my basket. I've had a wonderful day." She paused and glanced away as she said, "You know, Esther asked me the other night who I wanted to win. I lied to her and said it didn't matter... but the truth is, I was hoping it would be you."

Gabe's heart soared at her declaration. "I wouldn't want to share a picnic with anyone else," he admitted.

Emma's face pinked. She released his arm and took a small step back. "Goodbye... Gabe," she said softly. Then, with one last shy smile, she turned and walked toward her family's wagon.

As he watched her go, a sense of rightness settled over him. He could see now that Emma was a kind and caring person who didn't complain about her abrupt change in circumstances. And she was doing everything she could to fit into her new life. She was also charming and funny—not to mention the most beautiful woman he had ever seen. She was exactly the type of woman he wanted to marry. But he'd need to move fast if he wanted to do that. According to his friends, she already had men asking her uncle for permission to court her.

Looking around, Gabe spotted Edward speaking with Mr. Decker, and he took a few hurried steps toward the men.

"Edward," he said quietly, "could we speak privately for a moment?"

"Of course," the older man said, and he bid farewell to his companion.

Gabe stepped a few feet away, far enough to be sure no one would overhear, and Edward followed him, eyebrows raised in quiet expectation.

"I was hoping there would be a time this week that I could stop by and speak to you about Emma," he said.

"Ah, I figured this might happen when I heard about the bidding war on Emma's basket," Edward teased. "Come by Monday after dinnertime, and you and I can talk."

Chapter 21

The next morning, Emma woke before Mary, brimming with restless energy despite the little sleep she'd gotten. The cousins had stayed up all night, whispering and reliving every moment of the picnic, sighing over the men they'd spent it with. It still felt like a dream—a wonderful, impossible dream.

Not wanting to wake Mary, she quickly dressed and slipped downstairs to do her chores. When she made it back to the house before anyone else, Aunt Sarah looked surprised but wasted no time putting her to work. "Help me with breakfast, dear?" she asked, already handing her a bowl of eggs. "I'll start on the bacon."

Emma smiled and rolled up her sleeves. The familiar rhythm of the kitchen allowed her mind to wander as she tapped the hard shells against the bowl, and she recalled the moment she saw Gabe striding through the crowd, tall, handsome, and utterly confident. She thought her eyes were playing tricks on her, and she stood spellbound, heart pounding, watching the two men vie for her basket. And when Gabe won, the slow, heart-stopping smile he'd given her was so powerful that it stole the air from her lungs. It was the most romantic thing she had ever experienced.

"Emma, pay attention! You'll miss the bowl!" scolded Aunt Sarah.

"Oh, I am so sorry!" she said, bringing her attention back to the task in front of her.

"You were humming," Sarah pointed out a few minutes later. "Any reason?"

"Was I?" Emma asked, pouring the eggs into a pan on the stove. When her aunt nodded in quiet confirmation, she blushed. "I was just thinking about what happened yesterday. I've never had men fighting over me before."

"Ah. I can see why you are preoccupied then," her aunt said. "That would leave any young woman distracted." She bent to take a pan of biscuits from the oven. "I think everything is about ready. Once those eggs are done, take them to the table, and I'll call everyone to eat."

Knowing that she would get to see Gabe again at services, Emma raced upstairs after breakfast to change and flung open the doors of the wardrobe. She wanted to wear something that highlighted her best features, so she shuffled through her clothes until the perfect dress caught her eye. It was a rich, deep green silk that would beautifully complement the warm auburn tones in her hair like nothing else could. Smiling to herself, she pulled it out, and as she donned layer after layer of petticoats, she imagined what Gabe's reaction would be when he saw her again.

For Emma, the ride into town felt interminably long. It was only three miles, on the same fairly even road they traveled every week, but she was eager to get there. Her foot kept up a steady, impatient rhythm against the sideboard until Aunt Sarah turned with a firm, "Emma, enough of that fidgeting."

"I'm sorry," she murmured, her face flaming with embarrassment at being scolded like Esther or Ruth.

"It's all right, dear," Sarah replied, her tone gentler this time. "We're almost there. Have patience."

That was easier said than done, but Emma stilled her fidgety limbs and sat with a bit of decorum until they pulled into the churchyard a few minutes later. She was even able to wait for Uncle Edward to find a spot to park before she moved to the back of the wagon and hopped down unassisted. She had to pause and make a slight adjustment to her skirt as her indecorous descent caused her petticoat to show, but once everything was settled, she began looking around for Gabe.

"He's over there," Micah said, gesturing toward the church steps as he dismounted his gelding, Midnight—the name reflecting the inky darkness of its coat.

Emma turned to see him striding purposefully toward her, dressed in a crisp black wool sack suit, the dark fabric setting off the black-and-white pinstripes of his silk waistcoat and the subtle gleam of his silver paisley tie. He looked incredible.

"Oh my," she whispered.

She hadn't realized that she'd spoken aloud until she heard her cousin guffaw, and she had an almost overwhelming urge to stick her tongue out at him, as she'd seen his younger sisters do. Instead, she tapped him lightly on the arm and focused her attention on Gabe, who was standing before her now.

"Good morning, Miss Barnes," he said, tipping his hat, a wide grin crossing his handsome features. Then he nodded to her cousin. "Micah."

"Good morning, Mr. Moreau," she replied, giving a small nod. "How are you today?"

"Just fine," he answered with a warm smile. "And might I say, you look very pretty today?"

Emma felt a blush rise from her neck to her cheeks. "Thank you," she said softly. "You look very debonair in your suit."

Micah made a loud sound of disgust. "I'm going to go stand over there before I lose my breakfast," he grumbled, moving a few feet away.

Emma chuckled at her cousin's dramatic exit. "I think we embarrassed him."

"Or perhaps he's jealous of my new suit," Gabe said with a grin. "I walked into Mrs. Tandy's shop for one shirt and came out with this entire outfit, plus more. She must have seen an easy mark."

"She used her wiles on me as well," Emma confided. "I went to purchase fabric to make some dresses I could wear while working on the farm and ended up buying a ready-made one as well."

"That woman is amazing," he said with a slight shake of his head. "She could sell bacon to a pig."

The pun set them both off into a fit of laughter. Emma finally choked out, "She could sell hay to a farmer," and they laughed even harder.

"My! You two sure seem to be getting along," Martha May remarked as she joined them, a satisfied smile on her face.

"Yes," Emma answered breathlessly. "We were just singing the praises of Mrs. Tandy."

"Isn't she fabulous? I think she did an excellent job of making Gabriel here look like a real gentleman," Martha May said, as she gave Gabe a proud, maternal smile.

"Yes, now you can finally acknowledge me in public," he quipped, quickly dodging as his housekeeper tried to smack him with her purse.

"Oh, you rotten man! I've always been proud to be seen with you, and you know it." She rolled her eyes and looked at Emma. "Don't let his words fool you, dear; he is just the type of man you want to be seen with."

Martha May gave her a meaningful look and then tugged at Gabe's arm. "We should collect Henry and go take our seats. We will talk with you after church, dear."

Emma was grateful she managed to make it into the churchyard after services without another invitation to dine with Pastor Langley's grandson. She was sure he was a pleasant fellow, but there was only one man she wished to speak with.

And he was already making a beeline straight toward her, with his housekeeper and a handsome older man in tow.

"Emma dear, may I introduce my husband, Henry Rollings?" Martha May asked when they joined the Barnes family. "Henry, this is Emma."

"Pleased to meet you, Mr. Rollings," Emma replied, studying the handsome older man as they shook hands. Normally, she didn't like the way a man looked with a mustache, but somehow it fit him and improved his good looks.

"Just call me Henry," he said warmly. "Everyone else does. Gabe told me you were as pretty as a picture, and I see now that he didn't do you justice."

She grinned at the compliment and looked to Martha May. "Is he always such a flatterer?"

"Only when he wants something. Usually, it's an extra slice of pie." The older woman laughed while she patted her husband's shoulder fondly.

"Well, if she didn't make such excellent desserts, I wouldn't need to butter her up," Henry said, rubbing his stomach. "Speaking of desserts, Gabe says you might be interested in some cooking and baking lessons from my wife."

Emma nodded eagerly. "I would love to. That is, if it's alright with you, Martha May."

"Of course, dear," Martha May beamed. "I've already told Gabriel I'd be delighted to. Sarah, how should we arrange this?"

"I think I should accompany Emma to the ranch and stay to visit while she has her lessons," Sarah replied. "We could come by once a week. Would Friday work for you? I can make sandwiches for the family to have for dinner while we are away."

"That works fine for me. I'm looking forward to it," Martha May said, and then she turned to her husband. "Let's go get the wagon hitched, Henry. Gabriel can meet us when he is ready."

Emma heard Gabe chuckle as Henry and Martha May walked away. She quirked an eyebrow at him. "What's so amusing?"

"Martha May's not-so-subtle attempt to give us space to talk," he responded with a chuckle. "Look. Your family has all stepped over to the wagon."

She glanced around and realized they were, in fact, standing relatively alone, though still respectably chaperoned by her family a short distance away. "So you think they're all playing matchmaker now?" she asked, a smile tugging at the corner of her mouth.

Gabe grinned as he took a small step closer. "I know for a fact that your cousins are. I may have asked them for a little help finding a way to speak with you privately."

"I see. Well, I'll have to thank 'the trio' when I get home."

"The trio?" he asked, raising a dark eyebrow.

"Micah, Luke, and Joseph," she said with a smile. "That's what I've been calling them in my mind. It gets tiring saying all of their names, one after the other."

"That's fitting. I hope you don't mind if I refer to them that way as well."

Emma grinned. "Use it with my blessing."

"Do you have any other nicknames for your family members that I might claim as my own?" he asked teasingly.

“I do sometimes think of Esther and Ruth as ‘the Twins,’ even though they are a year apart. They are so close that I’m almost jealous,” Emma said. “At least until I hear them bicker.”

“I recall you saying you had a sister who passed away. Did you two never argue?”

“No.” She was touched that he’d remembered her mentioning her sister. “Abbey was younger than me, and I loved to dote on her. When she was a baby, I would carry her around everywhere—it terrified my poor mother.”

“I’ll bet,” Gabe chuckled.

“I was always very careful,” she told him, “but once Abbey got bigger, I had to stop because she was too heavy.”

“She was lucky to have such a caring sister,” he said softly.

“Thank you.” Emma felt her throat tighten with emotion. “She meant the world to me. I suppose that’s why I gravitated toward the orphan’s home. It was a way for me to have that same feeling of connection with the younger children.” When she caught sight of her aunt beckoning her to the wagon, she sighed. “I should be going. My family is waiting for me. Thank you for asking Martha May about the cooking lessons. I’m excited to learn all of her secrets.”

“It was a bit selfish of me,” he admitted, a hint of a smile playing at his lips. “This way I’ll have the chance to see you more often.”

Emma’s heart thrilled at hearing Gabe’s words, and she bid him a reluctant farewell, knowing time would continue to drag until she saw him again.

Chapter 22

Gabe had told himself he was prepared to face Edward, but as he rode up to the farm on Monday afternoon, his stomach was doing flips. What if Emma's uncle refused to let them court? It would be the ultimate irony: he was finally ready to take the next step with her, and her family might want nothing to do with him.

Sighing to himself, he swung down from Xerxes and led him to the stable, tying the reins to the hitching post. He had just finished loosening the cinch strap when he saw Emma's uncle coming from the house.

"Afternoon," he called out, hurrying forward to meet him in the middle of the farmyard. Forcing steadiness into his voice, he asked, "Do you still have time for that talk today?"

"I do," Edward replied with a smile. He extended his hand, and Gabe quickly wiped his sweaty palm on his pants before accepting the handshake.

"Great. Where should we..." His voice trailed off as he glanced around, searching for a good place for such a private discussion.

"Let's go to the barn," Edward suggested, already leading the way across the yard, past the chicken coop and garden. "We've finished our chores in there, so no one will bother us."

The wide double doors stood open, revealing the dim interior and empty milking stalls. Edward pulled one door partway closed behind them and handed Gabe a low wooden stool.

"So," the older man began once they were both seated, "you wanted to talk with me about Emma?"

"Yes, sir."

"Please, it's Edward. We've known each other much too long to get all formal now—especially if my guess as to why you are here is correct," he said as he smiled at Gabe encouragingly.

"Oh. Well then, Edward," Gabe said, drawing a breath. "I've come to you to ask for permission to court Emma. You're her oldest male relative now that her Pa has passed."

The older man studied Gabe for a moment before nodding. "So I thought. Gabe, since the day you stepped foot on the Lucky Strike, I believed you were a good man, like your Uncle Telly was. I just have one question."

He was a little taken aback by this. "Just one?"

"For now." Edwards' mouth quirked up at the corner in a smile. "What I'd really like to know is how you feel about her. I know your first encounter didn't go as anyone expected it to."

"It definitely didn't," Gabe chuckled. "We had a misunderstanding, but Emma and I were able to clear things up during our picnic. I know I've only known her a short time, but I'm coming to admire Emma."

He paused and met Edward's eyes steadily. "She's a kind and caring person. I saw her with Eunice Harper, and her compassion toward someone so often disregarded shamed me. I've lived here for almost a year and never saw Eunice the way Emma did."

No longer able to sit still, he got up and began to pace. "She's smart, utterly polite, and well-mannered, even to those who don't deserve it—and so darn beautiful it's hard not to stare. I feel like I could go on, but you get my point."

"Yes, I believe that sufficiently answers that question," Edward teased. He gave Gabe another assessing look and then stood to hold out his hand. "You have my permission to court Emma if she'll allow it, but between you and me, I do not doubt that she will. I'll talk to her soon, so be expecting an invitation to dinner to follow shortly."

The heavy weight of anxiety lifted from Gabe, and they shook hands firmly. "Thanks. I'll let you get back to your work."

He hurried from the barn, feeling like he was on top of the world, but paused when he saw Micah waiting a few feet away.

"I saw Xerxes," his friend said, tilting his head toward the stable. "How did it go?"

Gabe couldn't stop a wide grin from climbing onto his face as he said, "He gave his permission for me to court Emma."

"Oh, wonderful," Micah grumbled in mock annoyance. "That means I'll be seeing more of your ugly mug around here now."

He gave a nonchalant shrug. "Emma doesn't seem to think I'm ugly."

"There's no accounting for taste, I suppose." Then, more seriously, Micha said, "I'm happy for you, though."

"Thanks. Oh, before I forget. Here's the money you and your brothers lent me." Gabe dug in his pocket and brought out a few bills, which he handed to his friend.

"Lending you that money was the best financial decision I've ever made," Micah chortled as he stuffed it into his pocket. "I can still see the look on Gregory's face when you started bidding. He was so sure he would win."

"I liked seeing him walk away in defeat to a mere rancher," Gabe said. "He may never recover."

That evening at dinner, when Gabe told Henry and Martha May about his visit to Edward, his housekeeper screeched and jumped up from her seat so she could wrap him in a tight hug.

"Oh, I just knew this would happen!" she exclaimed. "Sarah and I..."

Her speech tapered off, and Gabe quirked an eyebrow. "What about you and Sarah?"

Martha May seemed to know that she had accidentally spilled the beans, so she sat back down in her seat, a guilty expression on her face.

"Well, Sarah and I have been arranging things between you and Emma a bit."

"What do you mean?" Gabe asked, narrowing his eyes in suspicion at her.

"When Sarah told me about Emma, we talked about how great it would be if you two met, fell in love, and got married. So we hatched a plan to get you to meet and spend time together. When you said you wouldn't come to the welcoming party, I panicked. I used the excuse of our longstanding friendship with their family to guilt you into being there."

Gabe knew he shouldn't be so shocked by this news, but he couldn't help himself. Martha May was good at getting her own way, but this took the cake. He was about to respond when she cut in anxiously.

"Can't you see? I needed you there to meet Emma before anyone else could catch her eye. It's the reason I asked you to get a new shirt. I thought if Emma saw you looking handsome and fashionable, she would take an interest. I was ecstatic when you told me you went to see Mrs. Tandy because I knew she had talked you into getting a new suit."

"And did you interfere in any other ways?" he inquired, trying to control his temper.

"Yes," she admitted reluctantly. "During the welcoming party, Sarah realized Emma hadn't met you yet, so when we got there she sent me inside and told me to keep her out of the way of the other male guests."

Gabe ran a frustrated hand down his face. "And since the party?"

This question was important to him. His shift in opinion and feelings toward Emma had changed since the party, and he didn't want that to be because someone else was playing puppeteer.

"No!" Martha May practically shouted. "Sarah and I decided that our attempts to bring you together weren't meant to be, so we left you both alone. We still wished for you to come together, of course, but promised we'd let nature take its course."

The amount of relief Gabe felt at Martha May's confession was indescribable. That meant everything that had happened since the party was their own doing. No one was forcing them together. Their mutual attraction and friendship were natural and powerful.

"And you? What was your part in all of this, Henry?" Gabe asked.

"I was clueless until my wife insisted you go to that party. Once I realized why, we talked about things. We both agreed that you needed a helpmeet. You've been so focused on the ranch; we were afraid that you would grow old and lonely out here. I approved of their introducing you and Emma to each other, hoping that you would get along. But I never snuck around or lied to you. I just gave a gentle nudge in Emma's direction."

"Martha May, I don't know whether to thank you for wanting to see me happy or fire you for trying to force things with Emma." Gabe rolled his eyes to the ceiling and then huffed out a breath. "I think I'll just have to forgive you. I know your heart was in the right place."

"Thank you, Gabriel!" Martha May once again sprang up from her seat to smother him with a hug.

"Good. Now let's have our dessert before it gets too late," Henry grumbled.

With the feeling of celebration restored to the house, Martha May served up the raspberry tarts she'd made that afternoon. As they ate, the talk turned to plans for the week, but all Gabe could think of was that Emma would be visiting soon.

"If you don't pay more attention, you are going to hurt yourself again," Miguel stated, bringing Gabe out of his wandering thoughts.

"I know, I know," he sighed.

He and Miguel had been out riding the fence line that morning when they found a section of barbed wire lying on the ground. They'd stopped to repair it, but Gabe kept getting lost in daydreams and had already smashed his finger twice.

"I don't like the look of this," the ranch hand said. "I think someone cut your fence. Maybe another rancher who wants open range?"

"Maybe," Gabe replied. "But Telly put up the fence years ago, so I would think that if someone had a problem, this would have happened a lot sooner. With any luck, this is the only spot. I'll have the hands keep a closer eye on things."

"Hopefully you will too. You're distracted today."

Gabe grinned and rubbed the back of his neck, feeling self-conscious. "I guess so. I didn't realize it was that obvious."

Miguel guffawed and slapped him on the back. "A blind man could tell. This is because of the woman we spoke of, sí? Miss Emma?"

"Yes. I asked Edward if I could court her."

"That's wonderful news!" Miguel's face broke into a broad smile. "Hopefully soon this place will be filled with babies for us to spoil."

Gabe felt heat rise in his face. He turned back to the fence, suddenly flooded with new—and very pleasant—thoughts of Emma.

Chapter 23

On Thursday evening, after supper, Emma was in her room chatting with her cousin when there was a knock on the door. She exchanged a curious look with Mary and hopped up from her spot on the bed. When she opened the bedroom door, she was surprised to see Uncle Edward standing in the hall.

"Emma, may I speak with you privately?" he asked.

"Of course," she said instantly, stepping back to allow him inside.

Mary gave her a stricken look as she left the room, but Emma shrugged to her cousin, shutting the door behind her.

When they were alone, her uncle glanced around the room for a moment before he asked, "Do you mind if I sit on the bed?"

"No, not at all. Is everything all right?"

"Yes, of course," he replied as he perched on the edge of the bed, looking extremely uncomfortable. "It's just that Gabe came to speak to me the other day."

"He did?" she asked, surprised to hear he'd come to the ranch. No one had breathed a word of it to her. "What did he want?"

"Well, he came to ask my permission to court you, since your father isn't able to answer for you himself." Edward let the statement rest as he watched for her reaction.

"Oh," she whispered.

All the excitement that Emma had been feeling when her uncle first revealed Gabe's intentions fled at the mere mention of her father's death. She was no stranger to grief. She'd lived with it most of her life, but she hadn't stopped to think about the full shape of what she was missing.

Her father wasn't here to give his permission for Gabe to court her. He wouldn't walk her down the aisle on her wedding day, nor sit proudly in a church pew with tears in his eyes. He would never cuddle her children close or bounce them on his knee. Every major milestone in her life would carry a permanent hole where he should have been—where her whole family should have been.

With the upheaval of closing out her father's estate, leaving Denver, moving to Elk Ridge, and building a new life for herself on the farm, she had kept her deeper sorrow at bay. She'd even told herself she was handling it well.

But now, suddenly, the dam broke.

Her chest ached, sharp and hollow as the realizations hit her, and before she could stop it, heavy, wracking sobs tore out of her. She pressed her hand to her mouth to muffle the sound, but the tears continued to roll down her cheeks, hot and unstoppable. Years of silent grief were finally coming to a head.

Edward leaned over, concern lining his tanned face, and set a gentle hand on her shoulder. "Emma, dear..."

Unable to speak, she just shook her head as sobs shook her whole body. If he tried to pull her in for a hug now, she was afraid that her tears would never end.

As if sensing her need, he sat next to Emma and let her cry.

When the worst of her tears had eased, Emma wiped her eyes with the back of her wrist, her breath still hitching. "Forgive me," she managed to get out, voice thick. "I thought I was over the worst of it. I didn't expect to hurt like this all over again."

"You don't have to apologize for missing him," her uncle said kindly. "I miss him too."

"You do?" She asked, drawing a shaky breath.

"Very much. We were as close as brothers once."

"What happened?"

"Life," he said, shrugging his broad shoulders. "After his parents died, he traveled by steamboat down to Missouri, loaded up a wagon with all the supplies he could carry, and set off for Colorado. I stayed in Wisconsin to work on the farm. He was drafted into the war, but as the only son of a widow who depended on me for her means, I was exempt."

He looked down at his hands, his voice quieter now. "Things like that created a distance between us. We stayed in touch as much as we could through letters, but those became less and less frequent once your mother and sister passed away. I think it was hard for him to hear about my growing family after he'd lost so much of his."

"He still carried you in his heart," Emma said, her eyes still damp. "He was deliberate in his choice of my caretaker; of that, I'm sure."

Now it was her uncle who had tears in his eyes, and his voice cracked as he softly said, "Thank you."

For a while, they both sat in quiet reflection, each coming to grips with their own heartache until she looked up at him, eyes red but steady. "Gabe... he really asked for your permission?"

"He did," Edward nodded. "He's a good man, and although things didn't start as either of you would have liked, he seems to be very taken with you. From what I've observed so far, you get along well together. You make each other laugh. That's a valuable element in any relationship." Then, with a lopsided smile, he said, "I gave him my blessing."

Emma's breath caught. She stared at him, tears welling anew, but this time from gratitude. "Oh, Uncle Edward... thank you," she whispered, and she threw herself against him, hugging him as fiercely as she could.

"You're welcome," he laughed, patting her fondly on the back before gently disengaging himself from her hug and standing. "I told Gabe to expect a dinner invitation soon. Perhaps tomorrow, on the way to his ranch, you and Sarah can make plans."

"That's a splendid idea," Emma said, grateful for the gentle way her uncle had steered the conversation to something hopeful. "She'll have all sorts of suggestions."

"I have no doubt," Edward laughed. "Goodnight." He was about to leave the room when he paused and turned back to her. "Thank you," he said.

She looked at him in confusion. "What for?"

"For letting me practice this discussion. I'm sure before too long, I'll be having it with Mary, and eventually her sisters."

Feeling pleased by his comment, Emma smiled. "I'm glad to be of help."

Her uncle gave her one last warm look before he left, but she wasn't alone for long. Mary came bursting into the room not even a minute later, out of breath, her eyes wide with curiosity.

"What did Pa want?" she gaped between breaths. "Are you in trouble?"

Emma looked up, her eyes still a bit swollen from crying, and felt a grin climb her cheeks. "No," she said, as joy broke through the last remnants of sorrow. "He told me that Gabe came by and asked for permission to court me."

"Oh, my word! Emma, this is so exciting!" Mary cried as she grasped Emma's hands.

"I know. Oh, Mary, I'm so happy. I truly didn't think that this would happen after our first meeting."

Even as they lay in bed that night, their enthusiasm was still humming as the cousins talked about Gabe and what things they might do as a courting couple. Emma's vote was, of course, for more romantic picnics.

As Emma and Aunt Sarah were riding over to The Lucky Strike the next day, they made plans to have Gabe over for Sunday dinner.

"We should wait to discuss what to make for the meal until we talk to Martha May," her aunt said.

"I agree. Then we can ask Martha May what his favorite foods are."

"He's a man, Emma. Any food that you make will be his favorite as long as he doesn't have to cook it."

"Yes, but I wouldn't want to serve fish if he disliked it."

When they finally approached the ranch, she saw a large stable and corral, where several horses were grazing lazily. Just beyond that, she could make out a large barn, as well as a long, narrow cabin set across from a beautiful two-story clapboard house. Its navy-blue shutters were a lovely contrast to the white siding. And the porch, with its railings also painted white, wrapped around the home with meticulously kept flower beds.

Emma adored Gabe's home, especially all the large windows, which would let in so much light. It was bigger than her aunt and uncle's place, which surprised her. His uncle, Telly, had been a single man with no children, and she wondered why he'd bothered to make it so large. She wanted to ask her aunt about it, but Gabe came hurrying out of the stable as they parked the wagon. He had a dazzling smile on his handsome face, and all her other thoughts disappeared.

Somehow, he looked even more attractive in a simple gray shirt, worn leather vest, and dusty blue denim trousers tucked into his boots—gun belt slung low around his hips—than he ever had in his Sunday suit. Here, on his own land, he seemed more at ease. More himself.

"Welcome! It's so good to see you," he said to both ladies, though his eyes were locked firmly on Emma.

"Thank you, Gabe. It's good to see you, too," she replied, enjoying the wide grin that spread on his handsome face when she'd called him by his first name.

"Here, let me help you down." He stepped forward and offered his hand so they could climb down safely from the high bench. "Martha May is all ready for you." Glancing at Emma, he said, "She has been anticipating your visit all week."

"Not as much as you have, I'm sure," Sarah mumbled teasingly under her breath as she strode toward the house, sewing basket swinging in her hand.

Gabe and Emma shared a smile when they heard her low words.

"She isn't wrong," he said, his voice warm. "I've been looking forward to seeing you all week. Did your uncle-"

"Gabriel!" Martha May's voice sounded from the front porch and interrupted his question. "Don't monopolize that girl. I've been waiting all morning to impart my considerable wisdom to Emma, and here you are mooning over her like a lovesick calf."

Gabe laughed easily. "I'm sorry, Martha May. Next time, I'll let you do your imparting first."

"Put that wagon away and go bother Henry until dinner is ready," his housekeeper scolded with a teasing scowl. Then she turned to Emma with a bright smile. "Come on into the house, dear. Sarah's pouring the coffee. We'll have a drink while we chat."

After saying goodbye to Gabe, she followed Martha May into the house, taking in every detail as they walked to the front parlor. It was tastefully decorated with sage-green floral wallpaper, and a three-piece silk tapestry-upholstered sofa set was arranged around the fireplace, made of huge, rounded rocks. Large bookcases flanked the fireplace on either side.

"This is a beautiful room," she said admiringly as she joined her aunt at the end of the sofa. "Who decorated it? Surely not Telly?"

Martha May laughed heartily. "Heaven's no! Telly had his house built at the same time ours was, and he asked me to decorate for him. He told me to spare no expense, so I picked what I liked."

"Well, you did a wonderful job. It feels quite comfortable in here," Emma complimented as she took a sip of coffee from the cup her aunt handed her.

"It makes me so pleased to hear you say that, dear. My own home is decorated similarly." Martha May said as she took her own seat. "Now, let's get down to business. Sarah tells me you want to invite Gabriel over for dinner and serve him his favorite food."

"Yes, we thought Sunday might work best. You and Henry are also invited to join if you'd like."

"As much as I appreciate the offer, I think I might like a romantic dinner of my own," Martha May tittered.

"Of course." Emma took another sip of her coffee to hide her amusement at the girlish laughter coming from the older woman. "Do you have any recommendations for a menu?"

"I think you would do well serving a roast, as he favors beef over chicken," Martha May said with perfect confidence. "To go with that, you can make bread rolls and mashed potatoes. Gabe always loads his plate with mashed potatoes and gravy. Maybe even add a simple cabbage salad too if you have a decent one in the garden."

"I think we can make that work," Sarah agreed.

"Good, now that we've dealt with that, let's get down to your lessons. Sarah has filled me in on the things she's taught you so far, and she says you're coming along well. I think we should do a bit of baking today. How do peach tarts sound?"

"Wonderful!" Emma's mouth was already watering at the thought. "I love peaches."

"Marvelous! I'm making chicken salad for dinner since it is so hot," Martha May said as she got up and bustled out of the room. "No one wants to eat soup on a day like this! I keep telling Gabriel he needs to build a summer kitchen."

As she followed the housekeeper through the house, she noticed that it wasn't just the parlor that had benefited from the older woman's touch. With pale yellow walls and a cream and gold wallpaper border, the kitchen felt bright and cozy. Six matching chairs sat around a large table in the center of the room, and there was still plenty of space to maneuver around it without being crowded.

As Emma scanned the space, she saw the same familiar sights: long wooden counters, pots and pans hanging from hooks on the wall, and a cookstove. She stepped forward to inspect it and saw that it was the same model they had on the farm. She recalled her aunt mentioning that her friend had ordered the same one, and she let out a small sigh. It was a relief to know that she wouldn't have to learn the workings of a new stove.

When Martha May stopped beside a hardwood cabinet placed under a window, which gave a beautiful view of forested mountains in the distance, she called Emma over. In front of them was a small sack of flour, butter, a cup of water, and a rolling pin. "I have all the ingredients set out," she said. "You already know how to make pie crust, and puff paste isn't much harder. The difficult part will be keeping Gabriel and Henry from snatching some before they are cooled."

"Maybe we can lock them out of the house until we are done baking," Emma suggested, which made both older women laugh.

"I may just do that at home," her aunt mused from her spot at the table. She planned on doing some mending while Emma had her lesson, and she'd pulled out her needle and thread. "The children are always running into the house to sneak treats."

"Well, we won't have any treats for Gabriel to sneak if we don't start working." Martha May declared, dusting a bit of flour onto the work surface. Then she guided Emma through the long, patient work of rolling the butter-layered dough, folding it neatly, and rolling it out again. They repeated the process three more times, with rests in the icebox between each turn so the butter stayed cold and the layers stayed crisp.

They used the tin cutter to shape the dough into perfect circles, and while the tarts were baking, they sat at the kitchen table with Sarah and chatted as they pulled the meat from two boiled chickens into a bowl for their cold salad. Emma's arms still throbbed faintly from the earlier pastry work, but she worked determinedly to whisk the oil and eggs into a creamy dressing, finishing it just in time to pull the dessert out of the oven as Gabe and Henry came stomping in the door.

"Well, hello there, Emma!" Henry greeted her cheerfully. He gave his wife a peck on the cheek and acknowledged Sarah as well.

"Hello, Henry. How are you today?"

"I'm doing fine, but I'll be better once I can get a taste of those tarts," he replied, and pointed to the pastries, which were cooling on the counter after being released from their pans.

"Oh no, you don't!" Martha May scolded her husband. "Go wash your hands!"

Henry gave a dramatic sigh and trudged to the sink while Gabe came to stand near Emma.

"Have you been enjoying yourself?" he asked.

"Very much. I'm so grateful you thought of asking Martha May to teach me."

"And I'm grateful for peach tarts," Henry said as he finished drying his hands. "I'd try one now, but my wife makes me eat all my food before I get dessert. She's a hard woman, Emma, but I still love her."

Martha May swatted playfully at his shoulder as he took up a spot at the table, a soft look in her eye. "I'm just trying to keep you from wasting away. Imagine how thin you would be if you did all of that backbreaking work on the ranch without a full belly."

Emma smiled at their silly banter and sat at the table. Gabe slipped into the seat next to her, and Henry gave the blessing over the food.

Like Uncle Edward, Henry seemed to favor a brief prayer, and as they ate, Emma watched Gabe to make sure he was enjoying the food she'd helped prepare. She hadn't realized she was staring until Sarah tapped her foot under the table. Emma felt her face go beet-red, and she made a concerted effort not to look at him unless he was speaking to her for the rest of the meal.

When it was time for dessert, she brought the plate of tarts to the table, but before she could set the dish down, Henry and Gabe reached for one. Their sounds of delight as they took their first bite made Emma swell with pride. She placed another one on their plates, and in no time at all, the tarts were gone. The men patted their slightly distended stomachs and declared that they couldn't eat another bite.

Martha May scoffed in disbelief, "Give it an hour, and you'll be back in my kitchen asking when supper is."

Emma agreed. She had seen how much her cousins could eat, and knew that if there had been more dessert, the men could have found room to eat more.

With the midday meal done, Henry and Gabe had no excuse not to return to work, and they gathered their hats and work gloves that they'd discarded upon entering the kitchen.

Emma picked up a plate, intending to take it to the sink, but Sarah took it gently from her hands and nodded toward the back door.

"Why don't you go say your farewells?" she said. "Martha May and I will finish up in here and meet you at the wagon in just a few minutes."

Emma hesitated, feeling guilty for skipping out on the cleanup, but her aunt shooed her out the door and into the bright afternoon sunlight. It took a moment for her eyes to adjust to the sudden glare, and once her vision cleared, she saw Gabe and Henry talking just a few feet away. As she descended the porch steps, Henry looked up, said a few quiet words to Gabe, and tipped his hat in farewell to her before striding off toward the barn.

"Uncle Edward told me you came to speak with him the other day," she said to Gabe once they were alone.

"I assume he told you what we discussed?"

"He did," she answered with a smile. "Would you like to call at the house for Sunday dinner?"

Gabe took a step closer to her, his handsome face alight with happiness as he said, "I wouldn't miss it."

Chapter 24

Though dark clouds had blanketed the sky and rain had fallen in heavy sheets on Sunday morning, by the time Gabe stepped out of the church, golden rays of sunlight were breaking through the clouds as they drifted away into the distance.

He was glad he wouldn't have to rush off to avoid the downpour. He wanted to see Emma. Her family had arrived late to services, and with the entire congregation packed tightly in the pews to avoid the rain before the sermon had started, they hadn't had an opportunity to talk yet.

It didn't take him long to spot where the Barnes family had congregated and began picking his way over. He had to be careful, as the ground was still quite slick and muddy, but he made it to them without incident.

"Afternoon, Gabe," Edward said, shaking his hand firmly. "Quite the little storm we had this morning, wasn't it?"

"The ground sure needed it, though," Gabe replied. "It's been too dry."

He exchanged pleasantries with Emma and her family for a few minutes before they subtly moved away, giving the new couple space to speak privately.

"I'm glad the sun came out," he said. "I was afraid I'd show up to dinner tonight soaking wet."

"Oh! I can't even imagine how uncomfortable that would be," Emma chuckled. "But I made roast beef for dinner, so at least you would have been consoled by that. Martha May told me you enjoy it."

"She's right. It's one of my favorites."

"Then let's hope it tastes as good as it sounds. She gave Aunt Sarah her recipe before we left the ranch, so I have a lot to live up to."

"I have no doubt it will taste just as good as Martha May's," Gabe told her, wanting to bolster her confidence. "She's already preparing for your lesson next week. She was impressed with how far you've come since you came to Elk Ridge."

Emma let out a light, tinkling laugh. "Well, when you start from nothing, even the smallest bit of progress looks impressive."

Her modest deflection made Gabe realize they weren't so different after all. Both of them had come to Montana as fish out of water—she learning how to live on the frontier and he learning how to raise cattle and run a ranch. The thought endeared her to him even more.

"It is gratifying to hear she feels that way, though," she said, pulling his thoughts back to their conversation. "It was different learning from Martha May."

"What do you mean?"

"She stayed with me the whole time and walked me through every little thing, slow and patient, like she's got all the time in the world. Aunt Sarah shows me how to do it once and steps back—expecting me to manage on my own. I appreciate both styles of teaching."

"Are we talking about the same woman?" he asked, eyebrows shooting up.

"Of course. Perhaps I see another side to her, woman to woman," she said with a delicate shrug.

"I reckon so," Gabe said. "She's always been hard on me, but maybe that's just how she shows she cares."

The conversation drifted on to other topics, and eventually they were joined by Micah.

"Emma, it's time to go," he said. "The wagon's all hitched up."

She nodded and turned to Gabe with a nervous smile. "I'll see you soon, I suppose."

"I'll say my goodbyes to Henry and Martha May and be right over," he assured her.

Once Emma had walked away, Micah motioned for Gabe to follow him. "I've got something for you," he said. "It's in my saddlebags."

"I don't know," Gabe said as he followed his friend, his eyes narrowed in suspicion. "The last time one of you Barnes brothers told me he had something for me in his saddlebags, it was part of a trick."

Micah looked back at him with a grin as they arrived at the hitching post. "No tricks this time." He flipped open the leather bag on Midnight's saddle and pulled out a sealed envelope, holding it out.

"You have something to say to me you can't say out loud?" Gabe asked, half-smiling as he took the proffered item and looked at it curiously.

"It's not from me, you dolt. It's from Emma. She asked me to pass it along to you, and Pa said it was fine."

Heart skipping a beat, he tucked it into the breast pocket of his coat. "Did she say anything else?"

"Nope." Micah swung up into his saddle, raised his hand in a two-finger salute, and said, "Don't take too long," before riding off.

With the admonition ringing in his ears, Gabe immediately set off in search of Henry and Martha May, feeling the note burn a hole in his pocket. He'd never had a woman give him something like this before, and he was eager to read it, but he couldn't do that here. There were too many prying eyes.

Henry was nowhere to be seen, but he found Martha May speaking to the pastor's wife. Gabe talked to the women politely for a few minutes before he pulled his housekeeper to the side to tell her he was heading to the farm for dinner.

"Have a good time, Gabriel," Martha May said as she smoothed the lapel of his jacket. "Emma is a lucky woman to have such a handsome man like you come calling."

He hesitated for a second before he said, "I'm feeling more nervous than I thought I would now that it's time for me to leave. Any last-minute advice?"

"Make sure to compliment her on the food. She's put a lot of thought and effort into making this meal, and don't forget to use your table manners." She patted his chest softly in a maternal gesture. "You'll be just fine."

"Thank you." He leaned down to kiss her cheek, which made her blush. "Say goodbye to Henry for me."

After leaving Martha May, Gabe collected his horse and set out towards the farm. There were still a lot of folks lingering in town and on the road leading in, but once he'd made it a mile out, he finally had some privacy to read the letter. With shaking hands, he broke the seal and pulled out the single page filled with a neat feminine script.

Dear Gabe,

My etiquette teacher would undoubtedly reprimand me for not addressing you as "My Dear Mr. Moreau," but as this is private correspondence, I feel safe enough to do so.

This morning, Matthew brought a frog into the kitchen, and the slimy thing jumped right into a bowl of flour I was holding. I was entirely covered in it, and so was the poor frog. Matthew, of course, thought this was the peak of hilarity until I told him I saw a recipe for fried frog legs in the cookbook I've been reading. Needless to say, he grabbed his amphibious friend and fled, while I was left to clean up the mess—myself included.

Gabe stopped reading and let out a loud belly laugh. The image of Emma covered in a dusting of flour while she threatened her youngest cousin was too much.

And if that wasn't bad enough, I somehow mangled crocheting my project so badly that I had to start all over. It was a bit humiliating, as the rest of the women in my family make it look so easy. I assure you I am much more accomplished at embroidery.

As I sit here writing this letter, I can hear Esther and Ruth squabbling over who gets to wear a dress they both favor tomorrow. I'm not envious of Aunt Sarah, as she is trying to mediate between the two. Just know that if you saw Esther at church in a green dress, she has won her prize.

Until Sunday dinner,

Yours sincerely,

Emma

Carefully folding the paper, he put the letter back into his pocket, smiling. He hadn't paid attention to what her cousins were wearing, but he would now.

Gabe's heart was pounding as he walked across the farmyard and knocked on the front door of Edward and Sarah's home. He thought he'd gotten all his nerves out on the ride over, but he was mistaken. There was a brief silence as he stood waiting on the porch, and then he heard a muffled shout through the door.

"I'll answer it!" came Matthew's eager voice.

"How come he gets to answer the door?" complained a young woman, whom Gabe thought was Ruth.

"She's right. Shouldn't Emma open the door?" agreed someone else.

"Well, someone should answer it; otherwise, Gabe's likely to starve out there on the porch," the quip unmistakably coming from Joseph.

There was a slight scuffling noise and an angry shout of protest before the front door swung open, revealing a disheveled Matthew, with his older sister Esther scowling down at him from behind.

"Afternoon, Gabe! Come on in," the young boy said, completely ignoring his sister's displeasure.

"Good afternoon, Matthew, Esther," Gabe said as he stepped inside through the tight gap they had left him.

"You were supposed to wait for Emma," Esther said, stamping her foot.

"But she's still busy in the kitchen. It's rude to make a guest wait, isn't it, Pa?" Matthew asked, looking appealingly at his father, who had just entered the parlor.

Edward looked slightly confused, but he said, "That's right, son." He stepped forward and shook Gabe's hand. "It's good to see you again. Dinner is just about ready. Why don't you have a seat while we wait?"

Gabe lowered himself onto the upholstered sofa and glanced around at all the eager faces. Not everyone in the family was present, but he realized they all knew he was courting Emma now. A heavy sense of expectation filled the room, as if they were waiting for him to make the first move.

Feeling more awkward than he ever had before, he said, "Dinner sure smells good."

"It does," Edward agreed, his lips twitching at the corners while Esther and Ruth giggled behind their hands. "Sarah and Emma have been hard at work. What are Henry and Martha May doing this evening?"

"They are having dinner together at their house tonight," Gabe said, relieved at having an easy topic of conversation to follow. "It doesn't happen often, so I'm glad they are getting the chance."

"Good for them. Henry tells me you are going to purchase some sheep. I bet he wasn't too pleased about that."

Gabe laughed. "He wasn't, but I explained my plans to him, and he's come around. I'm hoping this venture pays off, but if not, then I guess we can always have a big community dinner and serve lamb."

"Can I come pet your sheep?" asked Matthew, his interest piqued.

"Sure, once they arrive," Gabe agreed. "But only if you get all your work done at home and your Pa allows it."

They kept a polite conversation about the ranch and his plans for the sheep until Emma finally stepped into the room. She was patting her hair into place, apparently making sure she was presentable, but to Gabe, she looked perfect. She was still wearing the same wine-red dress with gold trim from church, and it made the rich auburn in her hair shine like polished copper in the soft lamplight. He popped up off the sofa and hastened to meet her.

"Hello, Gabe," she said warmly. "I'm so sorry I wasn't able to greet you at the door. The rolls took a little longer to bake than I had planned."

"It's all right. We were just jawing about work."

"Well, if you're all done, dinner is about to be served," she announced to those in the room. Then, in a graceful, practiced gesture, she pointed down the hall. "This way."

Not needing to be asked twice, Gabe followed her into the dining room. A matching set of china dinnerware was already arranged on a delicate floral tablecloth. The cloth napkins at each place setting stood tall and elegant, shaped like pointed crowns. Gabe imagined this was how her dinner table had looked every night in Denver, and he smiled. He liked having this small peek into her past life.

As the family filed in, Emma pointed to the chair near the middle of the table. "Why don't you take a seat? I still have to help Aunt Sarah bring the dishes out."

"Would you like some help?" he asked.

“That’s kind of you to offer,” she demurred, “but you’re our guest. Make yourself comfortable. I’ll be back shortly.”

Emma hurried away toward the kitchen, and Gabe took the seat she had indicated. Esther and Ruth sat together on the opposite side of the table, whispering and giggling as they glanced over at him.

When Micah took the seat to his left, he leaned in closer to his friend and, in a low voice, asked, “Do those two ever stop giggling?”

“Sometimes, but when they do, it’s arguing or whining,” Micah replied quietly. “It’s the curse of having sisters. Be glad you don’t have any.”

Gabe had always thought it would be nice to have siblings, but he was rethinking that now. The girls kept sneaking looks at him and laughing, and it was starting to make him uncomfortable. He couldn’t fathom what they found so hilarious.

He was saved from their scrutiny when Emma arrived with a steaming pot of roast beef. She set it in the center of the table, and he sniffed the air in appreciation as he stood to hold a chair out for her. “That looks delicious,” he said, craning his neck to see into the pot.

“Thank you,” she said, a soft flush coloring her cheeks at his compliment.

Once she was settled in her chair, Gabe took his own seat. Their arms brushed together accidentally, sending a rush of warmth through him. One glance at Emma told him she felt it too, as the flush on her cheeks deepened noticeably.

“Matthew! No eating until after the blessing,” admonished Sarah, as she trained a quelling look at her youngest son.

“Sorry, Ma,” the boy muttered as he pulled his hand back from the bread bowl.

“Edward,” she sighed. “Would you please say grace? Our children are apparently too hungry to remember their manners.”

“Of course, dearest,” Edward replied, immediately bowing his head and giving a quick blessing.

As dishes were passed up and down the table, Gabe filled his plate and tasted his first bite. It was heavenly. The tender beef was full of flavor, and he could taste the butter in the mashed potatoes. They were a bit lumpy, but he didn’t mind. Emma had done a good job of following Martha May’s recipe, and he used the clamor in the dining room to cover his words as he whispered, “I was right. This *is* delicious.”

"Thank you. I'm glad you like it. I also made more peach tarts for dessert since you seemed to like them so much."

"You are going to spoil me. I'll be as big as a house one day."

"I think if Henry can stay trim with Martha May's cooking, you will be just fine with mine," she said with a smile.

After a moment, he nodded across the table at her cousin, who was indeed wearing a dark green dress. "I see Esther prevailed."

Emma brought her hand up to stifle her laughter. "She did. It took over an hour, but she finally wore my aunt down."

"Poor Sarah," he chuckled sympathetically.

"She handles it well, but then again, she's had a lot of practice."

Not wanting to risk offending her family by carrying on a secret conversation in the midst of a meal, Gabe joined the talk around the table while he ate. It revolved mostly around benign topics: weather, cattle prices, and crop management. It was safe and familiar, and he appreciated that. Then, after dinner, Emma brought out the tarts, which were just as good as her first batch and gone just as fast.

Feeling pleasantly full, Gabe leaned back in his chair and rested a hand on his stomach. "That was a fine meal. Emma, would you care to take a short walk with me?"

She looked to her uncle, who gave her his nod of approval, and then back at Gabe. "I'd love to."

It took her less than a minute to collect her wrap, and they stepped out into the late afternoon sunshine side by side. They had made it all the way down the porch steps when a door slammed behind them. They turned to see Sarah settling into a chair on the back porch, her mending basket resting in her lap.

"I wondered who would come to play chaperone," Emma murmured.

Gabe grinned. "It could be worse; they might have sent one of the trio. We should count our blessings."

She chuckled at his answer, and he turned his steps toward the milking barn, making sure that they would stay in sight.

"I enjoyed reading your letter," he said, breaking the comfortable silence that had settled around them as they walked.

“I’m glad,” she replied, beaming a smile at him, her blue eyes sparkling. She looked so beautiful that he felt his heart speed up. “I wish I didn’t have quite so many incidents to write about. I’m still not sure I’ve gotten all the flour out of my hair.”

“Hmm,” he said speculatively as he stepped closer to her, pretending to examine her perfectly styled hair for flour remnants. “Looks as if you’ve done a good job. Hopefully, Matthew learned his lesson about bringing frogs inside the house.” He took a step back to keep their distance respectful and kept walking.

“He might not bring frogs in again,” Emma said, her voice resigned, “but he was sneaking one of the kittens from the barn into his room this morning.”

Gabe smiled as he imagined how Sarah would react once she discovered a barn cat lurking in her home. He feared Matthew was destined to find out sooner rather than later. They strolled contentedly through the yard for another half hour until a raised feminine voice could be heard from the house.

“I think your aunt is calling you,” he said as he stopped to listen when the voice came again.

“I suppose that means we should turn back,” she sighed, “but I’ve had such a pleasant time, and I’m dreading its end.”

“So am I,” he admitted, “but we’ll see each other on Friday.” He felt as if his heart were about to beat out of his chest, wondering if she was having the same growing feelings he was.

“I know. I’ll miss talking to you though,” she said shyly, looking down as she walked. “Our conversations seem to flow so naturally for two people who haven’t known each other long. It’s why I wrote you the letter.”

Gabe smiled, pleased that her feelings reflected his own. “Then I reckon I’ll just have to write one to you.”

They said their farewells once they reached the house, and as he watched her disappear inside, he realized Friday couldn’t come soon enough.

Chapter 25

To Emma, it felt like an eternity had passed before Friday arrived. She was grateful for the chores around the farm to keep her occupied. She might have gone crazy otherwise. Aunt Sarah must have been relieved as well, because as soon as the breakfast dishes were done, she wasted no time in grabbing her sewing basket and heading to the wagon.

When they arrived at the ranch, Gabe was waiting for them on the porch, looking ruggedly handsome in his brown canvas trousers and green chambray work shirt, its top button undone. He was beaming as he greeted both women, his hazel eyes almost glowing in the afternoon sunshine as he helped them down from the wagon.

When they were both safely on the ground, her aunt made a beeline for the house, but Emma stayed where she was, wanting a few more moments alone with Gabe.

"I see you made it through the week," he teased, a grin spreading across his face.

"I did," she agreed, "though just barely."

At that, he let out a deep laugh. "If I'm honest, I didn't do much better. I didn't sleep a wink last night. Martha May said I have bags under my eyes."

Emma stepped closer, studying his face. Aside from the faintest hint of stubble along his chiseled jawline, he looked perfectly fine. In fact, he looked rather perfect. Her heart fluttered wildly in her chest.

"I think they're here for you," he said, taking a step back from their close positioning, just as the night before when he'd come closer to look at her hair.

"Who?" she asked, pleased that her voice sounded normal and not as breathless as she felt.

"Sarah and Martha May," he said, pointing to the two women on the porch. "They just came out to collect you."

She turned, and lo-and-behold, she saw the two women standing on the porch, beckoning to her. "Emma dear, we are ready for you now," Martha May called.

"Coming!" she said, and then after a quick goodbye to Gabe, she headed toward the house. As she climbed the porch steps, she caught the look of satisfaction on the older women's faces.

"What's got you two in such a good mood?" Emma asked.

"We're just happy that you and Gabriel are getting along so well," Martha May said warmly. "He has been much happier lately."

Emma felt a rush of quiet pleasure at the idea that she was bringing him happiness. To hear such an observation from someone who knew him so well was deeply meaningful. Gabe was such a gentleman, and his careful attention to her reputation—even here in the privacy of his own ranch—only endeared him to her more.

"I'm glad to hear that, Martha May. What do you have planned for us to make today?"

"I was thinking you could look through some of my cookbooks and choose for yourself," Martha May replied. "It's one thing to plan a menu for others to follow. It's quite another when you're the one doing the work." She gave Emma a conspiratorial wink. "Part of being a wife is planning meals for your family. This can be good practice. Come, I have them all laid out for you."

Emma felt a flutter of nervous excitement at the thought, and she did her best to hide it as she followed Martha May inside. If she weren't careful, she'd be just as bad as Esther and Ruth!

On the long kitchen table, several worn, bound books and thin paper-covered pamphlets were laid out. Some of them looked quite old based on their publication dates. Emma gingerly picked up the one closest to her and began leafing through it, while Sarah and Martha May sipped their coffee and chatted quietly nearby.

By the time she had gone through half the stack, Emma was ready to call it quits. There were so many recipes to choose from, and even those with the same name often had different ingredients and preparation methods. It felt as though she had been given an impossible task. She was about to ask for help when she remembered Martha May's comment from the week before about not wanting to eat soup on a hot day. She began searching for recipes that required little to no use of the oven.

A half-hour later, she set the cookbook down with its pages still open and looked up with a smile. "I decided what I should make."

"That was quick! Tell me what we'll be serving the menfolk today," Martha May said.

"Sandwiches. Chopped ham and egg," Emma told her. "Then, for dessert, I can make rice custard. It's hot out, and this way, all I have to use the stove for is boiling the eggs and making the custard—if we have all the ingredients, that is."

"That is an excellent idea!" Martha May said, beaming with pride. "I've got some ham in the icebox. It should be plenty filling for Gabriel and Henry, and the house won't be stifling for hours afterwards."

"Good. I'll get started." Emma hopped up from her seat and got to work collecting the ingredients she would need. Because of its simplicity, dinner was prepared quickly, and Martha May gave her a paper and a pencil so she could continue to look through the cookbooks and write down any recipes that she'd like to try in the future. She had filled most of the page when Gabe and Henry came into the kitchen.

"Is it time to chow down?" Henry asked as he headed to the sink.

"Yes, everything's ready. Let me make you a plate," Emma offered.

While the men were washing up, she placed two sandwiches of each kind on their plates. She served more modest portions to the women, and after the blessing, they dug into the food. Emma was gratified to see Gabe and Henry enjoying their meal, especially when they each asked for second helpings.

"I have a rice custard for dessert if you are ready," she informed the men when they pushed their finished plates away.

"I think having two desserts in one day might be one of my favorite things about Fridays now," said Henry jovially.

"It's not like you're being deprived the rest of the week, dear," Martha May pointed out.

"That's true, but now I look forward to Friday as much as Gabe does."

Henry sent him a knowing smirk, and Emma could see Gabe's neck turn red as she served out bowls of custard.

"If he didn't look forward to seeing the woman he was courting, I would have to question his reasoning." Martha May shot back at her husband.

Emma couldn't agree more. In fact, she wished someone had said those words to her when she was being courted by Michael. It would have saved her a great deal of heartache. She was glad she didn't carry those worries now. Knowing that Gabe missed her and wanted to be with her had healed parts of her spirit she hadn't even realized were broken.

When supper that night was over, Emma excused herself to her room instead of staying in the parlor with her family. Aunt Sarah—and Martha May—had agreed to pass on a letter from Gabe, which she'd received on the ride home from the Lucky Strike, and she'd been looking forward to reading it all evening.

Once she was alone in her room, Emma lay back against the headboard, unfolded the paper, and read.

Dear Emma,

I've never written to a woman before, so I hope I'm doing it correctly. My letter won't be as humorous as yours because the things the ranch hands have said and done aren't for a lady's ears—or eyes, in this case.

This week at the ranch has been busy. We're preparing to build several sheds for a small herd of sheep that I am planning to purchase soon. Henry is still skeptical about having them on the ranch, but I think it will work out.

I spent last night out on the range with a few of my hands because we spotted some wolf tracks. We didn't see any animals, but we'll keep checking back every few days. Hopefully, all the cattle will stay safe because I'd hate for one of them to be hurt.

We also have a new colt that I'm eager to work with. His mother is a great cutting horse, and I'm hoping he will be too. I can already see that he likes to run fast.

I'll close this letter and hope you found at least some of it interesting. Maybe you can write back and tell me if there is anything you want to learn about the ranch.

Yours,

Gabe

Emma folded the letter and clutched it to her chest. She loved that he took the time to write to her. His daily life on the ranch differed from hers on the farm, but she could imagine herself there, waiting in the parlor for him to come home in the evenings. She fell asleep that night still clothed, clutching Gabe's letter and dreaming of her future.

On Sunday, after Pastor Langley had released the congregation, the Barnes family broke into smaller groups as friends and neighbors came to catch up. Emma was talking with her cousin Micah while she waited for Gabe to be done with his conversation with Cyrus, the livery owner and blacksmith, when a familiar voice interrupted them.

"Good day, Emma."

She turned around to see Gregory Callaway, smiling brightly at her. She was surprised to see him. He'd made himself scarce after the box social, and she'd assumed he'd given up in his pursuit of her.

"Oh, hello, Mr. Callaway," she replied politely. "How are you today?"

"Much better now that I am in your presence," he crooned. "I was sorry to have lost out on your basket at the box social. I was very much looking forward to spending an afternoon getting to know you."

"That's so kind of you to say. Were you able to enjoy the other festivities that day?"

"No," he said with a frown. "I, ah, went home to care for my aunt. She has a delicate constitution, you know, and as her only living relative, it's my duty to care for her. I've even taken to picking up her shopping for her, the poor dear."

After a moment's pause, he gave her a broad smile. "Perhaps I might speak to your uncle and get his permission for us to have a picnic sometime soon."

Micah, who had been standing quietly beside her, stepped forward. "That won't be necessary, Callaway. Emma is already being courted by Gabe Moreau, and we're all quite happy with the arrangement."

"Truly?" Gregory cried out, looking aghast as his gaze darted between Emma and Micah.

"Yes, it's true," she said, keeping her tone polite but firm. "I do appreciate your kind sentiments, though, and wish you luck in your search for a picnicking partner."

Emma hadn't noticed Gabe approach, but she felt his solid presence at her elbow. Just knowing he was there, quietly protective, brought her a surprising sense of comfort amid this awkward situation.

"I see," Gregory said coldly, brushing imaginary lint from his sleeve. "I didn't realize you preferred the rustic type. Good day."

Gabe and Micah both made sounds of protest and moved forward as Gregory stalked off in a huff, but Emma stopped them.

"It's fine," she said firmly. "Just let him go. His pride is pricked. He thought he could swagger over here with empty compliments and I would fall into his arms." She gave a small, wry smile. "Unfortunately for Gregory, 'once bitten, twice shy.' I don't need someone like that in my life again."

Emma noticed Gabe watching her with quiet curiosity. She sighed softly and whispered, "I'll tell you later."

He nodded, though concern still lingered in his eyes. Wanting to smooth the moment over, Emma decided distraction was best.

"Won't you join us for dinner?" she asked. "I think your invitation should become a standing weekly routine."

"I'd like that," Gabe said, sounding mollified.

Emma let out a relieved breath. She caught sight of Aunt Sarah beckoning her. "Oh, I see my aunt calling me, so I'd better go. I'll see you soon!"

She waved at Gabe and hurried toward the wagon. Once safely inside, she told her aunt about the impromptu invitation. To her relief, Sarah had been planning to suggest the same thing. Now all that remained was working up the courage to tell Gabe about Michael.

Chapter 26

Gabe had replayed the scene in the churchyard with Gregory over and over as he made his way over to the farm dinner. He'd been angered by the man's insult to Emma, but what bothered him most were the words she had spoken after. A knot of unease had settled in his stomach and refused to loosen. He was resolved to get to the bottom of things as soon as the meal was over. He'd ask her to take another walk so they could have the privacy to talk about what had happened.

When he arrived, Emma was the one who opened the front door. But when she smiled in greeting, Gabe could tell she was tense—not the happy, serene woman he was coming to know. The knot in his stomach suddenly felt like a boulder.

Thankfully, the family gathered in the parlor didn't seem to notice any stiff undercurrents, and the chatter around the dinner table was loud and upbeat. Even Emma seemed to have relaxed as the afternoon wore on, but something inside Gabe was still on high alert.

When the meal was finished and the dishes were being cleared, he asked Emma to take a stroll with him. Instead of answering right away, she hesitated. For a moment, he thought she might refuse, and felt his heart lurch. Finally, she gave a small nod. "Of course."

Unfortunately, there was little relief in her agreement—only the certainty that the serious conversation he'd been dreading all evening was finally coming.

Emma waited until they were clear of the house before she said in a small voice, "I suppose I should explain what I said in the churchyard."

Gabe nodded, desperate for an answer, but there was no rush now as they walked among the silent trees.

"After I finished my schooling, my father had his heart set on seeing me married," she explained as she wearily took a seat on a bench at the long outdoor table the family used during big gatherings. "We were at a dinner party one evening for Denver businessmen, where I was introduced to a young lawyer named Michael Cavendish."

Emma paused, and Gabe saw her face sour, as if the very sound of the name left a bitter taste in her mouth.

"He wasn't the first man to show an interest in me, but I was taken by his confidence and charm." She shook her head and gave a rueful laugh. "I must have been as naïve as Esther and Ruth, because I thought he was the perfect gentleman and immediately fell in love. We met a few more times at events before he asked my father if he could court me."

Gabe felt her declaration of love for another man like a physical punch to the gut. Part of him wanted to stop her, to never hear another word about this other man, but he knew she needed to tell the story—for her healing and for his peace.

"I was thrilled when my father told me Michael had asked for his permission to court me. I had these silly dreams of our wedding, what our children would look like, and what kind of house we would live in. Looking back, I can see just how innocent and trusting I was."

Gabe felt the weight of her heartbreak. He moved to sit beside her on the bench and gently took her hand in both of his.

"What happened?" he asked softly.

"We had been courting for about six months when Michael escorted me to a gala for local attorneys and their employees. I was talking with some acquaintances when he excused himself, and I thought nothing of it. When I realized he had been gone for quite some time, I went looking. It was merely by chance that I heard him talking with someone in an alcove near the coatroom. When I came closer, I saw he was kissing his typist. His *married* typist," she added for clarity.

Gabe shook his head at the other man's foolishness and studied Emma's face. There was such pain and disillusionment in her eyes, and he actively had to stop himself from wrapping his arms around her.

"Emma," he said, as his thumb stroked the back of her hand. "I'm sorry he hurt you. You deserve so much more than a man like that. I hope you know I would never treat you that way."

She looked up at him, tears shining in her blue eyes as a watery smile curved her lips.

"I know that," she said. "I'm just angry at myself for thinking Michael was this ideal gentleman, instead of the flawed human being he actually was. Looking back, I realize I was never actually in love with him, but the idea of having a family of my own. It was just my father and me for so long."

Gabe gave her hand a gentle squeeze. "I know it must have been very painful for you to go through that," he said softly. "But I'll admit I'm selfishly grateful. The thought of you married to another man—especially one who would have played you false—turns my stomach."

"I'm grateful too, though at the time, I never thought I would be." She sniffed and brushed a tear from her cheek with her free hand. "I've grown a lot from that experience."

She gave a wry little smile as she said, "Gregory reminds me of Michael in some ways. They're both much too concerned with appearances and status."

She turned and looked straight into his eyes, sadness lingering in her own. "It broke my heart when I realized you thought that of me after our first meeting."

Gabe briefly closed his eyes, the weight of her words hitting him hard. He had judged her so unfairly at the beginning. "I hope you know how sorry I am for that," he said quietly. "I always hated how people judged Mr. Flemming just for being an undertaker, without ever taking the time to know the kind man he is. He took me in and gave me a home when I was just a scrawny kid on the street."

Emma's expression softened with understanding. "He sounds like a very good man. I'm glad you had someone like that in your life when you needed it most." She paused, then added with a chuckle, "And as odd as it may seem, I'm glad we talked about Michael. I feel... lighter now. Thank you for listening."

They sat quietly on the bench in the late afternoon, watching the golden light play across the fields. It was so calm and peaceful. Gabe could have stayed right there for hours, but he knew it was time he headed home.

He stood and helped Emma to her feet, and she held onto his hand for a moment as she said, "I know you're busy on the ranch, but would you be able to come to the house on Thursday evening? It's my birthday."

"Of course," he replied, and gave her hand a light squeeze before dropping it and starting back to the house, letting the soft lowing of cattle fill the silence.

Sarah came to meet them on the porch, and Gabe said his goodbyes to both ladies. When they'd gone inside, Edward stepped out to stand beside him.

"I was expecting someone to be watching from the porch," Gabe said. "What happened?"

Edward smiled. "I know you aren't the kind of man who would take advantage of a young woman. Besides, it looked like you two were having a pretty serious talk. Sarah wanted to come out, but I talked her into watching from the window." He put his hands in his trouser pockets and rocked back on his heels. "Finding time for those kinds of conversations while courting can be tough, especially with eagle-eyed family members watching your every move."

"I can understand that," Gabe replied, "but there are rules for a reason, and I wouldn't want to violate your trust in me."

Edward clapped him on the shoulder. "Gabe, while you're in our farmyard, I think we can afford you both a little privacy. You want to make the biggest commitment of your life to each other someday, and you need to know that it's not just physical attraction driving you. Relationships are built on more than that. Now, if you're in town, I still expect a proper level of decorum, as Emma does still have a reputation to protect."

"Of course," Gabe agreed. "I appreciate your support. Emma revealed some things to me tonight that I know she wouldn't have wanted overheard, but I believe it brought us a better understanding of one another."

"Then I made the right choice," Edward said as he pulled a letter from his pocket and handed it to Gabe. "See you next week."

Gabe slipped the letter into his coat pocket, shook hands with Edward, and headed to the stable to collect his horse. On the ride home, he pondered all the pivotal moments that had brought him and Emma together. There were so many 'what ifs' that it made his head spin. He could only believe that God had been guiding them both along a path that led toward each other.

Gabe was still in a contemplative mood when he arrived home, so before he changed clothes and headed out to do evening chores, he read Emma's letter.

Dear Gabe,

I hate to inform you that my crocheting skills have not improved since my last letter. Poor Mary has been extremely patient with me, but I simply cannot make my needles do what I want them to do. My cousin advised me never to try tatting lace, as that is much more difficult, but I am more than happy to buy it pre-made.

On a happier note, Aunt Sarah says my cooking skills have improved so much that I can help make cheese in the creamery next week. I'm excited to be of more help to my cousins and to learn what they have known how to do for years.

Speaking of learning, I have something else to admit to you: I have never learned to ride a horse. There—I've said it; now you can laugh. I hoped that one day you could teach me, and then we could go riding together. I'll await your answer.

Yours sincerely,

Emma Barnes

Gabe smiled and set the letter back down. There was a lot to admire about Emma, but what he admired most was her eagerness to learn. And it meant a great deal that she wanted to learn from him.

Chapter 27

Emma was on pins and needles as she stared out the parlor window on Thursday evening. She and her cousins had decorated the parlor with paper flowers and banners earlier in the day, while Aunt Sarah made her birthday cake. All they needed now were the guests. Emma had invited Gabe, Henry, and Martha May to join them tonight, as well as Eunice Harper and her father.

"Emma. Relax—you're fairly shaking with nerves," her aunt gently chastised from her seat on a parlor sofa.

"I'm sorry," she said, taking a seat and picking up her embroidery frame. "This is my first time having guests over to celebrate my birthday in years. When my father was alive, we would go for a meal at the Windsor and then to whatever show was at the theater."

"Oh, well, I can understand your excitement then," Aunt Sarah said warmly. "I'm glad you're here with us now so we can celebrate you properly."

"Thank you. I'm glad I'm here as well." Emma smiled at her aunt and picked up the handkerchief she was making as a thank-you for Martha May. She worked in a steady, familiar rhythm for a few minutes until she heard the rumble of a wagon coming up the drive. "Someone's coming!" she exclaimed.

Sarah and Edward shared a smile across the parlor at her excitement, and Matthew darted forward to look out the window.

"It's the Harpers," he shouted before racing to throw open the front door.

Those family members who'd gathered in the parlor followed him out of the house and waved greetings to their guests as they pulled up in front of the house.

"Emma," Eunice shouted, waving wildly from her seat. "We came for your birthday!"

"I know!" Emma called back with a laugh. "I'm so happy that you're here."

Mr. Harper helped his daughter down, and she threw herself into Emma's arms, giving her a tight hug.

"Hello, Emma," Mr. Harper greeted jovially as he joined them on the porch. He handed her a small, paper-wrapped bundle of slim candles. "Eunice insisted we bring these for your cake."

"Thank you, Eunice," Emma said as she accepted the package. "That was so thoughtful."

"She has been talking all week about your invitation to everyone who comes into the store," Mr. Harper said with a friendly smile. "I can't thank you enough for including her. This is the first celebration she's been to for someone outside of our family."

"It's my pleasure," Emma insisted as she reflexively moved a strand of dark brown hair off Eunice's face. "I wanted everyone special to me to be here."

"Then you'll be happy to know that your beau is coming up the drive as we speak," Joseph said as he came around the side of the house, hands stuffed casually in his trouser pockets.

At his words, she turned and saw Henry and Martha May pulling the surrey up in front of the house, while Gabe followed behind on Xerxes. She excused herself from the Harpers, handed the package of candles to her aunt, and walked forward to meet him. Her heart leaped at the sight of him swinging down from his horse, and she couldn't stop the wide grin from spreading across her face.

"Just the one I was waiting for," Emma said, and instead of stopping in front of Gabe, she greeted Xerxes and gave him a scratch underneath his chin.

"Ha! She got you good, son," Henry called out as he helped Martha May descend from the fringe-topped wagon.

There were chuckles all around, and Gabe—being the good sport that he was—just shook his head and smiled.

"I suppose I should have known better than to bring this guy with me," he sighed. "He is a handsome devil after all."

Xerxes whinnied in apparent agreement, and Gabe tugged gently on his reins. "Come on, boy," he coaxed. "Let's get you settled in the stable before you end up stealing my best gal."

Emma blushed furiously at his words and watched him lift his hat to her in a gentlemanly salute before turning to lead his horse away.

It took her a moment to recall there were guests to entertain, and she invited everyone to follow her to the back of the house, where the long outdoor dining table sat. With this many guests, it would have been impossible to have them all eat inside. Luckily, they were blessed with clear skies and cooler temperatures than expected for this late in July, and she enjoyed a lively conversation with Martha May and Eunice while Mary and her sisters brought covered dishes of food outside.

It wasn't long before Gabe and the rest of the men rejoined the group, and he headed straight for Emma.

"Is this seat taken?" he asked teasingly.

"Not at all," she replied, gathering the fabric of her dress close so that it wouldn't be in his way. "I was saving it for you."

"That's only because Xerxes isn't allowed at the table," Gabe jested as he settled next to her.

Emma laughed at the mental image his statement brought and nodded in agreement. "He most certainly is not allowed at the table. Aunt Sarah and Martha May would definitely have something to say about that."

"You're right. Think of all the other animals Matthew would start bringing to the table if he saw that."

"Oh dear," Emma groaned. "I do *not* want to think about that. I'm still recovering from the frog incident. Although the kitten he snuck into the house has been sleeping in my room recently, and I rather like that. I've never had a pet before. In Denver, they were mostly for show, but this little one feels like proper company."

"Would you like to have one?" he asked.

"Maybe one day, though I'm not sure what kind. I like both cats and dogs, and it might be hard to choose."

"Who says you have to choose just one? You could have both. They're useful creatures in their own respects."

"I never thought of it that way," Emma mused. "But Aunt Sarah would never allow it."

"You could keep them at my place for now," Gabe suggested. "I've already got a few barn cats running around the ranch, along with Telly's old cattle dog, so what's a few more? Luke said that Sally's pups will be weaned soon, so maybe we could pick one out together since I'll need a pup to help herd sheep."

"But won't it be your pet then?"

"No, it would be yours. I'll just be taking care of it until you can do so yourself when you come over on Fridays."

"Gabriel Moreau," Emma gasped, sounding shocked. "Are you trying to sway my future decisions with adorable baby animals?"

A wide, handsome grin spread across his face. "Maybe just a little."

"You are diabolical, sir," she said, shaking her head at him. "Don't be upset with me when there are fifty cats and twenty dogs crowding into that big house of yours. You said I didn't have to choose just one."

Gabe chuckled. "If things work out the way I'm hoping, you'll never hear a complaint from me."

They shared a hopeful smile, and once everyone around the table had stopped their conversations, Uncle Edward said grace over the meal.

The conversation, as platters of breaded pork chops served with fried apple slices, cabbage salad, and freshly baked bread rolls were passed around the table, was boisterous and jovial. Everyone was laughing, making jokes, and reminiscing about old times in Elk Ridge, and it was one of the best nights Emma had had since her father passed away. She knew that he would have been right in the middle of everything, telling funny stories and handing out his trade cards to any potential business contacts.

It was still hard to accept that if not for a senseless gunfight between two drunk men playing cards, her father would still be alive. But if that were the case, she would still be in Denver, and she would never have gotten to know her cousins. Or Gabe. What a shame that would be.

Instead of the sharp pang that usually accompanied memories of her father, Emma felt more of a soft, wistful ache–still sad, but wrapped in fond reminiscence and gratitude for the life she had found here. She let the feelings come over her, accepted them with a small, cleansing breath, and turned her attention back to the table. The pain would always be there, but she was learning to swim in its currents of grief instead of drowning in its waves.

"Time for cake!" Sarah said as she brought out the two-tiered dessert and set it on the table.

All twenty candles that Eunice and Mr. Harper had brought were stuck carefully into the frosting. The wicks were lit, and all attention was turned her way as the children encouraged her to blow out the candles.

"Come on, Emma," Matthew shouted. "Wish for something good, like a big bag of licorice or a pocket knife!"

"Those are things you want, not what Emma wants," Esther chided.

"So," he shot back at his older sister. "Maybe she would give them to me if she didn't want them."

"Children," Uncle Edward scolded, "let's not quarrel."

Emma took that as her cue, and before another fight could break out, she made her wish and blew out all the candles in one breath. Everyone cheered, as this was a sign of good luck for the coming year, and Sarah began serving the cake.

Gabe leaned in and asked, "What did you wish for?"

"I can't tell you, or else it won't come true," she teased, accepting the plate that was handed to her.

As the warm afternoon sun began to sink behind the mountains, gifts were brought out from the house along with a chair. Emma hadn't been expecting to receive anything, but after a moment of surprise, she took her seat and opened each gift as it was handed to her.

She received a white satin fan with hand-painted flowers, gold-plated hat pins, embroidery supplies, caramel candies, a handmade bib apron, and several yards of tea-green fabric that she had eyed at the general store the last time she was in.

"Did I do a good job of picking your present?" Eunice asked, practically bouncing on the bench with excitement.

"Yes! You remembered the exact color of fabric I favored, too. Thank you so much."

"What about you, Gabe?" Isaac questioned. Everyone turned to the normally taciturn young boy, and he shrugged his shoulders. "Everyone else has given Emma something for her birthday. Did you not bring her a gift?"

"I was a bit different with my gift," Gabe informed him. "I planned on taking Emma to the bookstore in town to let her pick out however many books she'd like."

"Really? However many books I want. That could become quite expensive," she pointed out.

"It would be worth it," he replied easily. "I was thinking Sarah and Martha May could accompany us, and I could take you all out for dinner afterwards. Would tomorrow afternoon work for you, ladies? I know it's normally Emma's day for lessons, but I thought you all could use a break."

"That sounds like a fine idea to me," Martha May agreed happily.

"I think so, too. I haven't been to Jackson's in an age," Sarah exclaimed.

"That settles it," Emma laughed. "I can forgo one lesson if it means I get more books."

"Am I just supposed to starve then?" Henry asked grumpily.

"Well, you could always come with us," his wife suggested sweetly.

"And get roped into making stops at all the other stores in town when I could be getting in a day's work? No, thank you. I'd rather eat with the ranch hands."

Martha May rolled her eyes and huffed, "Then don't complain. It won't kill you to eat in the bunkhouse for one day. Why don't you go hitch up the wagon? If I'm going into town tomorrow, I have some preparations to make."

"I'd best go with you, Henry," Mr. Harper declared. "We have to be up early to open the store."

"Are you coming too, Gabe?" Henry inquired as he stood up from the table.

"I'll make my way home later," Gabe answered from his spot on the bench. "I'd like to stick around for a while."

"Sounds like a man with some serious courting to do," Mr. Haper snickered. "Come on, old man. We'll help each other out while the youngsters do some sparking."

Emma laughed at their teasing, but she felt a flush rise on her cheeks. She said goodbye to Eunice, promising to come visit her soon, and then to Martha May. She was about to help with the clean-up when Gabe came to stand by her side.

"Would you care to go for a walk?" he asked, sticking out his elbow for her to take.

"I'd love to," she smiled, looping her arm through his. "Which direction should we go?"

"I'll let you lead the way. I just wanted a bit of time with you," Gabe said with a small smile.

Emma's heart skipped a beat at his romantic words, but as they headed off across the farmyard, she couldn't help but recall Martha May's words on her last visit to the ranch. They walked in quiet for a few moments, the soft crunch of their boots on the dry grass the only sound between them. She hadn't noticed that she had gone silent until Gabe stopped and turned her to face him.

"Are you all right?" he asked. "You seem troubled about something."

"Did you know that Michael never once told me he missed me, even after being apart for weeks?" she said quietly. "Or that he was eager to spend time with me? In fact, he would constantly check the time when we were together. I always assumed it was because he had some important case to study for or a deadline to meet."

She shook her head and gave a bitter little laugh. "How was I so foolish?"

"I think he was the fool," Gabe said softly, giving her arm a light squeeze with his. "How could someone be around you and not want to spend every minute together? Even when I was stupid enough to think the worst of you, I was still drawn to you."

Gabe took a deep breath. "I know we haven't known each other for long, but you've become very special to me. I don't want to rush things, so I won't say more than that... but I needed you to know how I feel."

Emma's eyes filled with tears. Gabe was exactly the kind of man her father had wanted for her. Oh, how she wished he were here to meet him.

"Thank you, Gabe," she sniffed. "You don't know what your words mean to me. Some days I still can't believe that I was lucky enough to come to Elk Ridge after so much heartbreak and find you."

Gabe rested his hands on her upper arms and placed a brief kiss on her forehead. The gesture was so protective and sweet that more tears began to fall, and he pulled a clean handkerchief from his pocket to wipe them away.

"I didn't realize you were such a watering pot. Will I have to keep multiple kerchiefs on me from now on?" he asked teasingly as he dabbed at her cheeks.

"You might need to... just as a precaution," she sniffed. "I think I've cried more in the past year than in my entire life before."

"You've had some terrible things happen to you in a short amount of time," he said as he rubbed her arms soothingly. "No one will begrudge you a few tears. Hopefully, things will be much happier from here on out."

"They will be," she whispered, a quiet certainty growing in her heart. As they strolled back to the house, Emma felt as if she were stepping toward a brighter future—one with Gabe always at her side.

Chapter 28

The next day, as Gabe was hooking up the horses to the covered surrey, Henry sidled over and rested his large frame against the wall of the barn.

"You must like that gal something fierce to be willing to spend an entire day in town with the womenfolk, going store to store."

"It won't be so bad," he shrugged. "I need to send off some telegrams while I'm there, so they can shop to their hearts' content while I do that."

Henry chuckled and shook his head. "That's the mark of a man in love. He's willing to do whatever his lady asks of him."

"It was my idea in the first place," he pointed out.

"So you're saying that you aren't in love with her?" the other man asked incredulously. "Remember, there are still plenty of fellas who would be willing to hightail it to a preacher the minute she's set free."

"Then they're bound to be disappointed," Gabe said, a slight edge to his voice as he pictured that.

"Ah, so you *do* love her! I knew it," Henry crowed in delight as he stepped forward to pat Gabe on the back.

"If you don't mind, I'd like to speak those words to Emma first before you go off announcing it to the entire world," he said, keeping his voice low so it wouldn't carry far.

"You mean you haven't told her yet?" Henry asked, eyes wide. "Land sakes, boy! Everyone can tell that you care for her. It's written all over your face whenever you're around each other."

"We've talked about our feelings," he said, his neck heating, "but just not in those exact words. It's not the right time. I haven't known her for that long."

"That's balderdash. People have gotten married before they even meet in person, so why can't you admit your feelings now?"

"Emma isn't a mail-order bride, Henry. Lord knows I'd be a much happier man right now if she were—but she's not. Besides, I have a lot of things happening here on the ranch, and I want to have things secure before I become responsible for her. Emma deserves that."

"I can understand where you are coming from," Henry said, taking off his hat to run fingers through his graying hair. "But don't wait too long."

He stayed silent as the foreman placed his worn hat back onto his head and sauntered out of the barn, and from the corner of his eye, he spotted Miguel. The ranch hand had been trying to make his way out of the tack room surreptitiously, but stopped when he saw he'd been caught.

"I guess you heard all that," Gabe said with a sigh.

"Not on purpose," Miguel shrugged. "I came in to put up the mended tack, and when I came out, you two were talking. I didn't want to interrupt, so I stayed put."

"And what do you think?" he asked, plopping down on a nearby stool, his shoulders slumped. "Should I tell Emma how I feel now or wait until it's been more than a few months?"

"Only you know when the time is right. Don't do something just because someone is pushing you for it. Go with your heart."

"That's good advice. Thank you, Miguel."

"Any time, Jefe," the older man said, slapping him on the shoulder. "Enjoy your day."

Gabe was still ruminating on his conversations when Martha May came into the stable. When she stopped in front of him, she placed her hands on her ample hips and scowled.

"I've been waiting for you on the porch for ten minutes!" she said. "Have you been sitting here daydreaming this entire time, Gabriel?"

"I'm sorry," he mumbled sheepishly. "Guess I lost track of the time, but the surrey's all hitched up and ready to go."

"Then help me in, young man, so we won't be late picking Sarah and Emma up."

Gabe hopped up from the stool and assisted Martha May into the front seat of the wagon. Since Henry had declined to go with them, Gabe hurried around to the other side, got in, and set the horses in motion.

They made good time to the farm, as the surrey was light, and pulled into the yard just as Emma and her aunt exited the house.

"You have perfect timing," Sarah said as they made their way down the stairs.

"I am going to be the envy of every man today," Gabe said in greeting. "I get to escort three beautiful women around town."

"You mean two old women and one young and beautiful one," Martha May corrected as she stepped out of the wagon.

"No, I meant what I said," Gabe insisted as he stooped and kissed her cheek.

"Oh, you flatterer," she tittered as her face went beet red. "I'm not the one you should butter up. Now, help Sarah and me into the back seat. That way, you two can sit together as a sweet, courting couple should."

"Yes, ma'am," he said with enthusiasm at the idea, offering his hand to assist both women up.

When it came time to help Emma into the covered surrey, Gabe held out his hand. He relished the feel of her smaller one resting in his. Deciding to be bold—at least in the privacy the farmyard allowed—he pressed a quick, gentle kiss to the back of her gloved hand before helping her settle comfortably inside.

"You see, Sarah," Martha May confided in a not-so-subtle whisper, "we may be planning that wedding sooner than we thought."

Gabe pretended he hadn't heard the comment, but as he made his way around to his seat, he couldn't help but smile. Emma heard it, too. A slight flush colored her cheeks, and she stared straight forward as he climbed in and took off.

"So," he inquired, trying to think of something to break the awkward silence that had developed as they rode in silence. "Have you thought about which books you'd like to purchase today?"

"I have a few things in mind," Emma answered eagerly. "I usually like to buy at least one book that will help me learn about a new subject whenever I visit a bookstore, so I'm excited to see what they have today."

"What subjects interest you?" he asked, genuinely curious to know more about her.

"Well, when I was in Denver, most of the volumes I selected were related to business or law so that I wouldn't feel left out when attending social functions with my father or..."

Emma's voice dropped off for a moment, but she cleared her throat and continued. "Well, needless to say, I am in the market for anything else but those. Maybe I could look for a book about horses. I would still like to learn to ride... eventually."

"We could make that happen. Dotty here is a sweetheart and the most patient horse I have," Gabe replied, pointing to the mare on the right side of the traces. "She would be a perfect horse to learn on."

"I look forward to it," Emma smiled.

Gabe could tell that she truly meant it, too, which made him happy.

For the rest of the ride into town, he plied Emma with questions about her favorite authors or novels that she had read, and replied in kind with his answers when it was his turn. By the time they pulled up in front of the bookstore, Gabe was unsure if they would have any volumes that she hadn't read yet.

When they filed into the store, they were greeted by a short, stocky woman, around the same age as Martha May or Sarah.

"Well, hullo there, Martha May, Sarah," she greeted, a slight Scottish accent coloring her words. "I see ye brought in some fresh faces. Who, may I ask, is with ye?"

"This is my niece, Emma Barnes," Sarah replied, gesturing for Emma to move closer. "She's come to live with us recently, and we've kept her so busy that she hasn't had a chance to visit your shop yet."

"And this is Gabriel Moreau," Martha May said proudly. "He's Telly's nephew. He took over the ranch after his uncle's passing."

"It's a right pleasure to meet ye both. My name is Mrs. Paterson." She smiled kindly and then turned to address Gabe. "Your uncle was instrumental in helping me get this place up and running. He donated several crates of books, as well as paying a local carpenter to build the shelves. He was a good man and is sorely missed."

"Thank you, ma'am," Gabe said quietly. "I had no idea that Telly did all that. The more I learn of him, the more I wish that we could have met before he passed."

"Aye, I know what ye mean," Mrs. Paterson said with a kind smile. "But I'm sure he'd be right pleased that ye're here to take up where he left off. Now, what can I help ye find today?"

"Isla, you'll never believe it, but Gabriel promised Emma that she could come in and pick out as many books as she wanted for her birthday," Martha May chuckled. "They're courting, you see."

"Oh, and what a fine way to win a lassie's favor," Mrs. Paterson exclaimed happily. "Especially one who is already eyeing my shelves. I hope ye brought yer checkbook."

Emma looked guilty at being caught, but Gabe just smiled reassuringly at her. "I did indeed, and as I promised, she can have as many as she likes. Though I might have to take after Telly and donate a crate or two of books to restock the shelves when she's done."

"I'm not that bad," Emma insisted, though not with much force. "Besides, the surrey doesn't have enough room for that many books."

"I like yer spunk," Mrs. Paterson said approvingly. "Ye feel free to come back any time ye'd like. We're having a new book club meeting next Saturday, and I'd love for ye to join. We're reading *Heidi*."

"I love that book," Emma said. "My father bought it for me."

"Oh! Then I hope that ye'll come and maybe even share with us yer insights on the story."

"I will! That is—if we have the time," she said, looking to her aunt for confirmation.

"We do," Sarah acknowledged. "I haven't read this one yet, so I'll need a copy. Isla, can you direct us?"

Sarah gestured to a spot away from Gabe and Emma, and Mrs. Paterson seemed to catch on to her intentions, and she led them down an aisle to give the couple some privacy.

"Have you spotted something that catches your eye?" Gabe asked as he turned to her.

"More than one, but I need to pace myself. I don't have as much leisure time for reading as I did before."

"Well, you just lead the way," he said, "and I'll carry your books."

Emma gave him a gorgeous smile, her sapphire eyes sparkling with excitement, and turned to seek out her first treasure while he walked a few paces behind.

It didn't take long for the stack in his arms to grow quite heavy, and he wondered if he should make a pile on the counter. There were two books each on ranching and animal husbandry, a romance novel, a biography, and two mysteries, all with thick, hardback covers.

As Emma set the last book on her stack, she looked guiltily at her growing hoard.

"Are you sure you still want to buy all of these?" she asked, worrying her lower lip between her teeth.

"It's my pleasure," he insisted.

"But..."

She'd been about to protest when Gabe gently touched her arm. "Shh," he whispered.

For a moment they stood together in the quiet aisle, the air between them charged. Gabe had to force himself to step back, his arms full of books providing a much-needed boundary. He cleared his throat, trying to steady his voice.

"Emma," he said, a little hoarsely. "I want you to know that I can provide for you. Telly left me well off, and if I continue as he did, we won't want for anything."

"I'm sorry, Gabe. Please don't think that I meant to insult you. I suppose one day we will have to have a serious talk about finances."

"Yes, but today is not that day. Let me spoil you," he coaxed. When she still looked hesitant, he feigned a dramatic pout. "Please?"

"Oh, all right. I can't stand to see such a ruggedly handsome man look so hangdog."

This compliment perked him right up, and he gave her a rakish grin. "Ruggedly handsome, am I?"

"Yes, and you know it. Don't pretend," Emma replied in a scolding tone that he swore she picked up from his housekeeper.

As if her ears were burning from being talked about, Martha May rounded the corner, a bright smile on her face.

"There you two are! Did you find everything you wanted, dear?" she asked Emma happily.

"That and more. Mrs. Paterson has a wonderful collection."

"She does. Let's get these things purchased and head to dinner," Martha May suggested. "Sarah and I are absolutely famished and can't wait to have a meal that we haven't spent hours preparing."

Gabe took that to mean their private time was up; reluctantly, he headed to the front of the store, where he bought not only Emma's books but Martha May's and Sarah's as well. From the beaming smiles he received from all three women as he set their purchases in the wagon, he knew he had done the right thing.

Now free of his burdens, he offered his left arm to Emma so that, as they walked down the boardwalk, he was on the side closest to the street. As she slipped her arm through his, a pleasant shiver ran through him. Whenever she was near like this, he felt the same thrill—and it made him question his wisdom in waiting to take the next step with her.

When they reached the diner, he was saddened to let her go, but there was only room to stand single file in the entryway. The building was packed with local farm and lumber workers having their afternoon meal. Though the hum of conversation from the patrons never changed while they waited for a table, Gabe noticed that many of the men were staring at Emma.

He had mixed feelings about it. He knew she was a beautiful woman and any red-blooded man would find her attractive, but he didn't like how long some of them stared. *Maybe I should start listening to Henry more*, he thought grimly.

Gabe did his best not to let it affect his mood, and by the time they had been seated and ordered their food, he had put it from his mind. Today was about Emma and making sure that she felt appreciated and cared for—which was exactly what he intended to do.

Throughout the meal, the ladies chatted happily, remarking on the excellent food, the diner's décor, and local happenings. They insisted they were too full for dessert, but when Gabe ordered ice cream, they ended up stealing spoonfuls of his treat. He didn't mind sharing, though. He was pleased that they were having a good time.

As Henry had predicted, the women wanted to do some shopping while they were in town, so Gabe escorted them to the general store before he excused himself to run some errands of his own. He promised to be back at the store in half an hour to pick them up, but they told him not to hurry. Gabe knew Emma would want to spend some time with Eunice as well, so he took his time strolling down the street to the post office.

He made small talk with the telegraph operator, Mr. Everly, while waiting for confirmation of his purchase, and the reply came back after about ten minutes. Soon, thirty head of Merino sheep would be shipped into Butte by rail. The company would telegraph the exact date and time for pickup once it was scheduled. Gabe thanked the operator and headed back the way he had come with a bit of spring in his step.

When he arrived back at the general store, he found Emma wearing a work apron over her beautiful green dress and helping Eunice stock the shelves. They both had their backs to him, but when the young girl saw Gabe, she set her canned goods down and raced over to greet him, her long brown braids flowing behind her.

"Gabe! Pa says you are going to marry Emma! Is that true?"

The sound of metal cans hitting the floor rang out. Emma quickly knelt to pick them up and replace them on the shelf before gently taking Eunice by the shoulders.

"Sweeting, that isn't really a polite question to ask someone," she said kindly.

"But my Pa said you were courting, and that courting leads to marriage. Did he lie?"

"No, Eunice. Your Pa didn't lie to you," Gabe said, crouching down so he was at her level. "We are courting, and that usually leads to marriage if two people find they suit. I think what Emma means is that sometimes a question like that can put a gentleman on the spot, especially if he hasn't asked the lady to marry him yet."

The young girl's eyes went wide with understanding as she looked between him and Emma. "Oh, so you haven't asked her yet. Why not?"

"Eunice!" Emma exclaimed in embarrassment, though he just chuckled.

"Well, I guess I haven't asked yet because I want to make sure she really likes me." He leaned toward Eunice and whispered, "Do you think she does?"

"Yes!" she said, bobbing her head. "She gets all red in the face when someone mentions your name, or she lets out these long sighs."

"Oh my goodness," Emma groaned as she buried her burning face in her hands.

"Thank you, Eunice," Gabe said, standing back up with a wide, satisfied grin on his face. "You've been mighty helpful to me. Why don't you see if Emma will finish helping you with those cans before we have to leave?" he suggested.

"Good idea! Come on," the young girl said as she turned and tugged Emma's hands from her face.

She was indeed bright red from a furious blush, and while he thought it was delightful, Emma looked miserable. To save her from further embarrassment, he walked to the back of the store, where he took up his favorite activity of thumbing through the catalogs to pass the time and give her a chance to calm down.

It took another twenty minutes before all the ladies were ready to return home, but Gabe could tell that Emma was still feeling uncomfortable. He hadn't meant for his conversation with Eunice to upset her. He waited until they were driving back home, and the sound of the wheels upon the uneven dirt road could drown out their conversation before speaking softly to her.

"I hope you aren't still too upset by what Eunice said. She didn't mean any harm."

"Of course not," she whispered back with a small smile. "I know her questions weren't meant to embarrass us. I just hope you don't think I put her up to asking them."

Gabe stared at her in surprise for a moment before shaking his head. "The thought never even crossed my mind." He peeked over his shoulder and reassured himself that Martha May and Sarah weren't eavesdropping, then spoke again in a low voice. "We'll get there someday. I still have some things I want to take care of on the ranch before I take things further. I want to be able to give you the time and attention you deserve, and I can't do that yet."

He gave her hand a quick, gentle squeeze and then returned it to the vehicle's reins.

"Thank you for saying that," she murmured, giving him a charming little smile.

It was still early in the afternoon when they drove into the farmyard, and though he would have liked to stay and spend more time with Emma, he needed to get home. There was still a lot of work to prepare for his new herd.

Gabe parked the surrey and quickly came around to help the women descend. Martha May got out as well and began tugging Sarah inside the house, insisting that she needed to borrow a recipe for chicken and dumplings.

Gabe chuckled and whispered to Emma. "They need to work on their excuses."

"What do you mean?" she asked.

"Martha May already has Sarah's recipe. She's just trying to justify giving us privacy to say our goodbyes."

"Then I suppose we should do just that," Emma said, giving him a captivating smile. "Thank you for today. I had a wonderful time, and I thought it was very sweet of you to invite Martha May to come along as well. Two chaperones weren't necessary."

"She's like a second mother to me," he admitted. "She might have been hurt if I hadn't included her. Besides, she works hard to keep my house in order and deserves the break."

"You're being too modest, Gabe. You think of others first and treat them with kindness," Emma said earnestly. She took a small step forward, and Gabe felt his pulse tick up. "When I saw you with Eunice today, taking the time to patiently explain a rather complicated topic, it made me proud to be courted by you."

Gabe exhaled, steadying himself. "Emma..." The words caught in his throat, so he tried again. "Emma, it means a lot to hear you say that. I hope I can keep being the kind of man who deserves such praise." He took her hand and lightly brushed her knuckles with his thumb. It was just enough that they both felt the thrill of the contact. "Thank you."

They stood hand in hand, talking quietly until Martha May came back out of the house. "Come now, Gabriel," she called as she made her way to the surrey. "You've had plenty of time to say your goodbyes, and you'll see each other on Sunday. If I don't get home soon, dinner will be late."

Gabe said his farewells to Emma and dutifully helped Martha May into the wagon. Once she was settled, he climbed in himself and flicked the reins, sending the horses into motion. It was tempting to look back and see if Emma was still out in the yard, watching him leave, but he was afraid he might not be able to look away and accidentally lead his team into the creek that ran through both properties.

Chapter 29

The first week of working in the creamery had left Emma bone-tired, but full of gratitude. She never would have guessed how much time and effort went into making something that vanished from her plate in seconds. She found the entire process fascinating, even though it was hard and sweaty work, especially on these hot August days.

She stood over the copper vat—a farmer's boiler, Uncle Edward had called it—for what felt like hours, stirring as the contents warmed, steam rising in her face until her cheeks flushed and her arms burned.

"Is it done yet?" she asked breathlessly when her uncle came by to check on her progress.

"Well, the temperature's right," he said, looking at the thermometer. "Next, we'll stir in the rennet and a touch of coloring, then leave it to set."

Emma breathed out a sigh of relief and allowed Edward to help her with the process. She much preferred dipping the pressed wheels of cheese into the red or black wax that would seal them against mold, bacteria, and drying out. And the cheese house, built into the mountainside around a natural cave, was always a welcome respite.

She worked for another hour before Aunt Sarah came into the creamery to collect the girls for the book club meeting. Emma hurriedly took off her work apron, excited about the trip into town. There would be other young ladies close to her age who would attend, and while she had met a few in passing at church, she was eager to form some closer relationships.

After a quick trip to the house to freshen up and change into clean clothes, the girls collected their books and hurried downstairs. Sarah was waiting for them in the wagon, and by the time they rolled into town, the bookstore was already quite full, with women milling about outside, chatting with friends and neighbors. Once they'd parked, Esther and Ruth were off like a shot, while Emma, Mary and Sarah brought up the rear at a more decorous pace.

When they came inside the store, they spotted Martha May waving to them, and standing next to her was a very pretty, petite, young brunette woman whom Emma recognized as a waitress from Jackson's diner. She looked close in age to herself and Mary, but they had never been introduced.

"There you are!" Martha May said as they came to join her small group. "I was thinking you all weren't going to make it today."

"We had a bit of a late start," Sarah acknowledged, "but I was able to make up some time."

"Well, none of that matters now that you're here. Emma, have you met Rebecca Daniels yet?" Martha May asked as she presented the young woman next to her. "Her mother is a friend of mine, and I've known her since she was a baby."

"It's a pleasure to meet you," Emma said warmly, and the two shook hands.

"I remember seeing you in the diner last week," Rebecca said. "I don't usually work on Fridays, but Margaret was sick, so I came to help. Hello, Mary. Hello, Mrs. Barnes. It's good to see you two again."

"It's good to see you, too, dear," Sarah replied with a welcoming smile. "How is your mother doing?"

"She's doing better," Rebecca replied. "I was scared when she took sick with a fever and had a seizure this spring, but Dr. Philips said she can start taking in washing and mending again."

"That's good to hear," Sarah said, placing a hand comfortingly on the younger girl's arm. "You tell her that if she needs anything, to let us know, all right?"

"I will, Mrs. Barnes. Thank you."

It wasn't long before Mrs. Paterson came out from a back room carrying a tray stacked with cookies, muffins, and scones, along with two carafes, one of coffee and the other of tea. She set her heavy load on a sideboard next to clean linen napkins, delicate china teacups, and dessert plates, signaling that it was time for everyone to grab a drink and a sweet treat before finding their seats.

After selecting their refreshments, Sarah sat next to Martha May in a couple of plush tapestry-covered armchairs while Mary, Emma, and Rebecca settled on a burgundy velvet sofa. Esther and Ruth, who emerged a few minutes later from behind a freestanding bookshelf with their friends, sat on the floor, as the rest of the furniture was taken by the older women of the community.

"Well now," the librarian and owner called out, her Scottish accent coming through. "I think this is the most attended meeting we've had so far. Over thirty faces I see, with some new ones in the mix. I told my Angus that this book club would catch on, and he dinnae believe me. He'll be eating crow tonight!"

Loud cheers and laughter from all around the room accompanied this statement, and Mrs. Paterson raised her hand for silence.

"Aye, but let's not be distracted by my poor man having the misfortune of being so wrong. Today we've come together to share our thoughts on a lovely wee book called *Heidi*. Now, who would like to go first?"

Several women raised their hands, but she looked directly at Emma, who had just lifted hers.

"Let's have our newest member speak then, shall we? I'm sure by now everyone knows Emma Barnes, Edward and Sarah's niece. Go ahead, lass."

Emma was surprised to have been chosen first, but placed her hand back into her lap and nodded politely in acknowledgement to those around her.

"I was gifted this book last fall, and while I loved it, I never felt as connected to a story as when I lost my father earlier this year. Though our ages and circumstances were different, I too had to leave my home and go live with relatives whom I had never met before. I will admit it was terrifying, but as in the story, we were both lucky enough to have found a loving home." Emma cast a grateful glance around the room at her family members.

"I've found that I understand the book differently now. As I think about Heidi's fierce longing for her mountain home in the Alps, I know that I, too, would feel the same if ever forced to leave here."

There was a murmur of fervent agreement from around the room, and Emma was grateful that she wasn't alone in her sentiments. "I could go on and on," she laughed, "but I shall cede the floor as I'm eager to hear everyone else's thoughts."

The women took their turns speaking on what they found interesting in the story, with some mentioning the treatment the young heroine received from Herr Sesemann's staff, the hilarity of her unintended mishaps, and finally, the important lesson she learned and passed on to others: praying always to God and laying one's burdens before him.

The meeting ran much longer than anyone had planned, but there was still such an air of camaraderie that no one felt in a particular hurry to leave. Sarah and Martha May were in a discussion with Pastor Langley's wife, so Emma refreshed her tea and grabbed a few of the remaining cookies.

As she looked around the room, she saw Rebecca sitting alone in the same spot she had been during the meeting, quietly watching the people around her talk. Emma recognized this as a good opportunity to make a new friend, so she made her way over and offered a cookie to the young woman, who smiled and gratefully accepted it.

"I enjoyed hearing your thoughts earlier," Rebecca said as she nibbled her treat. "I would hate to leave Montana if something ever happened to my Ma. She's all that I have left in the world."

"How long has it been just the two of you?" she asked gently, knowing how sensitive the topic of loss could be.

"For a few years now. My Pa died in a logging accident along with my uncle. We've been getting on the best we can without them. Ma takes in washing and mending for the menfolk around town while I work at the diner."

"Do you enjoy working there?" Emma asked. "It seemed very busy when we stopped by last week."

"It's all right, I suppose," Rebecca said with a small shrug. "It was one of the few jobs in town that I could do at fifteen. Most folks didn't want to hire a young girl to do all the heavy lifting and hauling that most farm jobs require."

"They must not know how heavy those trays of food are," Emma said with a laugh. "My arms ached just watching them being brought out to each table."

Rebecca nodded, a shy smile tipping up the corner of her lips. "They are a weighty burden, but you get used to it."

"I imagine that's true," Emma replied. "I've had to get used to many things since arriving—such as cows wandering around at night, being a downright pest."

Seeing that her new friend didn't understand the reference, she retold the story of her midnight meeting with the hooved menace, Darla, and how she thought death was waiting outside the four small walls of a wooden outhouse.

"Oh dear," Rebecca choked out through her laughter. "You poor thing! I'm so sorry to laugh at your expense, but it is quite a story."

"I don't take any offense," she promised. "Once I got back to the house and had time to calm down, I realized it was quite hilarious. Surprisingly, it was Joseph who took me aside and tried to comfort me the next day."

"Joseph did?" Rebecca asked in surprise, her amber eyes growing round and her cheeks pinking as she said his name.

"Yes," Emma confirmed, as she noted the intriguing reaction to her cousin's name.

"Well, I suppose there's a first time for everything."

Then, before she could ask about the vague statement, Rebecca let out a gasp and hopped off the sofa.

"I must go!" she said, hastily gathering her purse as she glanced at the small nickel watch attached to the chatelaine at her waist. "I'm so sorry, but if I don't leave now, I'll be late for work."

Emma gave her new friend a little wave and watched as she hurried out the door. When Mary approached with her sisters a moment later, she asked, "My, what lit such a fire under her?"

"She needed to be at work. I believe my conversation distracted her for a bit too long," she replied sheepishly. "Speaking of work, I'm sure that we're needed back home. Is your mother ready?"

"Yes, she's waiting for us outside," Ruth answered. "We'd better hurry."

The girls quickly collected their belongings and thanked Mrs. Paterson before leaving the store. It had been a perfect afternoon away from the farm, and as they all took their seats in the wagon, Emma felt she was coming to belong here in Elk Ridge.

Emma was close to bursting with excitement as she waited for Gabe under the large, old cottonwood tree. It had become her favorite spot, offering shade on a hot day such as this, and it offered an unobstructed view of the church's doors. From here, she could easily search for him without craning her neck too much.

When he finally stepped out into the churchyard, looking so stylish and attractive in his suit, Emma couldn't help but sigh in appreciation. He truly was the most handsome man she had ever seen, with his dark, wavy hair and penetrating hazel eyes. As he walked purposefully toward her, she thanked God for her unanswered prayers. If the Lord had listened to her a year ago, she would be married to an unfaithful liar without even knowing it.

Unable to wait a second longer, Emma met him halfway.

"Hello, Emma," his deep voice rumbled as he lifted his hat in greeting.

"Afternoon, Gabe," she replied with a wide smile. "I have the most wonderful news."

"Do you?" he asked as he offered his left arm to her. "Then I can't wait to hear it."

Emma took his arm, the contact sending a pleasant shiver along her spine. She was momentarily distracted by the sensation, but she quickly recovered and said, "Sally's pups are finally ready to go to their new homes."

"That is good news," Gabe said as they strolled back toward her family. "Am I to assume that means you are ready to pick which one you want?"

"I've already decided," she said, as excitement bubbled through her. "Uncle Edward said I could have the first pick. We need to decide which one you want to take home today."

"Today?" he asked, one dark eyebrow lifting as he looked at her curiously.

"My uncle wants them to go to their new homes as soon as possible. Besides, you want to pick out the best one before someone else does, don't you?" she replied, gazing up at him.

"I won't ever be able to say no to you when you look at me like that," he said in a resigned tone, though his smile gave him away. "All right. We can pick out a pup for me."

"Oh, thank you!" she exclaimed happily. "I'm sure you won't be disappointed. And this way you'll have some time to work with the dog before your sheep come."

"True," Gabe said with a sigh. "I'll need to go home and make some preparations if I'm bringing home puppies. I might be late for dinner."

"That's all right. I'm making shortcake with raspberry cream for dessert, so be sure to bring your appetite."

"I'm hungry already," he told her, patting his stomach.

As they approached her family, she reluctantly took her arm from his, and Matthew came running up excitedly.

"Has Emma told you our news?" he asked.

"She has. You can show me which one is your favorite when I come by."

"You betcha. See ya at dinner, Gabe!" the young boy shouted before racing off to join Benjamin and Isaac as they headed for the wagon.

Emma said her goodbyes as well and followed her aunt, but before she climbed into the wagon, she glanced back to ensure her uncle had passed on her letter. She wished she could be the one to deliver it, but this would do for now.

Chapter 30

The first thing Gabe had done when arriving home was sit down to read Emma's letter, and with each line, he felt more and more connected to her. He loved how witty she was and that she wasn't afraid to share her struggles with him as she strove to learn and appreciate the new lifestyle she was living. In one passage, she wrote:

I've never felt more exhausted than when I retired after the first night helping in the creamery. My arms and shoulders still ache from the constant stirring, and my hands are even more chapped than when I started milking cows, but I know that all of this hard work benefits my fellow man.

I wonder, when you look out onto your herd, do you imagine the many people who will have food to sustain themselves and their families because of all your labor? I suppose a farmer must feel the same way as he gazes upon his growing crops.

To his chagrin, Gabe had never thought about ranching in such a way before. When Telly passed and he'd taken over the ranch, he'd viewed it as a job that he aspired to be good at. Emma's thought-provoking words gave him a new perspective on the legacy that had been handed to him.

He was still reflecting on it as he unsaddled Xerxes in the dairy's stable when he heard a familiar, soft, feminine voice.

"Oh, good! You're here. And you've brought my new friend."

Emma came to stand beside him, ran her palm over Xerxes' neck, and gave him a pat in greeting. "Hello, you handsome fellow. I've missed you."

The gelding softly nickered and nuzzled his forehead against her shoulder while Gabe watched in fascination as his wily and spirited horse turned to mush under Emma's tender ministrations. It seemed that he wasn't the only one who was falling under her spell.

Gabe chuckled. "Let me get him settled real quick. Come on, boy."

He guided the gelding to the corral and released him to join the other horses in the pasture, which were lazily cropping grass. As Xerxes galloped away, kicking his heels up as he went, Matthew yelled impatiently from the porch. "Are you ready yet? Ma says dinner is ready! The faster we eat, the faster I can show you the puppies."

He raised his hand in acknowledgment to the youngster and joined Emma, who had waited patiently for him. Throughout dinner, he watched as the Barnes family laughed and joked with one another. They genuinely enjoyed being together, despite the occasional quarrel, and Gabe knew that this was how he wanted his own family to be—with Emma.

"Are you all right?" she whispered.

"Of course. My mind was just wandering," he replied quietly.

"Let's take a walk to clear it," she said. "Matthew is chomping at the bit to go out to the stable, and I thought we should accompany him."

"That's a wonderful idea."

Gabe used the linen napkin next to his plate to make sure none of the shortcake or raspberry cream from dessert was on his face before he stood and pulled the chair back for Emma.

"I promised a certain young man I would go with him to see Sally's litter," he said, addressing the room. "Would anyone else like to go with us?"

Matthew jumped up eagerly, but the rest of Emma's family politely declined, so the small group set off across the farmyard toward the large stable.

High-pitched yips and playful growls could be heard as they entered, but the mother dog, Sally, didn't stir. She lay calmly in the straw and watched them approach while her ten furry black and white pups came charging out of the stall—barking and jumping to get their visitor's attention.

"Aren't they adorable?" Emma asked as she knelt on the ground in front of them.

"They sure are," Gabe agreed, and he took up a spot next to her in the dirt. "Which one did you choose?"

"This little boy right here," she said gleefully.

He watched her scoop up the animal and kiss its fuzzy head. The pup panted and grinned happily as it lay in her arms, and Emma beamed with pleasure.

"He likes to follow me around and sleep in my lap. How could I not choose him?"

"It seems like you both have good taste," he grinned, giving the pup a scratch. "Why don't you pick mine out too?"

"What! You're gonna let a girl decide for you," Matthew asked derisively.

"Emma isn't just any girl. We're courting, which means one day she'll be my wife," Gabe replied, casting a glance her way. He enjoyed seeing the blush creep up her cheeks. "As such, I believe she should have just as much say as I do."

"But what if she chooses one you don't like?" the youngster demanded, apparently unsatisfied with his answer.

"Well, then I guess I'd just get another. Not all of these pups are promised to a buyer yet."

"I guess that makes sense," Matthew acknowledged, and with his outrage eased, he left the stable for more interesting pursuits.

Emma gently placed her dog into Gabe's arms and began inspecting the remaining pups. Each one was picked up, turned this way and that, before being set down in favor of a different sibling. Finally, she picked up her last candidate and, after looking it over, set it down in front of him.

"This is the one," she stated proudly. "She's just perfect."

Gabe looked uncertainly at the creature before him and stifled a groan. Of all the pups she could have picked, of course, it was the runt of the litter. It definitely wasn't the one he would have chosen, but he supposed he could do as he told Matthew and buy another.

"All right," he agreed. "But she'll need a name."

"You could call her Tiny," Emma said happily. "It certainly suits her!"

Gabe looked again at the dog, who was wagging her tail enthusiastically and wiggling as if in approval of her new moniker.

"Tiny is it. Now, what of this guy here?" he asked, referring to the dog in his arms.

"Blue," Emma said without a second's hesitation.

"Blue," he parroted back, wholly confused as to how she came to this decision.

"Yes! One of his eyes is brown, and the other is blue; hence the name."

"Well, I'll be!"

Gabe looked down at the pup to confirm, as he had never seen such a thing in an animal before, but it was slumbering contentedly. He didn't want to wake the poor fellow from his nap, so he sat with Emma on the dirt floor of the stable, watching Tiny and her siblings play until they heard Sarah calling.

"I should be getting back," Emma sighed. "Let me take Blue so you can get up."

Gabe handed her the dog and got to his feet, dusting bits of straw off the seat of his pants. Then he held his hand out and helped her to her feet.

"I'll go saddle Xerxes. Can you bring both of them out to me?" he asked.

"Of course," she agreed.

Gabe thanked her and headed out through the open double doors. He'd been on his way to collect his horse when he saw Micah leading Xerxes toward him, already saddled and ready to go.

"I figured you might need a hand since you'll have some passengers to deal with on the way home," his friend said. "Where's the pups?"

"Emma's bringing them," he replied, taking his horse's reins. "It'll be a balancing act getting them home, that's for sure."

"Good luck," Micah said with a laugh, and the two shook hands.

When Emma emerged from the stable with a pup under each arm, her eyes suspiciously wet, Gabe felt his heart pinch.

"Don't cry," he soothed as he came to stand before her. "You'll see Blue again in a few days, and I promise to take very good care of him."

"I know," she sniffed. "I keep telling myself the same thing."

Gabe longed to wrap her in his arms and hold her as she cried, but he settled for a chaste kiss on her forehead. He stepped back, pulled himself onto his horse, and held his hands out for a pup.

Emma gave Blue a quick squeeze before passing him to Gabe and then did the same with Tiny. It was a trick to get them settled in his arms, but once they quit wiggling, he nodded to her in farewell. He would have tipped his hat, but both his hands were full.

Thankfully, Xerxes was well-trained and knew the way home, so Gabe used his knees to give the horse a light squeeze, and they were off.

Henry and Miguel were sitting in front of the bunkhouse, smoking their pipes, swapping stories, when Gabe arrived home. When they spotted the dogs resting in his arms, they came to investigate.

"What do we have here?" the foreman asked, tapping the pipe on the bottom of his boot to shake out any leftover tobacco.

"I brought home the pup I'm buying from Edward, and I've got Emma's, too," Gabe replied. He took his feet from the stirrups, swung his left leg over the saddle, and carefully jumped down. "I told her it could stay here."

Miguel reached out to scratch Blue around his neck. "He'll make a fine herding animal."

"That one's not mine," Gabe corrected as he set the pups down.

"You can't mean that little thing is your new sheep herding dog," Henry exclaimed. "Why, it's no bigger than a barn cat."

"I think you mean a starving barn cat," Miguel corrected, while trying to hold back his mirth.

"Be that as it may," Gabe said evenly. "I hope you don't disparage it when Emma's around because she chose it."

"Only a man who is head over heels in love would let a woman pick out his dog when she has no experience with such things," Henry chuckled. "If I were you, I'd pray that Edward still has a decent one left."

“It may not be so bad,” Miguel consoled as he crouched and offered his hand for Tiny and Blue to sniff. “Let them watch Dusty while he works with the cattle. He’s been slowing down the last few years, but he could still show them a thing or two.”

“I planned on it,” Gabe nodded. “For now, I’ll get them settled into the barn for the night. See you in the morning.”

He whistled to get the pups’ attention and led them to the barn, where he’d made a bed of hay inside a large wooden crate. After putting them in, he waited a few minutes to make sure they settled before he left for the evening. He just hoped that Emma wasn’t missing Blue too much.

Chapter 31

A telegram arrived a week later with word that Gabe's sheep were due at the Butte stockyard on Tuesday, on the 1 p.m. train. He let out a loud whoop, startling the young messenger boy, and hurriedly apologized. Digging into his pocket, he gave the boy two silver dollars as a tip and sent him on his way.

When Miguel and Henry came out of the stable to see what the hollering was about, Gabe showed them the telegram. His plans were finally coming together, and he was elated.

"I can't believe we're gonna be herding sheep," Henry said grumpily.

"It could be worse, Henry," Miguel consoled. "He could have chosen hogs, and they stink worse than Riley."

This comment brought a grin to the older man's face, and he laughed. "I suppose that's true. I'll go let Martha May know you won't be here for dinner tomorrow. Maybe you should make Gabe treat you to a meal in Butte, eh, Miguel?"

"And maybe ice cream too," the ranch hand agreed.

They continued to tease Gabe good-naturedly, but he didn't care. He was in such a good mood that he'd buy them each a whole pie if they wanted. With a wave, he left the men to their work and sought Tommy in the bunkhouse.

"Oh boy! Do you think we'll have some time for ourselves?" the young hand asked when Gabe told him they'd be heading into Butte in the morning. "I have a gal I'd like to meet up with while we're there."

Tommy wouldn't meet his eye as he said this, preferring to stare down at the floor. When Gabe realized what kind of "gal" he was referring to, his expression hardened.

"I keep a clean ranch, same as Telly did," he said firmly. "If you're engaging in that kind of behavior, you can collect your pay and be gone by morning."

"I haven't done anything," the young man protested, eyes wide. "We just talked last time I was there. That's all."

Gabe studied him for a long moment, then gave a single nod.

"Good. But if I hear you've been back to those places, you'll be heading down the road. Understood?"

"Yes, sir," Tommy said, looking as if he were on the verge of tears.

Gabe softened his tone slightly. "We still have morning chores to do on the ranch before we head out. We'll have time to find a place for dinner and maybe do some window shopping before the train arrives, but that's about it. Once they offload the sheep, I want to head home right away so we can get them settled before dark."

He patted the young man on the shoulder and left to make final preparations for the new herd.

When he finally came home, long after the sun had set, he found that Martha May had left him a plate of food on the table. It was cold now, but Gabe didn't care. He shoveled the food into his mouth, grateful that there was no one there to reprimand him for his poor manners.

He put his dish in the sink and dragged himself to bed, where he fell into an exhausted sleep, waking just as the sun was rising over the mountains. He closed his eyes for another moment before forcing himself to get out of bed. There were too many things to do and barely enough time to do them in.

Martha May was adding a few extra hotcakes to his plate when he came downstairs for breakfast. Gabe smiled appreciatively at her.

"Thank you. I feel like my stomach is playing catch-up from not eating yesterday."

"Well, I can't have you fainting while you're riding into Butte because I underfed you," she said. "Now eat up; the hands have already started their work."

"Yes, ma'am," Gabe replied, giving a sharp salute, and Martha May snapped his arm with a towel for his cheekiness.

By 10:30 in the morning, Gabe, Miguel, and Tommy were ready to ride out. They waved goodbye to Henry, who'd come to see them off, and headed north on the eight-mile journey to Butte.

It was an unseasonably hot mid-August day. The wide blue Montana sky held only a few wisps of clouds, much to the disappointment of farmers, ranchers, and homesteaders in the area who were praying for rain. With the ground so dry, dust from their horses' hooves hung thick in the air, nearly choking them. Even with their bandannas pulled up over their faces, they could taste the gritty soil in their mouths.

By the time they made it to their destination an hour later, their shirts were soaked with perspiration, making the fabric cling to their chests. They were more than ready for a respite from the glaring sun, and once the horses had been taken care of, they made their way to an eating house just up the road. They enjoyed hearty beef steak with mashed potatoes and string beans, followed by as many desserts as they could manage.

With their bellies full and the bill paid, Miguel took Tommy with him so they could send some telegrams off to family, and Gabe was left to explore the town on his own.

As he wandered through the busy streets of the burgeoning mining town, maneuvering around delivery wagons and folks on foot, he spotted a large store with a wooden sign proclaiming, "Height & Fairfield—Jewelers, Opticians, and Stationers." On a whim, he decided to see what they had for sale.

The store was filled with so many items that it was overwhelming at first glance. Aside from all the goods the sign suggested, they sold fine cutlery, scissors, razors, and more.

Gabe made his way through the displays and looked over the pocket watches and scarf pins but decided he didn't need anything new. When he noticed a covered glass display of rings, he wandered closer, curious.

There were dozens of gold and silver rings, all lined up in neat rows on black velvet trays. Some had plain bands, while others were engraved or set with precious stones or pearls. He bent closer to inspect them.

"Can I help you find what you are looking for, sir?"

Gabe glanced up to see a well-dressed man looking expectantly at him. "Oh, I wasn't looking for anything in particular," he replied, straightening up. "I just wanted to see what you have to offer."

"Well, we have a variety of unique rings available for purchase, but I also do custom work. Do you have a lady you are looking to buy a ring for?"

"I do," he admitted, rubbing the back of his neck. "But we've only been courting for a short time. It might be too soon to be looking at rings, don't you think?"

"It's never too early to think about what your lady love might like," the jeweler said with a knowing smile. "After all, out here on the frontier, good women are in short supply. They get married much sooner than one would back east, where I'm from. What month was she born in? Perhaps we can narrow your search down."

"Her birthday was almost three weeks ago," Gabe supplied. "The twenty-third." He smiled a bit as he remembered how happy his gift of book shopping had made her.

"Then you could look for something with an onyx or ruby," the jeweler suggested. "Both of which have been used to represent July birthdays."

Pulling out one of the velvet-lined trays from the glass display, he proceeded to show Gabe over a dozen rings. They were all finely crafted, with gemstones that cast a fiery glow in the light, but none of them seemed right for Emma.

"Thank you for showing these to me," Gabe said. "But I think I will wait on purchasing one until the right time." He held out his hand to the jeweler, and they shook hands. "I'll be sure to come back."

"I'll look forward to it. Good day," the man replied cheerfully as he returned the rings to their proper place.

Gabe left the store, and after a bit more exploring, he purchased an embroidered handkerchief for Martha May and a new pipe for Henry. They didn't need the gifts, but as they were the closest thing to parents he had, he wanted to do something nice for them.

Miguel and Tommy were waiting at the depot when Gabe arrived, and he pulled out his pocket watch to check the time. There were still ten minutes to spare. He clicked the cover shut and, after placing it back in his pocket, made his way to an empty bench. Some had left a recent edition of the Butte Daily Miner on the seat, so he opened it and read a few articles aloud to the ranch hands to pass the time.

Slowly, the platform filled with people. In the distance, a whistle sounded, alerting passengers to the train's approach, and the chugging of the engine grew louder and louder. Then the sharp, acrid scent of coal smoke drifted on the breeze, and when the brakes finally squealed and the massive metal locomotive came to a stop in front of them, a thick cloud of steam and soot billowed around the platform.

Gabe folded the newspaper and dropped it back onto the bench for someone else to read as he stood up. "Well," he said to his ranch hands, "let's get to it."

Tommy ran off to grab the horses, while he and Miguel walked the length of the train to where livestock was being unloaded from the cars. He showed his collection slip to the man in charge, who gave it a cursory glance and let them into the stockyard. They continued past the large pens for the horses and cattle until they reached the sheep pen.

There, huddled together in a tight circle and looking like one giant fluffy cloud, were Gabe's new Merinos.

He stood there for a moment, just watching them. It was surreal. He'd been planning this for so long, and now it was finally real. Shaking his head with a laugh, he opened the pen's gate and began inspecting them one by one. They made sure to bleat their displeasure at being handled, but aside from being a little annoyed, they seemed to be in perfect health.

Tommy joined them with the horses, and once everyone had mounted, Gabe opened the gate to the sheep pen. The plan was to drive them out of the corner where they'd huddled and out into the lane of the stockyard. But when the young ranch hand gave a loud yell to get the flock moving—the same one he used when driving cattle—the sheep fled in every direction.

Gabe watched the spectacle from the fence, rubbing his forehead. "Well... that didn't work," he muttered.

Tommy hopped off his horse, calling out apologies as he tried to round up the nearest bunch. The second he got close, they bolted again, slipping under fences and darting between the legs of the confused cattle. It looked like the sheep were playing a chaotic game of peekaboo among the bigger animals.

Gabe trotted over to help, and he and Tommy worked together to get all the frightened animals into a knot so they could lead them out of the stockyard while Miguel followed behind to make sure they didn't have any stragglers.

The ride back to the Lucky Strike took three times as long as it should have. They kept having to chase down sheep that broke away from the group. This would have been far easier with a good dog or two, but Tiny was still just a pup. Training her would have to become a much higher priority than he had originally thought.

As they made the final turn up the long dirt drive, Henry rode up to meet Gabe.

"Did they give you any trouble?" the foreman asked, wiping perspiration from his face with a bandana he'd pulled from his vest pocket.

"A bit," Gabe replied, "but we got it under control."

Tommy snickered, and Miguel smacked the back of the young ranch hand's head to keep him from spilling every detail about their rough start. Henry quirked a brow at the strange behavior of the two men and looked to Gabe.

"You know," the foreman drawled. "You might go speak to Angus Paterson. He was a crofter in Scotland and had some experience raising sheep. He might have some tips to help get you started on the right foot."

"I think you're right," Gabe sighed. "If today has shown me anything, it's that no matter how much time and energy I spent researching, it doesn't beat hands-on experience."

"Of course I'm right," Henry chuckled. "For now, though, let's get these woolies settled before the dinner bell rings. I'm starving."

"You heard the man," Gabe said to the hands, and as he nudged Xerxes into a trot, he realized he was in for some long, hard days.

Chapter 32

"My word," Emma exclaimed as she sat back in her chair at Gabe's table on Friday afternoon. "I can't believe I ate so much."

She'd made fried chicken, potato salad, and roasted summer squash for dinner, and there was hardly a crumb left. Even the graham gems she'd made for dessert—served with fresh butter and huckleberry preserves—had quickly disappeared.

"That's what happens when you make good food," Aunt Sarah chuckled. "A nice walk always helps me feel better when I've eaten too much."

"That's an excellent idea," Gabe said as he stood up and looked at Emma. "Why don't I take you on a tour of the ranch before you have to leave? Or, at least, the parts you can see from the house. I'll introduce you to the hands, and then you can say hello to Blue."

"That's right," she gasped, "I haven't seen him yet." She felt guilty that she'd forgotten to check on her pup when she'd arrived at the ranch. But Gabe had been waiting on the porch when she arrived, a handsome grin on his face, and she'd forgotten about everything else.

"You go along with Gabriel, dear," Martha May said, making playful shooing motions with her hands. "Sarah and I will clean up this mess. You two enjoy yourselves."

"Well, if you insist," she agreed, getting up from her seat. "It'll be nice to take a better look around and meet the men who work here."

He grabbed his hat from a peg by the back door before opening it for her. "After you."

Emma stepped off the porch and out into the bright afternoon sunlight, squinting against the glare. She was just about to raise her hand to shield her eyes when something heavy and dark settled over her head. The relief to her vision was immediate, and she glanced up to see that she was wearing Gabe's hat.

"Gabe! What are you doing?" she exclaimed. "This is yours."

"True, but you need it more than I do right now," he said, a crooked smile on his face. "You look fantastic in it."

"I do?" she asked curiously, touching the wide brim.

"Yes. I think it suits you, actually," he said, adjusting the hat so it sat more securely on her head. "There you go. Now you're ready to go exploring."

Emma wasn't sure if the butterflies in her stomach were from the look of admiration Gabe was giving her, or because he inconvenienced himself when he saw her need. The caring gesture reaffirmed what Emma already knew: Gabe was steady, kind, and thoughtful. It was one of the many reasons she was coming to love him.

"Shall we?" he asked, holding out an arm.

"Of course!"

Emma slipped her hand into the crook of his elbow, feeling the warmth of him through his sleeve, and they set off across the yard. Sitting on the bench in front of the long wooden bunkhouse she had noticed on her first visit were two men. When they saw Gabe and Emma approaching, they stood.

"Afternoon, boys," Gabe said as he nodded to them in greeting. "I'd like to introduce you both to the woman I'm courting. This is Miss Emma Barnes. She's Edward and Sarah's niece. Miss Barnes, this is my head ranch hand, Miguel Alvarez, and that's our cook, Stew."

Emma nodded first to Miguel, a tall, good-looking man with warm brown eyes and thick black hair with just a little gray showing at the temples. She guessed him to be in his late forties, but he was still very fit and would probably still be working twenty years from now. Then she turned to Stew, who was younger, shorter, and stouter than his counterpart. He had receding sandy blonde hair and watery blue eyes, though that might have been from the smoke that was curling up from the lit cigar he'd set aside when she'd joined the men.

"Ah! We finally get to meet your Miss Barnes," Miguel said happily, and he came forward to shake Emma's hand. "I have heard so much about you. I especially enjoyed hearing about how you handled Mrs. Callaway."

Her cheeks warmed as she accepted his handshake. "It's nice to meet you, Mr. Alvarez. I suppose I should have known word of my little scene had reached the ranch. I promise, I'm usually much better behaved."

"Don't mind him none, Miss Barnes," Stew said with a friendly smile. "We're mighty glad to meet you."

"Thank you. I'm glad to meet you as well, Mr..." Emma's voice trailed off. Surely "Stew" wasn't the man's given name.

"Stuart Henderson," he supplied, "but everyone around here just calls me Stew."

"Well, it's lovely to meet you both," she said. "Have you worked here long?"

Though it was a polite follow-up question, she was genuinely curious to hear their answer. She had spent little time with the seasonal workers they'd had on the farm earlier in the year. Uncle Edward tried to keep them separate from the girls, unless they were bringing meals or hauling buckets of water to the fields.

"Since the beginning," Miguel stated proudly. "I was working for an outfit in New Mexico, but the man in charge was a nasty piece of work. When I heard that the man we were delivering the cattle to needed hands, I quit and came to work here. It was the best decision I ever made, though I still miss my family back home."

"I came on shortly after," Stew said. "I was working in the mining camps, serving hot meals to men who'd had more luck than I had. One day a fellow who'd refused to pay pulled his gun on me." He chuckled and shook his head. "That fool Telly stepped between us and offered to pay for the food himself. Then he offered me a job cooking and cleaning for the hands on his ranch."

"How fortunate that he was there when you needed him the most," Emma said, thinking how terrified she would have been in that position.

"It was," the cook agreed. "And let me tell you, we were all glad that Gabe here has shown himself to be the same kind of man."

Miguel echoed the sentiment, and she glanced at Gabe, who was looking distinctly uncomfortable with the praise, and she smiled. "I believe you're correct, but let's not embarrass him any further by going on and on. He's promised me a tour of the ranch, and we should continue."

Emma said her goodbyes to Stew and Miguel and let Gabe guide her as they strolled through the yard. She was in no hurry to get back to the house. She was having a wonderful time just listening to him explain all the improvements that he'd made since taking ownership of the ranch. His passion for the land, the animals, and the people working here made her admire him even more.

They visited the stable, where she got to see the colt that Gabe had written about, and meet other ranch hands, Riley Dunn and Tommy Miller. Emma enjoyed talking to the younger men, even though it was only for a few minutes, and before she left, she made sure to say hello to Xerxes.

"Would you like to see the sheep now?" Gabe asked. "They've only been here for a few days, but I think they're settling in nicely."

"I would," she said eagerly. "Matthew will be so jealous that I get to see them first."

As they neared the large enclosure where the sheep were being kept while they adjusted to their new home, loud barking filled the air, sending the animals scattering. Emma turned to find the source of the noise and saw two black-and-white streaks heading straight for her.

"Oh, my goodness!" she exclaimed. "Where did you come from?"

Dropping to her knees to pet the wriggling pups, she happily received the sniffs and licks they were showering her with. She picked them up one at a time and hugged them to her chest. Blue couldn't contain his enthusiasm at being reunited and tried to climb onto her shoulder, almost knocking Gabe's hat from her head. Emma quickly raised her hand and held it securely while she set Blue on the ground.

"They're acting as if I've been gone for weeks," she laughed. "I hope they have been behaving themselves."

"As much as a young dog can," Gabe replied with an easy grin. "They've been following Telly's dog Dusty around all day, and the old boy is exhausted. I think he looks forward to when I train with Tiny because he gets a bit of a break."

"What about Blue?" Emma asked in confusion. "Won't he be learning as well?"

"Well, I wasn't sure how you would feel about that," he answered with a shrug. "He's supposed to be your pet, remember?"

"Well, yes," she agreed. "But if he's going to be living here on your ranch, shouldn't he help?"

"You mean *our* ranch," Gabe corrected gently. "The Bible talks about 'two becoming one,' and I believe that applies to our lives in more ways than one. It won't just be *my* ranch when we marry; it will be *our* ranch, which means you get a say in how it's run and if Blue is put to work."

Emma took a moment to think about his words and slowly nodded her head. "In that case, I think you should train both dogs. It'll be good for him to have a purpose."

"All right, then," Gabe said, a soft smile tugging at the corner of his lips. "As long as you're sure."

"I am," she stated, standing up and brushing her hands off on her skirt.

The pups at her feet began to wrestle with each other, so she moved to the wooden fence and leaned her forearms against the top railing as she gazed at the rams and ewes grazing on the fresh green grass and wildflowers. Gabe came to stand beside her, and they watched the scene before them in companionable silence, each lost in their own thoughts.

"We should head back," she sighed a few minutes later.

"We should," he agreed. "I'm sure Henry is chomping at the bit to get back to work."

With one last look around the pasture, Emma pushed off the railing, and they headed back toward the house. The dogs followed behind, nipping at the hem of her dress before getting bored and scampering off to the stable.

They had almost reached the house when a small buggy with a folding top came up the drive. It was pulled by a massive horse that was even taller than Xerxes, and Emma recognized the driver at once as Mrs. Paterson. She wondered what the librarian was doing here on a Friday afternoon.

"Just the man I was coming to see," Mrs. Paterson called down to Gabe as the conveyance stopped in front of them. "Oh! And ye have yer lovely lass with ye as well. Hullo there, dearie."

Emma returned her greeting, and Gabe helped to the ground, holding the reins of the vehicle.

"Thank ye, Mr. Moreau. Yer such a gentleman," the Scotswoman said. "I hope I'm not being too forward, but my Angus said that ye came to speak with him about yer new flock of sheep, and I wondered if ye'd thought of hiring a shepherd to keep them."

"I'd been giving some thought to it," Gabe replied with a nod. "Why do you ask?"

"Well, my sister's boy, Alastair, came over from Scotland a few months ago, and he's been struggling to find work in New York—the city's overflowing with people looking for jobs right now. But he's helped his Da herd since he was a lad, and he has a talent for calming any frightened beastie. Do ye think ye would consider him for the job?"

"Yes. It would be good to have someone around who actually knows what they're doing," Gabe laughed ruefully. "Mind you, it would be on a trial until I know he's a fit for the job."

"Ye won't be disappointed in him, I promise," Mrs. Paterson rushed to assure him. "I'll telegraph him right away so he can be on the first train out here."

"That sounds fine, but I'd like to pay for his fare," Gabe offered. He returned the reins and said, "Just give me a moment to collect my wallet."

Emma watched him quickly stride toward the house, and she smiled. "Well," she said to Mrs. Paterson. "You certainly seem to have made his day."

They shared a laugh and began discussing which book to choose for the next book club. For Emma, it was a toss-up between *The Lamplighter* and *The Wide, Wide World*. She resonated with parts of both stories.

Gabe returned a few minutes later, with Martha May and Aunt Sarah trailing behind him.

"Here you are," he said as he handed Mrs. Paterson a roll of bills. "This should cover his ticket and any expenses he may incur. And if it's all right, I'll stop by your place tonight, and you can tell me a bit more about your nephew."

"Aye, that'd be just fine," she said, still looking astonished at the amount of money he had given her. "I can't thank ye enough, Mr. Moreau."

"Call me Gabe, please. I'm sure we will be seeing a lot more of each other, and I'd hate to stand on formality every time."

"Then ye must call me Isla. And ye as well," she said, turning to Emma. "Well, I must be going now. I left Angus at the store, and who knows what havoc he's caused."

There was a chorus of laughter at that, and once Mrs. Paterson's buggy started rumbling down the drive, Emma smiled warmly at Gabe. "It was very generous to pay for her nephew's trip out here."

"Don't go inflating the boy's ego," Henry called out as he steered Aunt Sarah's wagon out of the barn. "He just wants to get help with those animals that he insisted he had to have."

"When you see how much profit we can make off of them, you won't be so upset about it," Gabe replied confidently.

"I look forward to being proven wrong then," the foreman said as he halted the cart and climbed down. "Now, hurry and say your goodbyes. We have work to do. Emma, Sarah, it was a pleasure to see you both again."

Emma said her goodbyes to Henry and Martha May, giving the older woman a quick hug, and then climbed into the wagon. Sarah got in next to her, and they were about to take off toward home when she remembered she was wearing Gabe's hat.

"I almost forgot to return this," she said as she handed it to him.

Gabe chuckled and placed the weathered felt hat over his wavy brown hair. "I forgot too. Are you sure you don't want to keep it?"

"You need it more than I do," Emma replied, echoing his words from earlier, and she could hear his rich laughter as the wagon pulled away.

Chapter 33

It took two weeks for Gabe's newest employee, Alastair Watt, to arrive in Montana. The train ride itself was only a few days' journey, but Alastair had been hired to haul cargo on the West Street piers until the end of August and was determined to honor his commitment. Gabe felt it showed great integrity, but the actual proof of his worth would come when he began working with the flock.

As luck would have it, he and Henry were just leaving the house after breakfast when a familiar buggy—pulled by a massive Shire—came rolling to a stop before them. Mrs. Paterson was waving cheerfully from the driver's seat as a tall, broad-shouldered man in his early twenties hopped down. Long days spent in the sun had faded his red hair, but his beard remained fiery. Dressed in sturdy denim trousers and a white linen shirt rolled up at the sleeves, he looked every inch a man who was born to work sheep.

"You must be Alastair," Gabe said, coming forward to offer him his hand. "I'm Gabe Moreau, and this is my foreman, Henry Rollings. It's good to have you here."

"Aye," Alastair replied in a thick Scottish burr, shaking Gabe's hand firmly. "'Tis grand to have a job so close to family. I was gettin' a wee bit homesick surrounded by so many folk and buildin's in the city, but seein' the wide open land and green hills made me feel right at home. Though Auntie Isla's cooking may have had a wee bit to do with that as well!"

"Ha! A woman's cooking will set any man to rights," Henry chortled, shaking hands with their new shepherd. "But our cook, Stew, does a pretty good job fixin' up his vittles. At least I have heard no complaints."

"After a hard day's work, it doesnae matter much what it tastes like, as long as it's warm and fillin'," Alastair remarked with a grin.

"I think we can all agree on that," Gabe laughed. "I'll let you say your goodbyes, and then we can get you settled in the bunkhouse."

"If ye dinnae mind, I'll sleep out with the sheep for the first wee while, so they can get to know me."

"Are you sure, son?" Henry asked as he scratched his head in confusion. "I'd guess you didn't have a proper night's sleep on the train and might want a real bed."

"Aye, I'll be fine. I slept out with the sheep many a night when I was back home in Scotland."

"It's all right with me," Gabe said with a shrug. He'd spent most of his nights under the stars or in a farmer's hayloft after he'd lost his home. It didn't seem like such an unusual request.

While Alastair said goodbye to his aunt, Gabe headed to the stable to get ready for the day. He could hear Blue and Tiny's high-pitched barks as he approached, and when he opened the large sliding doors, they ran to greet him. He bent, gave them each a scratch on their furry bellies, and brought Xerxes out of his stall. The energetic pups followed and began wrestling at the horse's feet as he was being saddled, but the gelding stood still, allowing them to have their fun.

"Tis a fine cuddie ye have there," Alastair commented as he walked into the stable with a canvas drawstring bag over his shoulder. When Gabe gave him a blank look of confusion,

Alastair shook his head and clarified, "Yer horse. I've been tryin' to speak plain American since I landed, but the old words slip out now and then."

"Don't let Xerxes fool you," he warned. "He can be docile as a lamb one minute and a demon beast the next. You know how to ride, I assume?"

"That I do, though I've never used one while droving. I've always had a dog to help get the beasties where they needed to go. I suppose that's what these two are for, eh?" He dropped to his knees and held out a hand to the pups, who instantly stopped what they were doing to come and sniff him. "Aye, these'll do just fine."

"Both of them?" Gabe asked skeptically as he eyed Tiny.

"Oh, aye," Alastair replied as he got to his feet. "Her size can be an advantage as long as she's trained well."

"I've taught them some basic commands, but I'll be relying on you to fill in the gaps since you have more experience than I do," he said, grabbing Xerxes' reins and leading the way out to the sheep's enclosure.

"Nae bother. I'll have them trained up in no time. Do they have names yet? I dinnae want to confuse them."

"The one there is Tiny, and her brother is called Blue," Gabe said, pointing to the pups who'd raced ahead of them. "He belongs to the woman I'm courting, but Emma asked that he be trained right alongside his sister."

Alastair nodded, seemingly unbothered by the news, and when they reached the temporary enclosure where the sheep were contentedly grazing, he whistled to the dogs. "Come on, ye wee ones. Let's see what ye can do."

Gabe was in such a good mood on Friday that he began whistling to himself as he cantered off toward the southern range, where his cattle were grazing. Emma was coming that afternoon, and he couldn't wait to show her the progress Blue and Tiny had made in their training. Whether that was due to the dogs' natural intelligence or Alastair's skills, he wasn't sure. But the shepherd had already proved his worth.

As he crested the hill and spotted Miguel and Riley standing together at the fence line, their faces grim, the cheerful tune died on his lips. Gabe felt the fine hairs on the back of his neck stand on end. Something was wrong.

“What’s going on here?” he asked, his voice ringing with command as he pulled Xerxes to a halt.

“It looks like the fence has been cut again. We have a few dozen cattle missing,” Miguel informed him gravely. “It looks like they were driven off to the east.”

Riley let out a harsh curse and kicked at the ground. “Those thieving varmints,” he spat in anger. “Let’s go get them.”

“Don’t be too hasty,” Miguel cautioned. “We don’t know how many men are out there. We should get help.”

“You’re right,” Gabe agreed. “Riley, you ride back and have Tommy come out to fix the fence. I don’t want any more of the herd wandering off. Then head into town and get Sheriff Bell.” He glanced back down at the tracks again. “Miguel and I will head out and see if we can catch up with them.”

“You got it, boss,” Riley said with a sharp nod. He swung up into his saddle and raced off toward the house, sending clumps of dirt and grass flying in his wake.

Gabe let Miguel lead the way, and they cautiously followed the cattle’s trail, eyes scanning the surrounding terrain for any sign of ambush. So far, there was nothing—only the freshly churned earth and the steady pounding of their horses’ hooves.

As they rode, he turned the situation over in his mind, but the answers that came left him unsatisfied.

“Do you think that this was done by the same person who cut the fence before?” he asked when they slowed to study the ground.

“Sí,” Miguel replied, his voice grimmer than Gabe had ever heard it.

“But they didn’t take any cattle before,” he said, frowning. “Why now?”

“I don’t think those were the only times someone has tried to tamper with your herd.”

“What do you mean?”

“We heard a gunshot during that bad storm a few weeks back. The cattle were already stressed, and it spooked them into a run. Tommy had to ride ahead and get them to circle up before they started a stampede.”

“And you didn’t think to say something about it to me?” Gabe asked sharply.

Miguel shrugged. “It’s Montana. Everyone here owns a gun, and if I came running to you every time I heard one go off, you would be sick of me. I thought little of it at the time, but now... it seems like it was done on purpose.”

Gabe let out a frustrated exhale. "That still doesn't explain why. There are other outfits in the area that free-range. It'd be a lot easier to cut out a few heads from one of them without anyone noticing. I'll have to speak to the Sheriff and see if he knows of any rustlers in the area."

They rode on in silence for another half hour before Gabe finally spotted a small group of cattle with the Lucky Strike brand hidden in a shallow gully surrounded by chokecherry trees. The distinctive marking of a three-leaf clover with a horseshoe in the middle was proof that the herd had been taken in this direction. But for some reason, these had been left behind.

"Well, at least we know we're on the right track," he muttered, pulling back on Xerxes' reins.

"Still, we must be wary," Miguel advised as he slid down from his horse to study the surrounding tracks. Frowning, he headed down into the ditch and reappeared a few minutes later. "I don't think this rustler is very experienced," the ranch hand said. "There were too many cattle for one man to move alone—especially if you're drunk." He tossed an empty liquor bottle into Gabe's lap and gathered his horse's reins.

Gabe looked at the empty glass container, and a nagging unease stirred in the back of his mind. He didn't partake in spirits, but something about the discarded item sent chills racing down his spine. Not wanting to carry it any longer, he dismounted and set the bottle in the middle of the path.

"We should go," Miguel urged. "We're gaining on him."

"I know. I'm going to leave a message for Riley to find when he and Sheriff Bell catch up," Gabe said, pulling a small leather notebook and pencil out of his saddlebag.

He scribbled quick instructions to round up the cattle and drive them home before ripping the paper out and rolling it up tight. He stuffed it into the neck of the bottle and hurried back to Xerxes, tucking the writing implements away before climbing into the saddle. With a nod to his companion, they galloped off, leaving a cloud of dust in their wake.

It wasn't long before Gabe heard the thundering of hooves behind him, and he turned in the saddle to see who it was. When he saw Sheriff Bell riding hell-for-leather toward them, he slowed Xerxes, and Miguel followed his lead.

"See any more signs of him yet?" the sheriff asked, as out of breath as his stallion. His weathered face was bright red, and sweat beaded on his forehead.

"No, but he shouldn't be too far ahead," Miguel said with a shake of his head. "The tracks are still fresh, and there are only so many places to go before you hit steep inclines into the mountains."

"Let's ride on then," the lawman pressed. "I don't tolerate thievery, and when I catch this son of a—." He stopped short, cleared his throat, and straightened in the saddle. "Well, when I catch him, he'll be going straight to jail."

With that stern pronouncement, they set off again, their horses' pace ate up the miles until the sheriff pulled up short. He pointed ahead where the rest of the herd grazed in a small field that spread out before a sheer incline of rocky terrain and clinging evergreens. Raising his hand to signal silence, he dismounted with care and pulled the Colt Army revolver from the gun belt. Gabe and Miguel followed his lead, their eyes scanning the treeline.

"We don't know if that rustler is still around, but if he is, I'd like to get the drop on him," the sheriff whispered. "Miguel, you have a lot of skill with tracking, so I want you to circle to the right while I come around from the left."

"What do you want me to do?" Gabe asked.

"I want you to stay here. If that coward tries to ride off, I want you to take off after him—so stay ready."

While this wasn't what he wanted to hear, he resigned himself to the role of lookout. Obviously, these two men were more experienced in these matters, likely picking up their knowledge from the War Between the States. And while he was good with his fists, he'd probably be more of a hindrance than a help in this situation.

Miguel and Sheriff Bell slipped stealthily through the foliage in opposite directions, and Gabe moved Xerxes off the trail. He kept his hand on the butt of his revolver, straining his ears for any sounds of a scuffle, but all he could hear was the wind moving through the trees and the occasional low of a distant cow.

By the disappointed looks on the men's faces when they finally reemerged, Gabe knew that they'd had no luck finding the culprit. Frustration and anger swept through him;

he pounded his fist against his thigh, though that did little to ease his increasingly foul mood.

"I'll send some deputies out to comb this area tomorrow," Sheriff Bell said as they approached. "There was a campsite back there, littered with empty gin bottles and tin cans. It seems some drunk is hanging around, looking to make some quick cash by selling stolen cattle."

"Thank you, Sheriff," Gabe said, shaking hands with the lawman. "I appreciate your help."

"I'd think about having your hands take turns on watch. If this scoundrel tries to come back and sees that you are on the lookout for him, he'll probably move on and find an easier mark."

"I'll have Henry work something out with the hands and take my turn as well," Gabe said. "For now, we should get the rest of these cows back. Dinner should be ready by the time we get home, and I'd be obliged if you joined us. It's the least I can do."

"How could I say no to Martha May's cooking?" the sheriff asked with a laugh. "Let's get these cattle home!"

Chapter 34

Emma paced back and forth on Gabe's porch, wiping tears from her eyes as she prayed for his safe return. When she arrived at the Lucky Strike for her Friday lessons and didn't see him waiting for her, she'd known something wasn't right. Deep in her bones she'd know, and it had now been over three hours since he'd ridden out after a cattle thief.

"Dear," Aunt Sarah said gently, placing her hand on Emma's shoulder. "You're going to wear out the boards. Come inside and have a cup of coffee."

"I can't," she sniffed. "Not until he comes back."

"Emma, that could take all evening."

"I know, I just..." Her voice trailed off as she heard the distant lowing of cattle and the steady rumble of hooves against the hard-packed earth. She sucked in a breath, afraid that she was only imagining the sounds. But as she glanced down the long dirt drive, she saw a cloud of dust rising in the air and three men on horseback herding a small group of agitated cattle.

"It's Gabe," Emma breathed, her voice barely above a whisper.

Sarah let out a soft gasp and hurried inside, calling for Martha May as she went.

The raised voices must have caught Gabe's attention, because as he rode into the yard, he turned and looked toward the porch. For a brief moment, he looked confused to see her there. Then his face lit up with joy, and he vaulted from the saddle, running toward her.

Unable to wait any longer, Emma flew down the porch steps and met him halfway, launching herself into his arms. "Oh, Gabe, I'm so glad to see you," she exclaimed, pulling back just enough to look into his face as tears of relief slid down her cheeks. "Henry told us what happened, and all I could think of was something terrible happening to you."

"I'm sorry for worrying you," he murmured, gently pulling her closer and tucking her head into the crook of his neck. "We recovered all the animals, and no one was hurt. That's all that matters."

They stood together in the yard, Gabe slowly rubbing her back in comfort, until Martha May and Sarah joined them. Neither woman seemed bothered by the intimate embrace they witnessed. If anything, they looked immensely relieved that he was home safe.

"I hope you don't mind," Gabe said, finally stepping back but keeping hold of Emma's hand, "but I invited Sheriff Bell to have dinner with us. I figured he deserved a nice meal so we could show our appreciation."

"You were quite right to do so, Gabriel," Martha May agreed, sneaking in a quick hug of her own. "Emma made beefsteak and onions with mashed potatoes and rolls for dinner, along with lemon tarts, apple pie, and rice pudding for dessert."

When he turned to her with a questioning look, she shrugged helplessly. "Apparently, I bake when I'm upset," she explained with a sheepish smile.

"Well, I've never been one to turn away food, and we have a guest, so I'm sure nothing will go to waste. Why don't we move into the kitchen so I can freshen up?" he suggested. "I'm sure the others will be in any minute."

Martha May and Sarah's relieved chatter filled the kitchen as Gabe washed the trail dust off his hands. It seemed all the silence that had lingered in the room while they waited for his safe return came back at once, and by the time Henry and the sheriff arrived, Emma was actually laughing.

"My, my," the lawman exclaimed as he saw the variety of sweets laid out on the table. "Looks like you've been doing some baking today, Martha May!"

"It wasn't me this time, Joshua," Martha May chuckled. "It was Emma. You remember Edward and Sarah's niece? I've been teaching her how to cook for two months now, and she's taken to it like a duck to water. I'm very proud of the progress she's made."

"And I've gained ten pounds," Henry noted as he patted his still-fit stomach.

"Well, I think that's a sacrifice I'm willing to make," Sheriff Bell stated. "I can't wait to have a bit of everything."

"Let's dig in then," Henry declared. "I'm starving. Someone was late for dinner, and the womenfolk wouldn't let me eat without him."

Though the foreman's words were teasing, Emma could see relief in his eyes. Oh, Henry liked to act tough, but she could tell that inside, he'd been just as worried as the rest of them.

After the cattle rustling incident, Uncle Edward had told Emma she would have to forgo her Friday lessons at the ranch for the time being. She had been shocked and angered by his decision at first. But when she remembered how she felt sitting in Gabe's kitchen, praying for his safe return, she realized her uncle might be feeling the same way about her. Not to mention his wife. Looking at things from this perspective, she no longer felt so upset about staying on the farm.

She still missed Gabe terribly, but by the end of the second week of September, the spring wheat was ready for harvest, and Emma and her aunt were busily preparing for another round of workers. They had just finished making up the four beds that would be needed when Sarah let out a sigh.

"I wish we'd been able to hire a few more hands. We lost some of our best workers to that gold strike up north, along with most of the able-bodied men in the area."

"Do you always hire the same men?" Emma asked as she fluffed a pillow.

"We try to." Sarah nodded. "Especially if they've proven themselves hard workers in the past. Hopefully, by the time we're ready to build that cheese factory Edward and I have been dreaming of, the gold fever will have long passed."

"You want to build a factory? I didn't know that!" she said in surprise. "What's kept you from doing so?"

Sarah laughed ruefully. "Money, of course. With the cost of land, building materials, equipment, and supplies, it could take years before we've saved enough."

Excitement built within her as a plan formed in her mind. "Would it be all right if I contacted Mr. Chapman about this?" she asked. "He has several wealthy clients, and if I have learned anything from attending all of those business dinners with my father, it's that they are always looking to diversify their investments."

"Do you truly think someone would want to speculate on a cheese factory in Montana?" her aunt asked in awe.

"Oh yes," Emma said, nodding emphatically. "In fact, I know of at least one investor who would jump at the opportunity."

"Then I'll speak to Edward about it tonight and let you know when you can write to him. Oh, Emma, this would be such an answer to our prayers!"

Sarah pulled a handkerchief out of her pocket and dabbed at the corners of her eyes before she gathered Emma into a tight embrace. "You have been such a blessing in our lives, and we love you so much. You're like another daughter to Edward and me."

Those heartfelt words brought tears to Emma's own eyes, and before she knew it, they were both sobbing.

When the door to the bunkhouse opened, they turned to see Luke standing frozen in the doorway, staring wide-eyed at them. Then, without a word, he turned around and closed the door firmly behind him.

Emma and Sarah looked at each other in surprise and burst out laughing. This time their tears were ones of mirth. When they finally got themselves under control, they collapsed onto the freshly made beds, trying to catch their breath.

"Oh dear," Sarah sighed as she held a hand to her side. "Poor Luke. He looked like a frightened rabbit. He's never been one who deals well with emotions, especially tears. I pray for the woman who eventually marries him. She'll have a tough nut to crack if she wants to get him to open up and be vulnerable."

"Maybe we should tell her to lock the door and hide the key before she broaches any serious conversations," Emma suggested.

Sarah let out a bright laugh. "I would love to see how he handles that."

Emma envied the trio on mornings like this. While they'd been able to ride to town ten minutes ago, she'd had to wait for the rest of the family to be ready for church. This was the downside of having such a large family, she supposed: no matter where you went, you were always waiting on someone to find their shoes or use the outhouse before you could leave. She wanted to kick herself for not insisting that she learn to ride a horse.

"Martha May," Emma called out as she climbed down from the wagon bed with Benjamin's assistance. She hadn't seen Gabe anywhere in the churchyard, and if anyone knew where he would be, it was his housekeeper.

"Good morning, dear," Martha May said with a warm smile. "My, it's good to see you."

"And you as well. It feels like ages since I've been out to the ranch. Do you know where Gabe is? I don't see him anywhere."

"Don't worry, dear. He's safe. He took watch last night and was plumb tuckered out. I'm not sure he's going to make it today."

"Oh. Well, thank you for telling me," Emma replied, trying to keep disappointment out of her voice. "That puts my mind at ease."

"Of course, dear." Martha May reached out and patted her arm. "Hopefully, this will all be over soon."

Emma nodded in agreement, afraid that if she opened her mouth to speak, she'd start throwing a fit that would rival Esther's. This forced separation had been wearing on her normally pleasant demeanor, and her lack of sleep from worrying about Gabe's safety certainly hadn't helped.

With a heavy sigh, she joined her family as they made their way into the chapel and slipped into a back pew. As they waited for the sermon to begin, Matthew and Issac started a game of rock-paper-scissors to her right. Though they'd played quietly, they didn't sit still, and Emma got elbowed in the side more than once. She was at the end of her rope with the boys when she felt someone drop onto the pew and sidle next to her.

Reflexively, Emma gathered her skirts and scooted over to create a proper distance. Scowling, she turned to see who'd been so rude.

"Gabe!" she gasped, her irritation instantly vanishing as her spirit soared, and her heart beat with giddy excitement. "What are you doing here?"

"I'm attending services," he replied with a roguish grin.

"I meant here, with me," she clarified, her lips curving into a smile at his playful answer. "What will everyone think?"

It was one thing to be seen strolling with him in the churchyard. But sharing the pew as the rest of the congregation looked on? That was a very public declaration of his intent.

"They'll think that we're courting, which we are," Gabe said, his hazel eyes warm and steady, "and that I have your family's blessing to sit with you. See for yourself."

Emma turned in her seat and saw Uncle Edward nodding his head at them in clear approval.

She couldn't help the elation that swept over her, or the wide smile that tugged at her lips. She faced the front of the church as the booming notes of a hymn rang out, but she found it nearly impossible to concentrate with Gabe sitting so close beside her. Every time their hands accidentally brushed while sharing a hymnal or passing the collection plate, her heart would beat wildly. By the time the service ended, she felt almost lightheaded.

Thankfully, the warm afternoon sunshine and fresh air in the churchyard, as she stood talking with Gabe and her aunt and uncle, helped Emma to regain her composure.

"Will you be joining us for dinner today, Gabe?" Edward asked. "I know you've been worried about things on the ranch, but you can still be home quickly if any trouble comes. We missed having you last week."

"I suppose I can't argue with that logic. Let me tell Henry my plans so he and Martha May won't be waiting around."

Emma was pleased that Gabe would spend the afternoon on the farm, but she also felt a bit panicked. Normally, she took great care in planning the menu for Sunday dinner, but she hadn't prepared to have company today. She hoped he wouldn't mind the roast chicken and vegetables.

Gabe returned a few minutes later with Xerxes and followed the family home, keeping his horse in pace with the wagon so he could talk with Emma. Then, once they were back on the farm, she and Aunt Sarah headed straight for the kitchen, while he joined her uncle and cousins in the parlor.

Though she didn't need much help to prepare meals anymore, Emma still cherished the chance to bond with her aunt. Especially now that she was spending more and more time in the creamery than in the house. As they worked side by side in the kitchen, she noticed Sarah seemed in a lighter mood than she had been the past few days.

"You seem happy today," Emma commented.

"I am," Sarah said with a bright smile. "Edward and I have discussed things, and last night, he agreed to let you write to your attorney. Depending on how many investors he can find, our dreams can finally come true." She paused and glanced toward the parlor where the family was still gathered, their laughter drifting in on the air. "It would mean that Edward could finally take things easier. We'd also have more time together as a family. Maybe even take a trip to visit relatives back east that we haven't seen in twenty years!"

"That's wonderful news! I'll write to Mr. Chapman this evening. Is that why you let Gabe sit with me this morning?"

"No. We suspect he'll propose soon," Sarah replied with a conspiratorial smile.

"He will?" Emma asked excitedly, almost dropping the sharp knife she held in her hand. "Did Martha May tell you that?"

"She hasn't said a word," her aunt said with a shrug and a teasing smile. "It's just a feeling."

As the afternoon progressed, Emma almost wished her aunt hadn't mentioned anything about a proposal. It was all she could think about now. Every time Gabe's fingers lingered over hers while passing a dish down the table, or she felt a gentle press of his thigh when he leaned in to whisper a witty comment, she felt her heat rise to her cheeks. Thankfully, she held herself together admirably until the end of dinner when Gabe asked her to step outside for a walk.

"Are you all right?" he asked as they strolled through the yard. "You seem preoccupied."

"I'm fine," she squeaked. Then, in a steadier voice, she said, "I was just thinking about something Aunt Sarah told me earlier. It's no worry." Not wanting to lie about what they had discussed, Emma changed the subject. "How are Blue and Tiny doing?"

"Very well, though I can tell Blue misses you," Gabe replied. "Alastair says they're learning their commands quickly and that he will take them out with him when he grazes the sheep further afield."

"I'm so glad Mrs. Paterson thought to suggest him to you," she said. "You seem pleased with him."

"I am. He's doing a great job," Gabe replied. "I'll introduce you to him on Friday. I spoke with Edward while you were making dinner, and he has agreed that you can resume your lessons."

"That's wonderful news!" she exclaimed happily. "I can't wait."

They walked in a wide, lazy circle around the farmhouse, talking about anything that came to mind—like what book they'd read, or a funny story about one of her cousins, or the antics of the ranch hands. The topic didn't matter. It simply felt so good to be together again.

Emma didn't think she could explain just how much being in his presence calmed her. So much of her life had gone into disarray after her father's death. Her future had seemed so uncertain, but when she was with Gabe, it was as if all her worries drained away. He brought instant peace to her soul.

Eventually, the mid-September sun began its slow descent toward the western horizon, and they headed back to the farmhouse. Emma waited while he saddled his horse, and when they reached the house, she paused at the base of the porch steps.

"Don't forget to ask Micah for your letter before you leave."

"I've got it right here," Gabe said, patting the breast pocket of his suit. "And I gave him my letter to you when I arrived."

Emma's breath caught as he took her hand in his. Slowly, he raised it to his lips and pressed a gentle kiss to the back of it. A pleasant shiver ran down her back at the contact.

"Until Friday then," he murmured.

"Y-yes," Emma stammered, thrown all into a tizzy by the romantic gesture. "Until Friday."

He gave her a wicked grin, as if he knew exactly what his kiss had done to her insides, and then swung up into the saddle.

With her heart beating wildly and her skin still tingling where his lips had brushed, she gave him a last wave. Gabe nudged Xerxes into motion and rode away. Emma watched until he was out of sight, then turned and hurried back into the house, eager to find Mary and fill her in on what had just transpired.

Chapter 35

As September came to an end, the residents of Elk Ridge were abuzz with the prospect of a husking bee on Friday. Walter Robins, a local hog farmer, had invited anyone who could spare the time to come to his place and help shuck the corn that had been snapped from the stalks and left lying in his fields. In return, he'd provide the food, and a dance would be held once all the work was done for the day. While the thought of dancing with a pretty gal was tempting, the biggest draw for many men was the five dollars Walter offered to whoever husked the most corn.

Since there'd been no suspicious activity on the ranch for weeks, Gabe felt it was safe to let some ranch hands attend, too. Since Stew and Miguel offered to stay behind, Gabe made the trip with Riley, Tommy, and Alastair. When they arrived at the Robins' farm around three o'clock, there was already a lively crowd: children were darting around near the house, and women were chatting with friends or setting up the tables for the food, while men were hauling empty baskets that would soon be filled.

Ears of corn were stacked in two massive piles, with short stools set along each one for people to sit while they worked. Having taken part in the husking competition last year, Gabe knew the routine: Walter would pick two of the best huskers to be captains, and after a coin toss to determine who went first, they would pick among those assembled to form their teams. Once all the men and women willing to join had been chosen and were in place at their respective piles, a signal would be given, and the contest began.

Gabe weaved through the gathering, looking for Emma, saying hello to folks he knew and being introduced to a few he didn't. He was surprised how far some of them had come, just for a night to let loose. He didn't envy the long, dark ride home they had ahead of them, knowing they'd be up before sunrise for morning chores.

When he finally spotted Emma standing next to her cousin, he made his way over. Peter McCoy was there too, but he only had eyes for Mary.

"Hello," Emma said with a welcoming smile. "I was wondering when you would show up. Mary and I were just telling Deputy McCoy that this is my first cornhusking. I'm worried I might not even fill my basket."

"You'll do just fine, I'm sure," the sandy-haired young deputy assured her. "The women join in, but they're much less competitive than the men."

"Oh! Do things get rowdy?" Emma asked, a trace of concern in her voice.

"No, it's all in good fun," Gabe promised. "The actual competition begins once the dancing starts."

"I'll be sure to save you a spot on my dance card," Emma laughed.

A few minutes later, the men who'd been picked as captains came to the front and began choosing their teams. There was friendly banter thrown around as the workers sorted into two groups, with people vying to be chosen, while their friends or neighbors called out teasing remarks. Gabe was hoping he'd be on the same team as Emma so they could talk as they worked, but he was disappointed when she was chosen for the opposing side.

Eventually, Micah and Peter joined his team, and once everyone had been assigned a side and they were spread around their respective ricks of corn, a gunshot sounded as the signal to begin. All up and down the line, men and women began grasping the silky tassels at the top of the cob and ripping them down to expose golden kernels. Once all the husks had been cleared, they tossed them into their basket and grabbed another piece.

An hour into the work, a matron came around with a bucket of cool water and a ladle while her husband offered a jug of rye whiskey. Gabe politely declined the spirits but gratefully took several long swallows of the refreshing water before wiping his mouth with the back of his hand and returning to the pile of corn.

As the pile of cobs dwindled halfway down, the motions became almost mechanical. He husked a new cob, getting ready to throw it in the basket when he saw the ruby hue of the kernels. Gabe's hand stilled, and he stared at it in disbelief. The treasure he was holding would grant him a kiss from the woman of his choosing. When his mind finally caught up, he let out a loud whoop of joy.

Micah, who had been working next to him, looked up. "What are you hollering about..." He stopped speaking when he saw what Gabe was holding in his hands and stood up to examine it closely. "You found a red ear," he exclaimed. "You lucky dog."

Peter joined them, and the three men stared at the cob as if it were some mystical object until they all seemed to come to their senses at once and began trying to wrest control of it from the others.

"Give it up," Micah grunted. "You already have a woman to court."

"Yeah," Peter panted as they struggled against each other. "Let the rest of us have a chance."

"Okay, wait. WAIT!" The other men froze at Gabe's raised voice, and they each took a step back. "Do either of you have someone specific in mind to give this to?"

"Yes," came Peter's instant reply, but Micah shook his head.

"Fine," Gabe sighed resignedly. "Peter, you can have it then."

"Thank you," the deputy replied, his face brightening. "I owe you one!"

Nodding in acceptance, he and Micah returned to work while Peter hurried away. They were right, Gabe thought. He already had a wonderful woman to court, so he didn't need the corn. But when he'd seen the gleaming red kernels, he'd been filled with excitement. He was trying very hard to be respectful and follow social etiquette, and the opportunity to steal a kiss without any damage to Emma's reputation had been difficult to pass up.

As the sun set over the distant mountains and soft pink and orange hues painted the sky, the last of the cobs were husked, and Walter Robins climbed onto a nearby wagon.

"I want to thank everyone for coming today," the young hog farmer said, raising his voice to be heard. "You all worked real hard, but since I've only got the five dollars to spare, that's going to Cyrus Douglass as the winner of the shucking competition."

Loud cheers and whoops erupted as the burly blacksmith came forward to collect his prize money. Walter shook his hand firmly, then turned back to the crowd with a grin.

"Let's eat!"

Supper was served at the front of the farmhouse on long makeshift tables that groaned under the weight of the feast the women had prepared. As everyone gathered in a line, Gabe sought Emma, who was standing with Rebecca Daniels, looking worn out from the day's drudgery.

"Well, how did you enjoy your first corn husking?" he asked, joining the women.

"My arms feel like lead weights, but I enjoyed it immensely," Emma said with a happy sigh.

Gabe chuckled and turned to Rebecca. "How's your mother doing? Martha May told me she went to visit her this week."

"She's doing much better. I even convinced her to attend today. She and Martha May spent most of the afternoon on the porch, reminiscing about old times."

"Sounds like a much better day than we had," Gabe laughed. "Where is Mary? I thought she would be here with you."

"She and Peter were talking with Uncle Edward and Aunt Sarah last I saw. I'm sure she will be along soon," Emma answered, a glimmer in her eye. "I know she's favored him since before I arrived, so I was very pleased when he showed up, looking like he'd struck gold."

Gabe was begrudgingly pleased by the news. If he couldn't have his kiss with Emma, at least it could be between two people who obviously cared for one another. They moved through the food line, filling their plates to the brim, and invited Rebecca to join them for supper.

"Are you sure?" she asked uncertainly. "I wouldn't want to impose."

"Nonsense," Emma replied, putting her arm through the other woman's. "You're the first friend I've made here, and I'd enjoy having you spend the meal with us. Besides, Mary promised to join us as well."

Knowing that she wasn't ruining an intimate evening seemed to ease Rebecca's worries, and they found a mostly flat spot to sit and have their meal. A few minutes later, Mary and Peter joined the group, looking pleased and a bit flushed. No one commented on the budding romance happening before their eyes, but he and Emma shared a knowing smile.

The most anticipated part of the evening came as the sounds of musicians tuning their instruments floated out of the freshly swept barn. Excited chatter spread through the gathering, and folks began lining up on the dance floor as the promise of dancing hung in the cool evening air.

"May I have the first dance?" Gabe asked Emma as he helped her up from her spot on the grass.

"Of course," she replied, a soft smile on her face. "I wouldn't have it any other way."

Noticing that Rebecca was standing nearby, a look of yearning on her face as she glanced at the barn, Gabe asked if she'd save the next dance for him.

"Me?" she asked incredulously.

"Yes," he confirmed. "Unless you don't feel like dancing."

"Oh, I'd be happy to! I was just surprised, I suppose. No one's ever asked me to dance before."

"Then save the third one for me," Peter insisted. "Before you know it, the rest of the men will be lining up to take you for a spin."

As the first notes from a fiddle rang out, Gabe slipped an arm around Emma's waist, holding her smaller hand in his, and led her around the dance floor. It was wonderful to have her so near, close enough that he could smell her lavender soap. He spun her gently, and when he brought her back, he held her a bit closer.

"You're a wonderful dancer," she complimented. "Wherever did you learn?"

"Martha May taught me," he said with a grin. "She told me I'd need to if I ever wanted to take a beautiful woman for a spin."

"And how many of these women have there been?" Emma asked cheekily.

"I've lost count," he said teasingly. Then, leaning close to her ear, he whispered, "But you're the only one who matters to me."

He spun her around again in time to the music, and when she returned to his arms, she gave him a soft smile. "I'll have to thank her. She's an excellent teacher, no matter the subject."

The song ended much sooner than he would have liked, but he led Emma to the sidelines where Henry was waiting to ask for her next dance. Gabe found Rebecca waiting for him just a few feet away, and he offered his arm.

"You didn't have to do this, you know," she said as they took their places. "I'm sure you would rather dance with Emma."

"We will have other chances to dance tonight. Besides, any friend of Emma's is a friend of mine. Now," he said with a grin, "let's see if I can outdo my foreman!"

The music began, and Gabe twirled Rebecca around the dance floor with playful energy. Every time she was spun away, she dissolved into laughter, and eventually she had to ask him to stop before she became too dizzy. Gabe immediately relented and settled into a steady rhythm for the rest of their turn together. When he led her off the dance floor, Peter was there waiting for his turn.

Since it would have been poor etiquette to dance every dance with Emma, Gabe took Martha May out for a spin, followed by Sarah and Mary. He was more restrained with the older ladies, but he made sure to give Mary some lively twirls. When he felt enough time had passed, he asked Emma for another dance and swept her into his arms as a nice, slow waltz began.

"I know this differs from the events you told me about in Denver, but are you having a good time?" Gabe asked.

"I am," Emma grinned. "I don't have to worry about the constant scrutiny. No one here cares if I have perfect posture or perform all the right steps. It's freeing."

"Did you even enjoy going?" he asked. He would have hated all the attention.

"To be completely honest, no," she sighed. "But I did it for my father."

"I suppose that's what happens when you love someone," Gabe mused as he looked into her beautiful sapphire eyes. "You do whatever it takes to make them happy."

They had taken only a few more steps when Emma suddenly stopped moving and bent down to grab her foot.

"Emma, what's wrong? Did I step on your toes?" he asked.

"Oh, no! I think I've turned my ankle," she said, her voice carrying over the music. "I must sit down."

"Let me help you," Gabe said, putting his arm around her waist and letting her lean her weight against him.

Emma gave him a grateful smile, and he led her off the dance floor, drawing looks of concern from the couples they passed. With the barn packed full of people, they had no choice but to make their way out into the chilly farmyard to look for a seat.

"I think I should try to walk on it," Emma said, standing to test her weight on her injured foot.

"Are you sure?" he asked, watching her face for any signs of pain.

"I'm sure it will be just fine with a bit of movement," she insisted, slipping her arm through his as they set off.

As the crickets chirped in the fields, and the distant music from the barn floated on the night air, she looked over at him with a tender smile. "Peter told me what you did for him," she said. "That was very generous of you."

"Well, it was pointed out to me that I already have a woman to court and didn't have as much need of it as some other man might," Gabe replied. He chuckled to himself as he remembered the scuffle he'd gotten into over it. "I just hoped it was put to good use."

"I think it's safe to say that it was, but I can't help thinking that you should have what's rightfully yours."

Gabe's heart ticked up a beat, and he moved them closer to the treeline. With it being so dark outside, this was all but guaranteed to hide them from prying eyes, but he checked anyway. Then, once he was sure no one was looking, he gently cupped Emma's face and kissed her. It was a brief meeting of the lips, lasting only mere seconds, but shivers raced down his body at the contact.

"Thank you," he whispered hoarsely as he pulled back. "We should probably return to the barn before someone wonders where we are."

Emma nodded, still slightly out of breath, and they left their wooded sanctuary hand in hand. Music was still playing when they returned, so he swept her back onto the dance floor, and they enjoyed what was left of the livelier tune. By the end of the night, they had danced together five times, and Gabe knew one thing for certain: it was time to stop procrastinating and make Emma his wife.

As soon as he could find a spare moment the next day, Gabe rode out to the farm to speak with Emma's uncle. When he found his neighbor in the milking barn, Edward was sitting on a short stool, engrossed in his tally books and completely unaware that he had a visitor.

Gabe knocked on the open door. "Is this a bad time?"

Edwards's head popped up at the noise, and he smiled when he saw Gabe. "No! By all means, come inside," he said, gesturing to the stool across from him. "I was just going over some things before I sent off a letter to my late cousin's attorney in Denver."

"Is something wrong?" he asked, concerned that this had something to do with Emma.

"It's the opposite, actually. We are trying to find investors for a cheese factory, and Mr. Chapman is helping with that. Once it's up and running, I plan to increase our herd size. Gotta meet the new demand."

"I didn't know you were looking to do that," Gabe said as he sat on the stool. "Have you found anyone to put up some money yet?"

"At least three, but the first one was the most generous. If I can secure a bit of land that's halfway between here and Butte, we should be able to build next spring."

"That's great news. Congratulations!"

"Thank you." Edward grinned. "It was actually Emma's idea to contact Mr. Chapman and ask him for help. He still manages her father's investments. I admit I was against the idea when it was first brought to me. But when I received his first letter and saw how much was being offered, I changed my tune. It would have taken us several more years to come up with that kind of money."

"She's a remarkable young woman," Gabe acknowledged, "and the reason I've come to speak with you today."

"You know, you're the second young man to come see me this morning," Edward chuckled. "Peter McCoy stopped by after breakfast to ask my permission to court Mary, which I granted. Though I suspect you are here for a slightly different blessing."

"You're right. I'd like to ask Emma to marry me," he stated. "I'm not an extremely wealthy man like her father was, but I can provide for her and any children we may have." Gabe paused to collect his thoughts. "Edward, I love her very much, and I'll do everything I can to make her just as happy as she makes me."

"That gives me great peace of mind and makes my permission that much easier to give." Edward stood, smiled widely, and held out his hand. "Welcome to the family."

Gabe got to his feet and shook the other man's hand firmly, excitement flooding through him.

"Thank you. I wish I could stay and speak to her today, but I have some things I need to prepare. Please don't say anything to Emma."

"You have my word," Edward promised. "I'm done here for the day, so I'll walk out with you."

They exited the building, talking more of the plans that were being made for the factory, when a wiry older man in unwashed denim pants and a wrinkled linen shirt approached them. Gabe wasn't sure who this was, but he didn't get a good feeling from him. The man's eyes were hard and intense.

"How can I help you, Jasper?" Edward asked firmly.

"Reaper broke," the disgruntled man said bluntly.

"I'll be right there. I've got some business to take care of first."

Jasper, as the man was apparently called, grunted in response and walked back toward the fields. Gabe opened his mouth to say something when Edward sighed and held up a hand as if to ward off his comments.

"I know. He's not the most pleasant person, but he'll be gone in a week. He's a temporary hand to help with the wheat harvest. We had trouble finding enough help this year, so we had to take what we could get. My boys promised to keep an eye on him until he leaves."

Knowing that it wasn't his place to say anything, Gabe just nodded. Edward and his sons were very capable of watching over their family. Shaking off his reservations, he said goodbye to his neighbor and galloped off to Butte, intending to see a certain jeweler about an engagement ring.

Chapter 36

Ever since the corn husking party, Emma had thought of little else but that stolen kiss with Gabe. She had never experienced anything quite so wonderful. Even days later, the memory of his lips on hers still made her heart race. She could tell by the look he'd given her when he'd joined her for services that morning—warm, knowing, and just a little roguish—that he remembered it, too.

Emma had to push those thoughts away as she and Gabe walked together toward Martha May and Henry, who were waiting near the edge of the churchyard.

"Hello, dear," Martha May greeted. "Your cousin looks so beautiful today. I think the deputy has taken notice as well."

Emma looked behind her and saw Mary and Deputy McCoy talking a few feet away. Her cousin was wearing a beautiful light-pink silk dress she'd purchased from Mrs. Tandy yesterday, while Peter wore a dark gray suit with his badge pinned neatly to his chest. His sandy-blonde hair was neatly combed, and he stood tall and proud beside Mary. They made a handsome-looking couple.

"He has," Emma said with a smile. "They're courting now."

"That boy sure didn't waste any time," Henry laughed. "I could tell just by looking at him at the corn husking that he was going to make a move soon. How early did he show up the next day, Edward?"

"Ten o'clock," her uncle replied as he and Aunt Sarah joined the group. "I don't think he could wait any longer."

"He was obviously eager to get your blessing," Sarah smirked. "In fact, he's coming for dinner."

"Why don't you all join us as well? It's been an age since you've dined with us," Edward suggested. "The more, the merrier."

"We'd be right pleased," Henry grinned.

"If you're going to be cooking for a crowd, you'll need every hand you can get," Martha May said. "We'll head right over. Come on, Henry. Let's get that wagon hitched."

With the plans settled, the group began to disperse. Sarah and Edward left to gather the younger children while Gabe followed Henry and Martha May so he could help hitch up the surrey. Emma lingered for a moment, watching them go before collecting Mary and telling her about their new guests.

Two hours later, as the young women worked to put the finishing touches on the meal, Joseph walked into the kitchen. He took a deep breath, inhaling the delicious scents that lingered in the air, and began lifting lids from the pots on the stove to see what had been made.

"Stop that," Mary scolded. "It's not finished yet."

"But I'm hungry," her brother complained, sneaking a biscuit from a tray that lay cooling on the counter.

"Joseph, did you come in just to snatch food?" Emma asked, exasperated.

"Of course not," he said, through a mouthful of food. "I came to tell you that Gabe has been asking for you, but I got distracted."

"What?" she exclaimed, fumbling to untie her apron strings. "Why didn't you say something sooner!"

He shrugged indifferently, and Emma almost threw the apron she had taken off straight into his face.

"Mary, would you mind if I stepped out?"

"No. I can handle things in here. Knowing my brother, Gabe's probably been waiting for ages."

Joseph didn't confirm his sister's suspicions, but Emma was sure that Mary had been correct. Placing her dirty apron on the cabinet, she did her best to pat her hair into place and walked into the front room.

"I'm so sorry I kept you waiting," she said to Gabe as he stood from his seat on the sofa.

"It wasn't that long," he shrugged. "I hoped we could take a walk before dinner if you're able to."

"Of course!" Emma said, pleasantly surprised by the offer.

"Good." Gabe looked relieved at her answer and gestured to the door. "Shall we?"

Emma felt there was something off about Gabe's actions today. He seemed nervous—fidgety. His hand kept drifting to his right trouser pocket, and when she told him about her humorous visit to Mrs. Tandy's with Mary, he'd barely reacted. He seemed to be capable of only short, one- to two-word answers. They were nearly at the milking barn before his strange behavior became too much, and she stopped walking.

"Gabe, is everything all right?" she asked, glancing up at him. "You're awfully quiet tonight."

"Am I?" Gabe replied. "I don't mean to be. I brought you out here to have a private word, and now it seems I'm clamming up."

He heaved a sigh and then took her hands in his own. The warmth of his skin sent shivers along her arms.

"I have been trying to find the right words to describe how I feel about you." He moved his thumb in a steady caress on the back of her hand. "From the first time I saw you, I thought you were the most beautiful woman I'd ever laid eyes on. But you're also kind to everyone—even those who might not deserve it—and you brighten the day of whoever crosses your path."

As he spoke, Emma felt tears well in the corner of her eyes. This shouldn't have been a surprise, given Sarah's words a few weeks ago, but she still hadn't expected it tonight.

"You have a true depth of character, and I'm constantly amazed at how you truly care for others. I miss you terribly when we're apart."

Her tears fell in earnest now. Gabe dropped her hands, using his thumb to wipe away the salty drops. Then he pulled a small velvet box out of his trouser pocket. He fumbled with the clasp for a moment. Dropping to one knee, he presented her with the most beautiful ring she had ever seen: a ruby set in the center of a delicate silver band, surrounded by small pearls forming the shape of a flower.

"What I'm trying to say is that I love you so much more than I even thought possible, and I can't imagine my life without you in it. I want you to be my wife. I want to build a life with you on the ranch, fill our home with laughter and children, and give you as many dogs and cats as your heart desires. Will you marry me, Emma?"

To overcome for words, she dropped to her knees and pressed her lips to his in a deep, heartfelt kiss. Gabe returned the gesture, tender at first, then growing a little bolder. For a few precious seconds, the world around them disappeared, and when they finally broke apart, their breaths were ragged.

"So was that a yes?" Gabe asked huskily, helping her to her feet.

"Yes," Emma chuckled, amused at his need to hear the words aloud.

He let out a loud whoop of joy, gathered her up in his arms, and spun them around until they were both dizzy.

"Oh, Gabe," she sighed happily as he placed the ring on her finger. "I love you too." She kissed him again, relishing the new freedom she felt to do so, and hugged him tightly around the waist. Lying her head against his chest, she said softly, "I never knew I could feel this happy."

"Neither did I," Gabe admitted as he returned the embrace. Then he placed a kiss on the top of her head. "Should we go tell everyone the good news?"

Emma nodded, and they hurried back to the house, hand in hand, where they found her entire family—all eleven of them—along with Peter, Martha May, and Henry waiting in the parlor. The look of eager anticipation on their faces was unmistakable.

"Well," Joseph said, breaking the hush that had fallen over the room. "Let's see the ring then."

Grinning from ear to ear, she proudly held out her left hand to show off the beautiful ring, tilting it so the ruby flashed in the mid-afternoon light.

“I knew he would ask you soon,” Sarah crowed in delight, rushing forward to pull Emma in for a tight hug. “Now we can plan the wedding!”

Right behind her was Martha May, tears already rolling down her cheeks. “I’ve been praying for this since the day I heard you were moving here,” she sobbed happily. “I couldn’t ask for a more perfect helpmeet for Gabriel.”

Once the older women had moved off, the rest of the family stepped forward to hug the couple and congratulate them. Even Isaac, who normally shied away from physical affection, gave Emma a quick squeeze.

The joyful, jovial mood continued as they gathered around the dinner table. As this was Deputy McCoy’s first visit to the farm, the family made sure he heard all their favorite stories—and no one, not even Emma, was left out of the retellings. They laughed and teased until their sides hurt, and the inevitable needs of livestock forced the impromptu celebration to end.

Henry and Martha May were the first to head home, and while Deputy McCoy and Mary were taking a short walk around the farmyard, Emma and Gabe made their way to the stable.

“How long before they follow our lead?” he asked, looking at the newly courting couple.

“I suspect they’ll be engaged before Christmas,” Emma grinned. “Aunt Sarah will have her hands full planning two weddings.”

“I’m sure she’ll have plenty of help,” Gabe said. “Especially from Martha May.”

“I suppose that’s true,” she nodded. “I’d be surprised if they hadn’t already started.”

“Sweetheart, as long as you’re the one I get to marry,” he said softly. “I don’t care who plans it.”

They stopped just short of the stable, and Gabe pulled her into his arms, giving her a warm, lingering kiss. When they parted, he rested his forehead against hers.

“I just hope they don’t make us wait too long,” he murmured.

Emma smiled, her cheeks flushed. “Me too,” she whispered.

Chapter 37

It had been almost four weeks since Gabe had proposed, and with the chilly late-October weather moving in, preparations for winter were in full swing on the ranch. The men had spent long days bringing in the last of the hay, repairing the barn roofs, and laying in firewood while Martha May prepared the root cellar. It was hard work, but with everyone pitching in, they were making good progress. And, since an afternoon off wouldn't do much harm, a plan began forming in his mind as he walked to the house for his midday meal.

Now that he and Emma were engaged, a bit of latitude was given to the societal restrictions of their courtship. They no longer had to be under the watchful eye of her family while in public. Of course, that didn't mean they could be indiscreet, but a drive into town and dinner at Jackson's would be perfectly acceptable. Excitement coursed through him at the thought.

He picked up his speed and burst into the house through the kitchen door. Martha May, who had been stirring soup in a large pot on the stove, gave a startled shriek as the door banged open. Hand to her ample chest, she turned with a glare and brandished her spoon at him.

"Gabriel! You scared the daylights out of me. What is wrong with you?"

"Sorry, Martha May," he said contritely. "I didn't mean to frighten you. I was coming to let you know I won't be staying for dinner."

"Now you tell me," she muttered crossly. "Where are you off to in such a rush?"

"Well, I thought I'd ask Emma to join me for dinner in town. I thought it would be a pleasant break for her. I'm sure she's been just as busy on the farm as I've been here."

"Oh! What a thoughtful gesture." The severe expression she wore changed to one of happiness as she lowered her utensil back to the pot. "I'm sure she'll be delighted. You go on then and have a good time, and I'll see you for supper."

"Yes, ma'am." Gabe kissed her cheek and hurried upstairs to change.

By the time he had finished hitching the horses to the surrey, the temperature had dropped noticeably as dark, heavy clouds moved in from the south. If rain fell on their drive, he could put the isinglass curtains down, but he grabbed a quilt for extra warmth before setting off for the farm along the worn path between the two properties.

He arrived just as the family was trooping up to the farmhouse for dinner, and Emma came hurrying forward to meet him as he descended from the wagon.

"Gabe! What a surprise," she said happily, her blue eyes dancing with excitement. "What brings you by?"

"Well, I hoped you would join me in town for dinner. I have a hankering for one of Jackson's pot pies. What do you say?"

"I'd love to! That is, if it's all right with you, Uncle Edward," she said, looking back at her uncle.

"Of course," Edward nodded. "It sounds like a fine idea."

"Thank you," Gabe replied. "We should be back in an hour or so."

"There's no rush. Why don't you go for a drive afterwards and enjoy the afternoon?" Edward suggested.

"That sounds like a wonderful idea," Emma said. "I'll go change." As she hurried off toward the house, she called back, "It won't take long!"

When Emma reemerged a few minutes later, she was wearing a clean dress and a deep green wool coat trimmed in white fur, and a matching muff.

"Shall we go?" she asked eagerly.

"Yes, but first there is something that I need to do," Gabe said seriously.

"What's that?" she asked, her brow wrinkling adorably in confusion.

"Greet you properly, of course."

He pulled her gently into his arms and slowly kissed her soft lips. When they broke apart, she grinned at him.

"I like this kind of greeting."

"As do I. Shall we do it again?" he asked playfully.

Emma laughed and stepped back a pace. "I would say yes, but I think we may scandalize my cousins, who are surely watching us."

Gabe glanced toward the house, and sure enough, multiple youthful faces were crowded around the kitchen window. When the curtain dropped, he let out a laugh, shaking his head in amusement.

"Then we should head into town," he said, offering her his hand. "I'm sure Jackson's will be filled soon."

"You're right," she agreed. "The last time we went there, it was packed to the rafters."

As the wagon trundled down the wide dirt road into town, they talked contentedly, pointing out the many hues of the changing leaves all around them. The contrast of bright red and deep golden yellow leaves against the unchanging evergreens was a breathtaking sight, especially as wisps of dense fog hung in the trees. The overcast sky made the perfect backdrop for the vibrant colors. When a chilly autumn breeze whipped past them, Emma shivered.

"Gettin' chilly, sweetheart?" he asked.

"A bit," she replied, though her teeth were chattering.

Gabe reached behind him and grabbed the quilt from the back seat he'd brought for this very reason. He handed it to her, and she unfolded the bright, patterned blanket, draping it across her lap.

"It's not much further," he said, tucking it around her legs.

Emma scooted closer and rested her head against his shoulder. "Mm. This is much better," she sighed contentedly.

Gabe smiled down at her. "Are you comfortable?"

"Oh yes, very," she answered happily. "You make an excellent pillow."

He couldn't help but laugh at her odd response. "I've never been compared to a pillow before."

"It was meant as a compliment," she insisted as she joined in on the laughter.

"If you say so," he teased. "Now, tell me what you've been doing without me."

"Aside from working in the creamery, I've pickled, dried, and canned just about everything you could eat. I find the entire process fascinating."

"I suppose that's a good thing," Gabe mused. "The work would be much more arduous if you didn't enjoy it."

"That's true. Which is why I've finally given up on crocheting. I'd much rather do embroidery."

"Then perhaps you could make something to go in the parlor to make it your own. After all, it will be your house too soon enough, and I'm useless with things like that."

Emma sat up and kissed his cheek. "I'd love to make something special for our home." She paused for a second, and then a wide smile bloomed on her face. "I enjoy saying that. *Our* home."

"I like it too," Gabe agreed, before leaning in to capture her lips in a light kiss.

Pulling back, he could see the buildings of the town rising in the distance and knew that their private interlude was over. He straightened in his seat and saw Emma was doing the same.

"I suppose we should be on our best behavior," he said.

"Yes, it wouldn't do to have false rumors being spread about town," she sighed, clearly put out that she had lost her warm resting place.

When they pulled into the livery a few minutes later, Gabe raised a hand in greeting to Cyrus, who was already waiting near the hitching post. After handing over the reins and telling him they'd be gone for an hour, the two men shook hands. Then he walked around to Emma's side of the surrey, helped her down, and leaned in just enough to brush a quick, tender peck across her lips.

"Gabe," she laughed, her cheeks warming despite the chilly air. "I thought you were going to behave."

"I couldn't help myself," he said in a low voice, offering her an arm as he led her out of the livery. "But I promise to try harder."

Emma shook her head, but a pleased smile still lingered on her face as they walked down the street.

Luckily, Jackson's wasn't as busy as the last time they'd had dinner here, and the greeting they received was warm and welcoming. Gabe asked to be seated at a table away from the clatter of the main room, and the waitress led them to an empty section in the back. The small space felt private and cozy, with a single lantern hanging above and the faint scent of fresh coffee drifting from the kitchen.

They slid into the chairs across from each other and placed their orders for pot pie. The waitress smiled cheerfully and left to get their drinks. Gabe reached across the table and held out his hand, and was pleased when Emma took it without hesitation.

"I like that we can be more open now," he said, caressing her knuckles. "Everyone knows we're engaged, so we aren't scandalizing the town."

Emma smiled warmly. "I suppose with a wedding on the horizon, folks are more relaxed."

"Not Martha May. She's been in a tizzy since the announcement and keeps pestering me about setting a date." He paused, eyes steady on hers. "Do you have one in mind?"

"I thought springtime might be nice," she answered thoughtfully. "The weather would be warm enough to hold a reception outside, which we would need to do since Aunt Sarah has already suggested we invite almost the entire town."

"Are we really inviting that many people?" he asked, eyes wide with shock.

"No," she chuckled, "but it feels like it. I know she's excited—this being the first wedding in the family—but I feel like I might have to put my foot down." She sighed and looked out the window. "Besides, how would we fit everyone in the church?"

Gabe shrugged. "I don't know. Maybe we can suggest a limit to the number of guests?"

"I'll bring it up with my aunt tonight."

The food arrived a few minutes later, and a companionable silence fell between them as they ate. The pot pie tasted wonderful and was so filling that neither of them felt like they had any room for dessert.

"How would you feel about taking a stroll over to the general store and saying hello to Eunice?" she asked, pushing her plate away. "We haven't seen her in a while."

"That sounds like an excellent idea. You can tell her I've finally worked up the courage to ask you to marry me," Gabe said with a teasing smile as he pulled out his wallet to pay the bill.

"She'll be very proud of you," Emma grinned. "I was thinking of asking her to be my flower girl."

"Eunice would be perfect for that," he agreed, standing up from the table. "I can't wait to see her reaction."

"Neither can I," she admitted. "Let's go tell her."

Gabe held her chair as she stood and offered his arm in escort as they left the diner, eager to share their news with friends. They had only made it halfway down the boardwalk when he stopped and stuck his hands into his trouser pockets. Not finding what he was looking for there, he searched his vest and suit coat.

"What's wrong?" Emma asked.

"I must have left my wallet back at the diner," he said, frowning. "Wait here just a moment while I fetch it." He placed a kiss on her cheek before turning back in the direction they had just come.

Chapter 38

Emma watched Gabe stride confidently down the boardwalk toward the diner, and she sighed happily. This was a perfect day away from the farm. The ride into town had been cozy and intimate, and she was already looking forward to the drive back. She wondered how long they could stretch out their afternoon together. After all, Uncle Edward hadn't even seemed worried about when they would return.

She was in the midst of dreaming up a plan for the rest of their afternoon when a familiar voice called her name. Turning, she saw Gregory Callaway hurrying across the street. He was waving eagerly at her, a wide, pleased grin on his face.

"There you are, Emma," he said. "I saw you from the window in my office," he gestured vaguely to the bank across the street, "and knew this was the perfect opportunity to speak with you—alone."

"I don't think that's a good idea, Mr. Callaway," Emma said politely but firmly. "I'm engaged now, and it would be disrespectful of us to carry out a conversation without my fiancé or family member present."

She gave a slight nod and tried to walk down the boardwalk to the general store, but he stepped in front of her.

"What kind of man would leave his intended in a position where her reputation could be compromised?" Gregory asked, his tone dripping with false concern. "Truly, Emma, I'm surprised he ever let you out of his sight."

"I don't think he expected me to be accosted on the street," Emma replied coolly.

"There's no need for dramatics," Gregory huffed. "I came to tell you the good news. You no longer have to toil away on that farm and ruin your delicate hands. I've been offered the position of Senior Loan Officer at the First National Bank of Denver. I'd like you to go with me—as my wife."

Emma stared at him, stunned. "What? You want us to marry?"

"Yes," he said in that maddeningly patronizing tone. "It wouldn't be appropriate for us to make such a journey without becoming husband and wife. Think of how scandalous that would be."

"I can't believe this is happening," Emma muttered, closing her eyes as if she could block him out.

When she opened them again, he was still there—still smiling down at her, looking unbearably self-satisfied.

"I know. It's an exciting prospect," Gregory continued, completely oblivious to her distress. "You can finally return to the lifestyle you're accustomed to. With you by my side as the perfect hostess, I could become president of my own bank, investing in silver mines and railroads, perhaps even running for the state legislature."

"You can hire someone to plan your dinner parties, Mr. Callaway; you don't need me for that," she pointed out, desperate to make him go away. "Besides, there are plenty of other women in Colorado that you could marry."

"I have met no other woman who can even come close to having your beauty and charm," he insisted.

Emma shook her head at the foolishness of trying to reason with Gregory when she knew he wouldn't listen. It was like arguing with a brick wall. She supposed his tenacity would serve him well in politics, but right now she just wanted this all to end.

"I cannot marry you, Mr. Callaway," she said tightly, her patience wearing thin. "I'm already engaged."

Gregory let out a short, incredulous laugh. "Ha! Do you think that you'll be happy living in this God-forsaken wilderness for the rest of your life? No, I'm afraid you don't know your own mind, my dear Emma."

He shook his head sadly. "It was obvious to me when you accepted the suit of that rancher. You deserve someone who can provide better for you."

"I deserve someone who loves me," she retorted hotly, past caring about her manners.

"Then I intend to do whatever I can to change your mind," Gregory replied smoothly. "After all, engagements can be broken, and love can grow in time."

Emma was about to really let him have it when she heard Gabe's voice calling out to her.

"I'm sorry that took so long, sweetheart," Gabe said as he snaked an arm around her waist and held her gently to his side. "Hello, Gregory."

Gregory ignored the proffered greeting and, after giving Gabe an assessing look, he turned to Emma. "I'm sure you'll come to your senses soon. But for now, I'm off to enjoy a drink."

Before she could reply, Gregory strode away toward the Tipsy Miner Saloon.

Emma stood in silence as he disappeared from view, and then broke into tears, her entire body shaking. Instantly, she felt Gabe gather her into his arms and gently rub her back.

"Shh. Everything will be all right," he murmured. "There's no need to be sad."

"I'm not sad," Emma corrected as she sniffed back her tears. "I'm angry. He's the most infuriating man. Did you know he asked me to marry him? Just like that—right here on the street?"

She wanted to stamp her foot and kick at something to vent her frustration, but Gabe's low laughter distracted her.

"How can you find this humorous?" she demanded.

"I don't find him harassing you on the street humorous at all," he replied as he stepped back from their embrace. "What I do find funny is that the sweetest person I know just looked like they were ready to do violence."

"If I were a man, I would have punched him right in the nose," she responded crossly.

"Trust me, I thought of doing the same thing myself," Gabe said, casting a dark glance in Gregory's direction. "But I'd rather not be thrown in jail today."

"It might be worth it," she muttered.

Gabe chuckled. "I didn't realize you were so eager to see me behind bars."

Emma sighed and shook her head. "No, of course not. I'm sorry. Gregory has me at sixes and sevens."

"That's understandable," he said gently. "Would you still like to go see Eunice?"

"Oh dear, I completely forgot that we were on our way to see her." She threw her hands up in the air and huffed out a breath. "Do you see what I mean? I feel completely upended. Would you think it terrible of me to just go home? I promise I'll speak to Eunice when I come back into town Saturday to see Mrs. Tandy, but for now I want to be as far away from Gregory as possible."

"Then that's what we'll do," Gabe agreed.

He put his hand gently on Emma's back and walked close to her all the way back to the livery. After helping her onto the bench seat, he tenderly laid the quilt around her shoulders and lap, making sure it was snug. The extra care and attention he was giving her after the ordeal on the street almost brought her to tears.

"Thank you," she whispered as she caught his hand in hers.

"Of course. I can't have you taking a chill on our first trip out together."

He kissed the back of her hand and hurried around the front of the vehicle to take his place. Instead of driving down the main road to get back home, which would take them directly past the saloon, he turned down a side street and used the road on the next block over to leave town.

"Now, where were we?" Gabe asked as he grabbed the reins. "Ah, yes, I remember now."

He drew Emma to his side and held her close with one arm. As they left Elk Ridge, a feeling of relief washed over her, quickly followed by exhaustion. Emotional upsets always made her tired. When Gabe caught her stifling a yawn, he tucked her head into the crook of his neck.

"Rest your eyes for a spell," he murmured. "I'll wake you when we get back to the farm."

"Are you sure?" she asked, her eyes beginning to droop of their own volition.

"I'm sure, sweetheart."

Gabe dropped a kiss on her head and began slowly rubbing his hand up and down her arm, which apparently was all she needed, because within moments her eyes closed, and she drifted off into a dreamless sleep.

"Wake up, sleepyhead," a deep voice rumbled. "You're home."

Emma groggily lifted her head from Gabe's chest and looked about. The surrey sat motionless in front of the large white farmhouse, and the team of horses lazily flicked their tails as they waited for instructions.

"I can't believe I slept the whole way here," she yawned, rubbing her eyes.

"I can," Gabe said with a grin. "Did you know that you have the most adorable snore?"

"I do not," she insisted, sitting up straighter on the bench.

"Are you sure about that?" he teased.

"Yes," she said firmly. "I've asked Mary about it, and she promised I don't snore."

"Ah, I must be mistaken then," Gabe said, his hazel eyes twinkling. "But at least now you are fully roused and ready to face the rest of your day."

Emma stared at him for a moment and then burst into laughter. "You're right. I feel very awake now."

"Then my job is complete," he grinned. "And just in time, too."

Gabe pointed to the addition, where Aunt Sarah had just exited, holding a large laundry basket—piles of folded sheets and clothing sticking out from the top. She noticed the surrey right away and came over to greet them.

"I didn't expect you two back so soon," Sarah said in surprise. "Did you have a good time?"

"We had a wonderful time," Gabe assured her as he hopped out of the vehicle to help Emma down.

"Until Gregory ruined it," she muttered angrily, kicking at the dirt with her boot.

"What do you mean?" Aunt Sarah asked, her brow furrowing.

"I think it's best if I let Emma explain things," Gabe said. "I need to get back to the ranch. Still got a lot of work left to finish."

He turned to Emma, tilted her chin up, and murmured, "I'll see you soon."

Tenderly, he pressed a quick kiss to her lips before climbing into the wagon and starting for home.

"Are you going to tell me what this is all about?" Sarah asked, one dark eyebrow raised.

"Yes," Emma sighed resignedly, "but I think I need a strong cup of coffee for fortification before I do."

"Then let's go inside and put some on," her aunt said, slipping an arm around Emma's shoulders. "We can even make a fresh batch of your favorite cookies while you talk."

Chapter 39

The Barnes family was already spread throughout the churchyard, speaking with friends and neighbors when Gabe rode up on Sunday. Emma was talking with her cousin and Deputy McCoy, so once he tied Xerxes off to the hitching post, he made his way over to the group.

He shook hands with Peter and Mary, then pressed a chaste kiss to Emma's cheek.

"How was your trip to Mrs. Tandy's yesterday?" he asked.

"It was fine," Emma said vaguely.

"Did you come away with any extra purchases?" Gabe pressed, knowing full well that she would have come away with at least one thing she hadn't planned on buying.

"Just one," she answered, a becoming blush spreading across her delicate cheeks.

"She must be losing her touch," Peter joked.

Gabe was curious about what would have provoked such a reaction from Emma, but he knew this wasn't the time or place to press her on the subject. Instead, he asked, "Did you visit the general store as well?"

"We did," she answered, looking relieved to change the subject. "Eunice said hello, by the way."

He inclined his head in acknowledgement. "And how did she react to our news?"

"She was very excited," Emma said with a fond smile. "Especially when I asked her to be in the wedding. She almost dropped the box of buttons she was holding."

"That would have made quite a mess."

"That's what a broom is for," Mary teased.

"So it is," Gabe laughed. "Silly of me to have forgotten."

"I suppose you can be forgiven if..." Emma's voice trailed off as her gaze drifted somewhere in the distance.

He put a hand on her elbow and frowned. "What's wrong?"

"Gregory is here," she grumbled.

Gabe glanced in the direction she was staring and caught sight of the finely dressed banker as he casually strolled among the crowd of worshipers. He had expected the other man to show up again, but his appearance was obviously upsetting to Emma.

"It's all right. I don't think he has spotted you yet," he assured her quietly. "Would you like to join your aunt and uncle?"

"Yes," she agreed readily. "I think that's a good idea."

Peter and Mary, who had obviously been informed of the unwanted suitor beforehand, followed them to join Sarah and Edward, who stood only a few feet away. The deputy moved to walk behind Emma so his much taller form acted as a shield from prying eyes. Gabe was grateful for Peter's forethought, and he sent the lawman a silent nod of thanks.

"Why the long faces?" Sarah asked when they approached.

"Gregory's back," Emma said grumpily.

"Did he say something to upset you?" Edward asked, looking around the yard.

"No. He didn't have a chance," she answered. "We came straight here once I noticed him."

"Let's find our seats then," Sarah suggested. "Services should be starting soon, anyway."

After parting ways with Peter, Edward guided the rest of their little group inside, calling for the younger children to follow. Everyone quickly settled into the pew as Mrs. Langley started the prelude music and the rest of the congregation—including the trio—began filing in.

When Gregory passed by on his way to the front of the church, Gabe felt Emma stiffen next to him. She seemed braced for some sort of acknowledgment or cutting remark, but the banker sauntered to the pew closest to the pulpit and claimed an aisle seat without so much as glancing in her direction.

"I can't believe he showed up here," Emma muttered angrily to her aunt. "He hasn't come to services in almost three months."

"Well, he's here now, and there's nothing we can do about it," Sarah pointed out. "Besides, he didn't bother us at all yesterday, so perhaps he's come to terms with things and is just here to worship."

"I doubt it," Emma replied skeptically, crossing her arms over her chest.

"Wait," Gabe said, turning to face Emma. "You saw him when you were in town?"

"We were on our way to Mrs. Tandy's when he passed us on the street," she explained quietly. "He didn't say anything to us. He just doffed his hat and looked at his pocket watch as if he were late for an appointment."

"I wonder where he was going in such a hurry?" Gabe mused.

"I did too," Emma nodded, "so I watched him from the shop window. All he did was cross the street and enter the saloon."

"Do you think he's a drunkard?" Sarah asked. "Perhaps he's picked up the habit. Oh, that poor man."

"What!" Emma looked at her aunt incredulously.

"Shh, the service is starting, dear," Sarah chided. "We'll speak about this later."

Gabe glanced to the front of the church and saw she was right. The gray-haired pastor was making his way up to the podium to begin his sermon, smiling kindly down at the congregation as he did. He waited for the music to stop before he began speaking, throwing his arms wide in welcome.

"Good morning! As you all should know, winter will be upon us soon, and that means it is time to raise money for charity boxes for those in our community who might need a bit of help to get by. Last year, we filled twenty boxes full of food and warm clothing to give to our friends and neighbors in need." There was a ripple of excited whispers, and

Pastor Langley waited for the talk to quiet down before continuing. "This year, I have set a new goal of thirty boxes so that we may bless more families. The collection plate will come around shortly, and I ask that you please give what you're able to. Every bit helps."

The pastor signaled to his wife, and she picked up the brass bowl by its wooden handle, passing it to the person at the end of the front row as the sermon began. The plate was passed down the pews, with folks dropping in whatever hard-earned money they could spare. When it eventually reached Gregory, he made a show of reaching into his vest pocket, drawing out three dollars and putting them into the bowl, one bill at a time.

Gabe rolled his eyes at the performance. Gregory was obviously trying to appear generous. And it might have worked if not for the showmanship that accompanied the gesture. By the looks on the faces of those around him, they were also unimpressed.

If the banker had bothered to pay attention, he would have seen that while some folks were dropping in spare coins, others like Gabe and Edward were putting in bills of a much higher denomination than a dollar. Instead, Gregory sat there with a smug grin, obviously not paying attention to the sermon as the pastor detailed Job's suffering.

It was one of the most sobering lectures Gabe had ever heard from Pastor Langley, and it reaffirmed his belief that it was God's plan for him and Emma to be here in Montana at the same time. Thinking about this filled him with gratitude, and as the congregation sang their closing hymn, he offered a silent prayer of thanks to his Creator for the woman beside him. They'd had a rough beginning, but now he couldn't imagine his life without her.

As they made their way out of the church, Gabe took hold of Emma's hand and kissed the back of it. She grinned, and a blush spread across her cheeks, which only made him want to kiss them as well. He held himself back from showering her with more affection in public and led the way to her favorite spot in the churchyard as her family followed.

"Ma, can we go find our friends now?" Matthew asked as he tugged on his mother's dress.

"Yes, but don't get your clothes dirty," Sarah warned. "Last week you were covered from head to foot in mud!"

"Yes, ma'am," the youngster replied dutifully.

The rest of the children took this as permission for themselves as well, while the adults, including the trio, stayed behind. It would have been a fine opportunity to speak with

Edward and his sons about how the plans for a cheese factory were going, but Gregory was heading straight towards them.

"Good day to you all," he called out as he neared the group. "I was hoping I could have a word with Miss Barnes."

"It's Miss Barnes now, is it?" Joseph said with a smirk.

Gregory smiled tightly, clearly not pleased about being questioned. "Yes, well... I came to offer my sincere congratulations to you and Mr. Moreau. After speaking with my aunt, I see that I have been overeager in my admiration. My apologies if I caused any offense." He turned to Emma. "I hope you will still consider me a friend, Miss Barnes. After all, we are neighbors, and I would hate for any unpleasantness between us."

"If that is truly your intention now, then yes," Emma replied cautiously.

"Thank you," he murmured, giving her a deep bow. "That eases my mind greatly."

"I'm just glad that we could come to an understanding," Emma said firmly.

"Of course, of course," Gregory replied. "And now I must bid you all farewell."

There was a polite chorus of goodbyes from Gabe and the Barnes family, but once they were alone, Luke was the first to speak up.

"I bet his aunt was hopping mad that he was still trying to pursue you after what happened at the general store," he said with a grin.

"She probably told him to leave you alone," Micah added. "And now he's pretending it was his idea to back off."

"Either way, I'm glad this is settled," Sarah said, putting a stop to their speculation. "We should head home and get started on dinner."

Before Emma left to follow her family, Gabe leaned down and pressed a chaste kiss to her cheek. "I'll see you soon," he promised.

She gave him a dazzling smile, which set his heart racing. "I'm already looking forward to it."

Chapter 40

Emma sat in the parlor of the ranch house on Friday afternoon in early November, poring over fashion plates in a magazine Mrs. Tandy had lent her while Aunt Sarah and Martha May held fabric samples up to her face.

She had originally wanted to wear her mother's gown, carefully packed away in a trunk she'd brought with her from Denver. But when she pulled it out, she found the fabric severely damaged and beyond repair. Thankfully, the Brussels lace and the pearl buttons were still in good condition, so her aunt had helped her salvage what they could to be used in the design of a new dress.

"I don't know," Martha May tsked as she held up a piece of fabric. "I think this color might clash with her complexion."

"Hmm, I think you're right. Maybe a darker shade of pink," Sarah suggested.

"I don't favor pink at all, actually," Emma cut in before either woman could run off with the idea.

"Well, that's all right," Martha May said easily. "We can find a different color. Which one do you like?"

Emma looked at the pile of swatches. A few caught her eye, but they were too bold for a wedding dress. Instead, she picked up a piece of cream satin silk and handed it to her aunt.

"I think this would go well with the pieces from my mother's gown."

"You're right," Sarah said, nodding approvingly. "And this color won't make you look sickly like plain white can."

Emma wasn't sure whether to be insulted by that remark, so she turned the conversation to the design. Lifting the magazine for the older woman to see, she showed them one of her favorites: an elbow-length sleeved bodice that buttoned to the neck with a tiny lace collar, and a skirt with large, gathered pleats at the bottom. The best part, in Emma's opinion, was that she wouldn't need to wear the dreadful bustle cage.

"You'll look beautiful in that, Emma," Sarah sniffed.

"Oh! I can just imagine it," Martha May sighed dreamily. "I know Gabriel will be stunned speechless when he sees you in it."

"Well, it's not made yet," Emma warned. "There's still plenty of time to change around a few details, but I like the overall look of this dress the best. It's simple but very elegant."

"We should get this design to Mrs. Tandy soon, then," her aunt directed.

"Actually," Emma said tentatively. "I was hoping that the two of you could help me make it. I've become much more proficient with the sewing machine, but with such an important piece, I'd like some more experienced hands at the ready."

Sarah was too choked up to speak, so she nodded her agreement while Martha May began sobbing. Emma was alarmed and looked to her aunt for help, but Sarah just shrugged helplessly.

"Oh, no! Please don't cry, Martha May. I didn't mean to upset you." Emma stood up quickly and began patting her on the back. "We can certainly hire Mrs. Tandy to make up the dress if it will be too much for you with your other duties."

"It's not that at all, dear. I'd be honored to help," wept Martha May, fishing out a handkerchief from her sleeve. "It's just that you don't know what it means to me that you would ask for my help. I could never have children, so I said goodbye to my dreams of helping my daughter prepare for the most special day of her life. Now you've given me that opportunity back."

The heartrending confession brought tears to Emma's own eyes, and she instinctively hugged the older woman tightly as Sarah joined in. How blessed she was to have two wonderful women in her life who loved her as one of their own. At times, it seemed so unfair that those who prayed for a child were denied, while others who would mistreat their offspring had more than they wanted, but she supposed only God knew the purpose behind it.

When Gabe and Henry stepped into the parlor a few minutes later, they stopped short at the sight of the women's red-rimmed eyes. Concern creased both their brows instantly.

"Is everything all right?" Gabe asked, his hazel eyes steady on Emma's.

"Yes. Everything's fine," she answered as she came forward to greet him with a quick peck on the lips.

"She's right," Martha May added. "We were just having a little heart-to-heart and lost track of time. Dinner is simmering on the stove, so why don't we head into the other room and leave this mess for later?"

"It looks like you ladies were busy," Gabe noted as they made their way into the kitchen. "Did you get much accomplished?"

"We've crossed the dress off the list at least," Sarah said.

"What more is there to need?" Henry asked with a grin. "Are you ladies planning some big fancy shindig?"

"Well, it certainly won't be as extravagant as a royal wedding, but we want to make sure Emma and Gabriel feel special," Martha May informed him. "Neither of them has parents to do this for them, so we're stepping in."

Henry nodded in agreement with this reasoning, and once everyone was seated and the blessing was given, the conversation picked back up.

"Is there anyone you would like to invite to the wedding from back home in Texas?" Sarah asked Gabe.

"The only person I keep in contact with is my old employer, Mr. Flemming," he shrugged. "But he doesn't like to travel."

"Oh, that's a shame," her aunt said sympathetically. "What about you, Emma?"

"I'd like to invite Mrs. Vance. She doesn't live too far away, so it shouldn't be much of an inconvenience for her to travel here and back. I'd love to meet her family as well. She talked so much about her son Rupert and his wife Rose that I feel like I know them already."

"This will be a much shorter guest list than we thought," Martha May remarked. "That's all right, though. It will still be a beautiful wedding."

"As long as there's cake, I'll be just..." Henry trailed off mid-sentence, looking confused. "Did you hear that?" he asked.

Everyone around the table went still, and in the quiet, they heard someone yell, "Fire! Fire!"

There was a collective gasp from Sarah and Martha May while the men leaped into action, scrambling up from the table and rushing out the door.

"Should we not be helping?" Emma asked frantically as she ran to the back porch, watching Gabe and Henry race across the yard. From this distance, she couldn't tell how severe the blaze was, but she could see tendrils of smoke coming out from the eaves of the stable.

"They know what they're doing, dear," Martha May said as she and Sarah came to stand next to her. "If they need help, I'm sure one of the hands will come and ask for it."

The women stood in the bitterly cold weather, watching the men work for several minutes before her aunt spoke.

"If you really want to help, we should collect some medical supplies. I'm sure they'll all have plenty of cuts and burns that will need to be seen to."

"Yes, that's a fine idea," Emma agreed, and she turned back toward the house.

They returned to the cozy warmth of the kitchen, and Emma rummaged through the broom cupboard for clean cloths while Martha May and Sarah stoked the fire for hot water and gathered medicines. They were so focused on the task at hand that they didn't notice someone had entered the room until the unmistakable click of a gun being cocked sounded behind them.

"Jasper," Sarah gasped when she turned around and saw the man who had once been her hired hand. "What are you doing here?"

"I'm collecting something for a new acquaintance of mine," he answered brusquely as he set a large sack down on the table with a heavy thud. "Now keep quiet. I don't want any interruptions."

Emma stood frozen as he peered out the window for a moment before turning and leveling his shotgun at them. She had met Jasper only once while he was working for her uncle. She hadn't liked the way he'd leered at her.

"You're robbing us?" Martha May demanded indignantly. "What a horrible man you are."

"I wasn't told there would be two old women I'd have to deal with," Jasper grumbled. "He owes me for this."

"Old women?" the housekeeper screeched. "You're probably the same age as we are!"

"Quiet, you, or I'll shoot you where you stand," Jasper threatened as his dark eyes took on a wild glint. When Martha May remained silent, he smiled, revealing his yellowed and rotting teeth. "That's what I thought. Now you," he gestured to Emma with his shotgun. "Stand nice and still while your aunt ties your hands behind your back."

He kept his shotgun aimed in their direction as he reached into the sack he had brought and pulled out a coil of rope and what appeared to be a note. He set the folded piece of paper on the table and then tossed the rope at Sarah's feet, jabbing the gun toward it. "Go on. I haven't got all day."

When she hesitated, Jasper stormed forward and pressed the cold muzzle against her side. "Do as I say. It's only the girl that I need. You're just in the way."

"It's all right," Emma said, her heart pounding in fright. "Just do as he asks."

Once he stepped back, Sarah retrieved the cord and began winding it around Emma's wrists with trembling hands. She was watched too closely to leave any slack in the bonds.

"I'm so sorry," her aunt whispered as she cinched the knots tight.

"It's fine," Emma said, wincing. "You have no choice."

As soon as Sarah was done, Jasper shoved her aside and stuffed a dirty bandana in Emma's mouth, tying it at the back of her head. With one hand holding his shotgun, he clamped the other onto her arm and pushed her in front of him.

"Both of you get into that broom cupboard," he warned the older women. "You make one wrong move, and she's dead."

Martha May grabbed Sarah's hand, and together they backed into the open doorway. When they were far enough in, Jasper moved forward and closed the heavy oak door, sealing them into the dark confines of the small closet. Then he wedged a sturdy wooden chair under the handle, grinning in satisfaction at trapping the helpless women.

The sight sent chills down Emma's spine, and as panic surged through her, she bolted.

"Oh no, you don't, Missy," Jasper growled as he lunged forward and caught hold of her arm again. "My new friend has a plan for you."

Emma screamed in terror, but the sound was muffled to almost nothing because of the greasy fabric in her mouth. It only enraged Jasper further, and he backhanded her across the face—the explosion of pain causing her to stumble. He caught her before she fell and shook her by the shoulders.

"That's enough out of you. The next time you act up, I'll just shoot you and deal with the consequences later. Now move!"

Jasper gripped her arm tightly and hustled Emma ahead of him as he hurried out of the house, where a lone horse stood waiting for them in the freezing wind. When they reached it, he plucked her from the ground and threw her none too gently onto the saddle. With her hands tied behind her back, Emma had no way of steadying herself; her stomach hit the pommel so hard it knocked the breath out of her.

For a few agonizing seconds, she couldn't draw air, then finally managed a stifled howl of pain.

"Quiet!" Jasper hissed as he swung up behind her.

The stench of stale alcohol and an unwashed body assaulted her, thick and nauseating in their proximity. She hadn't noticed it in the kitchen, but now it overwhelmed everything else. As he galloped off, Emma concentrated on slow, deep breaths through her nose, while the rushing wind carried the odor away. Eventually, the urge to vomit subsided, and she was grateful for the reprieve. Who knew what her kidnapper would do if she actually retched all over him?

Turning her thoughts from that terrifying outcome, she studied her surroundings. They had left the main road behind, and the trail they followed was leading them straight into the rising mountains to the south. The evergreens that dotted the land thickened, blocking any familiar building or landmark she might have used to find her way home if she escaped. Freezing to death in unknown terrain seemed more likely than rescue—especially as a flurry of snowflakes started to fall.

When she'd dressed this morning, she hadn't prepared for the possibility of snow. Her wool pantalets and silk stockings offered little protection, and the cold already burned her nose and ears. What she wouldn't give for a scarf and a wool coat right now.

The snow fell more heavily as they rode deeper into the mountains. By the time the horse finally slowed in a large clearing overlooking the valley below, large clumps clung to her hair and eyelashes. She blinked them away quickly; her vision was something she really couldn't afford. With her hands bound and her mouth gagged, the only things she really had left to depend on were her sense of sight and sound.

Once Emma could finally see clearly, she noticed another rider ahead of them. As they got closer, she could see that it was a man around her uncle's age, scanning the view below through a long brass telescope. He was so engrossed in observing the scene below that he didn't even stir as they pulled to a halt alongside him. Nor did he notice when Jasper dismounted and jerked her roughly from the saddle, sending her sprawling face-down into the snow.

Emma struggled to sit up, but with her hands tied behind her back, every movement was clumsy and painful.

Suddenly, Jasper grabbed her arm, hauling her to her feet with brutal force. An odd popping sound cracked through her right shoulder, followed by searing, blinding pain. A muffled scream tore from Emma's throat, but he only laughed and shoved her forward.

"I've been waiting here for ages." The man with the telescope muttered, still looking through the glass. "What took you so long?"

"I had an unexpected problem to deal with," Jasper grumbled. "I was told there was only one old lady in the house, but there were two. At least that fool we met at the saloon kept up his end of the deal. I thought for sure he'd complicate things."

"He has a powerful motivation to do a good job. Did you leave the letter?"

"Of course, and I brought the girl."

The stranger lowered his instrument, slipped it into his saddlebag, and then glanced at Emma. "A little worse for the wear, wouldn't you say?"

"You said you wanted her alive," Jasper pointed out, "not necessarily unharmed."

"True," the other man conceded. "You'd best hand her to me now. You've only got about ten minutes before he gets here."

Jasper grunted in assent, grasped Emma's uninjured shoulder, turned her to face him, and lifted her into the air by the waist. The stranger leaned down to take her, but as she was transferred, her right arm—broken or dislocated—was jostled violently. She cried out in muffled agony, nearly blacking out from the intense pain.

"You're sure he wasn't followed?" Jasper asked as he collected his horse's reins.

"Of course. I've been up here watching the whole time, and he definitely rode out by himself. Now, stop wasting time and hide. I'll see you at the cabin."

As they left the clearing, Emma said a prayer and asked God to safeguard whoever was coming after her, for he surely would need divine protection.

Chapter 41

Earlier

By the time he and Henry reached the stable, the fire was already roaring in the haymow, thick smoke billowing from the eaves while the horses inside squealed in terror. Gabe raced through the doors, shouting for Tommy to open the stalls to release the animals. He didn't want any of them trapped if they couldn't get the flames under control.

"I'm going up to see how bad it is," he told Henry as he reached the ladder up to the loft. "Hopefully, we can still save the building."

"From your lips to God's ears," the foreman declared before hurrying off to rally the ranch hands.

Gabe climbed swiftly, raising a hand in front of his face as a shield from the intensity of the heat. As he squinted through the thick haze of smoke, he could see that most of the blazing mounds were toward the front of the barn. Moving the burning grass could cause the fire to rage out of control when exposed to air, so he tied a bandana over his face and grabbed a nearby pitchfork to make a wide path through the salvageable hay so the flames couldn't spread.

A few minutes later, Miguel and Alastair joined him in the haymow, each carrying sodden blankets over their shoulders. The hands worked quickly to toss the bedspreads out, and as the wet fabric came into contact with the flames, a loud hissing sound filled the air. Large plumes of smoke billowed around the edges of the singed material, and Gabe could feel his stinging eyes water.

When the rest of the ranch hands arrived, the men formed a chain and began handing buckets of water up the ladder. Once it reached Gabe—the last link—he would toss the contents out onto the fire and then drop it back down to be refilled. With everyone working together, they were able to get control of the blaze before it had spread too far.

Fortunately, the damage was limited to the loft floor and a few rafters where the flames had been the highest. While they would have a lot to repair, Gabe was grateful that the building hadn't been razed to the ground, and that there was still enough good hay stored to last through the winter. It could have been so much worse if Riley hadn't spotted the fire so soon after it had begun.

"Keep dousing the area," Gabe instructed the hands, as he untied his bandana and used it to wipe his sweaty brow. "We don't want it to flare up. I should go check in with the ladies and let them know the danger has passed."

"I'll come with you," Henry said, climbing down after him. "If I know Martha May, she won't be satisfied until she sees me in person."

Gabe nodded, and the two men stepped out into the frigid November wind, tired and filthy from their exertions. The sky had darkened significantly since the mad dash to the stable, and he wondered just how long it had taken to put out. It had only seemed like minutes, but hours could have passed for all he knew.

They had made it to within a few feet of the house when a loud, continuous banging could be heard along with what sounded like a stifled plea for help. He looked to Henry for confirmation that he'd heard it too, and then they broke into a run, knowing that something was terribly wrong.

Gabe outpaced his foreman and vaulted up the porch steps, shouting. "Emma. Where are you?"

"We're in the broom cupboard," came the muffled reply. "Hurry!"

Panic surged through him. He wrenched open the back door and froze: a kitchen chair was wedged under the knob of the small closet. Henry ran in behind him as Gabe yanked the chair free.

"Oh, thank the Lord," cried Martha May as she stumbled out of the darkness and into her husband's arms.

Sarah followed, collapsing on her knees in front of Gabe. "He took her!"

"What are you talking about?" he asked, voice tight. "Where's Emma?"

"That's what she's trying to tell you, Gabriel," Martha May sniffed. "Someone took Emma."

Icy terror gripped his heart, and nausea rolled in his gut. "What?"

"One of the men that Edward hired during the harvest came in after you left to put out the fire," Sarah hiccupped. "He had a shotgun and was threatening to shoot us."

The hair on Gabe's neck stood on end at her words. A memory flashed—intense, angry eyes. "Was his name Jasper?"

Sarah looked up in surprise. "Yes, how did you know?"

"I met him. The day I asked Edward for permission to marry Emma," Gabe said. "I didn't get a good feeling from him."

"I still don't understand," Henry interrupted. "How did you all end up in there?"

"Jasper ordered us in there after he forced me to tie Emma's hands behind her back," Sarah confessed, voice breaking. "I was going to refuse, but he threatened to shoot me. I had no choice." She dissolved into tears again. "Oh God, forgive me."

"You did what you had to do," Gabe told her firmly. "You have a family that needs you."

"But Emma's gone," she wailed. "And we don't even know where he took her."

"I think we might," Martha May declared. She rushed to the kitchen table, picked up a folded piece of paper, and pressed it into Gabe's hands. "I saw Jasper take this out of the sack he brought before he locked us in the cupboard."

Gabe opened the note with shaking fingers. Rage and terror ran through him as he read the childlike scrawl:

I have your woman. If you want her alive, bring $1000 to the spot marked on this map and come ALONE. Don't bring the law, or I'll kill her. Tell no one where you are going.

It was almost unthinkable that someone would do this to an innocent woman, and as Gabe studied the crudely drawn map, his mind whirled with every outcome. This villain was giving him only one option, and he hated it. Tearing off the bottom part of the paper that held the map, he crumpled the rest in his fist and hurled it across the room.

"How long ago did he take her?" Gabe asked, his voice sounding strangely calm to his own ears.

"I couldn't say for sure," Sarah sniffed, moving to a chair. "It was pitch black in that closet, but it felt like we'd been in there for at least forty-five minutes before you let us out."

"If I ride hard, I might catch up to him," he said as he studied the directions again. "He won't be able to go as fast with another rider."

With his mind made up, Gabe shoved the map into his pants pocket and strode out of the kitchen. He returned a few minutes later with an envelope full of bills from his strongbox—meant for wages and expenses, to meet the demand.

At the back door, pulled on his outerwear. A glance outside showed that snow was just beginning to fall, so he grabbed a scarf and an extra pair of mittens and stuffed them into the pocket of his oilskin duster along with the cash before jamming his hat onto his head. Satisfied that he had prepared for the ride as much as he could on such short notice, he kissed Martha May and Sarah on the cheeks and hurried out the door.

Gabe could hear the women begging him to come back as he vaulted down the porch steps, but he ignored their pleas and sprinted across the yard.

He grabbed a saddle, bridle, and a heavy wool blanket from the haphazardly stacked pile of tack in front of the stable, then ducked under the corral railing. Xerxes was grazing nearby and gave a soft whicker in greeting. Gabe gave the horse a firm pat on the neck and began saddling him with more speed than he ever had before. He had just finished tightening the cinch strap when Henry appeared through the falling snow.

"You can't talk me out of going," Gabe warned.

"Figured not," Henry said. "Heck, I'd be feeling the same way if I were in your shoes, but you can't run off half-cocked. You need to think rationally about this," the foreman advised. "You're walking straight into a trap."

"I know, Henry," Gabe said solemnly as he guided Xerxes out of the corral and swung up into his saddle. "But I'm armed. And I'm good with my fists, if it should come to that."

"At least let me come with you. I don't want to lose the only son I've ever had."

Gabe looked away, throat tight, not wanting Henry to see how much those words had affected him. When he had his emotions under control, he gathered the reins and met Henry's eyes. "And I don't want to lose the man who showed me what a father should be. Look after Sarah and your wife. I'm sure they're tying themselves in knots over this."

Unwilling to waste another second, Gabe urged Xerxes into motion and galloped off without looking back. His focus now was on getting Emma—and himself—out of this situation alive.

The map Jasper had drawn took Gabe past an old, abandoned logging camp and then west. He had seen no sign of Emma or her captor, but that wasn't a surprise considering how thick the snowfall had become and how quickly the afternoon light had faded. At least two inches had already accumulated on the ground, and there was no sign that it would stop anytime soon.

After passing the last landmark on the map, Gabe rode for a few more minutes before the trees gave way to a wide-open clearing, which he assumed was the meeting spot. Slowing Xerxes to a halt, he looked around him in all directions to see if he could spot Jasper or Emma. As he scanned the area, an eerie silence descended upon the glade, and hairs rose on the back of his neck as he reached for his Colt.

"Hold it right there," came a voice from behind him, followed by the click of a hammer.

Gabe froze with one hand poised above his revolver, slowly turning his head to see who had got the drop on him.

The same disheveled and angry farmhand that he'd met at the dairy came strolling out of the forest, his shotgun raised and at the ready. Glee at gaining the upper hand was clearly written on his face.

"Did you bring the money?" he asked.

"Yes, but you're not getting it until I have Emma. Where is she?" Gabe demanded.

"Around," Jasper said vaguely. "But you'll never live to see her if you don't drop that gun."

Begrudgingly, Gabe lifted his gun out of its holster and tossed it to the ground, where it landed with a soft thump in the snow. So far, this ransom exchange wasn't going at all as he'd planned.

He watched in silent fury as the man who'd kidnapped his fiancée sauntered forward and picked up the discarded firearm, tucking it into the waistband of his pants and smiling victoriously.

"Good. Climb down and let me give you a once-over," Jasper demanded.

Knowing that his only other option was a bullet, Gabe slid from his saddle and waited as the other man came over and began patting him down, one hand still holding a gun for leverage. The outlaw—for that's surely what he was—searched every pocket that he could find fruitlessly. It seemed as if he might give up until he knelt and reached into the boots, chuckling to himself as he pulled out the derringer-style pistol.

"Oh, don't be too hard on yourself," Jasper laughed as he saw the look of defeat on Gabe's face. "I keep mine in the same place." He tucked the small gun into his own shoe, stood up, and gestured to Xerxes. "Mount up so we can go see your precious little lady, but don't even think about doing anything stupid."

After brushing off the snow that had collected on the saddle, Gabe climbed up and scowled at the other man. "Why are you doing all of this to me?" he asked as the outlaw brought his horse out from its hiding place in the trees and dug around in the saddlebags.

Jasper let out a sharp bark of laughter and stalked forward, a length of rope dangling from his hand. "You'll find out soon enough. Now give me your hands and hold still."

Reluctantly doing as instructed, Gabe held out his hands, and a minute later, they were bound and tied to the pommel of the saddle. It was humiliating to be so easily captured, and he couldn't help but feel like he was letting Emma down. How was he supposed to rescue her now that he had been completely disarmed? It was a question that replayed in his mind as Jasper led the way through the trees to an unknown destination where Emma was being kept.

Chapter 42

By the time they arrived at a small log cabin, Emma felt frozen solid. Her face and toes were numb, along with her right arm, though she suspected it had more to do with her injury than the cold. She desperately wanted to go inside and get warm, yet dreaded what would happen once the door closed. Who knows what evil deeds these men had planned?

In the end, she had no choice.

Jasper's partner dismounted and scooped Emma into his arms, roughly depositing her onto the ground. He wasn't gentle, but compared to her earlier treatment, it was almost a mercy. She was led to the front door and ushered inside.

The room was dark, lit only by the fading daylight struggling through the heavy snow clouds. Emma had to squint to make out her surroundings as her captor brushed past her, but he moved confidently in the gloom, clearly familiar with the place. Soon, he had a fire crackling in the stone fireplace.

The blaze illuminated the tiny, one-room cabin, revealing its neglect. The floor was thick with dirt, and the wooden planks were barely visible beneath it. Empty liquor bottles lay scattered; chairs from around the table had been broken and stacked near the hearth for firewood, and the small cot against the wall bore large stains and rips. In the corner, a rusty cast-iron stove stood beside a copper tub overflowing with soiled dishes—no soap in sight.

The more Emma looked, the more disgust rose in her throat, but she hurried to the armchair closest to the fire, grateful for the heat despite everything.

"Something bothering you?" the stranger asked, finally breaking the quiet.

Emma shook her head but kept looking around the cabin, wondering how long this place had festered in filth.

"What's so fascinating then?"

Unable to speak, she shrugged and turned her face toward the flames, relishing the warmth that slowly thawed her numb extremities.

"I hate talking to myself," he grumbled. "It's all I've done for months, holed up here. If I take that gag off, do you promise to behave?"

After she nodded her agreement, he knelt beside Emma's chair and began picking at the tight knots of the bandana. Up close, she could see the yellow tint of his skin and the puffiness under his bloodshot brown eyes. His distended belly pressed uncomfortably against her as he worked, and she caught the musty sweetness of his breath. She was no doctor, but Emma could tell that this man was not well.

As the cloth finally loosened and slid to the floor, she worked her jaw around to relieve the soreness of having it held open for so long. It was just one more ache to add to her list, which was already painfully long.

"Better?" he asked gruffly as he stepped back.

"Yes." Emma had almost thanked him, but remembered that he was part of this kidnapping plot and bore as much responsibility as Jasper. There was no way she would ever express thanks for that. "What's your name?" she asked instead.

"Louis," he told her, giving his name the French pronunciation: Lou-ee.

"I assume you know mine, since you went through the trouble of abducting me," she said tartly.

“Oh yes. I know exactly who you are, Emma,” he replied as he slumped into the other armchair. “That’s why you’re here.”

A shiver of fright shot down her back when he said her name, despite her attempt to sound unaffected. She supposed that word of her inheritance must have gotten out to the wrong ears, but these men were out of luck if they wanted her money—she received only a small monthly stipend; the rest was locked in a trust.

“I don’t understand,” she said, feigning ignorance.

“You will soon enough,” Louis chuckled. He picked up a liquor bottle from the table between them, took a long pull, and wiped his mouth on his sleeve before setting it down. “In the meantime, you just sit there quietly. I need to rest up.”

Louis rested his head against the back of the armchair, tugged off his sweat-stained hat, and placed it over his face to block the light. Apparently, he was unconcerned about her escaping, and he began snoring loudly within a minute.

This was her chance.

Moving slowly, Emma rose from the chair and tiptoed to the back corner where the rusty stove stood, hoping to find a knife or anything sharp enough to cut her bindings. She stepped carefully to avoid clinking liquor bottles or crunching glass. The last thing she needed was to wake him and be caught trying to free herself.

Unfortunately, the makeshift kitchen yielded nothing useful. All she found was a filthy spoon in an empty tin of beans, a heavy cast-iron skillet she couldn’t hope to wield with bound hands and a hurt shoulder. What she needed was something small and light, like a man’s shaving razor, though she doubted they owned one.

She glanced around for another spot to search and froze when she saw two silhouettes on horseback through the grimy window. Panic surged. Had they seen her?

Emma ducked low and hurried back to the armchair, struggling to keep her balance without making noise. She had barely settled into the seat when the front door slammed open.

The crash jolted Louis awake. He leaped up, hat tumbling to the floor, and drew his gun, aiming it at the doorway as two snow-covered men stomped in.

Emma had turned to look—and nearly fainted when she recognized the man standing next to Jasper.

“Gabe!” She sprang from the chair and rushed to him. She’d been expecting her uncle. He was the only one Mr. Chapman would release funds to. “What are you doing here?”

"Rescuing you," he said with a wry, disappointed smile, raising his bound hands. "Though I seem to be doing a poor job of it."

"You got that right," Jasper laughed, slamming the door and stomping snow from his boots.

He shoved Gabe further into the room, and Emma followed, unwilling to leave his side. Just being near him made her feel stronger—braver.

"I brought the money you demanded," Gabe said, voice steady and firm. He pulled the envelope from his front pocket and tossed it onto the floor. "We're leaving now."

"You aren't going anywhere," Louis told him. "I've got plans for you."

Emma felt her heart clench at the ominous words. She'd assumed this was about ransom money, but she was wrong. She was bait.

"Was it not enough to cut my fence, try to stampede my cattle, and then steal them?" Gabe asked, frustration and anger ringing in his voice. "Now you bring an innocent woman into your schemes? Just let her go."

Louis raised his eyebrows and turned to Jasper, his tone menacing. "What's this about you causing trouble? That wasn't part of the plan."

"It was fine," Jasper scoffed, swigging from his hip flask. "No one even saw me."

"You risked being seen."

Emma looked between them as they glared daggers at each other. The ranch troubles suddenly made sense—they'd been planning this for a while.

"Enough about me," Jasper snapped. "We got them both here, didn't we? You'd think that after all this time, you would be eager to finish things."

"Quit rushing me," Louis said threateningly. "I came here to speak my piece, and that's what I'll do. Go sit down."

Jasper's face was mottled with rage. "You can't order me around."

"Of course I can," Louis spat. "If it weren't for me, you'd be rotting in a jail cell."

"Ha! Well, I've been cleaning up drunken messes for years. Ya know what? I'm sick of it. You can have the ranch, but I'm taking the money and getting rid of these two right now."

Jasper stalked toward the envelope on the floor, but Louis raised his revolver and fired. The bullet struck him in the upper chest. The force of the impact spun him, and the second shot hit him in the back.

Gabe stepped in front of Emma, trying to shield her from the sight and any stray bullets, but she craned her neck, unable to look away from the chaos unfolding before her.

Louis lowered his gun and stared at the body on the floor. "Good riddance," he muttered, giving Jasper's leg a contemptuous kick. "I didn't need you anyway."

"Look," Gabe began, raising his bound hands in surrender. "I don't know why you want my ranch so badly, but if you let us go, I'll sign it over to you."

"You must think I'm stupid," Louis scoffed. He collected the shotgun from the floor and tucked it under his arm, then rooted around until he pulled out a revolver, sticking it in his belt. "Besides, with the two of you out of the way, I can get what I came for and never look over my shoulder again."

"I don't understand," Gabe said, exasperation edging his voice. "What have I ever done to you?"

Louis's eyes blazed with sudden fury. "You killed my wife and stole what was rightfully mine," he shouted. "My life was never the same after she died, and it's all your fault."

Emma gasped. She could never believe Gabe had committed those sins. Louis must have confused him with someone else in his grief, and now he was on the verge of carrying out two more murders.

"What are you talking about?" Gabe demanded. "I've never even met you before!"

A wild smile spread across Louis's face, and he began to laugh. The harsh, broken sound sent chills through Emma. When he regained control, Louis smiled at Gabe with cruel amusement.

"What's wrong, son?" he asked softly. "Don't you recognize your own father?"

Chapter 43

Gabe felt as if someone had punched him in his gut once his father's words sank in. Pa was older, heavier, with a sickly yellow tint to his skin and the whites of his eyes, but it was unmistakably the same man who had left him to fend for himself at fourteen years old.

"You've grown up since the last time we saw each other," Pa noted.

"Well, it's been almost ten years," Gabe said, voice steady. "Children do tend to grow. How did you even know where I was? I doubt you've been keeping track of me this whole time."

"I wasn't," his father said bluntly. "About a year back, I ran into an old friend from Kentucky, and he told me how sorry he was to hear that my brother had passed away.

Imagine my surprise when I found out—though of course I never let on that this was news to me."

Pa shuffled to an armchair near the fireplace, setting Jasper's revolver on a side table before flopping down heavily. He placed the shotgun on the floor but kept his own revolver firmly in hand.

"Once I discovered that my brother had come west and struck it rich," he said, voice rough, "Jasper and I lit out to claim my inheritance, only to discover from a local cowhand that you stole it from me."

"I didn't *steal* anything," Gabe ground out. "Telly willed the ranch to me."

"It should have been mine," Pa scowled, grabbing a liquor bottle from a side table and taking a long pull. "He must have done it to spite me for Charlotte."

"What does my mother have to do with this?" Gabe demanded.

"She was engaged to Telly for a year before the war," Pa said. "When word came in spring of '62 that he'd died at Shiloh, I saw it as my chance to woo her. Charlotte was instantly smitten," he boasted, "and we married two weeks later."

"But then a letter came from one of Telly's men, saying he'd survived and was recovering in a field hospital. I burned it before Charlotte saw it. Couldn't risk him coming back and claiming her. We left Kentucky within days, and by the time Telly got home, we were gone." Pa smiled with malicious glee. "It must have killed my brother when he found I'd won Charlotte's favor."

The delight that he was taking in his brother's misfortune was disconcerting, but despite that, his father looked exhausted from all the chaos. Gabe wondered if he could turn that weariness to his advantage. With Jasper gone, the odds had shifted. All he needed was time to find the perfect opening so that Emma could escape.

While his father continued to gloat, he looked surreptitiously around the room for anything useful. Jasper had stripped him of his weapon in the clearing. His pride still stung at being so easily disarmed, but he pushed that thought aside. Now was not the time for self-recrimination.

The only thing that caught his eye in the glowing light of the fireplace was a broken liquor bottle. The neck could be used as a handle, and the jagged edges looked sharp enough to cut rope. It wasn't ideal, but it was something. He filed the thought away and was turning to look back at his father when movement on the floor caught his eye.

Glancing over to where Jasper's body lay sprawled on the ground, he saw the dead man's fingers twitch—once, twice. Gabe sucked in a silent, shocked breath, forcing his face to stay neutral. The outlaw wasn't dead yet. He could use Jasper's sudden rise from the dead to his advantage and overpower Pa.

With a plan in place and hope surging through him, Gabe turned his attention back as his father shouted, "It's your fault that we couldn't have any more children."

"How was that my fault?" he asked, stunned by the accusation.

"You came earlier than we expected," Pa said, eyes narrowing. "She said she wasn't due until mid-January, but once her pains started, there was no stopping them. Charlotte had a hard time with the birthing. Something must have happened to her because we never conceived again."

"You can't blame an innocent baby for that," Emma blurted, stepping out from behind Gabe to stand next to him.

"Don't tell me what I can't do, girl," Pa spat, his voice rising with sudden venom, making Emma step back. "I was there. I heard her crying out in pain as she brought him into this world, and do you know how he repaid her? By killing her."

"I never meant for her to get sick," Gabe said defiantly. "I was just a child who had no control over whether she caught the fever. It was her choice to stay with me."

"And I begged her not to," his father declared, a look of hatred twisting his sallow face. "But she always loved you more than me." He stood abruptly, revolver aimed at Gabe's chest. "You've been a blight on my happiness since you were born, and after years of putting up with your presence, I finally washed my hands of you and left town. I assumed that hunger or the elements would have finished you off. But like a cockroach, you survived—only to surface again when I thought I was to be rewarded for all of my suffering. That all ends tonight." The mad gleam returned to Pa's eyes. "Once I kill you and a few months go by, I'll present myself as your grieving father. Everything you own will belong to me."

"If you wanted to kill me and take over the ranch, why did you drag Emma into this?" Gabe demanded, his fury rising. "Making it look like a robbery gone wrong would have been simpler."

"You're right," Pa laughed, a cold, broken sound. "I could have. But I wanted you to know the pain of watching the love of your life die before your very eyes—just as I had to."

Hearing the cruel and calculated reasoning made Gabe realize just how insane his father was. There would be no reasoning with this madness. No more time to wait. He had to act now or risk Emma being killed.

Taking a deep breath and sending up a prayer for guidance and protection, he took a step forward and brought his booted foot down on Jasper's fingers. The outlaw cried out in pain, jerking his hand back with a wet gasp. Emma screamed in fright and stumbled away. Pa froze, shock widening his eyes as his gun hand lowered.

Gabe seized the opening and launched himself forward, ramming his shoulder into his father's midsection, and the gun went off with a deafening crack as they crashed to the floor.

Emma screamed again. Gabe rushed to her, heart hammering, and examined her frantically. Her dark auburn hair was falling in wisps around her bruised face, and her right arm was still at an odd angle, but she hadn't been shot. Relief flooded through him, sharp and brief.

When he looked back, he saw Pa was already on his hands and knees, scrambling for the fallen revolver. Gabe lunged, kicking the gun skittering across the floorboards. He would have liked to use it, but the last thing he needed was to get into a tussle over the weapon and accidentally shoot himself.

Howling in frustration, Pa surged to his feet, swinging wildly. Gabe's boxing instincts kicked in, and he ducked, swiftly sidestepping as the momentum spun his father around. Clasping his bound hands together like a cudgel, Gabe brought them down hard on Pa's back.

The older man grunted and dropped to one knee. Gabe hit him again, this time landing a blow to the ribs. He was winding up for another punishing strike when his father rolled behind an armchair, putting some space between them. Then Pa crouched and lunged for the shotgun he'd confiscated from Jasper.

Gabe kicked the upholstered chair with all his strength, and the hardwood of the chair frame cracked against his father's skull. Pa dropped the shotgun and clutched his head, staggering sideways, and the revolver on the side table slid off and thudded on the floor.

Both men froze for a split second. Pa dove for it first, but Gabe was too far away to stop him from snatching up the gun and aiming it—straight at Emma.

She stood motionless, her wide sapphire eyes locked on the barrel. Her beautiful skin paled, making the mottled bruise on her cheek stand out even more.

Gabe knew that the only thing he could do. He raced across the room and threw himself in front of her just as the cabin door exploded open.

"Drop it," a familiar voice roared.

Gabe whipped his head around to see Henry and Miguel standing in the doorway. Snow was clinging to their coats and hats; their faces set in fierce determination.

"You heard what he said," Miguel added, his accented voice thick with resolve. "Put the gun down."

There was a tense moment in which Pa seemed to weigh his options, but the madness that had consumed him won out, and he pulled the trigger.

The shot went wide, and instead of hitting anything vital, the bullet grazed Gabe's bicep—a searing line of pain ripping through the flesh. He grunted, staggered back half a step, but stayed on his feet.

Pa didn't get a second chance to fire, as another gunshot cracked from the doorway, and he fell limply to the floor, dead.

A wheezing and gurgling laugh broke the silence, and Gabe looked down to see Jasper lying on the ground, staring at Pa.

"I always knew you would get me killed one day, Louis." The dying man rasped, coughing blood. "I'm just glad I got to see you go out before me."

Gabe, Henry, and Miguel watched as Jasper took his final breaths, but Emma stayed behind him, and he could feel her head resting gently against his back. He couldn't blame her for not wanting to witness the gruesome sight. Heck, he didn't even want to see it, but he needed to know—without a shadow of a doubt—that this nightmare was well and truly over.

A tight grip on his shoulder pulled him back to the moment. He turned to see Henry, face grim but relieved, steadying him.

"Are you all right, son?" he asked.

"Yes, I'm fine," Gabe answered slowly.

"You sure? You've got blood on your sleeve," Henry pointed out.

"He missed."

"Well, thank God for that. Let's get you untied. Miguel is helping to free Emma right now, but I know she'll want your comfort."

Gabe nodded and stood still while Henry fished out a pocketknife and sawed through the ropes. The cords had chafed his wrists raw, and blood had soaked into the fibers.

When he was finally free, circulation rushed back, stinging with pins and needles. Then he turned to Emma, her body angled away from the carnage, and gently wrapped his arms around her.

"Ah," she cried out, wincing.

"What's wrong?" Gabe asked, pulling back instantly.

"My arm hurts," she said with a grimace. "I can't move it, and I can hardly feel my fingers."

"It may be dislocated," Miguel said calmly from across the room. "I've seen it happen before on the ranch. I can try to put it back in place for you."

Emma looked skeptical for a moment, but then closed her eyes and sighed. "We might as well try. It's going to be a while until a doctor can see me, and I'm in too much discomfort to refuse help when it's offered."

The ranch hand gave Emma a small smile and moved to stand next to her injured shoulder. With one swift, firm motion, he pulled her arm straight out, then rotated it in a smooth arc across her body while pressing upward on the joint. There was a loud, sickening pop as the shoulder slipped back into place.

Emma sagged forward with a sharp gasp, knees buckling. Gabe rushed to scoop her up into his arms before she could fall.

"It's all right, sweetheart," he murmured to her as he cuddled her close, ignoring the fresh sting in his own arm. "You'll be just fine now."

"I know," she said, a little short of breath as she bent her arm at the elbow and draped it across her chest. "You saved me."

"I didn't want you to fall and bump your head," he explained softly, brushing a lock of hair from her face.

"Not just now—though that was also very considerate. I mean... you came all the way out here in a snowstorm to save me. You even took a bullet for me."

Gabe set her gently on her feet and used a knuckle to tilt her chin until they were looking into each other's eyes. "Emma, I love you. I would do anything for you, including laying down my life to protect yours." He paused for a minute and rested his forehead against hers. "I don't want to wait to get married. Let's talk to Pastor Langley and say our vows after services this Sunday."

"Oh, Gabe," Emma exclaimed, eyes widening. "How could we? Aunt Sarah and Martha May have been looking forward to this so much, and I don't even have a dress made!"

"You're right. I'm sorry." He heaved a disappointed sigh and lifted his head. "It would make them upset if we disregarded all of their hard work. I just... don't want to be apart from you any longer. I should have listened to Henry and married you months ago."

Emma chewed on her lower lip, deep in thought while her left hand fiddled with the top button of his shirt. Gabe's lips quirked in amusement. Finally, her fingers stilled, and she looked up at him with a tentative smile.

"What if we waited until next Sunday?" she suggested. "I'm sure that our surrogate mothers will forgive us for moving up the wedding date—especially after all this." Her eyes flitted around the cabin, carefully avoiding the spot where the two dead men lay before coming back to meet his.

"Do you mean it?" Gabe asked, sounding as eager as a young boy.

"Yes," she replied, giving him one of her stunning smiles. "I don't want to be apart from you either."

He dipped his head, and Emma rose to meet him. Their kiss was deep and full of everything they had almost lost. It lingered until a harsh clearing of a throat cut through the air.

Gabe pulled back, breathing a little heavily. When he looked over, Henry was standing in the doorway with a broad grin on his face.

"Sorry to interrupt," he said, not looking the least bit apologetic, "but we should go now. The storm has finally passed, and you two should both see a doctor right away. Miguel will stay here until Sheriff Bell arrives."

Gabe looked over to Miguel and saw the ranch hand take the soiled blanket from the bed and use it to cover the bodies of the dead men as best he could. Gabe gave him a nod of thanks and turned back to Henry, who was holding out a wad of clothing toward them.

"These are for you, Emma. Martha May insisted I bring these along with me so that you wouldn't freeze on the way home."

"Bless her," Emma murmured, accepting them gratefully. "She truly is an angel."

Gabe helped her into her coat, draping it over her right arm instead of threading it through the sleeve. Once he'd bundled her up the best he could, he led the way out of the cabin. The snow, which had been at his ankles when he'd arrived, was now up to his mid-calf.

He took Emma's hand to steady her as they trudged toward Xerxes and the other horses waiting nearby.

The gelding whickered softly in greeting. Gabe lifted Emma carefully into the saddle and climbed up behind her. As her body relaxed against his, Gabe kissed the top of her head.

"Let's go home," he whispered.

Chapter 44

Emma closed her eyes and relished the deep rumble of Gabe's voice as he spoke. She knew that for now, home meant the farm—but not for much longer. When he'd asked to move up the wedding date, she'd been ready to suggest that they wake the pastor as soon as they returned to town, but she knew how much this wedding meant to Aunt Sarah and Martha May.

Both women had become true mother figures to them, and Emma knew she couldn't, in good conscience, rob them of that joy. It would be a rush, but she was confident that they could all work together to get her wedding dress made in time. The menu for the reception had already been selected, and friends and neighbors would be happy to bring a dish if needed. There wasn't much else to worry about.

When she opened her eyes again, Emma realized that she'd drifted off. It was dark out, but she could see they were now on the main road, which had led up to the cabin. The heat from Gabe's body, combined with the cozy weight of her coat and gloves, had lulled her into a blessedly dreamless sleep. She shifted in the saddle to sit up straight and winced at the pain in her shoulder that had spiked as she moved. She must have made a noise of discomfort because Gabe leaned down at once.

"Are you all right?" he asked softly.

"I'm fine," she assured him. "My arm is just sore."

His hazel eyes still had a note of concern in them, but he dropped a gentle kiss on the top of her head and didn't press her further. Instead, he spoke to Henry, who was riding beside them.

"It's a good thing you showed up when you did. I was worried the storm would prove too much of a hindrance to Miguel's tracking skills."

"It almost did," Henry grunted, "but we heard Emma's scream, and that guided us the rest of the way."

"Wait a minute," Emma interrupted, turning slightly in the saddle to look at Gabe. "Do you mean to say that you knew Henry and Miguel would come?"

He shrugged and gave her a half-smile. "Not for sure, but I had a pretty good feeling that they would come after me. The note Jasper left instructed me to come alone, which meant that he or someone else would watch the ranch to make sure I didn't pull any tricks. I couldn't risk bringing them with me, but I knew Miguel was experienced enough to follow my tracks, and that they were smart enough to give me a head start."

Emma pulled the ends of her coat closer around her body. "Thank God they did," she murmured.

"Amen," Henry agreed. "The Lord was definitely with us tonight."

They rode quietly after that, each privately reflecting on the events of the evening until muffled hoofbeats broke the silence. A group of riders—about ten in all—had been thundering up the road but slowed as they drew close. Leading the charge was Sheriff Bell, who was followed by a few of his deputies, Uncle Edward, and the trio.

"It's Emma," Micah shouted. "She's alive!"

"Praise God," Edward cried out, and he pulled his horse up beside Gabe's. "You saved her," he choked out as a tear escaped and slid down his cheek. "How can we ever thank you?"

Gabe's lips twitched, and his eyes met Emma's for a brief, warm second before he looked at her uncle. "All I ask is that you be ready to support us when we tell Sarah that we've decided to move up the wedding date."

Edward looked confused for a moment, but then his handsome face split with joy, and he let out a loud laugh. "I can definitely do that."

The trio surrounded them, slapping Gabe on the back and taking turns clasping hands with Emma, their voices overlapping in relieved, joyful chatter. She felt tears of her own threaten, but she held them back and smiled through it all. It wasn't until the sheriff joined them that the talking quieted.

"I'm pleased to see you alive and well, Miss Barnes," the lawman said, looking her over. "I know you have been through a terrible ordeal, but I'll need to speak with you and Gabe."

"Can it wait until tomorrow?" Gabe asked, a note of impatience in his voice. "She needs to be seen by the doctor as soon as possible."

"Of course," Bell replied. "You take care of your fiancée, and I'll see you in my office sometime tomorrow. In the meantime, I'll be taking my men up to the cabin." He tipped his hat to Emma and rode off up the road.

"Thank you," she told Gabe. "I really didn't want to go over everything right now."

"I know," he said gently. "Neither did I. Let's just get you home so you can rest."

Emma nodded, and they followed Henry and her family the rest of the way back to town. It was decided that they would head to the ranch, since the rest of the Barnes family had gathered there to support Sarah as she and Martha May eagerly awaited news of the situation.

The women must have been so eager that their noses had been pressed to the window because as soon as Gabe and Emma rode into the yard, shouts of alarm rang out from the house.

"Is she with you?" Martha May asked, throwing open the back door and rushing to her husband.

"Of course she is," Henry grumbled, dismounting and pulling his wife into a hug. "Did you think I'd return home empty-handed?"

Sarah flew down the porch stairs after her friend. When she spotted Emma, she fell to her knees in the snow and wept.

"Thank you, God. Thank you, God," she repeated through deep, gasping breaths.

"Gabe, help me down," Emma pleaded. "I need to go to her."

He smiled tenderly, pressed a swift kiss to her cheek, then dismounted and gently lifted her from the saddle. As soon as her feet touched the ground, Emma ran to her aunt and joined her in the snow, wrapping her uninjured arm around the other woman's shoulders and shushing her softly.

"It's all right, Aunt Sarah," she whispered. "I'm here, and I'm safe. It's all right."

"Can you ever forgive me?" Sarah asked tearfully. "Oh, please say that you do!"

"There is nothing to forgive, Aunt Sarah," Emma insisted. "None of this was your fault. Please don't blame yourself any longer."

"I'll try, but I truly feel so awful," Sarah sniffed.

Emma searched for words, but all that came to mind was a Bible verse. "The soul that sinneth, it shall die. The son shall not bear the iniquity of the father, neither shall the father bear the iniquity of the son: the righteousness of the righteous shall be upon him, and the wickedness of the wicked shall be upon him."

Sarah blinked up at her in confusion for a moment.

"It's from Ezekiel 18:20," Emma explained gently. "What Jasper did was his sin, not yours."

"Come, dearest," Uncle Edward said, stepping forward to offer his hand to his wife. "Let's go get you warmed up."

Emma tried to rise, but the freezing snow had stiffened her already tired muscles. Gabe slipped his arm around her waist, giving her a steadying anchor, and she smiled at him gratefully. They stayed linked like that as they walked into the house.

"I just knew that Gabriel would bring you home safely," Martha May said, her plump face shining with tears. "He was so brave going out there on his own."

"He was," Emma agreed. "And so were Henry and Miguel. I owe them all so much."

"I'm just glad you're both back where you belong. Now, why don't you come sit down while I fetch you something to eat?" Martha May suggested as she gestured to the kitchen table. "Riley headed to town to get the doctor."

Emma and Gabe took seats next to each other while Martha May went to the stove to get some food for them. As they waited, the youngest Barnes children spilled into the kitchen and raced over to greet Emma. Mary trailed behind them, looking frustrated.

"I tried to keep them away until you rested a bit," she apologized, "but they couldn't be held back any longer."

"That's all right," Emma said with a tired smile. "The love of family is good medicine."

Emma spoke to each little cousin in turn, and by the time a big plate of fried chicken and mashed potatoes was set in front of her, Emma felt ravenous. It had been hours since she had sat at this very table having a rather enjoyable dinner, and her stomach was grumbling in its annoyance. She flushed a bit at how loud it was, but after her first bite of food, she forgot about her embarrassment and focused on satiating her hunger.

She had just finished her plate and was dabbing the grease off her mouth with a cloth napkin when Dr. Phillips was escorted into the kitchen by Riley.

"I hear my services are needed," he said, scanning the room for his patients.

Gabe stood and extended his hand. "Yes, sir. If you could please see to Emma first, I'd appreciate it."

The doctor shook his hand and smiled. "That sounds fine to me. Is there a place where I might examine her?"

"You can use my bedroom," Gabe offered. "It's right up these stairs. I'll go with you."

"Gabriel!" Martha May squawked indignantly. "You can't be in there while she's being seen by the doctor! It isn't proper."

"Considering she's going to be my wife in about a week, I think it's entirely proper," he replied calmly. "I'll step out of the room if she's required to undress, but I'm sticking close to her."

"A week?" Sarah asked in confusion.

Edward stepped forward and raised his hands in a placating gesture. "Let them see the doctor, and I'll explain everything."

Emma followed Gabe up the steep staircase as loud voices from the kitchen rose behind them.

"My poor uncle," she chuckled softly as they climbed. "We're leaving him with quite a mess to clean up."

"He'll be fine," Gabe assured her, glancing back with a small smile. "Besides, he owes me, remember?"

He opened the door to the first room on the right, gesturing for her to enter before him. It was a very spacious bedroom. Light blue walls, heavy walnut dressers, nightstands, and a large wooden bed frame that immediately drew Emma's eye. Heat rose in her cheeks as she stared at it. Thankfully, Dr. Phillips followed right behind, giving Emma something else to focus on.

He was a kind, older man in his sixties, with a calm, comforting manner. He asked questions about her injuries, and she managed a steady retelling of her ordeal without breaking down in tears.

Dr. Phillips carefully examined her arm, gently probing it with his fingertips and testing her range of motion before confirming it had been dislocated. He wrapped it in a sling and instructed her to wear it for a few weeks until he was satisfied that it had healed. Since none of her injuries required her to disrobe, Gabe was able to stay in the room and sit next to her while the doctor finished up.

When he was done with Emma, Dr. Phillips turned to Gabe and pointed to the bloodstained spot on his jacket. "I see you aren't without injury. Take that off, and we'll see how much harm was done."

Gabe shrugged off his jacket, and the doctor used a small pair of scissors he took from his bag to cut the fabric around the wound wider. "Hmm, not too much damage to the tissue. It doesn't even need to be stitched." He returned to the medical bag and pulled out a bottle of dark liquid and some clean white cloth. Emma watched as the doctor thoroughly cleaned and bandaged Gabe's arm neatly.

"My work here is done," he said, packing his bag. "Miss Barnes, I'd like to see you in my office in two weeks to check on that arm. No strenuous activity in the meantime," he said firmly. "I'll go tell your family the good news. Don't take too long to join us."

Once they were alone, Emma rested her head against Gabe's shoulder and sighed. "We should go back down... but I don't know if I have the strength to deal with the uproar our announcement caused."

Gabe gave a rumbling laugh, and he picked up her hand and brought it to his lips for a gentle kiss. "I'm sure Edward has taken care of it by now, but if we stay here much longer, Martha May and Sarah might frog march us to the pastor's house tonight."

"Remind me why that's a bad idea?" she asked teasingly.

He laughed again, eyes crinkling at the corners. "You wanted them to finish their planning, remember?"

"You're right." Emma drew a deep breath and forced her weary muscles to lift her from the bed. "Lead the way."

She followed Gabe down the stairs and saw Martha May and Sarah sitting at the kitchen table, each scribbling furiously on a sheet of paper. Confused, she came closer and looked over her aunt's shoulder to see that a list of things to do before the wedding was forming.

"Are you terribly upset that we moved up the date?" she asked hesitantly.

"No," Sarah answered softly. "We won't be able to do some things we had talked about, but as Edward said, all we really need is a bride, a groom, and a preacher."

Emma smiled at her uncle and mouthed a silent "thank you." He accepted with a nod before leaving to hitch up the wagon.

It didn't take him long. Once all the children had been herded into the back and tucked under heavy blankets, it was time for goodbyes.

Out in the darkened yard, she hugged Martha May tightly, then gave Henry a quick peck on his cheek. His face flushed a deep red, and he ducked his head, suddenly fascinated with his boots. It was endearing to see such a rough and tough man be so embarrassed, but she moved on so as not to make him more uncomfortable by staring.

"Do I get one of those?" Gabe asked, his lips twitching with restrained mirth.

"No, you get a better one." Emma went on tiptoe and gave him a lingering kiss before pulling away. "See?"

"You're right. That was much better," he agreed. "I'll gladly accept another tomorrow when I pick you up so that we can speak to the Sheriff."

"Oh, of course," she sighed. "I forgot about that."

"It'll be all right," he said as he walked with her to the back of the wagon. "Once we speak to him, we can put this whole mess behind us and focus on getting married."

"I suppose it's better to just get it over with as soon as possible," she said tiredly.

Gabe gently lifted her into the wagon, and when she was comfortably settled, Emma smiled at him. "Go get some rest. You deserve it."

"I'll try," he promised, and as Edward set the wagon rolling forward toward the farm, she gave him a last wave and closed her weary eyes.

When Emma awoke the next day, sunlight streamed through the window, warm and bright. She blinked and held up a hand to shield it from the light. She hadn't slept this late since she started milking the cows. It felt like she'd wasted half of the day in bed. Turning her head, she looked at the tiny clock that sat on her night table and saw that it was only ten o'clock.

"Well, at least I didn't sleep through dinner," Emma muttered to the empty room.

Taking a deep breath, she gritted her teeth against the pain she knew was coming and struggled to sit up in the bed. The muscles in her abdomen, which were bruised from Jasper's rough handling the day before, were protesting their use. She had just settled herself more comfortably when a soft knock came at the door.

"Emma, are you awake, dear?" came Aunt Sarah's muffled voice.

"Yes, come in," she called.

The door swung open, and her aunt bustled in with a tray of food and a large glass of water. The smell of eggs and bacon made Emma's mouth water, and she raised her hand to her mouth to make sure she wasn't actually drooling.

"How are you feeling this morning?" Sarah asked as she settled the tray on Emma's lap.

"As well as expected, I suppose. My arm is still very painful, but having it in the sling is helpful. The rest of me is just... sore."

Emma saw a frown flicker across her aunt's face. She looked as if she were about to apologize again. But Sarah mastered herself and set about straightening the bedsheet.

"Dig in," she encouraged. "Gabe will most likely be here soon to take you to town, and I'm sure you'd like to take a bath before he gets here."

"That sounds heavenly," Emma sighed as she scooped up her first bite of food.

"I thought so. I'll get the water heating in the summer kitchen while you eat."

Once Sarah had left, Emma devoured her meal in a most unladylike fashion. She was grateful that no one could see her lapse in manners. Especially when a bite of eggs completely missed her mouth and fell into her lap. It was harder to eat with her left hand than she had expected.

When her aunt returned with clean clothes, they slowly made their way to the addition, where the bathing room had been prepared. Emma sank into the wonderfully warm water, letting out a groan of satisfaction. It felt good on her aching muscles, and the tension she'd been carrying slipped away.

She had no idea how long she lay there, just relaxing in the water, but eventually she found the soap and carefully scrubbed her body from head to foot, readying herself to face the day ahead.

Chapter 45

If he hadn't been so exhausted from the day before, Gabe was sure he wouldn't have slept a wink. As it was, his dreams were haunted by his time in the cabin. He relived the events repeatedly, sometimes twisting to different, darker outcomes. Though he'd slept, he woke up feeling more tired than when he'd crawled into bed. Still, he tried not to show it.

The only thing that kept him moving this morning was the thought of seeing Emma. Everything was better when she was around. He looked forward to the day when he could wake up next to her, though that wouldn't be for another week. He sighed and went back to sweeping out the charred bits of hay that had remained in the loft, spending the rest of his morning cleaning it up so repairs could begin.

Instead of having dinner with Henry and Martha as he usually did, Gabe changed out of his soiled work clothes and bathed before hitching up the covered wagon and heading straight over to the farm. The ride took longer than usual, thanks to the thick blanket of snow that covered the ground. He wished he had thought to put on the sleigh runners, but it was too late now.

Gabe had pulled the horses to a halt in front of the farmhouse and knocked firmly on the door. A few moments later, Sarah opened the door and greeted him with a wide smile.

"Hello, Gabe. Come on in. Emma's upstairs at the moment."

She stepped back, and he removed his hat as he entered the parlor. "How is she doing?" he asked.

"Fine, I think," Sarah replied, a slight frown creasing her face. "She slept in this morning for the first time in months. She must have needed it. I hope you could get some rest as well."

"I got some sleep," Gabe confirmed.

"I'm glad," she said sincerely. "Wait here, and I'll go get Emma for you."

Sarah headed upstairs and returned a few minutes later with Emma, who looked more refreshed than he did. She was smiling brightly as she came forward to greet him, and even though her cheek had a large, mottled bruise, she still looked beautiful.

He kissed the uninjured side of her face and asked, "How are you?"

"I'm fine," she replied with a shrug. "Sore, but that's expected. Shall we go? I'd like to get this over with."

"Of course. Do you have everything you need?"

"I just need to get my coat. Would you help me into it? It's hanging on a peg by the front door."

Gabe spotted it immediately and retrieved the heavy garment, helping her slip her free arm into the sleeve and draping the other side over her shoulder. Then he swiftly buttoned it up so it wouldn't fall off and held out his arm to escort her outside.

Once they were in the yard, he looked down at Emma and asked quietly, "How do you really feel?"

She met his eyes and sighed. "My arm hurts like the dickens, but I didn't want to say so in front of Aunt Sarah. She is still chastising herself for what happened last night, and I don't want to make it worse."

"I understand how she feels," Gabe said, voice low. "Heck, my father was the mastermind behind the whole thing." He stopped beside the surrey and turned to face her fully. "I'm sorry this happened to you. You didn't deserve it."

"Gabe, look at me," she said firmly. "It wasn't your fault. Your father's anger and jealousy led him to abandon you when he should have been the one person in your life who was there for you." She lifted her good hand and cupped his face, thumb brushing gently along his jaw. "I don't blame you for what happened, and I certainly don't blame my aunt. You can't keep carrying this weight. I won't let you."

He smiled—small, grateful—and placed his hand over hers, holding it against his cheek. "Yes, ma'am."

"Thank you," she said with a satisfied little grin. "Now help me into the surrey, please. We have things to see to."

When Gabe and Emma entered the large red brick office, Sheriff Bell was sitting behind a solid walnut desk, looking over what appeared to be wanted posters. It took him a moment to notice them, but he quickly stood and greeted them.

"Thank you for coming in today," he said as he shook their hands. "Please take a seat."

He gestured to two plain wooden chairs in front of the desk. Gabe pulled one out for Emma, holding it steadily until she was seated, then took his own.

Once they were settled, the sheriff slid two pieces of paper over to them and looked at them with calm gravity.

"I'd like you both to look at these and confirm these were the men involved in the kidnapping. One of the bodies wasn't as... recognizable as I'd like."

Gabe saw Emma's face pale slightly, but she gave a small nod for the sheriff to continue.

"I believe I've identified his accomplice from these posters. Once you've confirmed my suspicions, I'd like to hear your version of events—one at a time."

Gabe hesitated. Right now, it was only a dark theory lurking at the back of his mind that his father had committed more crimes. The second he picked up that paper, it would be real. He felt Emma's hand slip into his, as if knowing that he needed his strength bolstered. He gave her hand a small squeeze in thanks and took a steadying breath before reaching for the sheet closest to him.

The drawing was unmistakably of Jasper. Somehow, the artist had perfectly captured the outlaw's intense, angry eyes.

"This is the man who took Emma," Gabe said quietly as he scanned the sheet.

Jasper, wanted in seven different states for a long list of crimes, including robbery and murder. He had a bounty of five hundred dollars. Gabe set the paper down and cautiously reached for the next one. As he saw the drawing of his father on it, his hand shook.

The sheriff seemed to have noticed his distress, because he sat forward, concerned. "Are you all right, son?" he asked.

Gabe nodded, his throat suddenly dry. "It's my father," he choked out.

Sheriff Bell's eyes grew round, and he let out a whistle as he leaned back in his chair, absorbing the news. "My, my," he mumbled to himself.

The wanted poster was similar to Jasper's—robbery, fraud, assault—but not murder. Gabe wasn't sure if he should be reassured that his father wasn't a proven killer or distraught because when he'd finally crossed that line, it was to kill his own son.

He tossed the paper back onto the desk and stared at the ground, feeling like someone had just ripped the rug out from under him.

"That's not what I expected to hear when I asked you to come in today," the Sheriff confessed. "Though it doesn't change my opinion of you, Gabe. My sire was a son of a-" He stopped abruptly, remembering Emma was in the room, and he cleared his throat. "Sometimes there are bad men out there, but you aren't one of them."

"Thank you," Gabe said, his voice thick with emotion.

"Any time," Sheriff Bell replied gruffly. He looked at Emma and smiled gently. "Miss Barnes, would you be so kind as to share your version of events first?"

Emma nodded, and they spent the next hour going over every detail that she could remember. It was hard for Gabe to hear how poorly she had been treated and how terrified she had been, but he was fiercely proud of her. She could have given in to fear and despair, but instead she had looked for a way out, despite the risk of being caught. If he hadn't already loved her, he would have fallen for her all over again right then. Even Sheriff Bell listened with obvious admiration.

Gabe's retelling took longer—so much history had led to this moment. When they were done, the sheriff sat back, intertwined his fingers, and laid them over his stomach.

"I thank you both for coming in today and letting me poke and prod at you. I know it wasn't easy to relive that."

"What happens now?" Gabe asked. "Will Miguel be in trouble with the law?"

"He killed an outlaw who was actively committing a crime, so no. Heck, I'm inclined to give him a parade." He chuckled at his own joke but stopped when he noticed he was the only one laughing. "My deputies will bring back the bodies, and they'll be buried in a cemetery outside of town—unless you'd like your father to rest out on the ranch."

"No," he said emphatically. "It might not be Christian of me, but I won't have the man who tried to murder my future wife buried on my land."

"Understandable," the sheriff nodded, unfazed by the refusal. "In that case, I just need to know what you would like to do with the bounties."

"I suppose we should split it between Henry and Miguel if they'll take it," Gabe said. "If it weren't for them, we would be dead. What do you think, Emma?"

"I agree," she said quietly. "They deserve to be rewarded for their heroism."

"Fine by me. I'll make sure they get it." Sheriff Bell stood and grabbed his jacket from the coat rack behind his desk. "Mind if I walk out with you? I have an errand to run for the missus, and if I don't do it now, I'm liable to forget."

They waited for the lawman to get his jacket on, then the three of them walked out into the frigid November air. Their breath puffed out in small clouds as they stood on the boardwalk saying their goodbyes.

Suddenly, a commotion erupted across the street, and their conversation cut off. The swinging doors of the Tipsy Miner banged open, and Gregory ran out into the street, looking panicked.

"My word!" Emma gasped. "What on earth is going on?"

Gregory must have heard her outburst because he turned to stare over at their little group, and he looked as if he'd seen a ghost. Then he bolted forward, clumsily mounted a horse, and kicked it into a frantic gallop, tearing straight out of town.

Gabe was too stunned to speak, but he heard the lawman heave a heavy sigh.

"Well," he muttered. "I guess I'll be tracking down another criminal today."

"What do you mean?" Emma asked.

Sheriff Bell harrumphed and crossed his arms. "He just stole my horse."

Emma had come by with her aunt for her usual Friday visit and was helping Martha May prepare food for the wedding in two days, when a knock sounded at the back porch door. Gabe, delaying his return to work after dinner, went to answer the door and saw Sheriff Bell standing there, tapping his wide-brimmed hat against his leg.

"Good afternoon, Sheriff. Please come in." Gabe stepped aside and let the burly lawman step into the warm kitchen. "How can we help you today?"

"Well, I was hoping to speak to you and Miss Barnes."

"Soon-to-be Mrs. Moreau," Emma said with a soft smile as she came to join them.

Sheriff Bell chuckled and slapped Gabe's shoulder. "That's right! Are you nervous, son?"

"Not in the slightest," he said, slipping his arm comfortably around Emma's waist. "Why don't we go into the parlor and talk there? Would you like some coffee? I think Martha May just put on a new pot."

"I won't say no to a cup, especially if it comes with something sweet."

Martha May, who had been standing by the stove, laughed at his wheedling tone and turned around to face him, hands on her hips. "Joshua Bell, have I ever served you coffee without a treat to go with it?"

The sheriff tapped his finger on his chin as if in thought and then shook his head. "Not in the twenty years I've known you."

"Well, there you go. Now go make yourselves comfortable in the other room, and I'll bring in a tray in a few minutes."

Following Martha May's command, they left the kitchen and took seats in the parlor. Gabe and Emma shared a couch, and the sheriff sat on a tufted armchair. They exchanged some small talk about the wedding while they waited for refreshments, but once they'd been served and were finally alone, Sheriff Bell leaned forward.

"I wanted to come here today to talk to you about Gregory Callaway. There are some things you might not have known that I think you deserve to hear."

He took a sip of coffee and continued. "When I caught up with him in Butte, he was trying to buy a train ticket out of Montana. I took him in for horse theft, but the second I started pressing him, he broke down and confessed to setting fire to the stable so Jasper could kidnap Miss Barnes."

"I don't believe it," Emma said, her eyes wide with shock.

“That’s what he said,” Sheriff Bell shrugged. “Evidently, he met Jasper at the saloon shortly after his run-in with you in town. He claimed the outlaw had tricked him—promised that if he helped get you out of the house, Gregory could press his suit once Gabe was dead. When he heard some of the boys in the saloon say that I was bringing in the outlaw who had kidnapped you, he panicked. He thought they were still alive and able to point the finger at him. That’s why he was in such a hurry to leave town that he stole the wrong horse.”

“Oh my,” Emma murmured. “How could he do something like this?”

Gabe could easily believe that Gregory would stoop to any low to get what he wanted, but he didn’t say it aloud. Instead, he slipped an arm around her shoulder and brought her close against his side.

“What will happen to him now?” Gabe asked.

“He’ll be sent to prison for a long time. The judge who oversaw his trial is known for wanting to reform criminals instead of hanging them, but he is still charged with arson plus accessory to kidnapping and attempted murder.” The sheriff looked about uncomfortably after delivering the news and stood up. “Well, hopefully now you can put this whole sorry business behind you. If there’s anything else I can do for you, just let me know. If not, I’ll see you on Sunday for the wedding.”

Gabe stood up as well and shook his hand. “Thank you for letting us know what happened. It answers some questions I had.”

Once Sheriff Bell had left, Gabe and Emma remained standing side by side in the parlor, letting the weight of what they’d just learned sink in. Finally, she turned to him and gave a small, determined smile.

“I know I might reflect on this later and have a different opinion, but right now I just feel relieved that it’s over. I want to make sure everything is ready for the wedding.”

“Then that’s exactly what we’ll do,” Gabe agreed. He pulled her close and gave her a tender kiss, wishing it were Sunday.

Chapter 46

Every spare minute since Emma had been brought home safely had been dedicated to preparations for the wedding, which mainly involved sewing her dress. To share the labor, Aunt Sarah and her daughters had cut the fabric, while Martha May assembled it. It had taken days to finish, but the dress had turned out just as Emma had hoped. She was pleased by her decision to ask for their help instead of taking it to Mrs. Tandy, though the seamstress would have done a wonderful job.

Now, on the morning of the wedding, she stood in the room that she had shared with Mary and looked around it in fond remembrance. They had spent many nights lying in bed and talking about Gabe and Peter when they should have been sleeping. It made for some groggy mornings, but Emma couldn't bring herself to regret a single one. Not when she was about to start her new life with Gabe.

In anticipation of that, her trunks had been packed and loaded into the wagon, waiting to be taken to the ranch after the wedding. A few essentials, including a new nightdress that Mrs. Tandy had sworn she needed, rested in the carpetbag. All that remained was to bathe, dress for church, and change into her wedding dress once services were over.

Mary came into the room a few minutes later, and with her aid, Emma washed up and slipped into a dark green wool dress before going downstairs. With her stomach fluttering in anticipation, she wasn't sure if she'd be able to keep down her food, but she ate anyway. It would be highly embarrassing to faint in front of the entire congregation because she had skipped breakfast.

As they set off for town with the wagon so full of food for the reception, Esther leaned close to Emma and asked, "Are you nervous?"

"No, I'm excited," Emma grinned. "I can't wait to marry Gabe. This week has felt like the longest one in my life."

"How can that be?" asked Matthew. "A week is always seven days long."

"You're quite right," she agreed, "but sometimes when you really want something and have to wait, it feels longer."

"Oh! Like when we had to wait for Sally to have her puppies," he said, nodding his head in understanding.

"Yes, exactly," Emma nodded.

"Will you still come around sometimes?" asked Isaac, his youthful face creased in a frown.

"Of course I will. And you're all welcome to visit me on the ranch anytime you want." She reached over and ruffled his hair, earning a shy smile. "We'll be neighbors now."

When they pulled into the churchyard, Martha May was waiting to greet them, her pleasantly plump figure wrapped in a deep purple velvet cloak.

"There you are," she said in a slightly exasperated tone. "Mrs. Langley agreed to let us use the rectory for the wedding preparations. Let's bring the food in quickly. The service is about to start."

While Edward, Sarah, and Martha May unloaded the wagon, Emma waited nearby. Since moving to Montana, she had become much more self-sufficient, and it frustrated her that she wasn't able to help. She was still indulging in a bit of self-pity when someone shouted her name, and she turned to see Eunice racing toward her through the snow.

"Eunice!" Emma said happily. "It's good to see you."

"I'm going to be your flower girl today," the young girl grinned as she came sliding to a stop. "I'm so excited."

"So am I. Did you know that I have a big basket of dried rose petals for you to use?"

"Oh, good! I was afraid that I wouldn't have anything to throw because all the flowers are gone."

"So was I, but my Aunt Sarah is very smart; she saves the biggest and most fragrant roses from her garden to hang up to dry so that she can use them all year round. Isn't that clever?"

"It is," Eunice agreed. "Don't you think so, Pa?"

Mr. Harper had finally caught up, a bit winded, and nodded his head. "Yes, of course."

"Why don't we go inside and get settled?" Emma suggested, taking Eunice's hand. "It's awfully chilly out here."

The three of them made their way into the church and joined Esther and Ruth, who were talking and giggling softly on a pew. Their whispered conversation was clearly about Gabe, who was sitting near the front talking to Henry. Just seeing him sent a thrill of excitement through Emma. She wished she could go speak with him, but Martha May and Aunt Sarah had been adamant about the tradition of them not seeing each other before the wedding. It was silly, but she had reluctantly agreed to make them happy.

A few minutes later, they were joined by the rest of the Barnes family, and as the congregation settled into silence, Pastor Langley made his way forward to the pulpit. He smiled at the collected assemblage and opened his arms.

"Welcome, everyone, on this fine morning," he called out. "I have an announcement to make before I begin. After our service concludes, I will perform the wedding ceremony for two of our beloved members, Mr. Gabriel Moreau and Miss Emma Barnes. The family would like to invite you all to stay and join them if you can. There will be a reception at the community center to follow, and I have it on good authority that Martha May has made the wedding cake, so you don't want to miss out. But now we must turn to the reason we are here today, which is to worship the Lord."

After what seemed like an endlessly long sermon, Emma was herded out of the church by her aunt, and they hurried through the crusted snow to the rectory just a few feet away. Martha May had brought the wedding dress in earlier, and they found it draped carefully across the bed in the guest room.

Not wanting to waste any time, Aunt Sarah closed the door of the room for privacy and helped Emma disrobe. They had done this so many times this week that it had become a well-known routine, and their movements were swift but executed with delicacy. Within minutes, she had changed into the cream satin silk dress with a matching arm sling—a late but practical addition to the ensemble. She was admiring the workmanship in the full-length mirror in the room's corner when there was a knock at the door.

"Who is it?" Sarah called.

"It's me," Martha May answered. "Let me in."

Emma saw her aunt roll her eyes at the command, but she opened the door widely and closed it once her friend was inside.

"Are we running late?" Sarah asked.

"No, I just came to see if I could be of any help." Martha May glanced at Emma with a slight frown. "I suppose there isn't much left to do."

"You can put on my veil," Emma suggested, picking up the delicate lace. "I can't do it on my own."

Martha May's face lit up with a bright smile, and she eagerly came forward to take the covering. Because of their height difference, Emma bent at the knees so the older woman could place the veil over her head. She waited patiently for it to be arranged, then stood up and faced the mirror once more.

"You look so beautiful," Sarah sniffed, taking a handkerchief from her sleeve and dabbing her eyes.

"Like an angel," Martha May agreed tearfully.

"Please don't cry," Emma begged them. "I'm likely to join you, and then I'll look a mess once I reach Gabe."

"You're right," her aunt said. "No more tears. Let's head back to the church."

Emma picked up her bouquet made from the soft tips of pine boughs and a few sprigs of snowberry and chokecherry shrubs. The white and red berries contrasted beautifully with the deep green needles, and were held together with a wide red ribbon. It wasn't a traditional bouquet by any means, but it would have to do.

Taking a deep breath to steady her teeming emotions, she followed the two women out of the rectory.

Uncle Edward was waiting in the vestibule when she arrived, along with Eunice, who was carrying her basket of dried rose petals. They both looked a little nervous, and Emma couldn't help but smile. Apparently, brides weren't the only ones with nerves on their wedding day.

While Sarah and Martha May left to take their seats, Eunice came to stand next to Emma.

"What if I throw out too many petals and I run out before I reach the end of the aisle?" the young girl asked.

"Let's see how many you have," Emma suggested, and she peered into the wicker basket. "Hmm, it seems to be full, but if you run out, it's all right—just keep going."

The door to the chapel cracked open a little. After a few whispered words from her uncle, it snapped shut again. Seconds later, the familiar strains of the wedding march swelled from the organ.

Emma's heart raced, and she clutched her bouquet of winter foliage a little tighter.

"Are you ready?" Edward asked, stepping beside her.

"Yes," she said softly. "I think I have been since he took me to the bookstore for my birthday."

Her uncle laughed quietly, eyes shining. "That sounds about right. I'm thrilled for you two, and I know your father would be too."

A lump of emotion formed in Emma's throat, and her eyes burned as pesky tears threatened to fall, but she held them back.

"Thank you," she whispered.

Edward kissed the top of her veiled head and wound her arm through his, straightening to his full height. A few moments later, the doors to the chapel were thrown open, and in synchronous steps, Emma and her uncle walked forward as the congregation stood.

All around her, people were smiling and nodding, but she only had eyes for the man who was waiting at the end of the aisle.

Gabe stood beside Pastor Langley, looking incredibly handsome in a new suit of dark gray wool. His face was split in a wide grin, and he rocked on his heels like an eager young boy. The closer she got, the more he fidgeted. Emma wondered if he, too, was feeling like throwing all propriety and tradition out the window and running straight into each other's arms.

The music ended as she completed her walk down the aisle, and she came to a stop before Pastor Langley. He asked those who had stayed to attend the wedding to be seated, and there was a brief rustle as everyone resumed their places. Once the chapel had grown quiet again, he began the ceremony by speaking on the significance of the vows that were about to be exchanged. His words were poignant but brief, and when he was done, it was time for her uncle to do his part.

"Who gives the blessing to this union today?" Pastor Langley asked.

"I do," Edward stated, his voice cracking just a little.

"Then please join their hands," the clergyman instructed.

Edward withdrew his arm, folded back her veil, and pressed a quick kiss to her cheek. Then he passed the bouquet to Mary, who'd stepped forward, and placed her hand in Gabe's outstretched one. Once that was done, he winked at her and retreated to the front pew.

Emma moved to face Gabe head-on and whispered, "Nice suit."

"Mrs. Tandy did me a favor," he murmured, his hazel eyes shining.

Pastor Langley spoke a few more solemn words on the importance of marriage, then asked the guests gathered for any objections. When none came, he moved on to the vows.

Gabe was asked to go first. He stood tall and proud as he recited the pastor's words, his voice steady and confident, just as he was. The look of pure devotion in his eyes as he pledged his love was so overwhelming, Emma had trouble speaking when her turn came. Somehow she managed to get through her vows with a minimum of tears.

Then the pastor called for the exchange of rings.

Gabe dug in his pocket, but Emma froze in sudden horror. In all the rush of preparations, she had forgotten to buy one. She was about to start panicking when Edward noticed her distress. He hopped up from his seat, quickly pulled off his own wedding ring and pressed it into Emma's hand with a whispered word of encouragement before heading back to the front pew.

Heat flooded her face, but Pastor Langley continued smoothly as if nothing out of the ordinary had happened. He instructed them to repeat, "With this ring, I thee wed," as they slid the bands onto each other's fingers. By some miracle, the borrowed ring fit perfectly. When they were finished, the pastor smiled widely and said in a booming voice, "I now pronounce you husband and wife! You may kiss the bride."

As soon as the words were out, Gabe gathered Emma up in his arms, and they shared their first kiss as a married couple. It was a wonderfully passionate embrace that lasted a little longer than what was considered proper for a public setting, but no one seemed to mind if the loud clapping and cheering were any indication. Apparently, a touch of impropriety was allowed on one's wedding day.

When they finally broke apart, breathing hard, Gabe grinned wickedly at her. "We'll have to continue that later, but in the meantime, Mrs. Moreau, I believe I was promised some cake."

Emma laughed and slipped her arm through his. "You're right. Lead on, husband."

His face brightened at her use of his new title, and together they started down the aisle on their first journey as a married couple.

Hours later, when the food had all been eaten and the reception was winding down, Emma sat happily next to Gabe, resting her weary feet. She had been asked to dance almost every dance, and now her body was paying the price. She didn't mind, though. This had been the happiest day of her life, and it wasn't even over yet.

As if he sensed her thoughts, Gabe leaned over to her and whispered, "Do you think anyone would notice if we slipped out the back door?"

"I don't think so," she replied quietly. "They're all having too much fun taking turns around the dance floor."

"Good," he grinned, taking her hand. "Come with me."

Emma stood up and followed Gabe as he led her around the perimeter of the room and out through the back door of the building. Outside, a flurry of snowflakes greeted them, and she shivered and pressed herself closer to her husband's side. His arm immediately came around her, and they hurried to where their surrey had been parked earlier.

"I should have brought my fur cape," Emma said as Gabe helped her in, "but it was so hot inside."

"It's all right," he consoled, climbing up to join her. "We're not going far."

She blinked at him in confusion. "Are we not going back to the ranch?"

"Not tonight," Gabe said, gathering the reins and setting the horses in motion. "We'll be staying at the hotel."

"Whatever for? We have a perfectly good room at home."

"We do," he agreed. "But I overheard the trio planning a shivaree, and I don't intend to be home when they come by looking to cause mischief."

"What's a shivaree?" she asked.

"It's where the newlywed couple is treated to a serenade of banging pots, pans, and other noisy instruments to interrupt their wedding night. Usually, the mischief-makers are invited inside for refreshments, but I'm not about to have those knuckleheads ruin our perfect day."

"Oh," Emma said, feeling mollified. "Well, in that case, I understand. Thank you."

"Of course." Gabe leaned over and pressed a slow, heated kiss to her lips. "I vowed to cherish you, and that is exactly what I plan to do tonight... and every night after that for the rest of our lives."

It was a solemn promise, as sacred as the vows they had spoken only hours before, and Emma knew she would never regret building her new life in Montana.

The End

Epilogue

September 1886

Gabe had just come in from working in the sweltering heat and was washing the sweat from his face when he heard his name being called from somewhere in the house. He turned the water spigot off and dried his face with a nearby towel before setting it down and walking out of the kitchen. He'd only made it two steps before he heard someone call for him again, but this time it was more urgent.

"Gabe! Come here! Quickly!"

Panic surged through him as he heard Emma's raised voice. He tore through the house, heart hammering, searching room after room until he finally found her sitting safely in the office. A pile of papers lay before her on the desk, but her swollen belly kept her from scooting the chair in all the way.

"My God," he breathed, shaky with relief. "I thought something was wrong with you or the baby. Don't scare me like that."

"I'm sorry," she said contritely. "I didn't mean to frighten you, but come see what I've found! You'll never believe it."

Gabe took in a few more steadying breaths. When he was sure that his legs would continue to support him, he moved further into the room. Emma picked up the stack of papers, handing them over gingerly as if afraid they would crumble to dust. He looked at her curiously but sank into the upholstered armchair—the one she used when she wanted to be near while he worked on the ledgers—and lifted the top page.

It was a typed letter from the Pinkerton Detective Agency, dated April 1865:

Mr. Moreau

After receiving your wire transfer and telegram with all the personal information of your brother and his wife, we have dispatched Detective Collier to their last known address to begin his investigation. He will update you on your case as pertinent details arise.

Sincerely,

Mr. Tolbert

Excitement bubbled up in him. He looked at Emma. "Telly hired a detective to look for Pa. Do you suppose he was trying to mend fences after he came home from the war?"

"I don't know. I'd only read the first letter when I heard you come in. Read the next one," she urged.

He smiled at her commanding tone and picked up the next paper in the stack.

It was a telegram reporting that there was no trace of Telly's brother. Gabe frowned and rifled through the stack—a dozen more reports, spanning years and several detectives. Each one of them echoed the same frustration: leads dried up, the trail went cold, and the case passed to the next man.

"This one's longer," Gabe murmured. "They must have found something."

"What does it say?" Emma asked eagerly, leaning forward as far as her belly would allow.

"Let's find out," he grinned and began reading aloud:

Dear Mr. Moreau,

I began my search for your brother's family at the last listed residence you gave the agency, and after interviewing the neighbors, I wasn't able to find out much more than my previous counterparts. That was to be expected, but I pride myself on leaving no stone unturned.

I expanded my search to anyone who was working in that same neighborhood during the time frame in question and found a man who remembered hauling some trunks to the train station for a young couple for a large amount of coin.

I then questioned the ticketmaster, and he recalled only that they had bought a ticket to somewhere in Mississippi. I'll follow this lead and write to you again when I have any more information.

Best Regards,

Detective Allen

"Mississippi?" Emma frowned. "I thought you were born in Texas."

"I was," Gabe said, and he picked up the next letter in the stack and read that to her as well.

Dear Mr. Moreau,

After much train travel and hours of talking to every conductor and ticket master who was present at the time, I found a few who remembered seeing your family.

Apparently, your brother Louis was seeking a way out to Texas, and he was rather upset that he couldn't take the train all the way there. The ticket master in Jackson recalled giving him the name of a man who was leading a wagon train to Dallas but was unsure if Louis had ever contacted him. I will head there on tomorrow's train.

Best Regards,

Detective Allen

"He was very good at his job," Emma said, impressed, leaning back in her chair and rubbing her belly absently.

"Yes—especially since none of the others had much success. Pinkertons have a reputation for being the best." Now completely engrossed in the mystery of his parents' journey, Gabe picked up the next letter without being prompted.

Dear Mr. Moreau,

Upon arriving in Dallas, I located the former wagon master, Thomas Keller. He's well known in these parts, and for the price of a drink, he answered all my questions.

Keller told me that your brother and his wife did join his wagon train, but they did not go all the way to Dallas. They settled instead in a town called Jefferson, not far from here.

Best Regards,

Detective Allen

"I wonder why they didn't go to Dallas," Emma mused. "Surely there were more opportunities for work. That's why you ended up there, wasn't it?"

"Yes, but my father never did anything that made sense." A tense silence settled between them. After a moment, he broke it by picking up the next letter.

Dear Mr. Moreau,

I regret to inform you that one of the people you tasked me to find, Mrs. Charlotte Moreau, has passed away. She succumbed to yellow fever in March 1871 and is buried in St. Matthew's churchyard in Jefferson, Texas.

Enclosed is a sketch of her tombstone and the funeral plot where it may be found. I looked for Louis and their son, Gabriel, at the address given to me by the pastor of their church, but it was vacant.

According to the neighbors and the current owner, the bank foreclosed on the property after a period of non-payment nearly a year ago, but Louis left town shortly before and abandoned his son. Abuse of the boy has been speculated by those who knew Louis, but I cannot confirm that unless I can find the young man myself. He was last known to be looking for work in a nearby town.

Please telegraph back if you wish the investigation to continue.

Best regards,

Detective Allen

Seeing his childhood put in such succinct terms by an outsider was difficult—but true. He wondered what his uncle had thought when he'd read this report. Had his stomach turned in anger the way Gabe's did now? Knowing it was pointless now to speculate on such thoughts, he picked up the next slip of paper, which was just a short telegram.

To Mr. Toulouse Moreau

Found the boy. Sending certified letter.

He found the promised letter and scanned the page detailing his movements after leaving Jefferson. It was impressively thorough, even mentioning his short time shining shoes at a train station. Near the bottom was an account of a conversation that the detective had had with him.

Gabe set the paper down and closed his eyes as a memory of a tall man with a neatly trimmed mustache and a bowler hat came back to him. He must have been about fifteen, just back after digging a grave at the cemetery. The stranger had come asking for Mr. Flemming, but with the undertaker out, he struck up a conversation with Gabe instead. The man hadn't asked any unusual questions, yet he'd made an impression on Gabe that had lasted almost a decade.

"I met him," Gabe said, opening his eyes again.

"Who? Telly?" Emma asked, her nose wrinkling in confusion.

"No, Detective Allen." He replied. As he recounted the memory to his wife, her blue eyes danced with excitement.

"Oh, how interesting! Is there anything else?"

"Just this last letter." Gabe held up a yellowed piece of paper that had been folded and tied with a red ribbon. It looked as if it had been handled a lot throughout the years, and the paper held a faint hint of roses.

Emma shifted uncomfortably in her chair and rubbed her belly. When he didn't respond right away, she sighed, "Well, aren't you going to read it?"

He had been distracted by her unrest, and her question brought his mind back to the letter before him. "Oh, yes, of course." He carefully untied the knotted ribbon, unfolded the note, and saw that it had been written in a feminine hand. This obviously hadn't been written by the detective.

Dearest Telly,

I know you will be far away by the time you read this, but I have some news that you must be given right away.

Our union has borne fruit—I am expecting a child. It is still early times, but God willing, I can bring forth a healthy child. I feel that if it is a boy, we must name him Gabriel, after your grandfather. I know how much you loved him and how his loss still grieves you to this day.

Please hurry home so that we may be wed properly and both our families may rejoice in our good news. I will continue to pray for your health and safety daily.

Ever yours,

Charlotte

Seeing his mother's name signed at the end of the letter made Gabe feel as if the floor had dropped away. Emma gasped softly. He read the page again to be certain and glanced at the date. April 1862. After a few seconds of silent calculation, he dropped the letter and put his head in his hands.

"I'm his son," he mumbled at last.

Emma reached out and touched his arm, and he looked up to see tears in her eyes. "He must have loved you—and your mother—very much. He paid the Pinkertons to search for you for years. I'm sure that didn't come cheap."

"I can't imagine how devastated he must have been," Gabe said quietly, "returning home to recover from his wounds, thinking that she'd be waiting, only to find she had married his brother." He shook his head and put the stack of papers back on the desk. "No wonder she married..." He stopped himself short of completing the word, jaw tightening. "No wonder she married Louis so quickly after she heard that Telly died. She needed a husband to avoid ruin, and I needed a father—even if he was a sorry excuse for one."

"Can you blame her?" Emma asked gently. "Being unwed and pregnant... it must have been terrifying."

"True," he sighed, looking at his wife. "Either way, what's done is done, and without them, I wouldn't be here today—loving you." He gestured to the papers. "Where did you even find these?"

"Oh," Emma said, rising slowly and pressing both hands to her lower back. "I was feeling like I needed to do a little cleaning in here, and I found a locked box on the top of that bookshelf." She waved vaguely at the tall shelving unit that reached nearly to the ceiling.

Gabe's eyes narrowed. "And just how did you get up there?" he asked, keeping his voice deliberately calm. "Sweetheart, you could have hurt yourself."

"But I didn't," she replied mulishly. "I was very careful, and I made sure I steadied myself on the chair before I stood up all the way."

Gabe growled low in his throat and crossed the room to stand beside her. "You should be more careful. I don't know what I would do if something happened to you or our child."

He placed his hand gently on her stomach, and she sighed in resignation. "Oh, fine. I promise not to do it again." She winced as if in pain, and when Gabe raised an eyebrow at her, she shrugged with a guilty expression. "It's possible that I might have overdone it today."

He nodded silently and kissed the top of her head. "Let's go to the parlor. I'll bring you something to eat if you promise to put your feet up."

"Mmm. Pickles and strawberry preserves?" she asked hopefully.

Gabe shuddered at the combination, but he couldn't help smiling at his wife's pleading expression. "I'll see what Martha May has available."

Emma kissed his cheek and then waddled ahead of him toward the parlor, hands still pressed to her lower back. Her progress to the parlor was slow, and Gabe was about to ask if she was feeling all right when liquid gushed out from beneath her dress and pooled on the floor.

"Oh, no!" Emma groaned. "I just cleaned these floors a few days ago."

Gabe stared at her in disbelief. "Emma, you're in labor! The floors don't matter right now."

"Well, you're not the one who scrubs them, *Gabriel*," she snapped.

He knew she was upset—she only used his full name when he'd truly exasperated her. "You're right," he said calmly. "I'm sorry. I'm just worried about you. How long have you been having pains?"

"I've been having twinges for days," she admitted, "but my back didn't start hurting me until today."

"*Days*?" His voice rose despite himself. "Emma, why didn't you say anything?"

"Because I asked Dr. Phillips about it, and he said that it was my body just practicing for the birth." She paused and looked up at him fearfully. "What if something goes wrong?"

"You'll be just fine," he assured her, voice steady even though his own fear was creeping in. He stooped and gathered her into his arms. As he headed for the stairs, he called out, "Martha May!"

His housekeeper hurried into the hall, eyes wide. "Land sakes, Gabriel, what's the matter?" she panted.

"Emma's water just broke," he told her, the words tight with worry.

"Oh, is that all?" Martha May chuckled. To Emma, she added, "Don't worry, dear. Let's get you upstairs and changed into a fresh nightgown."

Despite the urgency thrumming through him, she calmly led the way upstairs and opened the bedroom door wide. Gabe carried Emma inside and gently placed his wife on their bed, propping more pillows behind her head.

"Are you comfortable?" he asked. "I can grab another pillow from the other room."

"You'll do no such thing," Martha May said firmly. "Emma needs to get out of her soiled clothing, and *you* need to go fetch the doctor."

"I'll ask one of the hands to do it," he countered, his eyes fixed on Emma.

"No," Martha May insisted. "You'll go yourself."

When he opened his mouth to argue, she put her hands on her ample hips and scowled. "You'll have plenty of time to sit and worry while the baby is being born, but right now I need to help your wife get ready—and I can't do that if you are going to be a mother hen."

Gabe scowled back but realized she was right. Emma didn't need him in the way.

"Fine," he relented, and then turned to his wife. "I'll be back as soon as I can." He pressed a kiss to her lips and then smoothed a few stray hairs from her face. "I love you."

"I love you too," Emma replied, offering a shaky smile.

Gabe gave her one last kiss and then headed out the door, determined to ride to town and back in record time.

Instead of finding Dr. Phillips at his office and rushing him back, Gabe spent over an hour tracking him down from patient to patient using Mrs. Phillips's list of house calls. By the time he'd located the doctor, his mood was foul. It only worsened as he waited for the doctor to finish setting the broken bone of a mischievous child who'd done it for the second time in a year.

Gabe had known that he was being churlish about the delay, but all he could think about was Emma and their child. Thankfully, Dr. Phillips understood his angst and didn't hold it against him. Once the young hooligan had been tended to, they headed straight to the ranch.

Now, hours later, Gabe was pacing up and down the length of the parlor while Emma was making the most anguished noises from the floor above, and Henry sat stoically in an armchair, offering his support.

"You're liable to wear out that rug with all your worrying," the foreman warned.

"I can't help it," Gabe said, running his hand over his tired face. "She's in so much pain, and there's not a darn thing I can do about it."

"You can pray," Henry suggested.

"I have been, trust me. I just wish I could help."

"She's got the doctor and Martha May in there with her. She'll be just fine."

Gabe nodded, but another thirty minutes dragged on before the shrill cry of a newborn baby split the air. Relief and joy spread through him. He dropped to his knees to offer a silent prayer of thanks to God for the safe delivery of his child. When he'd finished, he wiped the moisture from his eyes and climbed back to his feet.

"Do you think it's safe to go up there now?" he asked. "The last time I tried, your wife threatened to toss me down the stairs."

"There's only one way to find out." Henry shrugged, a slight smile on his face.

Gathering his resolve, Gabe left the parlor and took the stairs two at a time. When he reached his bedroom door and knocked, he braced himself for threats of violence to be shouted at him again. None came. Taking that as a good sign, he opened the door slowly, peering into the room.

Emma was sitting propped up in the middle of the bed, dark auburn hair lying flat against her head from sweat, with a small bundle cradled gently in her arms. She looked up, exhausted but with a glowing smile. "Well, are you going to come see our son or not?"

"Our son?" he choked out through the sudden tightness in his throat.

"Yes," she laughed. "He even looks just like you."

Gabe walked past Martha May and the doctor, who were both busy cleaning up the room, and sank gingerly onto the bed next to his wife. From this position, he could see the baby—red-faced, scowling at the light of his new surroundings, with a full head of dark brown hair. When the tiny boy finally cracked one eye open, he seemed to stare straight at him.

"He's perfect," Gabe told her, leaning forward to press a kiss to his wife's forehead.

"Isn't he?" she sighed happily. "I counted all his fingers and toes just to be sure."

"Did you really?" He chuckled, picturing it.

"I did," Emma nodded, "but Dr. Phillips said that I'm not the only new mother to have done so."

"Surely not," the doctor said from the washbasin, drying his hands with a clean white cloth. He smiled at them. "You have a beautiful, healthy boy. I'll come back and check on you all in a few days to make sure everything is going well, but if you need me before then, send word."

He picked up his medical bag, snapping it shut. Before he left the room, he looked at Martha May. "I'm prescribing a few hours of rest for my patient, which means no visitors other than her husband."

"Of course. I'll make sure of it," Martha May agreed.

"No, *I'm* making sure of it," Dr. Phillips said firmly. "Out you go now. I'll be right behind you."

"If you say so, Doctor," Martha May replied demurely, marching out of the room with an armful of dirty laundry.

Gabe and Emma stared at each other in shock.

"Did you just see that?" he finally whispered.

"Yes, but I'm not sure I believe it." She shook her head. "She didn't even put up a fight!"

"I guess having a baby in the house has softened her already," he mused, stroking a finger over his son's soft cheek.

Emma gave a wide yawn and sank back against her mound of pillows. "Perhaps, or she was too tired to put up much of a fuss."

"She can't be more tired than you," Gabe insisted. "You should get some sleep. I'll hold him."

"You're a wonderful husband," she said sleepily, passing the baby over.

"I'll remind you of that the next time I upset you," he teased.

Emma mumbled in response as her eyelids closed. Seconds later, the tiny snore he loved so much sounded softly in the quiet of the room. Gabe smiled and took his son to the wooden rocking chair that sat next to her side of the bed and settled in to watch over his small family for the rest of the afternoon.

Later, once Emma had woken up from a long rest and they had lain in bed talking softly and admiring their son, Gabe asked Henry and Martha May to come up. The older couple agreed, eagerly stepping into the room.

"Say hello to James Allen Moreau," Emma said as she shifted the bundle in her arms.

"He's so beautiful," Martha May sniffed, sitting down next to Emma.

The baby let out a tiny wail, and Henry laughed. "I think he objects to being called beautiful. We'd better stick to handsome. Isn't that right, young fella?" He stuck his finger out, and James immediately grabbed onto it and quieted down.

The four adults gazed adoringly at the baby until Gabe cleared his throat.

"Emma and I have a question for the two of you."

Henry and Martha May looked at him curiously.

"We've had some time to talk about this," Gabe continued, "and we've both agreed that we would like our children to call you their grandparents."

"You've become like parents to us," Emma said softly.

Martha May burst into sobs, and Henry quickly gathered his wife into his arms. "Are you sure?" he asked shakily.

"More than sure," Gabe said. "Besides... I think my father would approve."

Instead of confusion, the new grandparents shared a look of relief. Gabe nodded to himself.

"You aren't surprised, are you?"

"No," Henry admitted. "I was the one who read your mother's letter to him while he was injured. She never responded to the one I sent back on Telly's behalf. After he came back from his convalescence, he never spoke of her again." He shrugged. "I assumed it was because she lost the baby and it was too hard to talk about. It's common enough. But when you showed up here on the ranch looking like the spitting image of him, I knew you were more than just his nephew."

"Do Sarah and Edward know too?" Gabe asked, wondering just how many people had known the truth before him.

"No one else knew but Martha May and me," Henry said. "It wasn't our place to say anything. If Telly wanted people to know, he would have said something, and I didn't want to go spreading rumors about my friend."

Gabe smiled and clapped him on the back. "You're a good man." Emotion welled through him, and to distract himself, he asked, "Well, what about it? Are you going to be Grandpa Henry?"

"That makes me seem too old." Henry frowned. "What about Papa Henry instead?"

"Sounds good to me," Gabe said, grinning.

Sneak Peak

Thank you for reading A New Life and Love in Montana, Book 1 of the Elk Ridge Brides Series. If you enjoyed Gabe and Emma's story, please come back for Book 2, where you can read about the newest couple in Elk Ridge—Addie and Micah.

Here's a small excerpt:

Prologue

Chicago, Illinois

October 1886

After another long shift working in the kitchen of The Delmont—one of Chicago's finest hotels—twenty-one-year-old Adelheid Devon, who much preferred to go by Addie, was eager to get home. Her feet ached from being on them all day, and if she didn't hurry, she'd miss out on dinner. Mrs. Jones, the proprietress of the boarding house where she and her best friend, Harriet Schulz, lived, was a stickler for punctuality. If you weren't at the table by six o'clock, you went to bed hungry, and no amount of pleading would change her mind. She wasn't a very kind woman, but the rent was low, and the building was close to the hotel, so Addie had learned to put up with her.

She was only a few blocks away from home and was about to cross the street when a young, scruffy-looking boy in patched wool trousers and a faded blue shirt slid to a stop in front of her on the wooden boardwalk. "Here, Miss," he said, panting to regain his breath. "Take this. It's the Matrimonial Times. It will help you find a husband."

"How do you know I don't already have a husband?" Addie asked as she accepted the newspaper, unsure whether to be offended by the boy's presumption.

"Because, Miss, you don't have a ring on your finger," he'd said, pointing to her left hand. "It's a shame, too, because you're a real looker. You have the prettiest blue eyes I've ever seen, and your hair looks like spun gold."

Addie scoffed and quirked an eyebrow at the boy. There was simply no way she looked attractive in her plain gray dress and stained apron. Her hair, which the boy had so fancifully described, was falling out from underneath her white linen cap and blowing in the gentle evening breeze. "I bet you say that to all the ladies you try to sell papers to."

"No, Miss! Honest! I usually say that they look like they could use a good man in their life. With the ugly ones, I just stick my hand out for payment and don't say a thing. My Ma would whip me good if I told them lies."

Addie couldn't help but laugh at the boy's radical honesty and dug around in her purse for a penny, placing it in his waiting palm.

"Thank you, Miss," the boy said, giving her a wide grin and shoving the coin into a pocket. "Have a good day!" He winked cheekily before hightailing it back to the street corner in time to offer his paper to another young lady, while Addie continued on home.

Made in United States
Troutdale, OR
08/14/2026

52524822R00196